Charles J Foster

The White Horse of Wootton

A Story of Love, Sport and Adventure in the Midland Counties of England

Charles J Foster

The White Horse of Wootton
A Story of Love, Sport and Adventure in the Midland Counties of England

ISBN/EAN: 9783337139711

Printed in Europe, USA, Canada, Australia, Japan

Cover: Foto ©Andreas Hilbeck / pixelio.de

More available books at **www.hansebooks.com**

THE

WHITE HORSE OF WOOTTON.

A Story

OF LOVE, SPORT AND ADVENTURE IN THE MIDLAND
COUNTIES OF ENGLAND AND ON THE
FRONTIER OF AMERICA.

By CHARLES J. FOSTER,

AUTHOR OF "THE HIGH-METTLED RACER," "THE LETTERS OF PRIVATEER," "FIFTY DERBY
WINNERS," ETC. EDITOR OF "THE TROTTING HORSE OF AMERICA," AND OF
"FIELD, COVER AND TRAP SHOOTING."

PHILADELPHIA:
PORTER & COATES,
No. 822 CHESTNUT STREET.

AS A SMALL TOKEN

OF GREAT ESTEEM AND DEEP PERSONAL REGARD,

THIS WORK IS VERY RESPECTFULLY

DEDICATED TO

R. W. CAMERON, ESQ.,

OF CLIFTON, S. I., BY HIS SINCERE FRIEND,

THE AUTHOR.

THE

WHITE HORSE OF WOOTTON.

CHAPTER I.

"I thought he was expounding the law and the prophets; but on drawing a little nearer, I found that he was warmly expatiating upon the merits of a brown horse."
Bracebridge Hall.

THE horses of the goblin and demon riders have almost always been black. It is so stated by the writers and historians who have recorded the events in which they figured and the scenes in which they appeared. He who carried Herne the Hunter under the hoary, wide-spreading oaks of the green glades of Windsor Park was black as night. Black as midnight thunder is the great steed ridden by the gigantic demon over the crags, through the brakes, by the gaping mouths of ancient mines, long unworked, on the slopes of the Hartz Mountains. Black was the stallion who bore the strange shape through the pelting storm, to demand the penalty nominated in the bond between the devil and Tom Walker. On the contrary, Spirits of Health of the equestrian order—founders of empires, demi-gods, and saints—have commonly appeared on milk-white steeds. White was the horse that carried Hengist and in the front of battle shook his snowy mane. White was he the good St. James bestrode when he fought before the ranks of Cortez against the heathen of America. To be sure some have hinted that St. James took no part in the battle at all, and that the man on the white horse was Francesco de Morla; but the same people would dispute the fact that the Great Twin Brethren appeared mounted and armed, and achieved victory for the Roman power at the battle of Lake Regillus. Yet what saith the ancient tradition?

" So spake he, and was buckling
    Tighter black Auster's band,
  When he was aware of a princely pair
    That rode at his right hand.
  So like they were, no mortal
    Might one from other know;
  White as snow their armor was,
    Their steeds were white as snow."

It may seem at the first view that White Surrey of Bosworth
Field was a notable exception, but the truth is that the character of his master, Richard III., has been grossly calumniated.
History and biography founded upon the writings of poets and
the traditions of players are always wrong. Shakespeare having for his patroness, Elizabeth Tudor of the rival house, dealt
unfairly with the Duke of Gloster, and the actors have done
worse. He was a wise, accomplished, valiant young prince, a
little unscrupulous, it may be, but on the whole, a good king,
as kings went in the Middle Ages and the wars of the rival
roses. He was killed in Leicestershire, at about thirty years of
age, and now the actors depict an elderly ruffian, a monster
of depravity and deformity, more like the boar, which was
his crest, than the wise young prince whom Warwick cherished, and to whom he gave his best beloved daughter, the
Lady Anne Neville. Therefore, White Surrey was no exception to the rule that white horses are the agents of love, beauty
and beneficence, as a thousand passages to young maidens and
princesses and milk-white palfreys go to show.

But for all that, the apparition John Bullfinch saw in his
ride, on a wild night, through the thick woods of Wootton,
came in semblance of a white horse—white as the sea-foam
that whirls about the bows of the Flying Dutchman when the
hoarse voice of Vanderdecken roars in the howling gale. The
White Horse haunted the memory of John Bullfinch for many
a day. He declared that it was white; he affirmed that it was
in the likeness of a horse; and as there was no better horseman within the borders of the counties in which the Woods
of Wootton lie than John, everybody said, " he ought to
know."

He affirmed, furthermore, that it was supernatural, and for
some time nobody ventured to contradict him on that point.
It might not have been altogether safe to do so, for John was
as positive as any other Englishman, of fair possessions and

past the middle age, in the Hundred of Ridingcumstoke. This
is saying a great deal. In fact John was seldom confuted in
his arguments or contradicted in his assertions. His landlord,
Sir Jerry Snaffle, was a mighty man in those parts—rich,
liberal, a great sportsman, an authority in the weighty matters
of the turf—an English gentleman after John's own heart.
From Sir Jerry John Bullfinch rented many an acre, and
many a rood of rich arable and pasture land, just as his forefathers had rented from former baronets of the Snaffle family
time out of mind. He likewise farmed his small patrimonial
estate of Hawkwell, a snug place, the nest of many generations of Bullfinches centuries before John himself was born.
Thus he was freeholder as well as tenant, a man of substance,
of that solid character that his opinions were just about as
easily shaken as one of the oaks which grew upon his land.
Like his landlord, John Bullfinch was a sportsman. Hunting,
coursing, and horse-racing he esteemed as the great delights,
not to say virtues, of the country, especially the last, in its two
branches—over the flat and over the steeple-chase course. He
also liked social conviviality and discourse of reason when the
day was well nigh done. His favorite beverage at night was
brandy and water, warm. At early morning he sometimes took
milk punch. In the middle of the day nut-brown ale, brewed in
March or October, and kept to a mellow age, he most esteemed.
He cared little for wine at any time, and held in contempt
the light productions of France. Claret, in his opinion, was
calculated to impair the British Constitution, a thing for which
he had profound reverence, whether considered corporeally, or
as existing in the three estates of the realm. He was a good
farmer in his own way, which was, in the main, that of his ancestors. He employed more laborers than any other occupier
of the same number of acres, and many of them had worked
for above a score of years at Hawkwell. He had as fine horses,
as fat oxen, as large flocks of massive, long-wooled sheep as any
man in the four counties of Buckinghamshire, Oxfordshire,
Northamptonshire, and Warwickshire; but he stubbornly resisted the notions which had begun to prevail touching scien-
tific agriculture and organized husbandry. Had not the fat-
test and biggest bullock ever fed in England, except one, been
raised and grazed at Hawkwell? Had not four of his men,

with their scythes upon their shoulders, and backed by Sir Jerry Snaffle and himself, challenged for a mowing-match against all England? These were the questions which, with a loud voice and a red face, John put to the advocates of artificial manures and mowing-machines. If at such times the famous Mr. Mechi had been present, and declared that Hawkwell was ill-farmed, John Bullfinch would probably have knocked him down. He had once been exasperated by a flippant youth from London, who depreciated the quality of his cattle, and recommended him to go and see Paul Potter's young bull. "Potter, Potter! who's he, and what's the breed of his young bull?" said John. With the country gentlemen, with his brother farmers, and with the laborers John Bullfinch was a general favorite. John Bullfinch was liberal in sentiment, generous with his means, a good rider across country, and known to the choice spirits of the land, from peers of the realm to prize-fighters. In his intercourse with the latter class John never failed to deplore the falling off of the Ring in respectability and usefulness since the days of that great man, Mr. Thomas Cribb, and his trainer, Captain Barclay. Though some modern professors of the fistic art succeeded in getting from him liberal contributions towards the "battle-money," they were always paid over with strong protests against the "dropping system," and formal notices that "The Ring" would be clean done for if ever there was "another cross."

The home of the yeoman, Hawkwell Farm, was a cheery place at the dawn of a brisk, wintry morning. The faggot on the wide hearth blazed and crackled as though it would leap up the chimney, and, like the devout Parsee, greet the first beam of the rising sun. The game-cock, full of valor and pride, crowed in the stack-yard. The house girls sang and swept; the cherry-cheeked milkmaids called up the lowing kine ; flails thundered on the stout barn floor ; geese screamed on the margin of the pond, flapping their wings as though about to mount to the upper air and join the flight of their wild kindred of the mist and cloud. The sow and litter clamored for the filling of the trough ; colts frolicked in the paddocks ; heifers in the straw yard. The rooks cawed hoarsely from the tops of the lofty elms. The pied bull, full-fronted and savage in aspect, bellowed over the ox-fence ; and, high over the ancient well in the blackthorn brake, the falcon wheeled and sailed.

The morning sunshine had just begun to glance through the windows and athwart the floors when May Bullfinch tripped down-stairs. She was a fair lass of midland English type, about nineteen, bright, brown-haired, and beautiful. She had hazel eyes, of a " punishing size," as her brother Jack remarked, and in her complexion there were blent the old favorites of the poets—the lily of the valley and the red, red rose! Her form was round, but light and graceful; her step firm but airy, like that of a young colt in the dewy pasture at the spring of day. May was the only daughter of John Bullfinch and the wife he had lost some ten years before, all too soon. As she grew up, the yeoman saw again, as in the light of love and memory, the fair lass he had wooed and won above a score of years before, and who had been the most blessed and best of women, a good wife and fond mother. The girl met upon the threshold her brother, a stripling, some years younger than herself, with the family features well marked. But there was this difference : what in her seemed gentle as well as gay, was in the boy impatient as well as lively. His cheek was of a browner hue, his hair of a darker shade. His hazel eyes were as bright but not as large and soft as those of his sister. He was tall for his age, well made, quick in action, and with that ease and confidence which horsemanship and the following of field sports in company with those of greater age always give to the young. The lad wore a tight jacket of brown moleskin, cord breeches, leather leggings and spurs, and carried a long-lashed whip in his hand. He was generally pronounced another excellent specimen of the good old family of the Bullfinches, sure to hunt, shoot and fight, and to cultivate the sciences of horse-racing and breeding game-cocks. The moralists of this day and generation may shake their heads, but young Bullfinch was a youth nearly half a century ago, and perhaps still lives in the home of his forefathers, worthy, wealthy and respected. True it is, that as he rode about his father's farm, and frolicked in the merry-makings of the neighborhood, Parkins the constable and the beadle of the parish, made moan over their beer, and pronounced him, in common with other youth of the same age and bailiwick, "a good deal too forrad!" The boy had just reached the time of life when ladies no longer called him by the coaxing and endearing name—"Johnny." "Johnny" had became plain "Jack" in everybody's mouth, never more to change until upon the fond lips of sweetheart and wife it should be rounded and softened into John. He was to all the country-side Young Jack, and sometimes, like the barons and squires, took particularity from his father's patrimony, and was called Young Jack of Hawkwell. At this moment the flush of exercise was upon his cheek, and the white hoar frost upon his curly hair. He had already ridden afield and returned for breakfast. The table was spread with the substantial fare of a country farm-house—eggs and bacon, cold chine, a brown loaf, and a dish of bread and butter. The lad was eager to begin. He looked at the chine and sniffed the fragrance of the broiled bacon. He went to the window and whistled, turned to the corner, and took up his gun from the side of the tall eight-day clock.

"Father's behind time, May, and I'm standing this bacon like old Dash at a leveret in turnips."

He might have added to this, but the solid tread of John Bullfinch was heard upon the stairs, and in a moment he entered the room. A ruddy, smooth-shaven man of forty-five or perhaps fifty, stout, muscular and active. Nevertheless, he stooped a little, and his legs were bowed from much riding in the saddle. There were a few threads of silver in his hair, but his face was unwrinkled, and his voice round and firm.

"Say grace, May," said the farmer.

With reverent, down-cast eyes and soft palms laid together, the maiden asked of the bountiful giver of all good a blessing. Little was said until the morning meal was ended, for neither the father nor the son cared to pause in eating for the sake of mere conversation.

"I think I shall do well enough now until lunch time," said the youth, rising. "The air of the hills in the morning gives an appetite. Father, I saw a fox steal into the Long Gorse just at dawn, and a pair of magpies chattered at him from the oak tree over the stile. A long-legged 'un! What a run he'll give us when the hounds come our way again, if he breaks and goes away for the open Otmoor country, instead of making for the woods at Wootton!"

"Jack," said May, "another half-year's run to school would do you good. You will be sorry some of these days that your father took you home so soon."

"My dear," said John Bullfinch, "I don't know that I have taken him home for good and all. It depends upon his behavior. Jack has as much learning now as most of the Bullfinches ever had, and we always managed to get through the run, be the day ever so long and the country ever so stiff. As Sir Jerry Snaffle says, men are not educated in school much. I shall not make my son a man before he's a boy. But he's the only one we have, May, and now that he can read, write, and cipher well, to my mind he is as well with us as he would be at boarding-school."

"I love to have him at home, father; I know that he is good at his books and figures, and plain English," said May; "people, however, think that for your son, heir of Hawkwell, certain accomplishments are desirable."

"Which," said young Jack, confidently and hastily, "I have got. Tom Scarlet says I'm the best rider in the country of my age; and as for the keeper, he says I can shoot too well by half."

John Bullfinch looked somewhat dubious at this last clause of the argument, and glanced at the light, double-barrelled gun which had been presented to his son by the Tom Scarlet mentioned. The farmer hemmed, looked from his son to his daughter, and from his daughter to his son.

"May, if I find it needful to take a pull upon the lad, it shall be done. He certainly has more liberty than I had at his age; but then I wasn't an only son. Besides, I trust him much to your guidance."

"And that," said young Jack, readily, "is quite right, for she can guide me and keep Tom Scarlet in the line of the hunt too."

"What d'ye mean by that?" said the father.

"Oh, nothing in particular! Tom is this way a good deal, you know," replied the boy, with a glance at his sister.

"I do know it. What then? What do you think brings him here? Come, now!"

"I think, father," said Young Jack, "that it's what they call instinct, which is the thing that makes young ducks hatched by a hen waddle straight off to the nearest water."

"Quack! quack!" said his sister, pinching his ear. "The accomplishments I mean are such as drawing, music and dancing."

"Music and dancing!" said Jack; "why I can play on the tabor and fife beautiful, and outfoot any man in the country in a jig or reel. Charles King says I ought to join the morris dancers come May day."

His sister laughed, and so did his father; but John then said, with a poor attempt at a frown, "Be silent, sir! On horseback Charles King is as good a man as ever sat in pigskin; but his fondness for music and dancing lowers his dignity as the best huntsman in the Midlands. I told Earl Spencer so myself, the last time I hunted with the Pytchley hounds."

Just then the clang of the gate outside, and the iron tread of a horse on the frozen ground, caused the farmer to rise, while his son exclaimed: "Here's Tom Scarlet himself, on Danger!"

CHAPTER II.

THE MAN ON THE RED HORSE.

THE new comer, Tom Scarlet of the Grange, a fine-looking young man, open and frank in countenance, about twenty-four years of age, rode a bright chestnut horse of great size and strength, one that to all appearance was very determined, not to say vicious, in character. His rider sat him with all the ease and confidence of a powerful and practised horseman, while the horse himself could hardly be said to be ever still. There was a constant weaving of his head from side to side, and flecks of foam flew from him when he threw it up as high as the martingale would allow. His forehead was broad and full, but his face below it was deeply "dished," and he showed much of the whites of his eyes. The rider was tall, thin in the flank, deep-chested, and strongly but not stoutly built. A forehead broad and high, and shaded with dark chestnut hair, rose over bright blue eyes. His complexion was florid, and his bushy whiskers, of a reddish hue, were such as were then seldom worn by young men of his class. Mr. Tom Scarlet, however, sanguine in temperament and independent in character, did not care as much for custom and precedent as many other people in that neighborhood, and his whiskers flourished to the discontent of some. His family name and appearance had led to his being often called "Scarlet and Gold," which nickname had originated with a damsel of gypsy blood and corresponding habits, an orphan, belonging to a tribe which often camped on the heaths and in the sequestered lanes of that part of the country. Her name was Miriam Cotswold. It was thought by some of the censorious that the master of the Grange was a little more familiar with Miriam and her tribe than beseemed the owner of a landed estate of small dimensions but great antiquity. But Mr. Tom Scarlet was not the man to care much about what the censorious and the gossips said.

John Bullfinch was his staunch friend. Young Jack idolized him. May Bullfinch was startled by discovering, of a sudden, how much she liked him. Sir Jerry Snaffle often consulted him. When Tom Scarlet's father, a gouty, choleric man, died—some years before the opening of this story—his eldest son John succeeded to the patrimony. It was an old family estate, which had once been much larger. Luckily, John Scarlet could not encumber it, as it was strictly entailed, for he was rather profuse in his expenditure. As the people, more especially his cronies and companions, said, he was a liberal, spirited young man, and lived like one of the old Scarlets. They might have added that he died like one too, for he broke his neck in a steeple-chase, and his brother Tom, then just twenty-one years of age, was heir to the Grange and the estate. It soon appeared that he had also inherited the bold family traits in full measure, for immediately after his brother's funeral he mounted Danger, the horse that had killed him, and galloped over the five-mile steeple-chase course on which the accident happened. Since then he had commonly ridden the horse, and it seemed that he had subdued him so far as his own management and riding went, though to every one else Danger was as uncertain and perilous as

before. The master of the Grange kept two other hunters
besides Danger. He trained racers for hunters' plates, and
he was the best gentleman rider in those parts. As such his
name was great in the mouths of Sir Jerry Snaffle, Master of
Hounds, John Bullfinch of Hawkwell, and most other people
of their way of thinking. Popularity of this sort, however,
has its drawbacks. If Sir Jerry and John Bullfinch had
often won money through Tom Scarlet's skill and vigor in
the saddle, some other people had lost it. So, on the other
side of the county, there were squires, parsons and farmers
well-to-do, who shook their heads and declared that " Ne'er a
jockey at Newmarket, nor anywhere else, was up to more
dodges, or prepared to take more advantages, in a cross-
country race, than Tom Scarlet." And then it was pointed
out by some, among whom were the leading attorney and
doctor of the neighboring town, that Scarlet had no proper
sense of his own place.

"Sir," said the attorney, " he clapped in before Colonel
Carbine at an ox-fence, and that was the reason the Colonel
got a cropper."

" And went over the Rev. Mr. Tallyho, horse and all, when
they were in Otmoor Brook," said the doctor.

" More than that, sir," cried the attorney; " the fellow actually pounded young Lord Doomsday and his thousand-guinea
mare, Scarlet being upon Danger, who ought to have been
shot long ago, and would have been if the coroner had done
his duty."

" Hem! I attended that case in my professional capacity—
the accident and the inquest, you know. John Scarlet's neck
was dislocated, and he must have died instanter.'

" Well, sir," said the attorney, " if you have to attend another such case, caused by the same horse, I, for one, shall
not go into mourning."

Nor was this all that came to the ears of Sir Jerry Snaffle
and John Bullfinch in regard to their young friend. Moleskin, head-keeper to the Marquis of Wootton, averred that
Tom Scarlet killed more pheasants in a week than could be
found upon the Grange farm in a year; besides which, he
was " hail fellow well met" with half the poachers and more
than half the gypsies in the county. But for all that, neither

Sir Jerry nor John Bullfinch would give up Tom Scarlet, though they sometimes gently and affectionately expostulated with him.

The calls of the master of the Grange at Hawkwell had become more and more frequent. What had at first been "lookings in" upon the farmer, to chat over good runs, great races, and other sporting topics, had gradually changed into visits to his daughter. While this was going on John Bullfinch had become somewhat perplexed. He liked Tom Scarlet; even his very faults secretly endeared him to honest John. But, then, John had his doubts whether "pounding" Lord Doomsday, riding over the Rev. Mr. Tallyho in a brook, and shooting more pheasants than the law allowed were just the gifts for a farmer's son-in-law. John procrastinated. He would think it over. May was a good girl, a dutiful girl; the image of her mother at the same age. There would be no difficulty in settling it all by-and-by. He would see Sir Jerry about it, and if it should become necessary, would consult Lady Snaffle, who was May's godmother, and whose word in that part of the county was never gainsaid. So John Bullfinch had let the matter lie, and meantime all the gossips in the riding had taken it up. Never had Tom Scarlet's misdoings taken such color at the tea-tables of Ridingcumstoke as when it was bruited about that he aspired to the hand of May Bullfinch, and that her father, "careless and stupid man," did not interpose to "forbid the bans," as one may say. The old ladies in black silk and lace caps, who had formerly applauded his most desperate leaps in steeple-chases, and laughed over his larks among the gypsies, now pronounced Tom a "bad 'un," and had "no patience" with May herself. Old Mrs. Oxenford, a notable woman and wise, summed it all up at the conclusion of a tea-party by saying, "Tom Scarlet, my dears, is just about such another as Danger, who broke his brother's neck."

"Why, aunt," exclaimed a merry young lady, "I have often heard you say that the wild colt makes the good horse."

"Well," cried the old lady, "so he does; but he throws a-many in the breaking."

May Bullfinch had given Tom Scarlet her maiden love and trust before she knew it. Matters had gone further then her

2

father imagined, though there was as yet no absolute plight of troth between them. In all probability Young Jack was the only one who knew how the land lay, and saw that Cape Matrimony loomed large through the mist in the distance. The daring qualities which made many people distrust and fear Tom Scarlet really endeared him to May Bullfinch the more. To her he was always gentle. An Indian maiden who has tamed a tiger may exult over the tusks and talons which are not dangerous to his mistress but terrible to other people. But May never called the young man "Scarlet and Gold," and never met the piercing look of Miriam Cotswold without some distrust.

A hearty greeting passed between John Bullfinch, Young Jack, and the master of the Grange. The former, surveying the chestnut horse all over, exclaimed :—

"If I were you, Tom, I should part with Danger. He is more trouble than he is worth, to say nothing of the risk, and of the memory of the accident which befell poor John."

"It is not so easy to part with him as you might think, sir," replied Tom. "People have a prejudice against him. Now, I don't deny that Danger wants watching, that he rushes at his leaps, and pulls a little."

"Pulls a little! Why he'd almost pull a church down, and you know it."

"Yes, sir ; but I can hold him for all that, and a better horse across country, when fairly settled to his work, there is not in the bounds of Ridingcumstoke."

"Very well—a good horse, no doubt—a very good horse. But the best I ever saw in the hunting field, for a man of my weight, is Cowslip, and here she comes."

As he spoke a groom led up to the porch a powerful bay mare, long and low, with great arched loins, heavy quarters, and long, strong thighs and gaskins, running into big, bony hocks.

"Ay, she's a good one, she is," said Tom. "A better mare was never seen at the cover side. No day too long, the pace never too strong, and when she rises at a fence she can lift a ton and take it clean over. Cowslip's the mare of my heart ! But I know of a stallion of another color, and may say I have got him, that is—*nearly* as good." He was about to say *quite* as good, but his eye fell upon May Bullfinch, as she came to the door, and he substituted "nearly."

John Bullfinch was much pleased. He was very proud of his hunting mare. It was well known—a matter of boast in and about Ridingcumstoke—that he had several times refused fabulous sums for her. Indeed, after young Lord Doomsday was "pounded" in a great run by Tom Scarlet, that youthful representative of the hereditary and collective wisdom of England sent word to John by Sir Jerry Snaffle that he could name his own figure for Cowslip—price was no objection.

"I am going to ride her to the cattle fair, merely for exercise," said John.

"Well, you needn't be afraid to send her along a little," observed Young Jack; "I have let her go a few smart canters whenever the ground has been good, since the long frost set in, and I'll warrant her not to blow at a hand gallop in four miles."

John looked at his hopeful son with symptoms of rising wrath, for his strong injunctions to him had been never to go more than a foot pace when exercising Cowslip. But May interposed, and by fondling the mare, patting her forehead, stroking her nostrils, and kissing her clean lips, drew John's attention.

"She knows as much as a man," said John.

"A precious sight more than some, and has experience that the best man in all England might be proud of," returned Tom Scarlet.

John thought he meant experience in the hunting field, while the Master of the Grange alluded, in fact, to the kisses and fond caresses lavished upon Cowslip by May Bullfinch. Young Jack, however, knew it all, and made a face at May as his father, Tom Scarlet, and himself walked slowly around the mare, surveying her proportions from every point of view, with great deliberation and intense satisfaction. It was as though they had seen her then for the first time, whereas all three had thus perambulated round and round her at least a hundred times, at different periods, and always with the same result— "there never was such a mare before!" from all three in chorus.

"You haven't heard that Sir Jerry thought of swapping The Bagman for Danger perhaps?" said Tom Scarlet.

" Did he ?   And you wouldn't take him ?"

" Well, I don't know that I wouldn't, for The Bagman is a good horse—a very good horse, though hardly up to the weight of such a man as Sir Jerry."

" You should have taken him for Danger," said May, looking at the restless chestnut, who had pawed and stamped a hole in the frozen ground at the foot of the apple tree to which he was tethered.

" I hadn't the chance," said Tom.   " Lady Snaffle broke up the bargain. ' Mr. Tom Scarlet,' said she, ' I do not want Sir Jerry Snaffle brought home on a hurdle.   Keep Danger for your own use.   You are the best rough-rider in the country."

" And what did you say to that ?" cried Young Jack.

" Say !" said his father, " why nothing, of course.   Do you think Lady Snaffle is to be argued with like a dealer at a fair ? I'll pound it Tom said nothing."

" You are right, sir.   I couldn't affirm that Danger is alto- gether a safe horse," replied Tom Scarlet.   " But I am to have The Bagman for a few weeks and try him.   A steeple-chase next winter is talked of, open to all horses that have been hunted in the Midland counties this present season.   Such a thing couldn't well come off without Sir Jerry."

" It couldn't come off at all without Sir Jerry.   Go on, Tom, and let us hear all about it."

" Sir Jerry will put in Danger and The Bagman, if it is a sweepstakes, and perhaps another."

" There will be no need for the other, and I should be un- willing to let her start if there was," said John Bullfinch, with his eye on the mare.   " Danger can beat any horse I know of that is qualified."

" I don't know about that," cried Young Jack.   " If the weights are light—that is, not up to welter weights——"

" Hold your tongue, sir !   Let Tom be heard.   One would think you knew more about it than either he or I."

" I prefer Danger to The Bagman at any weights, providing the chestnut has the right kind of a rider," said Tom.   " But between us here, I have as good as got a better horse for the five-mile journey over our bullfinches and ox-fences than either of them."

" Ah ! then he must be a rasper," said John.   " I must

mount and ride, **Tom.** Jack, go as far afield as the Long Hill and look over the wethers. May, my dear, kiss me. You get more like your mother every day. You need not sit up for me, my dear, if I happen to be a little late. Fury can be let loose before you go to bed. Any message for Mrs. Hickman?"

"Yes, love to her and Mary, father. Tell them they must be at our shearing, and I will send word when the cuckoo comes."

With a friendly nod to Tom Scarlet, and another kiss upon the cherry lips of his daughter, John Bullfinch mounted Cowslip and trotted leisurely away. His children and Tom looked at his stalwart retreating figure until it was hidden by the clump of blackthorn bushes around the hawk's well, from which the place took its name in old times.

"Dear father! he does so love Cowslip," said May.

"And with good reason. There never was such another mare," returned Tom Scarlet; "she's as good as Danger, and a little safer."

"A little safer—O, Tom!"

"Well, then, a good deal safer. Still, **Danger** is not half as bad as he is made out to be. He is not really vicious."

"O, no!" cried **Young Jack.** "Kind and docile, and just fit to carry a lady."

Tom Scarlet shook his head, told Jack to saddle Young Cowslip, a sister of the famous mare, and that he would ride with him to the Long Hill. Dismissing the boy with a wave of his hand, he followed May into the great kitchen of the farm-house, where the shepherd of the estate, old Will Dean, was already taking his early dinner. The sturdy old man—knotted, gnarled, gray as an aged oak, and almost as vigorous—sat at a table on one side of the wide fireplace, in which two or three billets of wood blazed. May Bullfinch stood before him, the Master of the Grange by her side. All around the shelves were glittering with pewter dishes. Flitches of bacon, great chines, and large plump hams filled the racks overhead, and hung upon spikes in the walls. The shepherd carved for himself from a gammon of bacon, red as a cherry and fragrant as a pear; while the daughter of the house poured for him good ale into a shining horn from a foaming flagon. Old

Will was a favorite with May, and he knew it. He often told her he was shepherd to her grandfather when her father was such another stripling as Young Master Jack, and affirmed with many a chuckle that Young Jack charged him with taking greater care of her ewes than he did of his.

"No lambs yet, Will?" said May.

"No, Miss, none; but there soon 'ull be. As soon as ever there be two or three couple I shall send for 'e. I have got a little hut built and thatched for 'e inside the fold."

"That's right. As soon as any of my ewes have lambs I shall be there every day to see them."

"And worth while, too, Miss! And well worth seeing they'll be, Mr. Scarlet, as you'll find out in a week or two. There ain't no such yoes as Miss May's in this county. I know there ain't, and I have been shepherd on this land more'n forty year."

"Young Jack's are good ones," observed Tom Scarlet, as if in doubt.

"Good 'uns! Ay, for him. But what do you think I said to Master and Sir Jerry Snaffle last autumn, 'bout the time of the fair? I said, says I, 'Be you two gentlemen a-going to exhibit any sheep at this here society? Because, if you be, don't you go and exhibit Cotswold yoes.'"

"Well, what then?"

"Why, then, they says, 'Why not?' And I says, says I, 'Because Miss May is a-going to show a pen of Cotswold yoes, and she can beat 'e both.' You should have heard the Master and Sir Jerry laugh. O, how they did laugh when I said, 'If the decision is fair and judgmatical, Miss May 'ull beat 'e both clean out o' sight.'"

With that old Will laid down his knife and fork, and roared till the rafters of the kitchen shook again.

CHAPTER III.

"The robin cheeped a dolorous note,
    And the corncrake from the lea—
The owlet gave an eerie skreigh
    As he leapt to the saddle tree."

IT was nine o'clock on a snowy night, and in the smoking room of the Wheatsheaf there were songs and other sounds of revelry. The Wheatsheaf was a substantial inn, kept by Mrs. Hickman, at Aylesbury—Aylesbury in the Vale, where the ducks come from, and where they held the real, straight-away steeple-chases of fifty years ago. The guests had reason to be content and merry. In the bar-parlor adjacent Mrs. Hickman sat in rustling black silk and the fine-thread lace made by the female peasantry of the neighborhood. In the bar itself, under her mother's eye, Mary Hickman presided. It was not like the bars of London gin-shops or New York hotels, but a snug little apartment, from which fine old wines and choice liquors were served to the waiter through a little window, and then carried to the guests in the bright, comfort-able smoking-room. The men of corn and cattle who occu-pied the room seemed to be loth to leave it. There was a huge sea-coal fire in the wide grate. Stout forms lined the high oaken settle which circled around it. The steam of hot grog mingled with the curling smoke from many pipes. The light flashed on spurs and buckles as the yeomen stretched their legs. There was laughter at passing jokes, and sometimes hammer-ing on the tables with the butts of hunting whips. Some think the men of corn and cattle are dull, heavy fellows, but it is a cockney heresy. They abound in jokes and dry humor, and have a vast capacity for drink and mirth; that is, they had at the time this company held revel in the Wheatsheaf, much to the delight of its head waiter.

The waiter was not a grave person in the rusty black of an undertaker's man, but a brisk and cheerful youth in drab breeches and gaiters, a green coat of the Newmarket cut, and a bird's-eye neckerchief, one of the sort named after the famous Mr. Jem Belcher. In fact, when not otherwise engaged, the

waiter sometimes put on the gloves with those of the Wheatsheaf's customers who belonged to the young aristocracy, and
it was whispered that no less a man than Jack Perkins, the
Oxford Pet, had offered to bring him out before the public in
that arena which was called the ring, mainly because it was
twenty-four feet square.   On this snowy evening the waiter
was in high glee.   He left no man unserved.   He laughed at
every joke, applauded every song, and was especially attentive
to the comfort and convenience of Mr. John Bullfinch of
Hawkwell.   Outside the snow fell fast and it had begun to
blow.   But John Bullfinch, with pipe and brandy and water,
and jovial companions, was as independent as Tam O'Shanter.
The minutes flew.   Stories were told of hard runs and great
leaps in the hunting field.   There were histories of fat beasts
and heavy crops, mingled with anecdotes of prize-fighters, and
eloquent tributes to the bravery and prowess of certain breeds
of game-cocks and bull and badger dogs.   John Bullfinch was
a sort of chairman to the company.   The narrators of the
stories addressed themselves chiefly to him.   The glasses were
often filled, and every time the jocund waiter carried that of
Mr. Bullfinch to the bar he said cheerily to his young mistress,
" Brandy and water for Mr. Bullfinch, just like the last."

The night waxed on.   One after another of the company
departed.   Many had to ride far before they got home, and
others had wives to explain to when they reached there.   So,
at last, except one or two townsmen, there remained only John
Bullfinch and a dark, lean, sinewy man, who sat at his right
hand, and answered to the name of Jack.   This man wore
cord breeches, a velveteen coat, somewhat old and weather-
beaten, with leather leggings and rusty spurs.   His look was
wary, yet daring; his eye was dark, very bright, and very
restless; and his long black hair fell over the nape of his neck.
Mr. Bullfinch and the gypsy—the man was a sort of horse-
dealer belonging to the tribes, and named Cotswold, though
seldom called anything but Jack or Gypsy Jack—were on very
good terms.   The latter was something of a pugilist as well
as a dealer in horses, and the farmer now told him some anecdotes of Jem Belcher and Cribb, both of whom he had seen
fight.   Perhaps the gypsy had heard the stories before, for he

did not appear to be especially interested, though he listened with deference.

"A wildish night, Mr. Bullfinch," said the ostler, as he came into the room and kicked the snow from his shoes at the grate.

"I've ridden home on Cowslip in a worse, but we may as well start," said the farmer. "Saddle the mare and bring her round. I'll say good-night to Mrs. Hickman, Jack, and then we will go."

"So you're going, Mr. Bullfinch," said the comely landlady, rising. "You will have a rough ride of it through the dark."

"The mare knows the road. Besides, I shall have company to the turn of the Wootton lands. Gypsy Jack is going so far."

"Queer company on such a night. You might as well be alone—perhaps better."

"Not at all, ma'am. Jack is a trustworthy fellow, and a deep hand. Between you and I, ma'am, very few understand Jack except Sir Jerry Snaffle, Tom Scarlet and myself."

"And how is Tom?" said the landlady.

"Well—very well! He was at my house this morning on Danger."

"I wonder he rides that horse, considering what happened."

"Now that reminds me that the last time I rode from here my horse shied abreast of the fence where John Scarlet was killed, and I was nearly thrown," said the farmer.

"You must be careful, Mr. Bullfinch; think of May. But it wasn't Cowslip?"

"Cowslip never shies, ma'am," replied John, with much gravity. "You may meditate upon her just as you may in your pew when the rector is in for a long, slow run, by way of sermon. Thank you, my dear" (this to Mary Hickman, as she handed him another glass), "I go over many things besides brooks and fences on Cowslip, ma'am. The back of a good horse, going home from feast, fair or market, is the best place for reflection and meditation that I know of. The action of the horse settles the thoughts; and the pace being good, sobers —that is, steadies—a man. Mrs. Hickman, your health, and Mary, yours, my dear. You are like my daughter, May— getting prettier every day."

The damsel of the Wheatsheaf glanced into the pier-glass over the fireplace with a smile and mantling blush, and then tripped into the little bar.   There she stood, fair to look upon, in the midst of glittering crystal and burnished silver, from which her face was reflected on every hand.   It glowed in the old wines, and where the potent spirit of Cognac lay, like a tiger in his den, it shone in the ruby flame.   It was an innocent little face! seen "through a glass darkly," in the lair of the turbulent essence, which held fixed the sunshine of a year. John Bullfinch stirred his grog and sipped, and stirred again, and as the spoon tinkled in the glass, he thought of wedding bells, Mary Hickman as a bridesmaid, his daughter May and Tom Scarlet.   The action of the horse was just about wanted to "settle the thoughts, and the pace being good, to steady the man."   John drank up.

"You are to come and stay two or three days at sheep-shearing time; but before that you are to drive over and spend the day among the violets and primroses, when the cuckoo comes. That's May's message, with her best love."

"Thanks! thanks!   Our love to her," said the landlady and her daughter.

"May will let you know when he's heard on the long hill. The cuckoo, in these parts, is first heard on our long hill.   It was so in my father's time and in my grandfather's.   It is so in mine, and so it will be in my son Jack's, and in that of those who come after him.   The philosophy of the matter is that the cuckoo's guided by instinct, which, as Jack observed this morning, makes young ducks hatched out by a hen toddle off to the nearest water.   Mrs. Hickman, good-night.   Mary, my dear, good-night.   Not a step out of the parlor.   'Good-by, sweethearts, good-by!'"

"Good-night! good-night!" exclaimed the ladies; and then Mrs. Hickman added: "Of all the graziers, dealers, farmers, and hunting men that visit Aylesbury in the Vale, John Bullfinch is the noblest man—a perfect gentleman!"

"Good-night again!" as John Bullfinch dropped a shilling into the ostler's hand.

"And a real good-night to you, sir," in which the waiter joined as the hunting mare struck into a canter, and the gypsy followed on his vixenish-looking nag.

Through the dimly-lighted town, and by the muffled, drowsy-looking watchmen, crawling like beetles under the eaves and gables of quaint old houses, the horsemen rode. Then leaving the baying of the watch-dogs behind them, they wound down the hill towards the north and west and into the rich vale below. It was about the last of a long and hard winter—a time when the old tyrant seemed to see, with rage, that men were getting ready to welcome joyous spring, and so determined to make the close of his iron sway felt while he had yet time. The wind blew keenly, and with it drifted a powdery snow. The sky was cloudy, but behind the pack there seemed to be a fitful sort of light, which now and again shone through. It couldn't be the moon, for there was no moon that night till later, and it shone mainly in the northern board of the clouded heavens. Commonly the horsemen could see dimly nothing but fields of snow and straggling hedges, and then again it would lighten up with a pale glare, and the cattle and sheep suddenly took shape and form for a moment. It was not a flickering light, but steady enough while visible, though coming and going like that thrown from a dark lantern. It was a light of which John Bullfinch did not much approve. Cats, bats and owls might fancy it, he observed, but for his part he would rather have good, black, honest darkness.

"Aye," said the gypsy, drawing nearer to the farmer, "this here light that comes just enough to make us blink and get blinder, 'ud suit churchyards, ghosts, grave-diggers and resurrection men better nor horsemen on the King's highway."

John Bullfinch did not like the suggestion. He repeated that good, natural darkness would be preferable, but thought the less said about ghosts and graves at such a time the better.

"The light," said he, "is just such as twenty 'Jack-o'-Lanterns' and twenty 'Will-o'-the-Wisps' might be expected to show through the mingled mist and snow of a winter's night."

With that he gave Cowslip the rein, and nothing loth she dashed along at a better pace, one which made the gypsy's nag gallop to keep up with her. Over the snow the horses and their riders went, mostly silent, always resolute, and still the long easy canter of the hunting mare kept the gypsy's nag at a gallop. They met the up night mail coach. They exchanged "Good-night," the universal benison, with the coach-man and the guard in passing. And at last they reached the turn of the lands, not a quarter of a mile from the Woods of Wootton. Here the gypsy said to his companion, "Good-night," and turning to the right, rode down into the shadow of a green lane, now white with snow, between tall hedges.

As the gypsy was about to leave him, John Bullfinch pulled the hunting-mare to a shacking trot and began to cogitate. The question was, whether he should ride home by the road, or through the deep woods and great preserves of the Marquis of Wootton. The woods were seldom traversed at night except by poachers and their enemies, the keepers and watchers. John, however, was on the most intimate terms with the head keeper, and was conceded the right of way whenever he chose to take it. The road, argued he, to himself, is further round and quite as lonely as the woods. It might be lighter, but he didn't want any more of the sort of light he had experienced upon it thus far. Besides, he remembered that he had busi-ness with the keeper, and should really be at home all the sooner for going through the woods and calling upon him. At the first gate he turned from the highway into one of the rides, between old oaks and thick underwood. It was not the first time by many, that John Bullfinch had ridden through these woods at night to call upon Moleskin. The keeper was a crony of his, and though they often disputed, they were at the bottom, staunch friends. John Bullfinch considered vulcipede a crime very nearly as heinous as murder, except when the death of the fox was brought about in the orthodox manner by a pack of hounds. Moleskin, on the other hand, had been suspected of shooting vixens and trapping cubs about the time the young pheasants were half grown. John had a sort of weak sympathy for poachers. Moleskin proclaimed with some ostentation, that he would shoot every known poacher he found in the preserves, out of hand, if it were not for the law. John denounced man-traps and spring-guns. Moleskin pretended that he had them set at all convenient places, and affected to look upon their inventor as a greater man than he who pro-duced the steam-engine. Their arguments were animated and long ; and neither ever succeeded in convincing the other that he was in the wrong. This, however, was nothing against their reasoning, for each was a man of obstinacy, and neither was inclined to give in upon compulsion. Moleskin was a bachelor. He had many tastes in common with the old hunters and backwoodsmen of our Western frontier. He lived alone in a sylvan lodge, deep in the great, solemn woods, some of whose oaks may have been as old as the era of the Norman Conquest. Sleeping much in the daytime, he was as alert, as watchful and as wary as an old dog fox by night. Like the sorcerer of old who entertained a familiar in a black bottle, Moleskin kept by him the spirit of old Cognac, and John Bullfinch knew it.

Silently and slowly the hunting-mare cantered over the soft carpet of snow that lay between the overhanging boughs of the great trees and the thick belts of bushes, until her eyes and those of her rider became used to the dim darkness of the woods. The ride was some thirty feet wide, and smooth as a bowling green, though with slopes and hills here and there. The snow hung heavy on the boughs and bushes, and still fell fast. The wind had veered to the westward, and the fall was now in thick, damp flakes. Sometimes John Bullfinch thought it had ceased, but whenever he threw back his broad-brimmed hat he found, by the spots in his face, that it was still falling. There was no wind in the ride, but now and then it swept through the vistas of the great trees with a melancholy sough, like a wail for evil things foreknown. Once in a while the yelp of the fox was heard, and the doleful screech of the owl broke the silence of the night. Then all was still again. The wood pigeons were silent, and the crows made no motion on the boughs. But there were murmurings deep in the thickets, as though the trees had tongues, voices of the ancient wood gods, heard ere old Pan was dead. A strange glimmer now came glinting down from the cloudy sky and up from the smooth snow, and lost itself in the shade of the tall trees and bushes. The oaks were often overgrown with ivy, and so were thick with foliage not their own. As his eyes got accustomed to this sort of weird gloaming, the farmer pricked more speedily along towards the hermitage where the stout keeper, after the manner of the Clerk of Copmanhurst, kept flagon and crust. Yet into the dark, beyond the space of his narrow ken, John Bullfinch now was ever peering. The hunting-mare, too, swerved always to the right, and pulled upon the near rein. John Bullfinch soon began to think that he had some sort of company in his midnight canter. More and more the notion grew upon him, until he was pretty nearly convinced that close to the bushes, on the left-hand side of the ride, there was something moving abreast of him. He rubbed his eyes and looked steadily; he drew the collar of his coat down from his ears and listened intently. Then he spoke to the mare. Cowslip quickened the stroke, but edged over to the right-hand side so far that the farmer's boot brushed against the bushes. John Bullfinch was not a man to linger long in doubt when action of his own could clear up an uncertainty. He touched Cowslip with the spur, gave her a cut with the whip down the shoulder, and pulled her suddenly across the ride to intercept that which seemed to be abreast of him. With a long leap like that with which she took a brook in stride, the hunting-mare bounded to the left side of the ride, but though she touched the bushes just where the shape which had perplexed her master ought to have been, it eluded her, as though it were a thing without corporeal substance to its form. This was passing strange. John Bullfinch pulled Cowslip into the middle of the ride and gave her her head. Fast now she went, faster and faster still, as she felt the close clip of the farmer's knees, and his delicate pull upon the snaffle bridle, but he soon found that the form he had been aware of rather than seen before was at her girths again, in the deep shadow. He looked over his left shoulder at the shape which was nearly shapeless and so swift, and knew not what to make of the matter. Again and suddenly he gave the mare a touch with the spur, and made her dash across to the left, so that he thought he could not fail to bring about a collision. But none came. He saw the glint of a fiery eye, and then, like a rack of cloud and mist in a driving storm, the thing swept by the mare's haunches and was gone. John Bullfinch was not a superstitious man. He knew no reason why a goblin shape, from the confines of the other world, should have power to vex and worry him. He was a true though unworthy son of the Church, paid his tithes without grumbling, was at the Communion-table at Easter, grace was always said at his board, through May he gave much in alms to the poor, and he was upon good terms with the rector and the curate. All this passed through his mind—but there was the shape again, and neither rector, curate, nor clerk at hand to exorcise it. John Bullfinch was a brave man, but now a chill went through him as though an ice-tipped arrow from the grim hand of Death himself had struck his heart and frozen up its fountain. The good mare, too, trembled between his knees, and John took this as an evil omen. What might it mean?

The farmer considered, and was sore distressed to find that he had forgotten, for the first time in his life, the order of the sublime sentences which constitutes the prayer of our Lord. There came upon his ear the sound of a church bell which he knew. Every night in winter it was rung at the same hour for thirty minutes, by provision of a dead man's will. In times long gone by, when that part of the country was mostly mire and wood and water, the haunt of wild fowl, birds of game, and beasts of chase, one lost in a wild night and in much distress, had regained his road through hearing the passing bell as it was tolled for some poor soul that had gone from the flesh. For the rest of his life, the man had it rung at the same hour, and when he died in due course of nature, not starved in the wild, buried in the snow, or smothered in the fen, he left property to pay for the continuance of the nightly ringing for all time to come. Strange to say, the sound of the bell, coming faintly and dreamily through the trees, brought small relief to the mind of honest John Bullfinch. He might not have heard that goblins damned and spirits evil can no more abide the sound of bell from gray church tower than they can stand the cheerful crowing of the early village cock. Something of the virtues of a horse-shoe as a talisman occurred to him.

"But," said he, "the mare can't have cast off all four of hers, and it's no good for this gear."

The efficacy of witch elm and witch hazel for the counteraction of ungodly spells, and to curb the cantrips of the servants of the evil one, was well known to him. But it was too dark to find a wand of either, although plenty grew thereabout. And besides, John would have been in no hurry to dismount if he could have found what he wanted. Rocked in the cradle of the saddle almost from infancy, the back of his horse was his place of vantage, the mare his tower of strength, and if he was to contend with things of diabolical origin he would meet them on her back. He thought, for just a moment, whether it would not be better to gallop back to the turnpike road, but scorning to retreat for ghost or goblin, he clucked to Cowslip and rode forward. As if in response to this resolute pluck, the moonlight now broke faintly through the flying scud above, and things became more distinct. Away went the good bay mare over the snow, while the night wind moaned among the tree tops. With the fumes of brandy dying in him, and the disordered thoughts and feelings that, swift as dreams, rushed through him, John's brain was a little confused. The great stride of the mare bore him rapidly along, and as he neared his destination he was about to devote to the Red Sea —whether the one of water or that whose billows are of rolling fire—all ghosts, goblins, and demons of the dark. But just then the owl shrieked, "the fatal bellman which gives the stern'st good-night." The moon, like a good ship scudding in storm and mist, sailed into the narrow strait between two dark promontories of cloud, and revealed the appearance again. It took shape and form—a phantom horse of great size and power ; white as the monumental tablets in the chancel of the church John knew so well—one erected to the memory of John Scarlet, another over the resting-place of a man done to death upon the highway. One flash from fiery eyes ! one glare from glowing nostrils ! the white mane waved in the wind, and the apparition vanished as the moon sailed behind the dark clouds again.

The farmer was aghast. He liked not the form of the apparition, and he was half inclined to say, " Take any shape but that !" He did say, " I have been charged with thinking more of horses than of my Maker, but that was all a lie, and if this *is* a visitation, it must be meant in mercy, not in wrath." He tried to remember whether any farmer, drover, or gentleman who rode a white horse had ever been murdered in the woods, but he could think of none. There came prancing into his mind the figure of a white horse on the sign-board of an inn that he sometimes frequentèd ; and then he thought of that pale steed who carries the fleshless King, with his all-slaying dart.

" If it's *that* white horse, *he* wasn't on him, which is a consolation," said John, as he touched Cowslip with the spur, and she sped away.

CHAPTER IV.

"But, Roman, when thou standest
Upon that holy ground,
Look thou with heed upon the rock
That girds the dark lake round;
So shalt thou see a hoof-mark
Stamped deep into the flint—
It was no hoof of mortal steed
That made so strange a dint."

IT may be doubted whether the hunting-mare ever went faster in her life than she did in the short space between the place where her master saw the neck and shoulders of the White Horse and the keeper's lodge. If the phantom and she had been running a neck-and-neck race for a horseman's soul, the one jockeyed by Apollyon and the other by an angel of light, she could scarcely have finished the heat with a more determined "rush on the post." John Bullfinch threw himself from the saddle with a loud halloo, and looked around. There was no white horse to be seen; nothing but the good bay mare, in a lather on the neck and in the flanks. Calling to Moleskin, who came out with a lantern, to bring him a blanket, the farmer led Cowslip under a sheltered shed and slackened her girths. He then wrapped her up, sponged her eyes and her muzzle, breathed into her wide nostrils three times, and, taking the keeper by the upper part of his sinewy arm, led him into the lodge without a word. The keeper's sitting-room was fitted and furnished suitable to his calling. Guns in racks, shot-belts and powder-flasks upon the walls, a white hare stuffed upon the mantel-piece, an old pointer lay before the fire, a cross-bred dog of the bull and pointer sat upon the hearth, and a tan-colored mastiff, of great size and strength, was chained near the case of the old eight-day clock. The keeper was a tall man, thin, but very muscular and sinewy, with a deep-gray eye and a grave, cast-iron sort of face—a watchful, wary, bold and determined-looking man. He had, perhaps, been taking a little brandy and water, for a black bottle and tumbler were upon the table, with a pipe and tobacco in a canister of lead. Contrary to his usual cus-

3

tom, which was to avoid the drinking of spirits neat, John Bullfinch poured out a dram of brandy, and drank it without any reference to Moleskin's health.

"Dick," said he, "bring another pipe."

The keeper did so. John Bullfinch filled it, lit it, took a seat, motioned Moleskin to another, and then said:

"What do you think I met to-night—this blessed night that still hangs over us?"

"How should I know? A couple of footpads, maybe. I have often said you carry too many notes and too much gold. The temptation to footpads, and, in a measure, to poachers, should be avoided."

"Footpads be hanged!"

"It's only transportation now, unless there is murder as well as robbery; and you are alive, I think," said the keeper.

"Don't you be a fool. It wasn't footpads—I could have dealt with them—but something much more serious," said the farmer.

"What! do you mean to say that there are poachers abroad? Have you seen or heard anything of poachers in this domain? Because, if you have, Tiger and I must be stirring."

The keeper laid his hand upon his gun as he spoke. The half-bred bull-dog rose and sniffed the air. The big mastiff looked at his master with sullen, bloodshot eyes, and shook his chain. John Bullfinch had let his pipe go out. He now lighted it again, and after a couple of whiffs, said:

"Moleskin, do you believe in ghosts—ghosts and goblins— what you may call apparitions?"

"Do I believe in ghosts? and in goblins and apparitions? Well, not in this domain—not in these woods and preserves. No ghost with a grain of sense would pick this for his tramping ground; for here, you see, he would meet with mastiffs, bull-dogs, double-barrelled guns, and so on, to say nothing of man-traps and spring-guns, which are set at certain convenient places on these premises."

"That's neither here nor there, sir. I ask, do you believe in such things in a general way?"

"In a general way I do not; but there may be such things in the proper places," replied the keeper.

"What do you call proper places for such appearances? Is this a proper place?" said Mr. Bullfinch.

"No, sir; it is a very improper place," replied the keeper. "To my mind the proper places are churchyards, old, solitary houses, in which misers have died of starvation among heaps of hoarded gold ; lone places where midnight murder has been done and the perpetrators have gone unhung; the foot of gibbets on heaths and moors where you hear the croak of the raven by day and the hoot of the owl at night. These are the situations for ghosts and goblins. I have no belief of any in these woods."

"Then I have, for I have just seen one," said Mr. Bullfinch in his most resolute manner.

The keeper saw that downwright contradiction would be of little service, but he shook his head as the farmer continued in a tone serious enough to command attention, if not partial belief.

"Look here, Dick! We are old friends. You have known me, man and boy, for many a year. Now, something very strange has happened since I turned into the woods to-night. Something followed me, or rather kept abreast of me from the gate of the ride until I drew bridle at this lodge. Twice it was close to me. Once when the moon broke through the drifts of clouds, I saw it quite plain, and perceived that it was as white as the snow itself."

"A fellow in a white smock-frock, with a pocket full of snares, and a short double-barrelled gun, the stock and barrels separated for convenience and concealment," said the keeper. "You ought to have seen the lurcher, too, for I'll pound it there was one. A mittimus to the governor of Aylesbury jail, or Oxford castle, lays ghosts of that sort for a time ; and the jaws of a man-trap, or a charge out of a spring-gun, nicely set and properly levelled, will do it sometimes more quickly and with less trouble."

"You are too knowing, by half," said Mr. Bullfinch. "A fellow a-foot keep up with Cowslip! I suppose that if you had been there it wouldn't have vanished into the air?"

"I don't think it would, especially as I should have had Tiger at my heels," returned the keeper, grimly. "But it is strange to hear you going on in this way, and to see you looking so solemn. You have ridden through these woods on nights quite as unkid as this, and you've met all sorts of men in all sorts of places."

"If this had appeared as a man I should not have thought so much of it," said Mr. Bullfinch, with great force and deliberation.

"Oh! it appeared as a woman! I have it! Miriam Cotswold, dark Janet, or some other gal of their infernal tribe, on the lookout while the men of the gang are after the roosting pheasants. Your friend Gypsy Jack is at the bottom of this here audacious job."

"It didn't appear as a woman, either. It came as a horse, a white horse!" said the farmer.

"Well, what of that?"

"A good deal of it," said John tartly. "I think I know a horse when I see one. I ought to, for I was born the night Pot-8-os was foaled, and have ridden for forty years. This wasn't a real horse, but the apparition of one."

"What makes you believe it wasn't real?"

"Two or three things. It didn't act like a real horse. Cowslip didn't act as if it was a real horse. I *felt* that it wasn't a horse with four honest shoes on, made by a mortal blacksmith at an earthly forge."

He then told the story of his ride from the entrance into the woods, and the earnest narrative was not without some impression on the keeper. Moleskin filled his pipe, replenished John's glass and his own, and looked fixedly at the farmer for some moments.

"It is very strange," said he, musingly. "What I can't make out is the white horse."

"Just so. I can't make it out myself."

"I don't mind telling you now," said the keeper, "but in strict confidence, people have thought they saw something in these woods before that was not just right. But then, you see, it wasn't a white horse, but a brindled dog—a deerhound. Some fifteen years ago one of my men was murdered by poachers."

"I remember it. I saw the body, and a shocking sight it was," said Mr. Bullfinch.

"So it was. Here lay the dog under a hawthorn bush, shot

through the head. A little further in the thicket was the man, with his breast blown in by a charge fired right over the heart, and close to him, for the powder burnt his clothes. Several fellows, well-known poachers, were arrested on suspicion, among them two gypsies, one of whom was the brother of your friend Jack, and the father of Miriam Cotswold. But nothing could be brought home to them, and the murderers were never detected. The Marquis, as in duty bound, provided for the widow and her children, but she was doleful in these parts, and soon moved away, down into Northamptonshire. Well, they say the man walks, and the dog along with him, though Hector was my dog, not his; and the story goes among the old women, who profess to know, that he will walk as long as the murderer lives. When he dies and goes to judgment they say the weary spirit will find rest."

" Do you believe this, Moleskin ?"

" I don't know whether I do or not. I am, as you may say, a lonely man, and my time is mostly spent in the gloom and shadow of the woods. I was born under these oaks, and hardly a night for fifty years but I have heard the hoot of the owl among the ivy. I don't know whether I believe in this reputed ghost or not, but I am sure I don't fear it."

" Did you ever see it ?" said the farmer.

" The man, never. I may have seen the dog. In these parts there are but few like him. Some years ago I came upon a brindled deerhound, near the spot where the man was murdered, three nights running. At first I thought he was self-hunting, but he always disappeared at that particular spot, and what's more, he left no tracks; I brought a dark lantern and examined the ground at night, as the rain would have washed the footprints away by morning. On the third night I shot at this dog, and what do you think happened ?"

" The gun missed fire or you missed."

" The gun did not miss fire and I didn't miss. I am not in the habit of missing. But I didn't hit, either. I shot at his haunches. Instead of making off, he turned and looked me in the face—full in the face ! John Bullfinch, as sure as you and I sit here alive, he was shot in the head, instead of the haunches; and it was my old dog Hector, the one that was killed when the man was murdered. Some say there's no soul, no spirit in a dog, to come back again; but this dog did come back."

"I have heard the same thing remarked about horses, and hold it to be all a lie, the invention of people who have not half the sense and affection of a good horse," said John.

"Still, this matter I have been relating throws no light upon the white horse. May it not have been a white cart-horse strayed?"

"Cart-horse!" said John, with some contempt. "Do you think there ever was a cart-horse that could keep alongside of Cowslip, and she at speed?"

"Well, I suppose not. But there's a white horse, an old hunter, over at the Barleymow."

"Flea-bitten gray, blind of an eye, and with a stringhalt," said Mr. Bullfinch. He continued: "This had a thoroughbred head, an eye like one bright star on a night of storm, and its action must have been perfect—perfect!"

"Tom Scarlet is always getting all sorts of horses. It may be a new one, escaped from The Grange and broke into the woods on the far side."

"No such luck. It was an apparition; that is what the white horse was, and it portends something, probably a death."

"Come, none of that. I ain't going to die, nor you either, you know," said the keeper.

"I hope not, Dick; but Death and the White Horse is a constant saying all the country through, and has been so ever since I was a boy."

"It's the pale horse in the Bible, which I take to be a shadowy sort of a cream. This saying about Death and the White Horse was all along of a picture painted for old George the Third," said Moleskin.

"I have seen it, and it is about as much like a real horse as a hen; not at all like the appearance of the horse I saw to-night. Besides, if this was King Death's horse, he had been throwed, for there was no rider on him," said John.

They sat and conversed for a short time further, but to no end. Among all the appearances they could remember to have heard of—some in old churchyards, some in crumbling mansions, some on lonely heaths, where men all unprepared for the taking off had been done to death; some beneath gibbets, upon which the bones of criminals swung in the moaning wind and hollowly rattled—there was none of a White Horse. At length John started out, tightened the girths of the mare, and, taking her by the bridle, led her along. The keeper, with his gun in the hollow of his arm and with the mastiff at his heels, walked with him, intending to go but a short distance. It was the dead time of the night. There was no yelp from the fox. The owl was still, among the ivy of his hollow tree. No cheerful crow came from a distant hen-roost. The snow fell silently. The wind was hushed. The leaden sky seemed to press down almost upon the tree-tops. Mist rose breast-high from the swampy ground. The men and the mare plodded along, with the mastiff in their tracks. The ride they took was a narrow one, and presently it fell into a deep swale, in which alders and willows were mingled with the hazel and the hawthorn.

"It was hereabouts that the man was——"

The keeper stopped abruptly, for with a noise like the rush of a whirlwind the mist was pushed aside, as it were, and a white horse, dimly seen, swept by them at speed. The mastiff followed with a savage howl. The men exchanged exclamations, and the keeper felt the caps upon the nipples of his gun.

"If I had had a silver bullet in one of the barrels I should have fired," said he. "No other metal will bring 'em down."

The dog came slinking back and retired behind them.

"Tiger's cowed for the first time in his life!" said the keeper. "John, come back and stay with me till daylight. There are things abroad that bode no good."

"Not I. Come what may I will go through!"

"Well, well, just come back till I melt half a crown and run it through the bullet mould. With this gun and a brace of silver bullets, I'd face the devil himself."

"And I will without them, if need be. I fear God, honor the King, and say confound the devil and all his works!"

With this John Bullfinch mounted the mare, and uttering a loud "Good-night," rode rapidly away. The keeper leaned upon his gun for a few seconds, then cast a look upon his dog and turned homewards.

CHAPTER V.

" Sir Leoline, the baron rich,
    Hath a brindled mastiff bitch.
    In her kennel, beneath the rock,
    She makes answer to the clock.
    Twelve for the quarters,
    Four for the hour :
    Sixteen short barks, not over loud ;
    Some say she sees my lady's shroud."

IT was not a very uncommon thing for John Bullfinch to be late at night, but it was seldom that he was late in the morning, and ill at ease as well. After his midnight ride with the White Horse, he was gloomy and depressed, feeling that something ill was about to happen, or to be disclosed. His daughter had aired the county paper, and folded it by his plate. He sat down to the meal with May and his son, but ate nothing, and let the paper lie untouched. His eyes were red, yet dull ; for the treacherous spirit of Cognac had changed from ruby to blue. He stirred his coffee and seemed in deep thought. The breakfast spoon in the cup made no such merry music as that which had tinkled in the glass the night before at the Wheatsheaf. He stared at the white cat and pondered. A pigeon, flashing past the window, like a wreath of snow, made him start. He looked at May.

" I was late last night—very late—much later than I intended to be. You didn't sit up ?"

" No, we did not ; but I was unable to sleep," replied May. " Fury barked the live-long night, except just when you came in. I can't think what ailed her."

" Tramps about, perhaps," said Young Jack ; " but I think she wants a licking, and I had a great mind to get up and give her one."

" It was well you didn't," said his father. " If you had licked Fury you might have got licked yourself. The bitch is a good bitch, faithful and bold. She acted after her kind, and, no doubt, had reason for what she did. I wish some boys were half as true and sensible."

"If they were no more sensible than to howl all night for nothing——"

Young Jack did not finish the sentence, for the door was flung open by one of the farm men, and John Bullfinch cried:

"What's the matter now?"

"Murder is the matter now," said Moleskin, striding into the room.

"No wonder Fury howled!" said May.

John Bullfinch sat aghast. What with the brandy blues, the White Horse, and the tidings brought by Moleskin, he was nearly confounded.

"Murder! Why, how, and where, and who?"

"As to who and where, it's easy to answer; but how, and why it was done, is another thing. I want you to ride over to my lodge while I go for the doctor. I have had Stevens taken there. He isn't quite dead, though senseless and left for dead. He was found within forty yards of where you and I parted."

"I knowed it all along. I told you so, Dick!" exclaimed John Bullfinch.

"Then, sir, if anybody else but you had said he knowed it all along, I should have took him up as accessory before the fact, which is just about as bad as the principal," cried another comer.

It was the parish constable, a little red-nosed man, voluble and restless, with high esteem of his own wisdom and station. Parkins, besides being inquisitive and meddlesome by "vartue" of his office, naturally was a busybody. He did not entertain such a fair opinion of many of his neighbors as of himself, but rather held in contempt many people who would have been much surprised if they could have heard some of his rapid soliloquies. He valued himself, in truth, very highly; first as "one of the authorities;" second, as *the* one who was, in his own expressive words, "not to be gammoned." His neighbors, high and low, were estimated by a sort of sliding scale, with which their liberality in dispensing malt liquor had much to do. Sir Jerry Snaffle, as one of the authorities, Chairman of the bench of Magistrates, stood high on that account, but higher still because his ale was of rare excellence, and was to be had at the Hall by whoever visited it, without so much

as asking.   Parkins often visited the mansion on one pretence
or another, and tersely expressed his opinion of the place and
its owner, thus: " Best quality, nut-brown, clear as amber,
sound as a bell—tap allus a-running."   John Bullfinch did
not stand as high as Sir Jerry in the constable's mental barom-
eter, by some inches.   John had backed prize-fighters, and
Parkins hated prize-fighters.   They had once or twice " pitched
into the authorities," instead of keeping the King's peace when
solemnly commanded to do so.   John suffered gypsies to camp
in his green lanes, and Parkins abhorred gypsies, especially
Gypsy Jack.   John had a sort of weakness in regard to punishing poachers, and a poacher was an abomination to Parkins.
Mr. Bullfinch had once interceded for a shepherd boy taken
red-handed, as it were, by Parkins, with a dead hare in possession, and had so " gammoned the higher authorities" that
the culprit was released with a nominal fine.   Still, there was
compensation, and Parkins summed it up as follows : " But his
brew is first-rate ; No. 1, brass tap, right hand side of the cellar !   Best malt, double strike to the hogshead.   East Kent
hops ; black horse brand !   Besides, his tankards is good measure—imperial.   None o' them disgustin' and disappintin' false
bottoms with which some low people try to gammon the authorities."   Such was the man who had hastily entered while
Mr. Bullfinch was speaking.

" Parkins, shut up.   I know what Mr. Bullfinch means and
it's all right," said the keeper.   " Go with him and examine
the tracks about the place where Stevens lay.   You'll find Mr.
Bullfinch's and mine at no great distance, and the tracks of
his mare, for it left off snowing as I got home.   But those are
not the tracks that are wanted.   You *may* find the track of
another horse, whether shod or not I can't say.   Report all
to me."

" Not shod—of course not," said John Bullfinch to the
keeper, in an undertone.

" Father," said Young Jack, " there's no use in letting
Moleskin go for the doctor.   I'll throw the saddle on Young
Cowslip, and go myself.   I can be there in no time."

" The gig, Jack—the gray horse in the gig," said May.
" The doctor will be there much sooner that way than upon
his pony."

The farmer looked round, and nodded acquiescence in what had been advanced by his son and daughter. He then gave his orders promptly.

"Saddle Black Hearty. Moleskin, you shall ride Young Cowslip. She is all ready, for Jack has been a-field. Parkins, you must come on a-foot."

"One minute," said May Bullfinch; "Stevens is a married man."

"Yes, with five children," returned the keeper; "and how to break this bad news to his wife I don't know. Of course, if it comes to the worst, the Marquis will provide for the family; but when the wife first hears of it there will be a terrible taking on; and I never could bear to see a woman in great and sudden grief."

"Nor I neither," said John. "But here's May; I see what she means to do."

"Yes, I will break this fearful news to his wife; and may Our Father in heaven see fit, in his mercy, to save this poor man to her and the little children."

"Very proper on her part," said Parkins, as May left the room. "I have always said she was a good 'un. A deal too good to be throwed away on such a scamp as Tom Scarlet," he added in an undertone. Then aloud, "As there will be much to do by the authorities—somebody to be took up and jugged—my opinion is that a horn of ale apiece, before we set out on the investigation, will be the right way to begin."

John Bullfinch made a sign to his housekeeper, and Parkins soon had his face buried in a tankard. Neither the farmer nor the keeper drank. The former betrayed signs of impatience, as Black Hearty and Young Cowslip were now at the door.

"We needn't be in a great hurry. We shall be there long before the doctor," said the keeper. "I only hope there is a chance for life. Stevens was one of my best men."

"A good, stout fellow, and feared nothing," replied Mr. Bullfinch.

"A quarrelsome blade, gentlemen, known to the authorities, and been had up three or four times for assault and battery," observed Parkins. "Now, who do you suspect of this here murder, master keeper?"

"I have not formed any suspicion yet—have you?" replied Moleskin.

With his head on one side, and the cunning look of a jackdaw, the constable laid his finger to his nose and winked portentously. "Mum's the word now. When the parties be took up and in safe holt, I'll let you know as much as I do."

"Which is just nothing at all, I expect," said the keeper, as Parkins went away.

John Bullfinch and Moleskin followed, and, being mounted, quickly passed the constable. They rode along some distance in silence, but as they neared the wood the farmer said:

"And you think he is fatally injured? Has anybody questioned him?"

"It's of no use; he is out of his senses, and all over blood from wounds in the head. I'm afraid his skull is broken."

"With what weapon, think you—a bludgeon or the stock of a gun?" said John.

"I didn't stay to examine, and it will be hard to say; he mumbled a little as I leaned over him, and I made out a few wandering words. What do you think he said?"

"Something about his wife and children, no doubt."

"Nothing of the kind; his mind seemed to be upon what he saw, or thought he saw, at the time of the attack. I couldn't understand much that he muttered, but he mentioned the name of Tom Scarlet, and spoke of a white horse."

"Dick, I'm amazed!" cried John Bullfinch.

"Well, I don't know that I am much. There was a white horse about there, we know. Now that violence has been done, I have chucked over the notion of anything supernatural. It's a good deal too natural when it comes to murder. The ghosts of men don't break heads in the dark, nor the ghosts of horses kick their brains out."

"But Tom Scarlet—I know he's rash and wild, but I cannot believe he did this thing; he had no enmity against Stevens," said John.

"He has queer associates for a man of his property and belongings, has Mr. Tom Scarlet," said the keeper; "he's hail fellow with the gypsies, and hand and glove with a set of men from London and Brummagem, who dress well, drink hard, ride fine horses, and live the Lord knows how. I wish I knew what sort of company supped at the Grange last night. This job was not done till nigh morning. I could tell that by the blood, and by Stevens's watch, which stopped at about four."

"It looks bad—it looks awkward; but I do not believe that Tom did it."

"He may have been with the man who did it, though," returned Moleskin. "But we will say nothing of this to Parkins. The first thing is to know whether it's death or some chance for life."

These were the last words that passed until they reached the lodge, where they found Stevens still in a heavy stupor. The doctor came, examined the wounds, and talked as doctors do.

"A critical case; compound fracture; great danger that inflammation would set in; concussion of the brain; the worst results to be apprehended, but still some hope, with judicious treatment. Good thing I was sent for instead of ————, a—a—a person of no experience!"

CHAPTER VI.

"The chough and the crow
  To roost have gone,
    The owl sits on the tree;
  The night wind makes its fitful moan,
    Like infant charity.
  The wild fire dances in the glen—
    The red star sheds its ray—
  Uprouse ye, then, my merry, merry men!
    It is our opening day."

WHEN John Bullfinch parted with Gypsy Jack at the turn of the lands, that worthy cantered along until he was two or three miles from the turnpike road. He then filled a short pipe, struck a light, and puffing away merrily, went briskly forward between the tall hedges of the lane. The gypsies seldom spare their horses, and Jack was about the last man in England to spare his when there was service to be done.

The wiry galloway, too, had good blood in him, and went gaily up to the bit as though he would never tire, unless the

pace was set too strong. The way the gypsy was travelling
was seldom used except by poachers, tramps, and the people
of his own roving race. Gypsy Jack, however, had no desire
for company, and the loneliness of the situation and the mur-
kiness of the night rather suited him than otherwise. A
smart canter of five or six miles brought him to the verge of
a wide, wild heath. It was a sombre-looking place, even when
the clumps of gorse, which grew here and there, could be seen.
Now it was one waste of snow below, and cloud above, save
far to the right, where a red glow rose like the reflection of a
fire from the mouth of a pit or a lime-kiln. The gypsy rode
towards it. He drew bridle, after some time, near a deep
hollow, in the bight of which a party of his people had pitched
their tents. The embers of the huge fire were all aglow in the
bottom of the glen, and though the tents, with their covering
of snow, could not be distinguished from the white ground,
Jack readily made out the forms of the horses and donkeys
hobbled at the camp. It was no part of his design to show
himself. He reined up under the lee of a thick clump of
gorse and gave a low whistle. Five minutes had not elapsed
before the gorse was parted where the gypsy sat on his horse,
and a boy of some fourteen years old stepped silently out, like
a young wolf, from his lair.

"I thought you wasn't a-going to come at all. You've been
away near a week, and me with such news as never was," said
the boy.

"I was detained. What is this news?" returned Jack.

"Jagger come down from Lunnon town," replied the boy.

"I know it. I met Harry Cox at the fair."

"Then you expected him, perhaps?"

"Perhaps I did, but not quite so soon," replied Jack. "However, as he's here, he must come to a settlement."

"He won't come to anything of the sort," said the boy, confidently.

"Why not, Ike?"

"Because he's gone again."

"Ah, but he'll return. He dare not try to give me the slip,
or Tom Scarlet either," said Jack.

"But he's done it. He's off by the north road to-night; and, what is more, Tom of Lincoln, who was in hiding, packs up his bundle, and goes off, too, by the Oxford road."

" Which shows that he ain't going with Jagger."

" Does it ?" said the boy. " I followed him at a distance. When he thought he was well away, he cut right across country for the Barleymow. I went upon the scout, and from what I heard they're off before now."

" What horses had Jagger ?" said Jack.

" Two—a bay and a gray."

" Dark or light ?"

" Dark—an iron-gray with black legs."

" You see they can't mean going fast or far, for, with the groom, they are three men to two horses. Tom of Lincoln and the groom must ride double. Tom Scarlet and I can start in the morning, and catch them this side of Stratford," said Jack.

" Aye ; but, uncle, it's my belief they know precious well where to find another horse ; for they had a spare saddle and bridle. Besides, Miriam wormed it out of the groom that he thinks they are bound to Liverpool, and so across the herring pond to North Ameriky."

The elder gypsy swore a great oath, and remained a few minutes in deep thought, while the boy stood with his hand on his uncle's knee.

" Ike, it's a do—a dead sell ! Jagger's an out-and-out villain, for which there's no excuse, as he's rich. He means to do Tom Scarlet, and what's worse, to do *me—me*, who have always been fair and honest as a dealer, and in other transactions."

" He does. So does Tom of Lincoln, who was harbored in our own tents."

" Aye ! he's another nice 'un. Wants to go over the herring pond. Well, so he shall, but in another direction, where there's a place well beknown to some of his kin, called Botany Bay. What puzzles me is the other horse ; yet he was in Lincolnshire, dark like and—but jump up. We must go to Tom Scarlet at once. So now ! clip me under the arms and away we go !"

" I say !" cried the young gypsy, as they galloped over the

heath, "didn't I make a good plant upon 'em? Where would you have been if I hadn't been on the lookout?"

"It was good—very well done; but no better than I had a right to expect, considering."

"Considering what?" said Ike, with some disgust.

"Considering your bringings up; the advantages you've enjoyed in having had an uncle like me to look after your edication, and put you up to the time o' day," replied the guardian.

"Now, you pull up and let me get down," said the boy. "If this is all you've got to say after I've been on the scout two nights and a day, laying in ditches and listening in at winders, without winking or flinching, you go on and rouse Tom Scarlet yourself. And mind that there bloodhound, for he's let loose o' nights, and if he grabs you by the throat——"

He did not finish the sentence, for his uncle seized him by the wrist and spurred rapidly on towards the Grange.

Gypsy Jack pulled up at the gate of a straw-yard, divided by a lane from an old orchard. The house itself stood apart from the farm buildings, a solid stone structure, frowning through the night upon these visitors, as it seemed. There was, however, a light stirring in a stable to the right.

"Now, Ike," said the gypsy, in a low voice, "you know all the dogs, and you know his room. Get him up, and bring him here without letting any of the men hear you. Stop! one word more: if you see anybody else tell 'em that——"

"The night flies apace, and there'll be the d—l to pay in the morning!" was said close to his side.

"You here, Miriam! By the heavens! but you startled me. Girl, I have told you to keep clear of Tom Scarlet. What brings you here at this time of the night?"

"What brings you and Ike, if it comes to that?"

"I may go where a lass has no right to go. I had business here," replied Jack.

"So had I," said Miriam.

"What business?"

"To put Tom Scarlet on the right scent," said the girl. Then she drew her shawl about her head and tripped away, singing,

> "O! the bonny White Horse,
> To Banbury Cross,
>   He gallops away, away!
> The Scarlet and Gold,
> And the chestnut bold,
>   May catch him by break of day."

Gypsy Jack and his hopeful nephew looked after their niece and cousin until her form was lost in the gloom, and a burst of light flashed forth from the stable.   First came a man with a lantern, then another leading by the bridle the horse Danger; and he was followed by Tom Scarlet, booted and spurred, and putting caps on the nipples of a brace of pistols.   They came on to where the gypsy and his nephew were posted, when the Master of the Grange said:

"This is a sudden move, Jack.   I'm glad you've come, that we may have a short talk before I go.   I did not know that Miriam had told you."

"She had not.   Of Jagger's being here, I heard at Aylesbury from Harry Cox.   Of course I thought he had come to square things; but now I learn from Ike, and partly from Miriam, that he means nothing but a double cross, one on you and one on me.   But what has Miriam said that you are in such hot haste?   She is my sister's child, Mr. Scarlet, remember that; and this scampering over the country by night and all alone, is not good for her."

"Miriam can take care of herself, Jack; and you may swear she'll never come to harm, if I can help it.   She's as true as steel in every way.   The lasses of your race are unlike the country girls of our folk."

"True enough," returned the gypsy, "but people have said that she is too free with you, and I stand to her in place of her father and mother, both of whom she lost when young. But now to this business!   Ike, stand further off and no listening to what passes between the gentleman and me.   It's a private affair."

"Private be blowed!   I know more about it already than you do," said the boy.

"Silence, you scamp, and cut it, until I call you.   Now, Mr. Scarlet, what do you mean to do—shall I go with you?"

"No, better not.   I find from what Miriam says that Jagger brought the White Horse into this neighborhood, and hid

him away somewhere until he got the quittance I had left for
him at Oxford. He's also got a pot of money. Instead of
delivering the horse to me, as the bargain calls for, he means
to run him off to America and chisel all his creditors in this
country. Tom of Lincoln is glad to get away, and having a
natural bent towards roguery, is now in with Jagger."

"I'll have him in Aylesbury Jail or Oxford Castle before
he's four-and-twenty hours older," said the gypsy, vindictively.
"I've sheltered that fellow for months, and the London and
country beaks all after him. Besides, this here villain, Jagger, owes me a matter of above eighty pounds, thirty for a
gray gelding, and the other cold money—lent, paid down on
the nail. Now, what are you going to do?"

"I shall ride straight to the Barleymow. If I find Jagger
there I will take him by the throat, and make him tell where
the White Horse is. If he is not there I shall follow him.
He cannot get away from Danger and me."

"I had better go with you," said the gypsy. "Tom of Lincoln may show fight if you are alone, but before me he'll be as
quiet as a lamb."

"The people of the house will be on my side," replied Tom.
"Besides, I am man enough for Jagger and the Lincoln man
together. Then I have these," he added, pulling one of the
pistols from his pocket.

"Beware of using 'em," said the gypsy. "It makes no end
of trouble, the pulling of a trigger does, even when one is in
the right. Remember, my claim against Jagger is more than
eighty pound—a little more. Tell him to settle it if he wants
to escape the beaks, and save his companion from making a
voyage in a transport ship."

"I will get your money. Meantime, stay here and send
your scouts out. When they find I am sharp on their track
they may double back."

"Every road and byway shall be looked to," said the gypsy.
"I'll set a plant for them they little think of. Did you ever
hear of such a rogue as Jagger, and him rich? If a poor
man gets strapped, and has to bolt, it is another matter."

"Jack," said Tom Scarlet, "I must be moving. Ike, here's
a couple of half crowns for you. Good-night!"

He mounted the chestnut horse. Danger gave a snort and

a buck jump into the air, but his master was in the saddle.
He landed on all fours, and went away at a gallop.

"Jump up," said Gypsy Jack to his nephew.

"There goes a good 'un!" said the boy.

"Ay, a thoroughbred 'un! A cock of true game, but too
hasty for real serious business. You see, for some matters it
takes a deep, cool head," said the gypsy.

"Yourn, I suppose," returned the boy, with some irony in
his tone.

"Ay, mine. Now, look here! you think Tom Scarlet's gone
after Jagger and Tom of Lincoln."

"I sartainly do," said the boy.

"Well, then, he isn't. Particular business, which you and
I know nothing about, has called him down into Warwickshire," said the gypsy, coolly.

"I never heard that the Barleymow was in Warwickshire
afore. I thought it was in Northamptonshire," said the boy.

"And I tell you it's none of your business where it is. Tom
Scarlet isn't gone there."

"Do you think you can gammon me like this here?" said
the nephew, with huge contempt.

"Well, you are one of our family, and we ain't easily hum-
bugged, that's true. But mind now, mum's the word for the
present! Recollect, you're asleep in the tent this blessed minute, and have been ever since dark, if anybody axes you."

"I know what to say. But nobody will ax me; they know
it's of no use," said Ike.

"All right! Hand over them half crowns; I'll take care
of 'em for you," said Jack.

"Walker! I'll take care on 'em myself."

"You'll play at pitch and hustle, and lose every penny, besides being pulled by Parkins, or the beadle, for being at it in
church time," said the gypsy.

"How do you know as I won't win?" cried the boy.

"Why it stands to reason," returned Jack. "Here are you,
a boy of twelve——"

"Fourteen!" cried Ike.

"Well, here you are, a boy, playing with men, grooms, and
helpers, and what not, that have been at Newmarket, and
Epsom, and Melton Mowbray——"

"Ain't I been there, too?" said the nephew, interrupting him. "Besides, if I am a boy, I'm a gypsy boy, and up to things. Do you think them chuckle-heads can do *me?* You're a-thinkin' of your own losses when Young Dutch Sam walked into you for the price of a good horse at cribbage."

"If you say another word I'll pitch you off," exclaimed his uncle, in a rage. Then, after a long pause, he added: "The cards fell agen me that night."

"They generally do when you play with Sam," said the boy.

"Sam's a Jew," replied the gypsy, "and they're a people that have got a genius for games of that sort—it comes natural. However cute and wary a man may be, he can't *do* the Jews, and in the long run they'll *do* him, if he tries it on. Therefore, Ike, avoid 'em through life in ticklish transactions; but in matters of buying and selling deal with 'em. There's no better or more liberal business men than the Jews, when they know you're on the square yourself."

In all probability this wisdom was the fruit of experience, but it may also be that the "liberal business men" the gypsy alluded to had very seldom found that he was "on the square" himself.

CHAPTER VII.

"Which be the malefactors?"

FOR the creation of sensation wide and deep in a quiet rural neighborhood, nothing is so effective as murder, arson, highway robbery, housebreaking, or violence which appears to have been attempt at murder. Ministries may go out; dynasties may change; foreign thrones may topple; great convulsions of nature may happen, and the rustic goes on ploughing, sowing, reaping, mowing, and keeping his beasts afield without much concerning himself in such matters. But let Sir John's keeper be shot at in the ash spinney, Farmer Bullock's stack-yard be fired, the steward be knocked off his mare and robbed of forty pounds, or even Gaffer Goodman's geese be stolen, and the whole country side is aroused. Squire, parson, yeoman,

constable, beadle and bumpkin seize upon the one theme for
gossip and declamation. The landlord thrives. There is vast
consumption of nut-brown ale and tobacco. Magistrates ride
to and fro. Officers wear an air of portentous mystery.

For weeks after the events before related there was but one
topic in the hundred of Ridingcumstoke, and no more to speak
of in the hundreds adjacent. The attempt to murder Stevens
was on every tongue, and so was the flight of Tom Scarlet.
And yet, according to the majority, these things were what
they had always expected and confidently predicted. For a
few days Parkins had maintained an air of cautious wisdom
and frozen silence, but under the influence of the tap at The
George and Crown he thawed, and revealed to a chosen few
the ramifications of a great conspiracy in which Tom Scarlet,
Gypsy Jack, Miriam Cotswold, and Young Ike were the principals, and John Bullfinch, Moleskin, and perhaps the Marquis
of Wootton, the intended victims. The Radicals, Parkins
thought, were at the bottom of it. The Marquis was a known
" Church and King " man, so was the keeper, so was John
Bullfinch. It was true that the Scarlets had always been
staunch Tories time out of mind, but Tom was known to have
been in communication with men from London and Birmingham, and, besides, having been flatly refused the hand of May
Bullfinch, he had come into the plot, partly for revenge and
partly with a view to carry her off to foreign parts. Then
again, the gypsies, as Parkins had always declared to the
authorities (and more's the pity that he wasn't listened to),
ought to have been transported long ago. Having hit upon
this theory, the constable turned it over so often in his mind
that, by a natural process, he came to believe it, and not only
revealed it to the chosen few at The George, in whose age and
discretion he could confide, but to the butler and page at Sir
Jerry Snaffle's, where he called every day to report progress.
He enjoined secrecy, but of course the page hurried with the
news to the housekeeper, the ladies' maid, and the cook ; while
the butler was on thorns, as he metaphorically expressed it,
until he had the opportunity of telling it to the steward, a man
of much sagacity and decision of character, charged with the
collection of the rents of Sir Jerry Snaffle's two estates. The
page was rather large for his livery, and much communication

with the huntsman, the whippers-in, and the hunting-grooms had so excited his ambition in regard to sport, that he was really above his buttons. He addressed the eager ladies, after having related what Parkins had said with a few embellishments, after this manner:

They knew something of poachers and poaching—he (the page) did, for unfortunately his mother's brother had been taken up for it, unjustly, four or five times. None of his father's relatives—bar two—had ever been charged with it, and they were acquitted. Therefore, it must be admitted that poachers were up to anything. The ladies were, of course, familiar with gypsies——

"Not at all!" cried the cook and the ladies' maid promptly, though the fact was that Miriam Cotswold had told their fortunes for a shilling a-piece, and cheap at the money.

The page meant familiar with their disposition to depredation and crime. Perhaps they had heard of pirates. Now, he had it from the postboy at the Wheatsheaf that a sailor of dark and sinister appearance had held a long consultation with Gypsy Jack in the inn-yard the very day before Stevens was assailed, and there was no doubt he was one of the gang.

"Why ain't they arrested?" said the cook.

"Because they ran away—bolted," replied the page, "before the warrants were out."

It was true that Tom Scarlet had left the neighborhood, and that the gypsies, after the manner of their people, had silently disappeared, so that, in the glen where their ponies had browsed and their fires had blazed, there was nothing but white ashes when the keeper went to reconnoitre the ground.

"And so," said Farmer Stubbs, after listening to the recital of Parkins for about the tenth time, "all this here has been done and nobody took up."

There was that in the farmer's tone which might imply some doubt of the constable's vigilance and activity.

"You see," said Parkins, "when there's a case of this kind, people mustn't be took up haphazard. They must be pulled according to law, and they can't very well be pulled when they have cut away and given leg-bail for security. Now, Scarlet has cleared himself out of the country, no doubt; Gypsy Jack is also out of our jurisdiction, besides which, the magistrate's clerk and Moleskin say there's no evidence to keep him, if I had him in holt."

"Then the amount of it is, that as Stevens is getting better, nobody'll be took up at all," said Stubbs.

"Won't there, though? From information I have received, I think I may venture to say, that I shall pull somebody in less than three days."

"On this account?"

"On this here account. You just wait for two, or, say, three days."

But though Parkins had it cut and dried, and many agreed with him, there was a minority who either remained in doubt, or were satisfied that Tom Scarlet had had no hand in the crime. This minority included John Bullfinch and the keeper. Still, they could not account for his prolonged absence from the Grange, and could gather nothing from his men as to his whereabouts or probable return. Moleskin, silent, active and wary, pushed his quest in every direction, but nothing had come of it.

"I can't account for his not being here," said John.

"I can't account for that white horse being there," replied Moleskin. "Gypsy Jack, Miriam, and Ike have disappeared, too—gone like bubbles on the stream. The tribe is now in Bedfordshire, but neither Jack nor Miriam nor the nevy is with them. I have had a man among them, and I know it."

"He can't have gone off with Miriam—hey, Dick?"

"I think not," said the keeper, "for my opinion is, that he was dead struck after your daughter May. Still, as a bachelor, I don't pretend to much knowledge—I mean knowledge from experience—of that sort of thing. We must wait, and *we'll* say nothing about the white horse for the present Stevens is out of danger, and slowly recovering. He says he saw a white horse just before he was struck, but who beat him down he cannot say. As soon as I hear of anything to the purpose I will come over."

Mr. Parkins had examined Stevens many times, and had been sorely puzzled by this white horse. It was clearly implicated, and if he could have found one in the neighborhood answering the description, he would have thought it his duty to "pull it up." In vain he re-examined and cutely cross-

examined Stevens. In vain he had over from the nearest
market town a tippling, red-nosed man in rusty black, a lawyer's clerk, who plied the under-keeper with leading questions,
and consumed many tumblers of hot gin-and-water. All would
not do. They could neither get the white horse out of the
case, nor, properly saddled and bridled, into it. He was running loose. The turnpike man was questioned. Had he seen
Tom Scarlet on the morning in question? He had. The
young man had passed through his gate soon after daybreak.

"On a white horse?"

"Not a bit of it. On a dark chestnut—the hunter Danger."

The lawyer's clerk had another round or two of gin-and-
water, and then "summed up" by informing Parkins that if
ever the case came to trial, the counsel for the defence would
ride that white horse clean through the indictment.

May Bullfinch, innocent as the dove, if not timid as the
fawn, had been shocked and deeply pained by the affair. She
believed Tom Scarlet to be innocent, and her brother Jack
maintained the same with such vigor and emphasis, that he
greatly reassured her and fortified her conviction. Explanations! Did May think he should take the trouble to explain
a charge made by Parkins?

The truth was that Parkins had been much exasperated by
the conduct of Young Jack since the morning of the discovery.
He was "flying in the face of the law, manifesting contempt
for the authorities, and had better be careful—accessories after
the fact could be pulled."

May visited the under-keeper's cottage nearly every day,
taking him wine and such delicacies as the doctor allowed him
to have. She was greatly liked by Stevens and his wife, and
was the prime favorite of the children. So great and so apparent had her influence with the family become, that the
astute and vigilant Parkins, to use his own expression, "smelt
a rat" in that quarter. She would sway their minds and mould
the man's evidence so as to clear Tom Scarlet. Justice would
be defeated. The felony would be compounded and hushed up,
and nobody so much as pulled, even for a preliminary examination upon probable cause, unless he, Parkins, watched her
stratagems, detected her manoeuvres, and defeated her plans.

May sat in the front room of the cottage with the brown,

curly-headed little boys and girls of the Stevens household all about her. A feast of nuts and cakes, with bread and raspberry jam, was interrupted by a question to May from their father, as to whether any news had yet been heard of Tom Scarlet.

"There is none," replied May. "My brother was at the Grange yesterday. The men neither know where he is nor when he is likely to return."

"It's queer, very queer!" said Stevens, passing his hand before his eyes. "I have been considering things, and I think that he didn't do this job for me."

"Oh, Stevens, I am so glad—so very glad to hear this from you," said May. "I always felt certain that he was incapable of such a thing."

"Well, Miss, I dunno as to that. It was pretty well settled that he was a very hard hitter when his blood was up, and I don't doubt his capacity at all, but I think it wasn't him."

"I am sure it was not," said May.

"And I be sure as it was. Now, what have you got to say to that?" exclaimed the constable, rubbing his pimpled nose with the nob of his walking stick, as he stood in the doorway and surveyed the group.

The children hid themselves. Stevens told Parkins to come in, and the latter entered. May Bullfinch met him.

"What right have you to say that? What are your reasons? Where are your proofs?" The female Bullfinch seemed inclined to fly at him and peck him, as birds do those who molest their young in the nest.

"Reasons! I don't give no reasons to nobody; not even to their honors on the bench. Proofs! proofs ain't to be called for in this stage of the investigation," said the learned constable, in some heat. "I know he done it, and that's enough. If anybody else had done it I should have pulled 'em. If he hadn't abscondulated, I should have pulled him."

"If he hadn't what?" said May.

"Cut it, mizzled, bolted, run away!" The learned constable would no doubt have added "skedaddled," if that expressive word had been then in use, but it was not.

"I don't care for all that. I don't believe it was him," said Stevens.

"You don't believe it was him as done it," said Parkins, with slowness and severity. "Didn't you think you saw him? Ain't there a warrant out? You don't think he done it! What's the meaning of this here prevarication? Is it the result of a bargain, an unlawful bargain, to compound the felony?"

"Compound be blowed—there's no prevarication about it. I don't think he struck me, and so I shall swear," said Stevens.

"That's right, Stevens. It's the truth, and do you stick to it," said May.

"Miss Bullfinch, you be interfering with this case, and suggesting things to the witness, clean agen the law, and in opposition to the authorities and the course of justice," said the learned constable.

"Justice! to put the crime upon an innocent and absent man. Here is the only person that can know anything about it, except the perpetrators, and he says Mr. Scarlet is not guilty of it."

"I know he does, and it's a precious nice statement for him to make. But I see it all!" said Parkins, eyeing a bottle on a side table. "You've been giving him drink, and it's flew to his head. That's what's the matter with him."

"No more than the doctor ordered," said Stevens.

"This is merely sherry wine, and you may see that the cork has not been drawn," said May.

"Well, then, draw it at once. I don't care if I take a drop with him myself, Miss," said the placable constable. "Sherry wine, sich as your father keeps and has had on hand ever since your brother's christening, is suverin as a cordial for sick people, and wun't do them in health any harm. All the authorities agree in this."

"It was intended for the patient only, but here, sir," she replied, handing him a glass, after some movement among the bottles.

Mr. Parkins accepted, and drank a very fair dose of physic before he discovered the trick put upon him. He dashed down the glass with an oath, and was about to leave, when he was met in the doorway by John Bullfinch and the keeper.

"What's the row, now?" said John.

"Oh, nothing—nothing, except a plan to compound the

felony, and save Scarlet from transportation. That's all!"
said the indignant constable.

Moleskin pushed by him to the easy-chair in which Stevens
was seated.

"Bill," said he, "you seem to be doing pretty well under
the care of your wife and Miss May Bullfinch."

"Miss Bullfinch has done as much for me as the doctor, if
not more. I shall teach my children to say, 'God bless
her!'" said Stevens.

"We want to hear your account of this matter once more.
Every word and everything," said Moleskin, impressively.

"Stop!" said the constable, beckoning Moleskin to a corner.
"All this here'll be irregular, and, I may say, agen the law.
Mr. Bullfinch is not in the King's commission and confi-
dence."

"No, but he is in that of the Marquis and Sir Jerry Snaffle,
and, unless you are a fool, that will be enough for you,"
returned Moleskin.

Parkins assented, but not with a good grace.

"Have you made any further discovery, Parkins?" said
John Bullfinch.

"Seeing that Tom Scarlet done it, there's no more to be
made, except to find out his accomplices and pull 'em up," the
constable replied, with a dark look at May.

They then turned to Stevens. He recapitulated minutely
all that he remembered, winding up with the declaration that
he could not swear to anybody as having struck him, but was
satisfied, in his own mind, that Tom Scarlet did not. Whether
he was there or not he could not say.

The constable flew into a rage, but suddenly cooled down
at Moleskin's stern eye and the hot look of John Bullfinch.

"I have a great opinion of the practical experience and
sagacity of Moleskin in matters of this sort," said John. "He
has made a discovery and a suggestion——"

The learned constable was about to interrupt and protest
against this, but the farmer waved him aside and continued,
authoritatively: "I say, a discovery which is important and a
suggestion which is wise."

"What's the discovery? Never mind the suggestion!" said
the little man, with some sarcasm.

" The discovery is, that Gypsy Jack is in this neighborhood again," replied Mr. Bullfinch.

The constable was sorely vexed. Jack in his old haunts; the keeper and John Bullfinch with knowledge of it; and he, the constable, one of the constituted authorities, with a character for craft and vigilance at stake, in entire ignorance. He looked blankly at them and said, " He shall be took up forthwith."

" A bad plan," said the keeper; " there's no evidence against him; nothing to hold him on."

" No, none at all," Mr. Bullfinch continued, " but Moleskin suggests that, under the circumstances, he is sure to know more or less, and it is our business to get all the information we can out of him. We must draw for Jack as hounds draw a cover, for he's as cunning as an old dog fox."

" Of course he'll tell all he knows when *you* question him," said the ironical constable. " But it's all right; proceed in your own way; and when you have got his story, which is sure to be made up of the biggest lies he can think of, I'll clap in, and conduct the cross-examination. That's the only good that'll come of this here present investigation. But where is he, and is the gang back? the dealers, the tinkers, the fellows that sleep all day and rob and poach all night; and the fortune-tellers—be they back with him?"

" There is no one with him but young Ike, and he is at the Barleymow," said the keeper.

" The Barleymow! I think you said the Barleymow!" exclaimed the indignant constable. " Why, this is one of the most howdacious doings I ever heard of. Here he is, instead of hiding in a hedge, or a hovel, put up like a gentleman born at the best cross-roads inn in the country, slap under the noses of the authorities!"

" That's enough!" said Moleskin, taking up his gun; " come along."

The committee of inquiry proceeded on their mission. When they reached the Barleymow they found Gypsy Jack very much at his ease. He was sitting on the horse-trough, in the genial spring sunshine, entertaining his nephew and the ostler with what must have been a facetious story, as there was loud laughter among them. At the approach of John Bullfinch and his party, the keen black eyes of the boy lighted up with intelligence, perhaps with glee. Gypsy Jack was more wary. Without looking straight at the new-comers, he made a sign for the lad and the ostler to leave. He then rose, and met the farmer of Hawkwell with apparent frankness and cordiality. He flashed a side look upon the keeper, and then met his gaze in a way that plainly said, "Now, you know me, and I know you. What are you going to do about it?" The constable was regarded with a stare which might imply surprise, or might indicate contempt, but certainly not alarm. The gypsy's experience in various matters had, indeed, led him to form a rather derogative opinion of those Parkins commonly called "the authorities," meaning himself, four or five more constables and tithing-men, and as many beadles, in the vicinity. There was, in those days, no rural police. Gypsy Jack surveyed the constable very much' as an old gray badger or a wild-cat might look upon a noisy but not dangerous little dog in a wood. At a word from Mr. Bullfinch, they passed into the Barleymow, a large, old-fashioned, roadside house, full of all the comforts of the days of stage-coaches and post-chaises, and were shown into a private room. The gypsy, sitting opposite to Mr. Bullfinch, looked almost constantly, and always confidently, into his clear blue eyes. He took no notice of Parkins, and very little of the solemn-looking keeper. Mr. Bullfinch returned the gypsy's gaze with some unsteadiness, not knowing exactly how to begin to "draw for the old dog fox" before him. He said something about the "good of the house," and bad weather, and ordered gin-and-water and pipes. Bad weather! It was a beautiful day in spring. The sun shone through the latticed windows, the scent of the violets rose from the bank under the hawthorn hedge, the goldfinch sang among the blossoms of the plum tree to his nesting mate, and lambs were skipping at play in the pasture on the nearest hill. The gypsy's eyes twinkled, and the constable nodded approval, as the waiting-maid placed the liquor and pipes before them. Mr. Bullfinch lighted his pipe with almost Dutch deliberation, and then began:

"You remember the night of Aylesbury fair, Jack?"

"I've had no call to forget it, sir, as I know of," replied the gypsy.

"Something happened that night," said Mr. Bullfinch.

"Very likely," said Jack, with much composure; "something commonly *does* happen when gentlemen drink much of the strong brandy-and-water they serve at the Wheatsheaf, and ride home late."

"This here's prewarication," said Parkins, aside to the keeper.

"Moleskin's man, Stevens, was set upon that night in Wootton woods, beaten within an inch of his life, his skull fractured, and he was left for dead."

"Well, what of it?" said Gypsy Jack, with a bold and steady stare at the yeoman.

"Here's a villain!" said the constable to Moleskin.

"The next day," Mr. Bullfinch continued, "it was found that you had left the neighborhood?"

"I dare say it was, if anybody thought it worth while to inquire," said the gypsy. "I don't send the bellman round to tell folks when I am going to change camps, and I went off without saying good-by to Parkins or the keeper. I had business elsewhere."

"It was discovered that same morning that Tom Scarlet had left the Grange, and he has not been seen or heard of since," said John Bullfinch.

"Yes, he has," said Jack.

"By whom?"

"By me."

"Then you're the chap I be after as accomplice and accessory, both before and after the fact," cried Parkins.

"'Complice in what?"

"In the murder—the attempt! Come, none o' your nonsense. This may turn out a hanging matter."

"Hanging be d—d," said the gypsy, with contempt. "The man isn't dead, nor likely to die; and if he was as dead as mutton, I could prove a halibi by five witnesses."

"What sort of witnesses? Your gang that was camped at the heath won't do," said the constable.

"I've three without any of them; and here sits one," said the gypsy, pointing to Mr. Bullfinch.

"It is mainly as he says," remarked Mr. Bullfinch. "Parkins, be quiet, and make no further interruption. Now, Jack, where did you see Tom Scarlet?"

" In a good many places."

" More prewarication," murmured the outraged constable.

" I mean the last time," said the yeoman.

" Well, sir, I met him at a horse fair in Lancashire the last time I saw him."

" When was this, Jack?"

" I don't think I shall be able to remember when it was until I find out what is to come of all this cross-questioning," said the gypsy.

" Well, well! what did he say concerning this attack upon Stevens?"

"Nothing at all. I believe he did not know of it. He had other things to talk about."

" Well, *you* knew of it," said the keeper " and what did *you* say about it?"

"Nothing at all. It isn't such a wonderful thing for a keeper's man to have his head broke, that people should prefer it to their own business when in another part of the country. He isn't the first that has had a crack on the crown in one of the Marquis's covers, and I don't believe he'll be the last," said the gypsy.

" I dare say he will not," the keeper remarked, grimly.

" I think there's been enough said about Stevens," returned the gypsy. " In my opinion the breaking of a head or two is a very trifling matter."

" And in mine it's a lagging matter, when the head broke is that of a constable in the execution of his duty or a keeper in a preserve, watching in the night season," cried the irascible constable. " For why? because the law in that special case made and provided—as anybody may see by looking into the act—which means the statute—is broke too, and not all the currant jelly and sherry wine that May Bullfinch could furnish gratis in a twelvemonth could mend *that* again."

" Where do you think Tom Scarlet is now, Jack?" said the yeoman.

" Well, sir, if the wind has been fair, and the passage anything like good, he ought to be very near the coast of America by this time."

" America !" exclaimed Mr. Bullfinch. " What should he do in America ? What took him to America?"

" Particular business," replied the gypsy.

" Which," interposed the irate constable, " is the case with all of 'em. The particular business of nine out of ten that cuts away from this country to that is to defeat the authorities and avoid the service of a little docyment running in the name of our Suverin Lord the King."

" What is this particular business, Jack?" said the farmer.

" I can't say—that is, I won't say. It is private, but no harm," replied the gypsy.

" I don't know about that. Private and sudden business never took me over sea," said John.

" No, nor never will, sir!" exclaimed the admiring constable. " Forty years and more have I knowed you, and you never cut away for fear of a little docyment proceeding in the name of our Suverin Lord the King. Hows'ever, there'll be no splitting on the part of this here—party. You may believe as much of what he says as you like, but he won't gammon me—I ain't to be gammoned."

With this the astute constable walked out of the room. Mr. Bullfinch and the keeper, finding they could make nothing of the gypsy, soon followed.

The constable surveyed the front of the house. Thence he went into the garden bowers, among the bees and spring flowers. With some remarks upon the wisdom of the busy bee, and an allusion to the properties of honey, he took a seat which commanded a view of the back door, and soliloquized:

" The reward is sure to be liberal, and it will be all my own —no going halves. The keeper and him (meaning Mr. Bullfinch) can have no claim ; for, though they knew the gypsy was here, they haven't suspected, up to this time, what he's been up to. It took my experience and penetration to find that out."

He rose, went to the front of the house again and took a seat on the horseblock. Mr. Bullfinch and the keeper approached. Parkins, regarding them with an air of profound mystery, said in a guarded tone :

" Gypsy Jack must be took up. I'm going to pull him here and now, and may want your help."

"Nonsense! he had nothing to do with it," said John.

"Perhaps not with the Stevens case, but how about a higher crime? Murder will out! That is, when there's a certain sort of man to find it out."

"What murder do you mean?" said John.

"Hush! speak lower! The murder of Tom Scarlet. I have hit upon the key to the whole business, and it's as clear as day. The gypsy's cock-and-bull stories about horse fairs, business over the water, and what not, don't gammon me. I ain't to be gammoned! Tom Scarlet has been made away with, most likely by hocussing and burking. His body, sold to the resurrection men, has been biled by this time. Jack was one of the principals, and he must be took up."

This prompt and positive recital of horrors made Mr. Bullfinch open his blue eyes to the widest possible extent.

"What evidence is there?" he asked.

"Plenty, as I'll show when he's collared and handcuffed, and has no chance to cut away and get shet of the watch and other vallybles taken from the murdered man. I hope we shall be able to find the body—that is, the skeleton; for if we don't, the counsel as defends this here villain will pretend that there's no *corpus delicti—corpus delicti!* Mr. Bullfinch," added the learned constable, "the legal meaning of which I will explain some other time, if convenient."

"If there is plenty of evidence, let us hear a little of it," said the keeper, in his dry, matter-of-fact manner.

"Well, what be the facts to one used to such investigations? In the first place, this gypsy bears a noted bad character—a shocking bad character! He's up to all sorts of games against the law, and has no respect for the authorities. He meets Tom Scarlet in some out-of-the-way place. The young man has a large amount of money about him—it was his habit to carry a deal of gold."

"By George, Moleskin, that's true!" exclaimed John Bullfinch.

"Not so loud—not so loud!" said the watchful constable. "He pretends to be cutting a stick out of the hedge yonder, but's he's really a-listening to us, and can hear half a mile or thereabouts. Now, you can swear to Tom's carrying the gold yourself, Mr. Bullfinch. You can prove that."

5

" I can swear to the habit, but not to the fact, in this instance," said John.

" It's all one for that. The fact is to be inferred from the
habit, and so the counsel for the Crown will say, when this
here amazing and celebrated case comes to be tried. Besides,
Tom left but little money at the Grange, you say, and you
don't think his men have robbed the bureau, do you ?"

" No," said John Bullfinch, " they are honest lads—I know
them well."

" He always used to keep a deal of money in gold and
notes," said the constable, " and the old house would have been
robbed over and over again only for his name as a dare-devil
and the knowledge of double-barrelled guns and pistols all
over the premises, to say nothing of bull-dogs and bloodhounds.
Housebreakers, Mr. Bullfinch, picks their customers, just as
you picks the easy places to ride at in a hard run."

" Go on with your evidence," said the sententious keeper.
" The caps have snapped every time you've pulled the trigger
so far. Come to the point. Didn't I hear you say the gypsy
had Tom Scarlet's watch ?"

" I said, ' No doubt he had ;' and I say it again. Let him
be took up, and you'll see," replied the constable.

" No go !" said the keeper. " It's all just like the castles
children build with cards—take one away, and down come all
the rest. As for Tom Scarlet, I believe him to be alive and
well this minute, and, as the gypsy says, gone abroad on some
sort of a wild-goose chase that very few men would undertake."

" I'll see Sir Jerry Snaffle about this," said John Bullfinch.
" He's a great hand to puzzle out a faint scent and hit off the
true hunting line."

The constable heard Moleskin's remarks and the yeoman's
resolution with much disgust.

" Assault with intent to kill committed," said he to himself.
" Murder as good as proved, and nobody took up ! while one
of the principals is swaggering about like a lord in the land,
and regularly gammoning everybody but me. This comes of
the interference of farmers, keepers and the like with the *real*
authorities."

CHAPTER VIII.

"Then came faire May, the fayrest mayd on ground,
  Deckt with all dainties of her season's pryde,
And throwing flowers out of her lap around;
  Upon two brethren's shoulders she did ride,
The twinnes of Leda; which on either side
  Supported her, like to their soveraine queene.
Lord! how all creatures laught when her they spide,
  And leapt and daunc't as they had ravished beene,
And Cupid's selfe about her fluttered all in greene."

THE namesake of the nymph, who rode upon arms of Leda's twins, was not in high favor with society in and about Wootton and Ridingcumstoke, when the latter scattered her flowers and threw around her sweets. May Bullfinch had displeased many of those who had constituted themselves the inquisitors and censors of other people's conduct. If any one wants to incur the resentment of his neighbors, let him deny some proposition they have laid down as a truth. Let him have the hardihood to withstand "public sentiment" and insist upon holding his own opinions. This May Bullfinch had done by refusing to listen to those charges against Tom Scarlet, which had been proclaimed and enlarged upon over' almost every tea-table in the riding. In spite of his loose reputation, which had been fired at her a thousand times, point-blank, by all the gossips of her own sex; in spite of his sudden departure, just at the time of the assault upon the under-keeper; in spite of his continued absence, of his silence, and of the fact that Miriam Cotswold had also disappeared and still remained away, May's faith had never wavered. With a spirit like that of the old knightly challengers, she maintained his innocence and defied all comers. She was argued with, but not shaken in her belief and trust; she was coaxed, but it was of no avail; she was scolded, and she laughed at invectives. At last the old ladies gave her up as "past praying for," pronounced her a very suitable match for Scarlet himself, and fell to pitying the blindness and weakness of the stupid man, her father. The farmer had held several interviews with Sir

Jerry Snaffle, but the baronet, after much beating about the bush, had confessed that he was unable to hit off the scent. Young Jack was altogether of his sister's mind, and Parkins was in doubt whether the boy was "gammoned" by his sister, or was trying to gammon other people within the metes and bounds of Ridingcumstoke.   Another staunch friend of Tom Scarlet was the busy and influential landlady, Mrs. Hickman, of the Wheatsheaf. The good lady, with her daughter, pretty Mary, had driven over to Hawkwell in her gig, and held counsel with May Bullfinch. She knew Tom Scarlet and Gypsy Jack well, and assured May that Tom would come out all right in the end. She also knew Parkins well, and told May that he was a fool, a "tippling, conceited fool of a man, who ought to be ducked in a horse-pond; and she had a great mind to have it done." May thought so, too, and parted from Mrs. Hickman much comforted.

Old Winter now had fled in perfect rout before the front of brisk and lusty Spring. The fields were green with grass and growing crops, the trees thick with expanding leaves, the hedges whitely powdered with the fragrant May, the clustering blossoms of the hardy hawthorn; and here and there were warm tints of buds of the crab, and the blush of the wild rose bedecked the bending briar. The cowslip, the crocus and the daisy spangled the smooth pastures. Under the trees of the copse the delicate primrose bloomed; over the thriving wheat fields cloud and sunshine and the vernal breezes chased each other. So looked the Vale of Aylesbury as John Bullfinch, with his daughter and son, rode along it, on a bright May morn, to Gosford races. It was an annual event, and one of moment. John could never remember that there had been a race meeting at Gosford at which he was not present. The races, perhaps, might have been brought off without him and Sir Jerry Snaffle, but it may be doubted. The farmer rode Black Hearty. On one hand May was upon Cowslip; on the other, Young Jack upon Young Cowslip. Nature was in a merry mood. Up, up! the lark towered up, and sang as though he would pour out his very life aloft in melody. They heard the cuckoo on the hill, the golden-fluted blackbird in the hedge, and deep in wood and grove swelled the many varied carols and wild notes of the thrush. They lingered on the way, John Bullfinch and his daughter May, content to enjoy so fine a morning and so fair a scene. But this sort of thing was far from suiting Young Jack. It was a race morning, the occasion was momentous, and he was fiery hot with haste.

The little jockey boots, the white buckskin breeches, and the jacket of violet silk under his loose coat indicated that Young Jack would take a prominent part when the proceedings on the heath began. He was, indeed, to ride a certain thoroughbred pony called Maid of the Vale, in the Ladies' Cup, two miles, for ponies not more than fourteen hands high. Three times before he had ridden the little mare to victory, but never in a race of so much interest and importance as the one about to come off. Her chief antagonist would be a famous brown pony, with a bald face, a noted runner, brought on from Whittlebury Forest. He was the joint property of a gypsy and a dealer in bridles and whips, an immense fat man, twice as big as his own horse. This pony, Creeping Joe, had won many races, and had furnished occasion for frequent quarrels and one or two fights between the worthies who owned him, the gypsy and the fat man. In the altercations the fat man generally had the best of it, for he was exceedingly loud and voluble ; but in the fights the strategy of the gypsy prevailed. He lowered his head, and by butting his antagonist in the pit of the stomach reduced him to mere helplessness. This gypsy was a crony of Gypsy Jack's, through whose suggestions Creeping Joe had been brought up to Gosford Heath to run against Maid of the Vale for the Ladies' Cup.

"We shall be late. I know we shall be late, and Mr. Birdbolt will be waiting. Put Hearty to a canter, father, and let May send Cowslip along a bit. I declare that many people would go faster to a funeral than we are going to Gosford Green on the race morning," said Young Jack.

"And I shouldn't blame 'em, if the funeral was that of some boys," said his father. "You'll go fast enough before the day is over, if you beat Creeping Joe, for he is a nailer. Between the gypsies, the big fellow and Young Ike, they have got him in rare condition, I am told."

"So much the more reason that I should be with the mare, to see how she feels and have another consultation with Jim.

But, father, do you really think that Creeping Joe can outrun the Maid?"

" I've no doubt of it, and you must depend on her bottom. Now, the way to ride this race is to go along for a mile at a——"

" Ah! I know all about that. I talked it over with Mr. Ransome, from Lord Jersey's, at the Barleymow, and we came to the conclusion to make the running strong. Now let *us* make a little running here," said Jack.

" We'll just jog along as we are doing. I see Sir Jerry Snaffle's chariot in front, and I won't pass him and her ladyship, if we never get there," said John.

" Then all I can say is, that I wish Sir Jerry Snaffle would go a little faster," said Jack, with some discontent.

" Sir Jerry, sir," said John Bullfinch, " has a right to make the pace as fast or as slow as he pleases. Why, when I was a boy I should no more have thought of passing Sir Jerry's father on the road, than I should have thought of flying. But times have sadly changed—butcher boys spatter the mud over gentlemen's carriages, and gypsies go spurring by the best in the land."

This last observation was drawn out by the fact that the young gypsy, Ike, who was to ride Creeping Joe, had just turned out of a green lane in front, on his uncle's galloway, and dashed by Sir Jerry's carriage, as if he was nobody. Half an hour brought John Bullfinch to the front of a small but elegant domain on Gosford Green. It was the residence of Mr. Birdbolt, a short, stout old bachelor, hot in disposition and hearty in manner, with white hair and a face as red as a beefsteak. He was a great connoisseur in flowers, singing-birds and racing ponies; owned Maid of the Vale and often declared that he wouldn't swap her for any sixteen-hand horse in the Kingdom. He now rushed through the front garden, and assisting May to alight, kissed her on the cheek. " Beautiful, beautiful!" said the old man, holding her at arm's length.

" Yes, the month for singing-birds and flowers—the spring flowers!" said May.

" Ay, you charming rogue, for bullfinches and roses. But come in to lunch, and then I'll show you the nesting gold-finches and canaries," said Mr. Birdbolt.

" Never mind them to-day, sir," cried Young Jack; " any day will do for them. This is the mare's day. What I want to know is——"

"Confound the boy! What do you mean by interrupting a gentleman at his own house?" said his father. " If I was Mr. Birdbolt, I think I'd make you strip those colors off, and get another rider. Still," he continued, " I should like to look at the mare myself before we lunch, for on a racing morning the less we have to do with birds the better, unless it be carrier-pigeons, to instruct friends in London how to put the money on."

" There are cold fowls and tongue already on the table," said Mr. Birdbolt.

" They won't fly away while we look at the mare. Come along!" cried Young Jack.

They found the stable door locked, and the key in charge of a short, bony man of fifty, who had once been a jockey, and was now trainer to Mr. Birdbolt's ponies, in which weighty affairs his chief counsellor and adviser had usually been Tom Scarlet. The man was somewhat hoarse and at first so grave and taciturn that you would have thought something ill had certainly befallen the mare.

" All right, eh, Jim?" said Mr. Bullfinch.

" Yes, yes! she's tol'able well," replied the trainer.

" Good at her feed, and pulls up well after her gallops?" said John.

" Yes—yes! she's eat what I gave her, and she's took her work, but——"

" But! what d'ye mean by but? You don't mean to say that she's amiss in any way?" cried Mr. Bullfinch.

" Why, no. Not exactly amiss, but she's had a good deal easier races; and if Tom Scarlet was here, just to look her over and advise young master how to ride it, I should be easier in my mind. However, you look her over yourself."

With this, he threw open the door of the box, and there stood Maid of the Vale, with her muzzle on, ready for her war paint. She was a pony, but with all the length and elegant proportions of a thoroughbred horse of high quality. A rich bay, long and low, with a glowing coat, full, meaning eye and broad forehead—a mare well worthy of some of her ancestors, who, stouter than the sailors and men-at-arms of Spain, breasted the billows of the stormy Channel, and swam ashore from the wrecks of the Armada. She answered May's caresses, and looking round at the visitors, as if to collect their sentiments, seemed to know that her time had come again—that Young Jack was there to take her to another struggle.

"She's fit! She's up to the mark. We shall win it, Jim—I know we shall win it," said Young Jack.

"And I know we shan't, if you underrate your adversary," returned his father. "Of all the perilous and fatal errors made in regard to racers, boxers, and the like, there is none worse than underestimating those who are to oppose you. I've seen it proved a hundred times. Look at Old Dutch Sam, the winner of a hundred fights, and licked at last by a journeyman baker! Look at Jem Belcher, never beaten until he underrated his own pupil, the Game Chicken!"

"Ay," said the trainer, "but I have always heard that Belcher would have won the fight, only he had lost an eye a short time before, playing at rackets, and Pierce got in on the blind side of him. It's always been the belief in the racing stables that Jem would have won if he had had two eyes."

"I know it," said Mr. Bullfinch, with a sigh, "but I have heard competent judges say—I didn't see the fight myself—that he couldn't have beaten Pierce on that day if he had had four eyes. But he was a great man—a very great man was Jem Belcher! The best in my time, or any other time, for that matter. There's no such men nowadays."

"Well, never mind him *now*," said Young Jack; "it's a race and not a prize-fight that's going to come off."

"In regard to the race," said Mr. Bullfinch, "much depends upon the riding of it. You have had but a limited experience. Now, I could have got a boy from John Day's——"

"I don't like them Days," said the trainer gruffly and positively. "They call old John 'Honest John,' and, to my mind, it is because he's the d—dest rascal in all England."

"Well, well, let it pass! No boy from John Day's is here, and Jack is to ride—my son is to ride. Now the mare, though perhaps not as fast, is better bred than Creeping Joe, and the way to win is to come away and make running."

"From the start! right from the start," said Mr. Birdbolt.

"And so diminish Creeping Joe's speed before it comes to the finish," said May.

"Now, this is all wrong," said Jack, expostulating. "You all talk as if you had made a grand discovery, when Tom Scarlet and I and Jim have always known that the little mare's strong point is her ability to stick over a long course. I don't want instructions as to that matter. I've ridden her before without instructions of that sort—eh, Jim?"

"Ay, and *against* instructions, and won, too," said the trainer, "for at Cotesford Mr. Bullfinch said, ' Wait and win,' and the guvner said, ' Nail 'em on the post' but Tom Scarlet and you and I said, ' If we wait for them big horses they'll outstride her at last, with all their weight; so we'll just go along and keep 'em moving all the way.'"

"That was it—precisely it!" said Young Jack, as his father and Mr. Birdbolt began to retreat. "I cut out the running."

"And kept the pace good," cried May.

"And won in a walk," hallooed the trainer, whereat John Bullfinch and Mr. Birdbolt quickened their pace towards the house.

This matter at Cotesford had long been rather a sore subject to treat upon before John Bullfinch and Mr. Birdbolt, and for that reason it was to the trainer, like a long suit at whist—he never neglected an opportunity "to bring it in."

CHAPTER IX.

> She was not foaled on the Northern wold,
>   But dropped in the lap of the midland vale;
> And the gypsy there, with the coal-black hair,
> And the eye well read in the fates, they said,
>   Told them next morn of the time, and tale.

IT could hardly be averred that John Bullfinch took as much interest in the plates and stakes run for at the rural meetings near the Vale of Aylesbury as he did in the grand event which came off at Newmarket, Epsom and Doncaster, but it is very likely that they afforded him as much enjoyment. In a certain sense he was of the upper circle, the inner ring of a great section of the turf. He had for years been intimate with Mr. Ransome, a sort of Master of the Horse at Middleton, the favorite seat of the great racing magnate of that age, Lord Jersey. All Sir Jerry Snaffle's racing doings and secrets were confided to John Bullfinch. With the Days he had long been friendly. With Will and young Sam Chiffney he was hand and glove. Isaac Sadler had great respect for him, the more so, that John always had a balance at his banker's, and Mr. Sadler sometimes had none. It was not likely that one who had discussed with Ransome the merits of Cobweb, Middleton, Mameluke, Glenartney and Glencoe, with the Chiffneys the memorable triumphs of Zinganee and Priam, and with Sadler the glorious doings of Defence and Dangerous, should prefer hunters' plates and pony stakes to the national events. John's hat had been thrown up too often after the great turf victories of Lord Jersey, Sir Jerry, the Chiffneys and Isaac Sadler for that. It was a truth, however, that after a race of heats at the country meetings, in which the struggle had been long and close, John's satisfaction was intense. The trainer, the jockey, and the owner of the winner always received his congratulations in the order named. In the great steeple-chases, for which the beautiful Vale of Aylesbury was then famous—real cross-country contests, quite unlike those over the artificial courses of the present day—John was in his glory. A bold and skilful rider and a fine judge of that rare animal, the weight-carrying hunter, Mr. Bullfinch felt himself on solid ground when steeple-chasing was in order. Concerning the Derby, the St. Leger, the Ascot Cup, and so forth, he was never very confident, but inclined to listen to the suggestions of his friends Ransome, Edwards, the Chiffneys, the Days, Robinson, Isaac Sadler, &c. None of these great men attended the little meetings of Gosford Green, save Ransome and Sadler. The latter commonly had horses to run, and at such places they were generally coarse-looking creatures, sometimes string-halted or knuckled behind, almost always running in bandages, and *quite* always set down by Ransome in his own mind as "dangerous." He might know nothing at all about them, but his theory was, "Isaac Sadler knows precisely what sort of a horse to bring here."

As our party cantered along from Mr. Birdbolt's to the heath, the scene was highly animating. Scores of farmers on horseback, and their wives and daughters in gigs and carriages, were on the road. Now and then a barouche, bearing from the country mansions fair dames and damsels, bright with rich colors, and with ribbons gay, went rolling by. On either hand there was a continuous crowd of country folks a-foot. Sturdy men in smock frocks and leather gaiters; young fellows in velveteen coats, upon whom the recruiting sergeant cast a longing eye. Lads and lasses, ruddy and dusty; troops of children with May garlands in their nut-brown hands, and no fear whatever of the beadle before their eyes. It was always a general holiday. On the heath, scattered over the open sward among the gorse, and as near to the course as might be, were booths, from which the clamor of voices, the scraping of fiddles, and the sound of tabor and pipe, were already audible. The thimble-rig, and other games of skill and chance, were going on, in nooks and corners, among the bushes. About the vehicles, drawn up on each side of the roped run-in, there was Punch and Judy; and the hoarse bawling of ballad-singers was almost loud enough to drown the voices of the gypsy girls, crying, "The correct card of the races, with all the running horses, and the weights, names, and colors of the riders!"

John Bullfinch and Mr. Birdbolt were recognised on every hand. The latter was now as hot and earnest as Young Jack himself. May was the cynosure of many eyes, as she sat on Cowslip with admirable ease and grace, bowing right and left to the compliments showered upon her. Soon she became aware of the near presence of Gypsy Jack, who, with a companion, was intently regarding her from a short distance. The gypsy's companion was a man of thirty, much scarred from small-pox, sinewy and long-armed, dressed as a sailor. It seemed as though they had something to tell May or her father, for after exchanging some words together, the sailor nodded to the gypsy, and the latter made three or four steps towards her. But just then Sir Jerry Snaffle rode up on a gray gelding, and paid such a compliment to May that she blushed and looked down. When she raised her head again, the gypsy and the sailor were gone. Sir Jerry, a tall, florid man, with reddish-brown whiskers, bushy as the brush of a fox, was one of the

stewards—in fact, the leading man of the meeting. After a few
words with John Bullfinch, he mentioned Lady Snaffle's wish
that her goddaughter, May, should join her in the carriage.
Dismounting and throwing his reins to a groom, the baronet
assisted her to alight and conducted her to his wife's chariot.

Lady Snaffle was a little stout, fresh and fair, with a merry
eye, a rich, joyous voice, and a kind heart. She was the only
daughter of a fine old Admiral, who had fought at the Nile
and Trafalgar and scores of other places. He had come inland
at last, bringing with him the rustle of reefing breezes and the
rich flavor of the combing seas of the main ocean. Lady Snaffle
had no children. During the lifetime of John Bullfinch's wife,
a quiet, ladylike, superior woman, she had often called at
Hawkwell, and thus it was that she was godmother to May.
After the death of Mrs. Bullfinch, when John took his children to the Hall and presented the little girl, in her deep
mourning, to Lady Snaffle, the lady clasped her to her heart
and vowed that she would be a second mother to her. This
was a source of great relief to Sir Jerry, who hated sadness
and sorrow, and whose well-meant endeavors to console the
widower had, somehow or another, failed. His exhortations
to John to "cheer up" had been wholly unavailing. Seeing
the little girl in his wife's arms, the good-hearted baronet took
charge of the little boy and carried him and John off to the
stables. Ever since that time May had spent a day now and
then with Lady Snaffle, and Young Jack had come to have
the run of the gardens and paddocks. The families had more
in common than people in the towns would at first comprehend, for the Bullfinches were as old in the county as the
Snaffles, and had marched to battle in the wars of the Roses,
side by side with the chiefs of that ancient house. Besides,
whenever the Admiral was at the Hall he frequently called at
Hawkwell and chatted with John and his daughter. After
his visits he would say to his daughter, "Good man, John
Bullfinch, Laura! Like the cut of his jib. Politics right—
true blue! Knows the ropes about horse-racing and farming.
Very handsome girl, May Bullfinch—beautiful! and so well-
behaved! Reminds me of the landlady's daughter at Port
Royal when I was a midshipman in the Sea Horse frigate.
Does, by Jove! She used to wait upon us middies and mix

our grog. You should have heard her sing 'All in the downs.' Smart boy, that Young Jack—ought to go to sea. Topman, by George, by the time he's twenty; might be captain of the foretop at five-and-twenty. Or we might get him appointed midshipman, only our party is not in, and there's an over-supply of them."

" He is heir to Hawkwell, papa, the estate of the Bullfinches —very old family."

" What signifies a few acres of muddy land, Laura, when the lad can own, as you may say, millions of acres of dark-blue water?"

Even Tom Scarlet was looked upon by Lady Snaffle with a certain sort of favor, through the Admiral. On one occasion the old sailor was at the Hall when the anniversary of the battle of Trafalgar came round. Soon after break of day, " two bells in the morning watch," the Admiral rose and found the whole front of the mansion bedecked with laurel boughs; he roused out his daughter and Sir Jerry, and then the crowd upon the lawn gave three cheers and began the stanza which is, for simplicity and pathos, almost sublime:

" By Britons long expected great news from the fleet,
    Commanded by Lord Nelson the French for to meet—
    At length the news came over, through all England it soon spread,
    That the French were defeated, but Nelson was dead."

Tom Scarlet had been the prime mover in all this, and Lady Snaffle appreciated the pains he had taken to celebrate the fame of her veteran father.

May had not long been seated by the lady's side when she noticed the sailor looking hard at them.

" A blue-jacket, May, but not a man-of-war's-man, my dear; he seems determined to know us again. What can the man be staring at us for?"

" Perhaps he is not a sailor," said May.

" O, yes, he is. I can tell at a glance the real tar from the impostors who put on sailors' clothes to beg in. This man is a sailor, but not one of our men—a man-of-war's-man."

Just then the bell rang to clear the course for the first race. There was galloping up and down, smacking of hunting-whips, and pressing back of the foot-people behind the cords. Louder was the hubbub. Shriller the gypsy girls cried the " correct cards," as they pushed back their tangled locks and curtsied to the "gentlemen and sportsmen," who paid in shillings and half crowns, and got smiles and chaff for change.

Now the course and the horses riveted all attention. The ballad-singers bawled no more. Punch shrieked in vain. Pipe and tabor and catgut were silent. Tramp, tramp! swish, swish! six or seven horses go flashing by. Isaac Sadler's chestnut wins the plate for all ages, and Young Jack goes off to the quarters of Maid of the Vale, under a clump of elm trees a few rods from the course.

On his way the lad was accosted by Parkins.

"Master Bullfinch, what game, what *gammon* do you think the gypsies be up to now?"

"I don't know—I'm in a hurry. Is it something about Creeping Joe?"

"You've just hit it; he's to win easy, and Young Ike is to be made a great jockey. The fat man says he'll be one of the top-sawyers at Newmarket!"

"Do you believe that nonsense, Parkins?"

"Do I believe it? Master Jack, I hates the gypsies, especially the family of Gypsy Jack. They be bad 'uns, all bad 'uns."

"Well, no," said Jack. "Miriam Cotswold is a good girl and a merry one."

"What! A good girl! Lord, how you be gammoned! Listen to me——"

"Another time," said Jack; "no time now. The saddling-bell has rung."

Creeping Joe was first on the course, led by the gypsy owner, and followed by the fat man, Jack Cotswold, his nephew Ike, and some scores of the dark and sinister-looking men of the tribes. Then came Maid of the Vale; and she soon became the centre of a circle of rustic admirers. The old trainer held her by the head, Ransome buckled the girths, and Young Jack was as busy about her as a bee in clover. A tall groom in livery came up and said:

"I want Master Bullfinch! Where's Master Bullfinch?"

"Now, where do you think Master Bullfinch is likely to be at this minute, and the mare ready for her mount?" said Young Jack.

"Lady Snaffle wishes to see you for a moment, sir. The carriage is close at hand."

"I know. You tell her ladyship I can't come now, but after the race——"

"What! you send such a message as that to Lady Snaffle?" cried his father. "Off with that jacket! There's a boy here from Will Chiffney's just the weight. No boy that fails in proper respect for Lady Snaffle shall ride this mare."

"Go to her ladyship," said Mr. Ransome, "and keep cool; there's plenty of time. The fact is that her ladyship ought to know better when there's a race in hand; but ladies never *do* know better. Go on, Jack."

"I'm going," said he, with tears in his eyes; "but if this race is lost it won't be my fault."

Hurrying along, whip in hand, natty and spruce in breeches, boots, and purple silk, Jack passed by the carriages, and heard with some satisfaction such remarks as "There's Young Bull-finch. He rides Maid of the Vale. I hope he'll win." In one carriage there was a matron with three daughters, all fair and rosy, and beautifully dressed—Mrs. Southdown, her two eldest daughters, and Margery, a young miss just in her teens. Mrs. Southdown and the young ladies bowed and smiled. Margery jumped up and cried, "Jack! I say, Jack!"

"Ma! Ma! the idea! Shocking!" said the young ladies.

"Well, my dears, it may be improper in a sort of way. But children will be children; and your father has done his best to spoil Margery and Young Jack ever since they were babies."

The Baronet's lady received Jack very graciously, and all his discontent vanished. Lady Snaffle gave him the tips of her fingers, saying, "How d'ye do, Master Bullfinch? Pleased to see you in the Maid's colors again. How is the dainty little mare?"

"She's well, my lady; very well and fit," said Jack.

"They say the bald-faced pony is a wonder, Master Bull-finch. What do you think of the race?"

"He's fast, my lady, but the mare's the real sticker. She's better bred. You know her pedigree?"

"Well, yes, but really at this moment I do not recall it."

"Got by Master Henry out of Miss Stays, by Whalebone;

Master Henry by Orville. Lord Jersey and Mr. Elwes bred him. The mare will win. Has your ladyship got anything of value on?" said Jack, with solemnity.

"Got anything of value on! May, my dear, am I expensively dressed to-day?" said the lady, laughing.

"I don't mean that, my lady. I mean any money on the mare. Because if not, put a little on."

"But I don't know who to put it on with. Everybody in this part of the course is for the Maid."

"So much the better for them, my lady. Bet with Sir Jerry; he'll stand it. Somebody has gammoned him into the belief that Creeping Joe can't lose it."

"A good idea, I declare! Here comes Sir Jerry, and I'll adopt it. May, it will be a rich joke, and I shall win twenty guineas."

The Baronet rode up, and gave his opinion of the race. Creeping Joe was probably the fastest horse of his inches in the Kingdom since Little Driver's time. The mare was a good one, but might not be quite up to the mark. He would have been more confident if Tom Scarlet had been there to train her. And then the Baronet added, "A very clever young man, Miss May."

May blushed and looked a little confused, while Lady Snaffle said, "I believe the mare will win. Master Bullfinch is very confident."

"Boys always are," replied Sir Jerry. "He'd be confident if he had no more chance than a man a-foot."

"Sir Jerry, I will back our county, and lay you twenty to forty," said her ladyship.

"Not taken. Say twenty even, and it's a bet."

"I'll do it," said Lady Snaffle.

The start was at the head of the straight run-in, half a mile from the judges' stand. From the latter the course turned in a half circle for a mile among the gorse, and then there was the straight run-in again. As the ponies came along towards the carriages and went sweeping by, it was seen that Maid of the Vale, going with a long, measured stroke and her head low, was leading two lengths. Creeping Joe, higher and more rapid in action, was second, and two others who had started were already outpaced. Away they went, between the bushes and clumps of green gorse, nothing of them to be seen but the caps of the riders. A mile had been run, and still the little mare forced the pace. A mile and a half, and still she was leading two lengths as they entered the straight. Now the excitement began to rise.

"She'll win! I know she will! May, my dear, the mare is winning!" cried Lady Snaffle.

"I *do* think so!" said May, in a flutter of hope.

"The boy rides well, and she sticks hard; but the great pinch is yet to come," said Sir Jerry, galloping away.

They were three parts of the straight run home, when the gypsy called upon his pony for a great rush, and there was a loud shout as the bald face of Creeping Joe was seen a little in front of the mare. The ladies trembled with excitement, and some shook with fear. But that shout was nothing to the swell of the prolonged roar which shook the bushes when Maid of the Vale came again, and won the race by a length. Then laughing, smiles, bright flashes, shaking of hands, and a rush around the weighing booth, as Young Jack and Ike, with their saddles on their arms, came out. The mare was the great local favorite.

"Sir Jerry, the race is mine by rights. He rode foul. He did indeed! My uncle can prove it," cried Ike.

"Sir Jerry, it's a lie!" said Young Jack. "Ask my father —ask Mr. Ransome—ask Isaac Saddler—ask Lady Snaffle! O, Sir Jerry, do ask Lady Snaffle!"

"Ike, there's half a guinea for you. The race was well ridden and fairly won. It was not your fault that you lost it."

The Baronet then took Young Jack by the arm and said, "My boy, you're a credit to your father, and he's as good a man as ever put foot in stirrup. You ride extraordinarily well."

"So I ought, Sir Jerry; it was Tom Scarlet taught me," said Young Jack, full of pride and joy. "Ride foul, indeed! I'd scorn it, Sir Jerry, especially against *him*, Ike."

"Ah, I understand—clever fellow, Tom Scarlet. Come along, come along! You must receive the congratulations of your sister and Lady Snaffle, and I'll bring your father and Mr. Birdbolt there."

As they went through the crowd to the carriage, Young Jack's silken sleeve brushed the blue jacket of the wiry sailor.

6

He stood talking with Gypsy Jack. They were looking at May Bullfinch again, all unconscious of the astute Parkins, who watched them and muttered, "I ain't to be gammoned. You chaps can't gammon me!" He took good care, however, to keep behind the sailor, who showed such a rough and resolute countenance, as he smoked his cheroot, that Parkins said, "A bad 'un! A very bad 'un!"

After the sports of the day were over there was more noise, more merriment, and more bustle. The brown, bare-legged gypsy boys and girls ran shouting here and there. Tall racers in their clothes, led by little grooms, trod stately by. Red-faced farmers, with their buxom wives and daughters, pressed forward in the throng, and hallooed, "By your leave! by your leave, there!" In the booths faster went the fiddles, more merrily sounded the tabor and pipe. Punch chuckled more richly as he cudgelled the beadle and hung Jack Ketch. There was the thundering of the drum, "and the vile squealing of the wry-necked fife." And loud bawled the ballad-singers. Lady Snaffle threw sixpences among the gypsy boys and girls, clapped her hands, and laughed. Young Jack and Mr. Birdbolt had gone away with the trainer and the victorious little mare. Sir Jerry Snaffle's horse, Black Hearty, and Cowslip were held in readiness by grooms near the chariot; but the Baronet and the yeoman just then were elbowing their way into the thick of a vast crowd, where a fight was going on, in which Gypsy Jack and the sailor acted as seconds to one of the brawny principals.

It was the twilight of the long summer day before John Bullfinch, with May and his son, sat at the board of Mr. Birdbolt. They had a pleasant and a jocund time. The piping bullfinch sat on May's finger and whistled "Coming thro' the Rye," with such art and emphasis that he was encored. The trainer was had in with his lads to join in drinking to Maid of the Vale. Young Jack, for the tenth time, went over all the incidents of the race, and declared that he knew he had it safe when Ike challenged a furlong from the post, instead of waiting till close at home. John Bullfinch was in high glee. Sir Jerry had passed warm encomiums upon Young Jack to his father, and the latter now exclaimed, "No more boarding school, Jack! No more, May!

Sir Jerry says he don't need it; he is in the right way of education—the school for men."

Then John declaimed at length upon the glories and uses of
the turf; the principles of breeding; the art and the science
of training; and the mysteries of jockeyship. Many anecdotes he related, and much information he communicated, concerning the Darley Arab, the Godolphin Arab, Bloody But-
tocks, the Byerly Tuck, the two True Blues, Flying Childers,
King Herod, Eclipse, Pot-8-os, Waxy, Whalebone, and Web;
and finally wound up with an eulogium upon Tom Searlet and
Cowslip.

Mr. Bullfinch had just concluded when it was announced
that Gypsy Jack was at the door and wanted to see him on
business.

" If his business is to claim the Cup, it won't do, you know,"
said Young Jack. " I rode fair, and the mare won. Sir Jerry
and the other stewards have settled it, and the matter can't be
re-opened."

" Hold your tongue !" said his father. " Mr. Birdbolt, shall
we have Jack in and treat him ?"

" By all means," replied Mr. Birdbolt.

The gypsy looked as if he had been in a hot encounter, and
had washed at a horse-trough. His black hair was matted,
there was blood upon his shirt, and a cut over his eyebrow.
He came forward with his usual self-assurance, looked at each
of the company in turn, gave a sort of patronizing nod to
Young Jack, and in compliance with the invitation of Mr.
Birdbolt tossed off a steaming bumper of gin-and-water with
much relish.

" That's the right stuff !" said he. " Gentlemen, I made so
bold as to call, being bound up the country instead of down
the vale, and having business which may prove of interest to
all concerned."

With this he set down the glass and looked steadily at May.

" Well, what is the business? Is it about the race, Jack ?"
said Mr. Bullfinch.

" No, sir, it ain't. The race is over; I've paid my bets, and
that's enough. The mare," he continued, with a glance at
another tumbler of gin-and-water which Mr. Birdbolt was
mixing, "is a d—d sight better than I took her for, and your

son rode like a captain, he did; like a professor of the jockey art, which is a'most as noble as that followed in the twenty-four-foot ring. The owners of Creeping Joe have quarrelled and fought. Luke licked the big fellow by butting—which I don't count quite fair, though within the rules—and has took the pony all to himself. But that ain't the thing. My business here is to deliver a letter—I may say two—from foreign parts."

"A letter from foreign parts! Why it must be from Tom Scarlet," said Mr. Bullfinch.

"I shouldn't wonder," said the gypsy, with a grin, "seeing they was brought over from America—there's one for Miss May, too—by a sailor cove, a friend of mine that was in the clipper brig Tom Scarlet took passage to Baltimore in."

"Is the sailor outside? If he is, let him come forward and splice the mainbrace," said Mr. Birdbolt.

"Well, he's outside, but not here; that is, outside of the lock-up," said the gypsy. "You see, there was a little mill, and after that a jolly row all round. Parkins, being cheeky and officious, had his head punched by this sailor, and went off to get a warrant out. So the sailor, not wanting to be jugged, has cut and run into another county."

"I saw the man," said Mr. Bullfinch. "Were not you and he seconding one of the men in the ring?"

"O, ay! he belongs to the profession, as you may say," returned the gypsy. "You used to know him well some years ago, when he was a clever lad and a lightweight—fought by the name of Harry Cox."

"The Oxford Sailor Boy! And he went over in the same ship with Tom Scarlet, eh?" said Mr. Bullfinch.

"That a did," returned the gypsy, "and introduced him there to one of the right sort; a man from the West, some-where or another, away up the country among the mountains and prairies. A good horseman! a knowing cove! a racing cove! and one as can fight above a bit! He got Cox out of trouble with the beaks in New Orleans once, when they brought off a little battle for a thousand dollars a side, and the other man happened to die. Tom's all right."

"Take another glass, Jack, while I read this letter," said Mr. Bullfinch.

The gypsy readily complied. After a long look at May he

addressed some observations to Mr. Birdbolt and Young Jack, touching America, the vast quantities of unappropriated land there, the absence of game laws, and the cheapness of rum: "Tuppence a glass and help yourself! My eyes! what a country!"

The letter to Mr. Bullfinch was brief, and being very legible, which is more than could be said of many letters in those days, was soon read. It seemed to be satisfactory, for John laid it on the table before him, and surveyed the company. "It is," said he, "a letter from America, written by Tom Scarlet, sure enough, and is just as much to the point, and goes as straight to the purpose, as if it had been written at his own desk at the Grange. The voyage seems to have made no more difference to him than a journey to Aylesbury, Banbury or Oxford would to me."

"Very likely not as much, if it was winter time, and a white horse happened——"

"Hold your tongue!" said Mr. Bullfinch, peremptorily, to the gypsy, pointing to a third glass of gin-and-water. He then resumed: "Tom is quite well. He is gone to the West. I don't precisely know what *the West* means."

"It is like our going to the west of England," said Young Jack.

"I dare say it is. Tom means to make an extensive tour in company with a man of those parts with whom he has become friends—a *very* good man, a capital horseman!"

"Meaning for America, of course," said Young Jack.

"Hold your tongue, sir! A good horseman to Tom Scarlet is good anywhere. During his absence he requests me to look after some matters at the Grange."

"Sensible notion, that there," said the gypsy.

"And," continued Mr. Bullfinch, raising his voice, "to tell Sir Jerry he need not be afraid to match The Bagman across country, for Tom himself will be home to ride him."

"That's very good!" said Young Jack. "I wish he had seen the race to-day. Father, I should like to ride over to the Hall with you when you go to tell Sir Jerry. I caused him to lose twenty guineas to-day, and if I can help to put him on a good thing, by letting him know the real, *private* opinion of Tom Scarlet as to The Bagman, it——"

Mr. Bullfinch had been so struck aback by this statement from his son, that up to the point of the private opinion about The Bagman he had been unable to interpose. He now cried, "What d'ye say? Did I hear aright? Were you the cause of Sir Jerry's losing money? Went halves with the chap who won it, I suppose. You are a nice one for my son!"

"Went halves—no! I am only to have a new saddle and bridle. Her ladyship told me that since the race. She laid the bet with Sir Jerry through my advice."

"O!" said John, opening his eyes very wide, while a smile ran over his face, like the ripple of the sunshine across a meadow in the spring, when light chases shadow, and is in turn chased itself. "If her ladyship won the money, it alters the case. I like to see the ladies bet, especially when they put it on the right horse."

May came forward from the window with a bright, liquid eye and a flushed cheek. She said:

"Tom—Mr. Scarlet, I mean——"

"Always called Tom," put in the gypsy.

"Mr. Scarlet writes very kindly. He wishes to be remembered by all his friends. Sends his love to Jack; and mentioning having written to you, father, says, tell him that as yet I have heard nothing certain of the WHITE HORSE!"

John Bullfinch winced and cleared his throat.

"Heard nothing of the White Horse!" said Mr. Birdbolt.

"Heard nothing of the White Horse! He must be gone over about the White Horse," exclaimed Young Jack.

The gypsy fixed the yeoman with his piercing eye, and said, with great emphasis and deliberation:

"'Tell him that as yet I have heard nothing certain of the White Horse!' Now, this is curious! If this here White Horse was only a goblin horse, a sort of Will-o'-the-Wisp, leading people astray, I could have him charmed and laid by some of our folks. But Tom couldn't have been led off by that sort of thing, and we shall hear more of the White Horse.'"

"I hope I shall hear that he's ringboned and spavined," said John Bullfinch, with some acerbity.

"Then I don't," said the gypsy, "for though Tom has heard nothing certain of him yet, he *will* hear of him, and if the White Horse is sound, I'll bet a trifle he never comes back without him."

CHAPTER X.

"She was so loved, the fairy!
    Like a mistress or a child,
For she was so trim and airy,
    So buoyant and so wild.
Although so young a rover,
    She knew what life might be,
For she had wandered over
    Full many a distant sea."

A CLIPPER brig lay, in the moonlight, a little out in the stream at Baltimore, and two men stood upon the wharf abreast of her. The brig was low in the water, broad in the beam, and very heavily sparred. It seemed that she had lately met with heavy weather, for part of her bulwarks had been washed away and her decks had a bare look, which indicated that they had been swept by green seas within a few days. Yet the spars and standing rigging were all right, and there was no want of trimness in the coiling of the falls of the running rigging upon the belaying pins and cleets. The fact was that the swift clipper, after wrestling with the ocean in its fierce and angry moods for three weeks, had at last reached her port, with all on board well and no damage done save to the paint and upper works, and two or three sails blown out of the bolt ropes. She was a favorite with her officers and her gallant crew, though a very wet vessel, and one that from the height of her masts, the reach of her yards, and the great length of her main boom kept the watch on the alert, and in heavy weather required all hands and the cook to reduce her canvas. She had never made a more marked impression upon the nautical mind by reason of her swift, staunch, and weatherly qualities than upon the passage just concluded.

"A good brig she is; and by the powers, the skipper and mate know how to drive her. The passage was fast and good. We are here ahead of Jagger ever so much. The brig lay her course, you know, all the way——"

"To tell you the truth, Cox, I know very little about it.

Whether it's a week or a fortnight or a month since I came on board, I hardly know."

"Ay, ay! 'twas a rough passage from first to last, for we got it in the channel, and the last gale off this coast was a heavy one. Danger must be a pretty good sea-horse by this time, for he was under water much of the way. I fed him myself all the passage, and he ate well, which is more than you did. He's a very knowing horse. When he smelt the land he almost talked, and the way he struck out for the shore when we shoved him overboard was beautiful. The fact is, that the Roanoke in a breeze of wind is a lively craft. She ducks down a little often, and points her flying jibboom up at the stars once in awhile. But what then? She is safe and swift. She lay her course all the way, which is a d—d sight more than the liners and regular traders could have done. Whichever Jagger may be in, he isn't this side of the Grand Banks yet."

"Now I've had time to reflect," said Tom Scarlet, "I must say that it was imprudent in me to come off at red heat. You see, while I lay below, and the brig was tossing between sea and sky, buffeted about, as it seemed to me, by all the winds and waves in the world, I had nothing to do but consider."

"I know. That's all over now. Another twenty-four hours on land and you'll consider again. I have pondered over this matter in the watches—at the wheel, mind you, and on the look-out, and I've got it made up by day's reckoning. Now, there's one thing sure. Jagger won't go to New York, because there are men there who know him, and he would sooner see the d—l himself than meet them face to face. They had transactions together in England, and when these men were obliged to cut and run he cheated them. Boston's very unlikely. Canada he is sure to avoid. He may go to Mobile, or to New Orleans. Meantime, you are in as good a place as any to hear of him. Kelly here, up at the house, has acquaintances all along this coast. But, better than that, he tells me the Western man I told you of is in Baltimore. Of all the millions in America he's the man to show you the ropes and help you to overhaul Jagger."

"But why should he take trouble and interest himself in me, a complete stranger?"

"Because he's that kind of man. He will carry you off to

his plantation, and once he gets upon Jagger's track he'll hunt him to the Rocky Mountains or to Texas, but what he'll have him and recover your horse. Come, we'll go up and see if he is there yet. Kelly expects him by this time."

They walked a block or two into the city and entered a long room, from which flashed forth ruddy light, with the sound of music, and vigorous feet tripping in the dance. Some dozen men were lounging and smoking, most of them sailors. Some were dancing to airs from two fiddles, a fife, and a harp. At the farther end of the room there was a bar, behind which stood the proprietor of the place, a stout fellow of five-and-thirty, with his shirt-sleeves rolled up. To his right, in a little recess, there were two men over a stove, with pipes in their mouths. One of these was an old sailor, weather-beaten, gnarled and knotted. His hair was grizzled, and his face was as red and hard as salt junk which has been a time or two around the world. The other man was rather tall, very brown, very sinewy, and very quick in his movements. His hair was black, his eye a dark hazel, bold and bright. He had neither beard nor whiskers. His dress was neat, not expensive, but decent, like that of a countryman, and any one could see by his cap of rich fur and his spurs that he was not a Baltimore man.

"And so you say, old man, that you know of millions of money which may be come at for a trifle of outlay?"

"Ay, he does! that is, says so," said Kelly; "but does it stand to reason that they'd be there long and him without enough to pay for his grog and tobacco?"

"Young man, I do know of it, and what's more, nobody else does; so it's all my own. If you was a sailor man, we'd go halves. There's nothing but an outfit wanted; and if Kelly here don't plank down something towards it, none of the money'll be spent in this place; that I'm settled upon—not a doubloon, not a joe, shall he have. Now, what is wanted is a fore-and-aft schooner and six men, a puncheon of rum, a hogshead of bread, and some beef and pork."

"I say, you can furnish them last," said the landlord.

"Well, I have beef cattle (but they are on the hoof) and a drove of live hogs. Old man, whereabouts is this treasure?"

"Well, *young* man, did you ever hear of the Grand Cayman?"

"Did I hear of it? Why, I have been there, and, more fool I, after such a treasure as you tell about. We found the inside of a Spanish calaboose instead of the money. But I hear Cox's voice, Kelly, and I suppose that's the Englishman with him. He looks like a lost man."

"That's him. They came ashore last night from a clipper brig, one as has had a hard but fast passage—a diver, you know—one of them as only comes up now and then to blow. The Englishman has brought a horse with him—such a horse! They swam him ashore. He'd suit you to death, only you couldn't ride him."

"I can ride anything that has a mane," said the Western man, positively.

"No, I'll swear you can't!" replied the ancient mariner; "for to say nothing of the lions, the sea-serpent we made out off the Mauritius had a mane three fathoms long. It's true as I'm alive—as true as the treasure down there by the Grand Cayman. 'Twas in the morning watch—larboard watch —I was at the wheel, and I says to the mate——"

"Hullo! what's the row now?" cried Kelly.

The music had ceased—oaths, the breaking of glass, and the interchange of blows were heard, and a man or two fell to the floor. Those who had interrupted the dance then went hastily into the street, and the musicians, after a time, prepared to play again. But suddenly the door was flung open, and a party of men, armed with slung-shots and clubs, rushed into the room. Their leader was a huge fellow, with a powerful club. He struck down Tom Scarlet, and another was bending over him with a slung-shot about to strike a blow which might have brained him, when the Western man and Kelly sprang forward together. A kick upon the jaw of the man with the slung-shot drove him in among the fiddlers, and then the frontier man faced the intruders. Cox and several sailors had been stricken down at the first onset, as well as Tom Scarlet. The whole party were about to close with the Western man. But he did not wait for them. Retracting his left hand into the sleeve of his coat, so as to fend off with that arm, he drew a knife from some part of his person, and with a fierce cry, sprang at the gigantic leader. Twice the clubs came down upon his head. Twice his knife flashed, and the glitter of the blade made some of his assailants draw off. But at last the large man struck, two-handed, with force enough to fell an ox, and down went the countryman. His opponent uttered a shout of triumph, and hove up his club to finish the work, but then came his own swift destruction. The frontier man rose quickly upon his left knee and right foot, and with an upward, backhanded stroke at the giant, "yerked him under the fifth rib." With a yell of fear and pain the man dropped his club and rushed out of the place, followed by his companions. Kelly sprang to the door and threw two stout oaken bars across it. He had no sooner done so than there were shouts outside of "Help! murder! watch!" and knocking at the door.

"I say, Sassafras, you've killed that fellow," said the landlord.

"He would have killed me, if he could. Look at this club, with lead run into the head of it. If the man who made that ain't a murderer at heart the Mississippi don't run towards the Gulf. Who is he?"

"A fireman and a politician—that is, his friends have got political influence. You must clear out at once, and take the Englishman with you. It won't suit you to lay in jail."

"No; but I doubt whether the Englishman could cut his way through the gang at the door if I could mine."

"I'll manage it all. Come here. Billy, get up."

A young boy arose from a berth near the bar, and the landlord said:

"Go to your uncle's; tell him to have the Englishman's horse saddled and bridled and in the alley in no time. Then go to Carrol's and take Sassafras's horse there. Wait till they come to you."

He then put the boy out through a little window at the back.

"Now, Cox," said the landlord, "you three must go out over the roof, cross the alley, and down off the tobacco warehouse. You have been out that way before."

"I have; but there was a plank and fifteen fathom of rope."

"They are there now. You'll find Mike in the attic to bring them back again. Sassafras, you'll be pursued—no time to lose. Never mind money. This'll soon blow over, and you can settle when you come East again. Take that Englishman home with you, and keep him out of harm's way until he has got the hang of the country."

In less than half an hour Sassafras and Tom Scarlet mounted their horses behind the stable of Kelly's brother in the presence of Cox, a man from Carrol's, and the boy Billy.

"You'd better come with us, Cox. I can get another horse at Pierce's, outside the city. Fine, free air t'other side of the mountains, and I'll show you sport."

"The breezes from the blue water are healthier for me," replied the sailor. "I could lay in this town all snug for six months. But there's no call for it. In the stream, waiting for the turn of the tide to trip her anchor, there's a vessel bound to New Orleans. I know the mate and I mean to sail in her. Direct letters to me at the old place and I'll take 'em to England."

"You won't go with us, then?"

"No; it's not to be thought of."

"I say, Sassafras, I'll go. I want to go to the West," said Billy.

"Good boy! So you shall when I come East again. Goodnight, boys."

CHAPTER XI.

Dogberry.—You shall comprehend all vagrom men; you are to bid any man stand in the Prince's name.

Watchman.—How if a' will not stand?

Dogberry.—Why, then, take no note of him, but let him go; and presently call the rest of the watch together, and thank God you are rid of a knave.

SILENTLY and slowly through the city, keeping to narrow and unfrequented streets, Sassafras and Tom Scarlet rode together. Presently the former explained in brief terms that when they reached the road they could make speed, and with such horses as they rode could easily keep ahead of all pursuers. Arrived at the straggling suburbs, Sassafras leaped his horse over a low fence and led the way across an open space of ground to a good road leading towards the West, through an undulating country. Another leap took them into the road, when Sassafras assured his companion they might now consider themselves safe. They would ride briskly for about five miles, when he would call upon a friend of his for a few minutes, after which they would push on farther. He should consider himself bound to be a friend to Tom; he would carry him first to his plantation, to get the whistle of the winds and the roar of the waves out of his ears, and then aid him to pursue Jagger and recover his White Horse. Time enough for talk afterwards, he added; they would canter along now and get a piece away from those who might follow.

" Do you think the man is dead?" said Tom Scarlet.

" He may be, but he had thick clothes on, and the life lies low in some of these heavy, burly fellows. Besides, I felt the knife cut through a rib or two, and I doubt whether it went far home. But you would have been dead enough by this time if I had not struck in. I have heard something of your history from Cox. Reckon me your friend. I will take chances but what I'll see you righted; the more so, because at this, our first acquaintance, we were in a little difficulty together. Nothing like being on the same side in a little fight to make friends of men upon short acquaintance."

Tom Scarlet expressed his gratitude in suitable terms, and declared that he resigned himself to the guidance of Sassafras. The young men shook hands, and put their horses to an easy hand-gallop.

Sassafras was a Virginian; but his home was now so far towards the West, that it may be doubted whether his new-found friend would have consented to accompany him, if he had known that the plantation to which they were bound was some twelve hundred miles away, and west of the great river which, running a course as far from north to south, is called the Father of the Waters. Sassafras was the youngest of a family of three children, the eldest of whom was a girl. He lost his mother young, but not before the excellent woman had planted and cherished in his mind the sound principles of morality and simple piety by which she herself had always been governed. His father, after the death of his wife, grew discontented, and moving across the mountains with their stock and negroes, they settled in Kentucky. The daughter

married a well-to-do farmer when she was eighteen. Not long
afterwards the father and the eldest brother were cut off untimely in a desperate encounter with fellows called " Regu-
lators," who, under pretence of supplementing the laws, carried on all sorts of depredations and violence. Young Sassafras killed the leader of the gang before the blood of his
father and brother was well off the ground, and desperately
wounded two others. They had relatives and friends, and
after carrying on a bitter, bloody and vindictive feud with
extraordinary daring and constancy, the young man—he was
hardly more than a youth—sold off most of his effects to his
brother-in-law, and started for Missouri with the negroes, who
might be considered the survivors of his family. He also took
a lot of blood horses. He settled on the Missouri river, near
St. Joseph's, the old city founded by the French explorers and
traders. There he now owned a large plantation. He did not,
however, spend much of his time upon it, but made excursions
to the Indian country, and sometimes visited New Orleans.
Meantime his land and stock were honestly, if not thriftily,
looked after by his negroes, at the head of whom was a sage,
white-headed grandsire, who had "always been old," as Sassafras said, which meant as long as he could remember. Most
of the produce raised on the estate, save the tobacco, which
flourished much in the rich bottoms, was consumed upon it.
In fact, if any one had made it a matter of reproach to Sassafras that he owned slaves, he would have replied, " If it comes
to that, they own me."

He was passionately fond of horses and horse-racing. He
was a bold, skilful and enduring rider, a sure shot with the
rifle, and a mighty hunter. He was not a quarrelsome man,
but he was a quick, tenacious and severe fighter when engaged.
He revered the memory of his mother, and sometimes curbed
his tongue in altercations and broils with the reflection, " My
mother would not have approved of this." He was intensely
devoted to " Old Virginia," and it is to be remarked that the
most thoroughgoing and unselfish admirers of some states,
commonwealths and countries, are to be found among those
who have left them. Sassafras would sometimes laugh at a
reflection upon himself; but let anybody say anything against
the name, the fame, the honor or the wisdom of the " Old

Dominion," and his blood was up. The calumniator was required to retract or fight upon the spot.

About once a year Sassafras visited Baltimore, passing down the Mississippi and up the Ohio by steamboat to Wheeling in Virginia, and then riding across the mountains on horseback. His business was to settle his accounts with an old Scotch merchant to whom he sent his tobacco and his furs, and who shipped to him sundry supplies. Two days before he had met Tom Scarlet, Sassafras had presented himself, without notice, as usual, at the merchant's warehouse, and had been ushered into the inner office, where the old man sat at one desk and his trusty bookkeeper, a canny Scot, at another. After a warm greeting, there was some such colloquy as follows:

"Ye've sent no tobacco the year, Sassafras. How's that, man?"

"I was off in the Indian country, Mr. Leith. The tobacco is all right, and a good crop it is. It will be sent on after the spring freshets have run out of our rivers."

"'Tis good, is it, Sassafras? And how many hogsheads?" said the old gentleman, taking a pinch of black rappee, imported from "Edinboro' Toon."

"I don't precisely know how many, sir."

"Hear till this, Duncan! hear till this! Here is a planter who don't know how many hogsheads of tobacco he's got to ship!"

"I didn't count 'em. I know more about the furs, because I brought them from up the Missouri river myself."

"And what will they be, Sassafras?"

"Why, there's mink and otter and beaver and fox, and there's two silver fox, but they are not for you."

"Not for us! How's that, man?"

"I'm going to make a present of them to a lady—a young lady, sir."

"Present to a leddy—a young leddy! Nonsense, man! The value is very large—much too large."

"Very likely, but for all that I shall give 'em to your daughter."

"Duncan, heard a man ever the like o' this! Sassafras, there must be an invoice o' the furs."

"Very well, you can make it yourself."

"And we maun settle our old account. Ye'll have had the statement, Sassafras?"

"O, yes, sir, I have the statement you sent."

"And ye've fund it correct?"

"I have. I have added up all the figures, and the totals are right. The statement is a beautiful statement, only I can't quite make out whether we are even, or whether I owe you about a thousand dollars or you owe me a thousand."

"Good Lord! Duncan! hear till this! Draw the man a check for $1161.18, and let's get him oot o' this toon as soon as may be."

"Never mind the odd cents, Duncan."

"But he must mind the odd cents. How the devil do ye think the books can be balanced and the check no' show the cents? Sassafras, ye'll dine wi' me the day. Duncan, ye'll come and cut your mutton wi' us. And noo, as it's past the hoor of noon, a wee drap of the auld stuffie from over yonder will be no that ill to take. Bring out the Ferintosh, Duncan. See ye draw the curtain close, too. Ye see, Sassafras, there's a wheen young lads in the ooter office, and I'll set no bad example to youth. Doon wi't, man! Ye get na such dram as that in the Indian country. Here's till ye!"

When the old merchant took his seat at the desk the following morning, he said:

"Duncan, we mun gi' credit to Sassafras at the full market price when his furs come to han'."

"Ay, sir; and he mun get full weight in the entry of his tobacco."

"Wha said anything about weight, ye fause loon?"

"Weel, sir, I did. You chiel, Sassafras, accepts everything we put doon without question, and he's no skeel in figures beyond adding up. 'Twould be a shame not to gi' him full weight. Besides, we'll mak' it up oot of them ower-cute Yankees fra' the North that come here haggling and objecting and speering, and wushing a reduction of this, and demanding an explanation o' that—we'll mak' it up oot o' tha cunning bodies wha think a' body as unprincipled as theirsels."

"So we will, Duncan—so we will! My certie, Duncan, but ye're well grunded in the true mercantile principle, to which, by the by, we'll take a wee drappie."

The education of Sassafras had been elementary only. But

it had been improved and enlarged since his early school days.
He had derived much general information from several classes
of men. The chief of these were Catholic priests at an insti-
tution near St. Joseph's, and certain Jesuit missionaries among
the Indians. Sassafras was not himself a Catholic. His
mother had been a member of the Episcopal Church of the
Old Dominion, and that was good enough for him. But he
respected the priests he knew, especially the missionaries.
Besides, when stricken with fever at New Orleans, after
the expedition to the Grand Caiman, he had been nursed and
cured by the Sisters of the Charity Hospital. You might as
well abuse the Old Dominion as declaim against priests and
nuns to Sassafras after that. He gave money to help build
churches. He furnished the fathers with horses. Every year
at Christmas he overwhelmed the larder of the Lady Superior
(a French Countess) of the Sisters' House at St. Joseph's with
hogs, hindquarters of beef, turkeys, poultry and bucks, such
as delighted the heart of Father Abbot at Bolton Abbey in
the olden time. Sassafras was fond of books at leisure times.
He read but few, but these were good, and his taste had mainly
been guided by a good old Jesuit from the Canada side of the
line, who was as much English as French, and had been a
soldier in his youth. The last time the old man parted from
him was at an Indian encampment among the spurs of the
Rocky Mountains, and then the missionary said:

"Sassafras, my son, farewell! We shall probably not meet
again. To say to you be brave, honest, and truthful I deem
unnecessary. But, Sassafras, be temperate, merciful and just.
Shed no blood, save upon absolute necessity. May God have
you in his keeping."

Sassafras and his English friend drew bridle in front of a
large frame house, with straggling out-buildings, which stood
back from the road. The moon was sinking in the West, but
there was light enough for the practised eye of Sassafras to see
that a herd of cattle lay in the yards adjacent to the out-buildings. He put his fingers to his mouth and whistled low but
shrill. A man came out, attended by a stout negro bearing a
lantern. The man was thin and tall. His face was expressive,
now grave, then lively and gay, and there was humor in his
gray eye and the lines about the corners of his flexible mouth.

7

"Halloo, Sassafras!" said he, "what now? You are back very soon."

"Ay! and a friend with me, but we shall not stop here now."

"Not stop! why you won't go on to Smith's! Your friend is an Englishman, I see, and on a good horse. He's brought money with him. They all do it. Don't let him go to Smith's."

"Pierce!" said Sassafras, sharply, "there's been a little difficulty, and a fellow got cut with a knife in the ribs."

"I say, Sassafras, so you've been at it again!" said Pierce, solemnly, and then he added with a grin, "and a knife, too! You ought not to have used a knife."

"Well, a pistol would have done as well and I had one about me, but the knife was handy to my grip. Besides, the difficulty was hot just then, and a knife never misses fire. Now, the man who was cut has got political influence, and they will send men after us. I don't want to fight any more to-night, and I don't want to be followed. Still, if we *are* followed we are not going to kill our horses by running away. You understand."

"I understand, Sassafras. You won't be followed beyond this house—that is, if them that follow have got a bit of sense."

"Good! who's here with those cattle?"

"Men from the West, who own them."

"From over the mountains?"

"No; this side of the mountains."

"Well, good-night, Pierce. Give my love to my cousin Elizabeth, and tell her the next time I come East I'll take her to the Old Dominion."

"Sassafras, stop that," said Pierce, with a gesture of alarm; "them words 'Old Dominion' wakes up your sweet cousin in the most astonishing manner, and her health is so precious that I object to having her disturbed."

Sassafras and Tom Scarlet rode away. Pierce returned into the bar-room of his tavern with the negro; and while the latter stood by the stove, the former made ready to refresh himself with a glass of liquor. Before he got it to his lips there was a patter as of little feet in slippers on the stairs at the back, and a female voice, not as low and soft as Pierce or Richard Grant White might have wished, exclaimed :

" Pierce !"

He shook his head and looked at the negro, who thereupon skook *his* head.

" Pierce !　*Mister* Pierce !"

No answer, until the frill of a night-cap over certain black eyes and black hair in curl-papers appeared round the balusters.　Mr. Pierce then exclaimed :

" I must have been dozing, my dear.　What do you wish ?"

" Who were you talking with outside, Pierce ?"

" Travellers, Elizabeth ; strangers going West."

" O, you bold deceiver !　It was my cousin — Sassafras. And there's been a fight.　Sassafras has whipped four or five more.　Acknowledge the corn, Pierce !　You know he has !"

" Well, my dear, *if* Sassafras was here, and *if* there was a fight, Sassafras got the best of it."

" Of course !　He's a Virginian, from the Old Dominion. So am I, Pierce !"

" My dear, I've heard that some thousands of times."

The footsteps retreated, and the good man was about to put the tumbler to his lips, when Elizabeth said :

" Pierce, if men come here from Baltimore, send them packing home again.　Tell them that there's a party of Virginians on the road ahead ; and say, too, that your own wife, a Sassafras by the mother's side, can hit a squirrel in a treetop with a two-grooved rifle—from the Old Dominion, Pierce !"

Mr. Pierce shook his head at the darkey, and listened like a cat at a cupboard door, until he heard a sound above which indicated that Mrs. Pierce had laid down again.　He then drained his glass, and, looking at the darkey, said :

" When a man, a Marylander, marries into one of the——"

" Fust families !" said the darkey.

" Fust *fighting* families of Virginia, he nat'rally wishes his member of the family to enjoy her sleep o' nights.　Jacob, there'll be men here from Baltimore.　They will have driven fast, and you'll have to look to their horses."

" Yes, sah ! and if dey trow a shoe, or break a trace, or start a tire—such will happen sometimes on de road, sah !"

" Jacob, I see you understand, but I hope none of these accidents will happen on the road *back* to Baltimore.　What will you take, Jacob ?　Here's whiskey, very pure, made in the mountains, Jacob; and here's rum, old, straight from Jamaica."

"De whiskey, Massa Pierce, is bery fine. For de ole Jamaicky I hab great respect, sah! But habbing been ras'd in Virginia, away down on de Eastern shoah, de peach and honey —real essence and true flavor ob de ole Domin——"

"Stop! Here you are—help yourself!"

The miserable man—he was in bondage sore—took the peach brandy in one hand and the honey in the other, and compounded a tumbler full. His eye dilated, his nostrils expanded, his mouth seemed to widen from ear to ear. And all over his broad ebony countenance there spread a glow like that of an African morning on the west coast.

"Jacob," said Mr. Pierce, "your missus is a singular good woman."

"Dar no better 'oman in de 'ole——"

"Stop!"

"'Ole United States, sah! Everybody say dat. De town trash negroes in Baltimore acknowledge dat."

"Jacob, you may live—far distant be the day—to see your missus in her coffin. You've heerd of people being buried alive?"

"I hab heerd, but not experienced, sah."

"Well, Jacob, if you live to see your missus in her coffin, jest whisper 'Ole Dominion' close to her ear. If nothing happens then it will be safe to proceed with the funeral."

No long time had elapsed before Pierce and the negro heard the sound of approaching wheels, upon which they fell asleep instanter, and it was several minutes before they suffered themselves to wake up and admit the new-comers. There were six men in the party, and the leader was a bluff, portly personage, with the air of one in authority, He was addressed by the others as Sheriff, but his office was only that of chief deputy.

"Any strangers in the house, Pierce?" said he.

"Yes, there are—five or six. They own the cattle in the yard and are going to the city at daybreak."

"Is there any stranger here, come from the city, a Western man, with a sailor and an Englishman in his company?"

"No such person in the house."

"No man by the name of Sassafras, eh? Do you know such a person?"

"I do. He stopped here some days ago as he went in. What of him?"

"He has killed a man, that's all."

"Then if he is on the road he's gone on to Smith's beyond any question. All such parties do. None but quiet, peaceable citizens stop at my place, but at Smith's——"

At this Pierce gave such an unutterable look and made such a gesture as to signify that Smith's chosen customers were none too good for Sassafras or any other man.

"We must follow him. How far do you call it to Smith's?"

"I call it a good deal too far for you to travel before daylight," replied Pierce. "If Sassafras and the sailor and the Englishman are there, they will have the backing of as desperate a gang as is to be met with on this side of the mountains. If I were you I should stay here until daylight certain. You are not strong enough to take these men at Smith's."

"The law would be on our side," said a timorous-looking man who was of the sheriff's party.

"You couldn't have a worse thing on your side at Smith's when the knives and pistols and rifles come into play."

"You think Sassafras will resist?"

"I know he will. He's been resisting somebody or something ever since he was fourteen years old, at which age he fought at the polls for Jackson. Besides, I doubt whether he won't be justified in resisting. Your warrant will not run at Smith's; his house is in another county—a Democratic county."

"And Sassafras is a Democrat, is he?" said a sprightly little man.

"I have it from his cousin, a noted shot with a two-grooved rifle, who is not far away, that he fought at the polls for Jackson when fourteen years old, and he's been at it pretty much ever since."

"Then I honor him," said the little man. "I'm a Democrat myself, and I now give notice that I have been mistaken. The sheriff inveigled me into joining this party by pretending that it was to go after a murdering ruffian, and I now find that he's a respectable gentleman, a worthy fellow-citizen of the West. This is a political manœuvre—another Whig plot against the rights of the people. Talk about resisting—I'll be d—d if I don't resist it myself."

"The real truth is that you had better stay here till morning and then go back to Baltimore," said Pierce. "How can it be expected that you gentlemen in buggies, responsible men of homes and reputation, can come up with such a set of dare-devils as Sassafras and Smith's gang, and them on horseback? Besides, if you could come up with them, you would be ambushed to a certainty. That cousin can hit a squirrel in a tree-top with a two-grooved rifle—that I know, for I've seen it done. The best thing for all concerned is just to let Sassafras go his ways. The state of Maryland will be well shet of him, and you'll take no damage in any respect."

"As a father of a family," said the timorous-looking man, "I look upon Pierce's advice as good."

"I have something else to say about Sassafras, which the sheriff ought to hear," said Pierce. "Look at this paper. I got it through the cousin I mentioned, copied it with my own hand from the original, which you'll find in the possession of Sassafras, if you ever get hold of him. Now listen:

"'GREENBRIAR, Virginia.

"'This is to certify to my friends that John Sassafras, Democrat and Jackson man, came to my aid in a time of great peril, and saved my life at the imminent risk of his own.
           (Signed)   HENRY CLAY.'"

"Let me see that paper," said the sheriff. "Ay! that's Mr. Clay's hand and style, sure enough!"

"Hand and style! Why, it's a copy!" said the little man.

"Very well, what if it is? Do you think Pierce can copy from Harry of the West and me not find it out? It will be of no use for us to put ourselves into trouble and danger in order to take this man. No jury will convict. Pierce, copy me that off. We'll stay here till morning, and then take the back track."

CHAPTER XII.

"The western sky was all aflame,
The day was well nigh done—
Almost upon the western wave
Rested the broad, bright sun."

AT the time of which I write, between forty and fifty years
ago, the Republic of the United States of America,
although vast in extent even then, had not embraced several
great regions which are now within its boundaries. Texas, an
empire in itself, so far as extent and fertility are concerned,
had not been annexed. Neither California, New Mexico, nor
Arizona had been acquired. Moreover, a vast portion of the
country, which is now partly settled and fruitful to the hus-
bandman, or valuable to the cattle-breeder and miner, was
then in a state of nature, wholly unsubdued and almost wholly
unknown. Great forests, immense prairies, wide as seas, lofty
and rugged mountains, and tracts wild and desolate as the
deserts of old Arabia or young Australia, were then part and
parcel of its territory. To the west of the Mississippi river the
population was very sparse, save towards its mouth, in low lat-
itudes; and it was largely composed of adventurers, trappers,
hunters, Indian traders, and the like. In the great state of Arkansas there were but a few thousand inhabitants, exclusive of
Indians. In Missouri there were not many. The settlements
were mostly upon the rivers. On the Arkansas, Little Rock
was the only place of note. On the Mississippi and Missouri
the old French towns of St. Louis and St. Joseph's were the
seats of population and trade. The latter was the northeastern
starting point of the famous Sante Fe trail, the route by which
the interior of the vast regions of the Southwest was reached,
and the bullion of New Mexico brought to the States. The
rich deposits of gold and silver in our own country were then
as unknown and as unsuspected as was the existence of this
continent itself when Christopher Columbus sailed from Palos.
The western parts of Missouri and Arkansas were the hunting
grounds of powerful and predatory Indian tribes, and the
resorts of buffaloes in immense herds. Beyond these western

boundaries there was, practically, a vast *terra incognita*, the home of the savage, the buffalo, the elk, and the grizzly bear. Explorers sometimes penetrated into the passes of the Rocky Mountains. Trappers and hunters sometimes ventured in the "Parks," which lie between their spurs, but their numbers were scanty and their visits far between. Indian traders had here and there, in this vast wilderness, what they dignified by the name of forts, but which were chiefly mere trading posts, erected for the purpose of traffic in buffalo robes, skins and furs. Almost all kept, as near as might be, to the Santa Fe trail, for that was about the only known route, and the sole means of succor and supply in times of danger and scarcity. The Indian tribes, though savage, improvident, turbulent and inconstant, were then much more powerful in numbers and organization than they are now; while their people were not nearly as debased, individually, as they have since become. Years after that period, many bands of Sioux, who hunted upon the upper waters of the Missouri, about Fort Benton, had never tasted the "fire water," and thought Charles Primeaux, manager of the western posts of the American Fur Company, the richest and the greatest man on earth. He received by a steamboat, which painfully struggled up the Missouri to Fort Benton about once in two years, such supplies of powder, lead, blankets, etc., as made the untutored savages think the wealth of the world was poured out at his feet. To the southward, the tribes, always nomadic in their habits, were almost constantly encroaching upon the grounds of other tribes, while what they called their own were encroached upon in turn; so that it would now be nearly as difficult to assign to any one of them its proper limits, as it was for Gibbon to trace the wanderings, the innumerable vicissitudes and changes of many of those hordes of barbarians who overthrew the Roman Empire. It is sufficient here to say that the Indians between the borders of Missouri and Arkansas and the Rocky Mountains were predatory, fierce, aggressive, and all horsemen. And it may also be affirmed that many of the whites with whom they were brought in contact were nearly as ignorant and savage, and quite as greedy and unscrupulous as themselves. The neighborhoods of the trading posts were sometimes the scenes of privation which bordered on famine. At other times they rang with drunken revelry, and barbaric profusion was mingled with brawl and slaughter.

On the afternoon of a clear, hot day, towards the end of August, a small train was passing over the practically boundless prairies to the eastward of the Santa Fe trail. It was trending to the southward and eastward, so as to point for those head-waters of the Arkansas river which rise in the neighborhood of the Ozark Mountains. The party had left St. Joseph's many days before, and having gained a good departure to the southwest along the trail, its leader had now inclined to the left, as if he meant to strike the northwest corner of Arkansas. The train itself consisted of four wagons, drawn by mules and driven by negroes. It was preceded by two men on horseback, and followed by two more. Behind two of the wagons there were powerful horses, clad in sheets and hoods of a light, striped fabric. The pace the travellers went was slow, for the afternoon was intensely hot; but they proceeded steadily along towards a thin fringe of cottonwood trees, or, rather, bushes, dimly seen in the distance, near which the leader knew he should find the great necessity of the prairie at that season—fresh water. One of the men who rode in advance was tanned so red, his beard was so overgrown and scorched by the summer sun, and he was so clad and armed in the fashion of the rovers of the West, that he would not have been known by his friends, nor even by his enemies, if some of them had met him there and then. It was Tom Scarlet, Master of the Grange, in the parish of Ridingcumstoke. His companion, the leader and captain of the band, was Sassafras, now in his proper element upon a roving expedition. As he sat his horse with the ease and freedom of the Indian, and the short stirrup and bent knee of all the real riding races, as contrasted with the long leathers and straight leg of those who teach equitation, he seemed to be almost a part of the animal he rode. Sometimes Sassafras had gone as far as New Mexico to the southwest. Upon other occasions he had spent weeks with the chiefs and head men of the Cherokee nation in their territory. Sometimes he hunted and camped, and if occasion happened, fought with the nomadic Indians of the plains and mountains. But whenever he went upon his Western expeditions he always took one or two thoroughbred horses with him, and was ready to run against anybody for anything. After spending some time at his plantation, Sassafras had taken Tom Scarlet to St. Louis. While there he received from some boatmen on the river certain information which induced him to hurry back to St. Joseph's. There he speedily equipped his train. Taking with him four of his negroes, and associating with himself two experienced frontier men, he crossed the Missouri and set forth boldly towards the southwest. The supplies for the needs of himself and men were neither expensive nor extensive. Ammunition, salt, coffee, sugar, bacon and a few bags of corn-meal composed their stock, as they knew they could mainly live by the game which would fall to their rifles. The wagons were loaded, in great part, with bags of oats and bales of corn-fodder, the latter plucked and cured while the stalk was green. These were for the race-horses. Sassafras had learned, by a long and wide experience, that grass and Indian corn would not suffice for the race-horse, if he was to be called upon to display his high powers of speed and endurance.

They journeyed on. The white men with knives in their belts and pistols in their pockets, their rifles ready to their hands in the wagons. The negroes laughed and sung, while the sweat rolled down their faces in thick streams.

"Is the weather always as hot as this in these parts?" said Tom Scarlet. "I protest, Sassafras, that I am roasted and basted, like a goose at Christmas, and before long I think I shall be done brown, if not burned to a cinder. It is terribly oppressive!"

"The weather is a little hot—hot even for these parts," said Sassafras; "but you'll get used to it in a little while, and think it very pleasant. For my part, a good deal of sunshine agrees with me. You'll get used to it, and come to like it."

"I think I *have* become used to it, but as to liking it, that is another matter. Does it never change here? Ever since we left St. Joseph's it has been unvarying—blue sky and blazing sun."

"Well, it does change a *little*, as you'll find out before very long," said Sassafras. "The moon is near the full. Before she passes into her decline we are likely to have a storm. Before it comes I hope to reach the timber belt at the foot of the Ozark spurs, for it rips heavy over these prairies sometimes, especially after a long spell of dry, hot weather."

"You seem to know this wild, lonely country as the sailors know the sea, aided by their instruments and the sun, moon, and stars, Sassafras. Were you born about here?"

"Born about here! Why, no white men have ever been born about here, and some think there never will be any. But I hold to another opinion. Where buffaloes can live and trains can subsist their men and horses on a passage, folks can make settlements and thrive. So I think this part of the country will finally be staked out and bounded, and towns built, but not yet for a good while."

"You are a Western man?" said Tom, inquiringly.

"A Western man, yes. But I was born in Old Virginia, a thousand miles and more to the eastward; some say nigh upon two thousand by the way we have to travel to get there. My father lived in King George county. I was but a boy when he moved his family to the West, after mother's death," said Sassafras, slowly.

"Tell me all about it," said Tom.

"The all is but little," Sassafras replied. "We were four— father, two sons and one daughter. I was the youngest. We crossed the mountains with two wagons—the big Virginia wagons with hoops and cotton tilts. We had two thorough- bred mares hitched to the tail of the wagons, and underneath there were chained two couple of the best hounds that ever ran a red fox through the underbrush. It's many years ago, but I remember all the journey. How the wolves used to howl away off from our fire at night! and how the panther screeched in the rocks and woods above!"

"And you went on in this way to Missouri?"

"No, no! we settled in Kentucky, and lived there; but we had ill luck after some time. My father and brother were killed in a fight. I have wiped that score out since," said Sas- safras, sternly, while there was a gleam of fire from his eyes that made his companion start. "My sister married and her husband is a very good man. After that I got restless and went further west."

They rode on in silence for some time. Then Sassafras cleared his throat, and said, "I visit the graves in Kentucky once a year, and my sister brings her children there to meet me. Sometimes I go to Virginia to the graves we have there."

" It is good," said his companion.

" So I find it. In old King George my grandfathers and grandmothers and all our kin before them, lie, as well as my mother," said Sassafras.

" I'm glad of that. Men should hold their forefathers in remembrance ; be proud of them. They have no reason to be ashamed to visit the places of their burial. Some have said that you Americans cared nothing for old homes and the graves of the households that were your ancestors."

" It's a lie !" said Sassafras, earnestly, " at least, so far as we of Virginia are concerned. Of the down-east people I don't know much, but from what I do know, I believe it to be a lie in regard to them, also."

They rode on a little further, when Sassafras said, " Look at our horses. What do you think ails them ?"

" I do not know. There's something unusual," replied Tom. " Perhaps they smell the water, or a wild beast has passed here."

" It isn't the water," said Sassafras. " They have been here before, and know where that is as well as I do. No wild beast has passed that I or they know of, although a wolf may have prowled by here last night. There are buffalo within a few miles of us. These horses are old buffalo hunters, and scent a herd long before we can see it. We may have tongue and steaks for supper."

The herd of bison, a small one, was soon seen leisurely grazing along one of those hollows of the prairie in which the grass was freshest. There were several bulls in the van, great fellows, with massive heads and horns, gigantic shoulders and withers, and wild, shaggy fronts.

" Keep quiet," said Sassafras. " We must let the Gumbos pass them to the right and left, and get upon their flanks. Our horses are pretty well tuckered out, and if the herd stampede the slowest of them will distance us."

" Gumbos ! are there Indians in sight, too ?" said Tom.

" Indians ! no. The Gumbos are the Frenchmen—our men. They are Gumbo French, which means the French of St. Louis and St. Jo. and all the frontier. First-rate men they are, too, for the plains, the rivers and the mountains."

" Can't we dismount, and stalk the buffaloes with our rifles ?" said Tom Scarlet.

"No, you can't stalk buffalo a-foot. They smell the powder in the gun, some say," replied Sassafras.

"I have heard the same of crows in England, but I don't believe it," returned Tom.

"Nor I. They can smell the man that carries the gun, and as he is out of sight they are all the more wary," said Sassafras. "A good many things concerning wild birds and animals are put down by men who know nothing about it."

This observation is as true now as it was then. It was gravely announced recently by the *London Spectator*, in an article on the power of sea-birds to estimate distances, that at a certain place they had calculated the difference of range between shot-guns and rifles as soon as the latter were introduced, and in two or three days kept just outside of the range of two thousand yards. The author of this valuable addition to natural history was evidently unaware of the fact that a hundred riflemen could not hit a sea-bird at two thousand yards once a week, if they shot every day and all day long.

The train was halted. The proper dispositions were made, and the men let their eager horses go for the buffaloes. A cow in good condition, and a yearling, fell to their fire. The sun now declined, slow and majestic, towards the edge of the western horizon, and all that quarter of the heavens was flooded with rosy light. The camping place at the stunted cottonwood, by the scanty pool of the creek, was reached. The weary horses were relieved of their riders, the mules hobbled and turned loose, and the race-horses watered and fed. The men ate their evening meal and smoked their pipes. Then the first watch was set; and while the sentinel remained silent and alert, the others stretched themselves upon buffalo robes and fell asleep. The middle watch was kept by Tom Scarlet. He paced to and fro by the wagon. The moon had risen high in the heavens, and now flooded the prairie, far and near, with a sea of silver light, whose even wave no shadow broke. A light fog, close to the ground, took the white beams, and looked like smooth water. The scene was grand in its sublimity and awful in its silent desolation. No sound broke the silence of the night. No howl of wolf, nor hoot of owl, nor cry of whippoor-will invaded it. The very men and horses might have been dead—they were so still and motionless—remains of a band of explorers, whose bones would whiten in the realm of the mighty and mysterious wilderness. The young Englishman felt the influence of the scene, the hour and the place—the place! one spot in what seemed boundless space. He thought of his home in the fair vale of the populous little island over the sea. The sadness of the solitude grew upon him. But Sassafras rose silently from the shaggy robe which was his couch, and broke the spell, saying:

"Watchman, what of the night?"

"Nothing; but it seems so lonely here," replied Tom. "We might fancy ourselves the only beings in a wide world shone upon by yonder moon. Sassafras, I am sad to-night."

They sat down together, and talked in the low tones befitting the pale hour and the solemn scene that lay before them. The Western man, in spite of his wandering life, had read much, in a *few* books. His memory was retentive, his penetration quick and deep. The young Englishman was surprised to find him well-informed upon topics of which he knew but little himself. Sassafras loved history, especially the history of England and of this country, as taught in the lives, the works, and the famous exploits of their great men. After some time, their conversation gradually diverged to the subject of their expedition.

"If we have been running a false scent after all, it will be very provoking, Sassafras. I shall, however, have had experience of a region vast and wild beyond conception to me before, and of a way of life glorious in its freedom and the absence of petty things and cares."

"All true, Tom," said Sassafras; "you have left petty cares behind you. But then you have also left the true-hearted girl, and the warm friends, and you will rejoice to see them again. We are on no false scent. We shall hit the head of the snake's trail, instead of beginning at the tail of it, that's all."

"You still think so, do you?" said Tom, anxiously.

"Do I? Ay, I do. It isn't a moonlight night in a lone camping place that'll shake my conclusions," replied Sassafras. "The information received from Orleans was mystical in words, no doubt, but true enough in substance. Staples was bound up the river and West by way of the Arkansas, making for the Ozarks. Your man, Jagger, was with him, and he had the White Horse."

" Suppose this information should be the device of an enemy, instead of the warning of a friend, and intended to lure me into these wild parts?" said Tom.

" There is not a bit of sense in supposing any such thing. I sent word to friends in New Orleans to make inquiries. This information comes not from them, but no doubt from somebody who heard from them, and who knows Jagger and all his moves ; who is also your friend, but don't want Jagger to know it just yet. This is the lay of it, as sure as my name's Sassafras."

" I hope it is so, but I have no friend in New Orleans," said Tom, after a pause.

" It must be so," said Sassafras, earnestly. " No enemy who wanted to decoy you into these parts to your harm would have decoyed me along with you, unless he was the biggest fool that ever sailed up the passes of the Mississippi river. Why, man, none other of my sort has as much influence with the Indians of these plains as I have. I can raise a ' power,' as they called it in Old England, in the days of the Roses and the Barons. Old Staples has as much influence as I have, if not more, in the Cherokee Nation ; but this business must be settled here, where the red horsemen, who roam and hunt all the way from the Ozarks to the Rocky Mountains, will be the referees. They don't like Staples a bit too much ; and he's no favorite at all of the Comanches and Kiowas, whose country is further to the Southwest. Enemy ! why I want to show you ! You've no enemy in all this land but Jagger. Nobody knows who you are but me and him ; and he won't know you when you meet again, if you keep a still tongue."

" He may have told all sorts of lies about me," said Tom. " The man is a villain, Sassafras, capable of anything. He knows that I was hard upon his heels at Liverpool, but unfortunately, by the advice of Cox, I took ship for Baltimore, while Jagger must have sailed for New Orleans."

" It was not unfortunate that you came to Baltimore, but all the other way. You and I met there, and I reckon myself a gainer by it," said Sassafras.

Tom thanked him warmly.

" Jagger would have had the best of you at New Orleans. I believe you said he had been there before?" said Sassafras.

"I said he had been in the West Indies."

"It's the same thing. Fellows of his hang and stamp always turn up at Orleans at last, when they visit the West India Islands—that is, the Windward Islands. When we got this news at St. Jo., concerning him and Old Staples, I said to myself, 'Boys, I know where you're pinting for, and you'll meet somebody at the post, about the spurs of the Ozarks, that you little think of.' Luckily an expedition was about to set out for the head-waters of the Kansas river, with supplies, and to hold a talk with some of the chiefs. By that I sent word to a fast friend of mine, a chief among the Cheyennes, whose main hunting-ground is now about Solomon's Fork. I requested him to cross the plains and be at an old rendezvous of ours early in September, or a little earlier if he could."

"And do you think the Indian will come?" said Tom.

"As sure as water runs down hill, Cinnamon will come, if alive, with a band of his young men—a band able to hold their own against the drunken, crazy set that are mostly in the neighborhood of the post at this time of year."

"Well, then, Jagger may have said anything, and may say what he will, and not harm me?"

"You are a young man of plenty of sense, in most ways, but as innocent as a baby in a venture of this kind," said Sassafras. "Jagger will never mention your name; he'll think you are a good thousand miles away, and probably four or five thousand—gone back to England. Why would he mention you? He would as soon see the d—l as you any of these days, because you know that he has run away with a heap of money belonging to other folks and stole your horse. Now, I can tell you that the people in these parts, whether about the towns, in the woods or on the prairies, don't hanker after horse-thieves, except at the rope's end or through the sights of a rifle."

There was great significance in the way Sassafras said this.

"You say Captain Staples is a shrewd man. Is he honest and fair-minded as well as shrewd?" said Tom.

"Honest! Lord bless your innocent heart alive! he's the d—dest rogue in North America! But it ain't everybody that can find him out though. I soon found him out. He's cunning as a fox and treacherous as a wolf."

" You describe a man without a single good quality."

" No, I don't," replied Sassafras. " I don't say he is without plenty of courage of a certain sort. He has it. Show him prey, and he's fierce as a tiger. But he grows old, and is no longer quick and prompt enough for open fight with a man like me."

" What hold can Jagger have established upon a man like this?" said Tom. " I have seen the fellow in a row at home; and when there were not strong odds on his side he was chicken-hearted."

" He has no hold on Staples. It is nothing but the attrac-tion of his gold. The old man swings to it like the needle to the north star. Staples has established the hold on him; and he is not likely to let go while the other man's money lasts. Some difficulty we shall have in managing the matter when we meet them at the post. Your countryman is of no account out here. It would be very easy to settle with him. Staples is the nut that is hard to crack. We might buy him off, but it would cost a sight of money; and I'm opposed, on principle, to paying him a red cent."

" So am I," said Tom. " The horse is mine. He has been paid for once, and he shall not be paid for again."

" Good! The next thing is, we may gamble for him, or run for him; and win him at poker, or in a race."

" But we might lose, Sassafras, and that would be equiva-lent to paying twice over and not getting him at last. We must find some other plan."

" Very well," replied Sassafras. " If no better way offers, we can take him by the art of war—a mixture of force and strat-agem. By making all the Indians, save a select band of Cin-namon's men, drunk, we can get up a free fight, and while h—l's bells are ringing can run the horse off to a *caché* I know of before Staples and Jagger can tell that the hair is still upon their heads."

" I do not think it will do," said Tom. " Innocent blood would be shed. The horse is my property. When I have found to a certainty where he is, cannot I recover him by the law?"

" The law! why bless your innocent soul, 'Old Father Antic, the law,' was never within some hundreds of miles of

8

this place. There's no law here but such as white men and red men can make good with knives and rifles," replied Sassafras, laughing.

"It is true, we are far in the desert, but the law has long arms. Are we not still in the United States?"

"Ay, lad, in the territory of the United States, that we be, and if we were to pass a thousand miles further to the westward we should be still. But only a little of this land is staked and bounded, like lots in St. Jo., and no sheriff or marshal has ever served a writ here. We are in what is called the Indian Territory, an immense country that white men know but very little about, as yet—prairies and forests; plains and mountains; then more plains and more mountains and barren wastes, and big rivers that in flood time come thundering down to make up the great streams of the Missouri and the Arkansas."

With this Sassafras rose, and the conversation ceased.

CHAPTER XIII.

"Fair laughs the morn, and soft the zephyr blows,
    While gaily sailing o'er the azure realm,
In gallant trim the gilded vessel goes,
    Youth at the prow, and pleasure at the helm,
Unmindful of the treacherous whirlwind's sway,
That, hushed in grim repose, expects his evening prey."

NEXT day, and the next, the journey of the party was continued towards the south and east, Sassafras and Tom Scarlet riding in the lead as before. The negroes, merrily carolling their old plantation songs, followed with the teams and wagons. The Frenchmen brought up the rear. The swells of the prairie now rose higher at almost every mile, and it was cut and scraped here and there by ravines, in crossing some of which the quick eye of the frontier man detected the tracks of wolves. Water was more frequent, and at some pools they saw where buffaloes had wallowed in the mud upon the marge. The dead stillness of the prairie left behind was exchanged for sounds and sights of life, even if it were but the hoarse croak and flight of ravens, which sailed in circles

overhead on ragged wings. At length Sassafras paused and
pointed out, in the distance, the loom of a range of hills to the
south-southeast. They were the spurs of the Ozark Mountains, and on the far side of them, Tom was told, where the
slopes were sheltered from the sweep of the prairie winds in
winter, they should find belts of timber, white oaks and black
walnuts.

The young Englishman had now grown very weary of the
blue above and the brown below. The heat still continued.
The same unclouded sky was over all; the fervent sun still cast
its burning rays upon the dry or reeking earth. It was sorely
oppressive. The mules stood it well, much better than the
horses. The approach to the uplands was good news to Tom
Scarlet. The notion of hills and groves, clear springs and
green trees, verdant slopes and grassy valleys, took possession
of him, and he began to lament that he had left Danger at
the plantation near St. Jo.

"Sassafras," said he, "I'd give a trifle if we had brought
Danger with us. He is a rare horse for a timber country."

"Horse for a timber country!" replied the man of the frontier; "the timber in the parts hereabouts isn't post-and-rail
fences, between grass lands, with a clump of oak trees here,
another of ash yonder, and another of elm a little further off.
It's woods; small trees, but many of them, about the rocky
ground; big trees, the growth of ages, in the rich, deep places
where the good soil has gathered thick. Underneath their
arms lie the mouldering trunks of other giants, grown long
ago and overthrown by the storms of other days. The squalls
come through the shutes between the hills with a power sometimes, and level miles of tall timber flat in a minute. Why,
the Indians can ride little better than a foot pace there; and
unless Danger is quicker than a cat, he'd be down before he
had gone five rods."

"But if we had him we might run him a race at the trading post. It's my belief he can give any horse in this part of
the country a stone of weight, and a beating. I fully believe
that," said Tom.

"I don't think he could give one or two a pound," said
Sassafras, glancing over his shoulder at the gray mare and the
bay horse that leisurely followed the wagons. "Good as he

may have been in England, I would not trust him here. Let him stay at St. Jo. My boys will gallop him along gently, and get him acclimated. Late along in the fall, when the corn shocks stand in the fields, and the shucked heaps are yellow on the black ground; when the leaves show crimson, russet and gold among the green, and the hoar-frost glistens on the grass in the first beams of the morning sun, we may perhaps bring him to a race; that is, if we get back to the settlements in time. Besides, you told me he was not altogether thoroughbred."

"Yes, he must be well enough bred for this country, as the stain is remote. He is by Stumps out of a mare by Sultan, her dam by Walton."

"Well, go on; that ain't half enough. What about the dam of the Walton mare?" said Sassafras.

Mr. Scarlet looked at Sassafras as if surprised. Then he answered:

"Concerning her there is some doubt; she was certainly got by Tramp, and many said that her dam was by Dick Andrews, out of a thoroughbred mare."

"That story won't hold. A Dick Andrews mare would hardly have been put to Tramp, as he was got by Dick Andrews," said Sassafras.

"That's true enough! In fact, Sir Jerry Snaffle and John Bullfinch say that the dam of the Tramp mare *was* out of a thoroughbred mare, but by a gypsy pony, instead of by Dick Andrews. This pony was well-bred himself, and got into the pasture where the mare was at spring grass. So you see, even if this is the true bill, Danger is almost thoroughbred," replied Tom.

"Ah, that *almost!* How many races have been almost won that would have been quite won if the horse had been *quite*, instead of almost, thoroughbred! I go in for a clear pedigree, especially for stock to run over a distance of ground and repeat heats. When there's a black drop in it, it is sure to show itself some time, and it generally happens at a very inconvenient time."

"Do you mean to say that your horses—these behind us—have full, clean pedigrees, according to English rules?"

"I certainly do. As clean as any in your Stud-Book. They

are without a cold cross, right back to Eclipse and King Herod, Matchem and Snap," said Sassafras.

"Why, how can that be, Sassafras?"

"In this way: our forefathers in Virginia, Maryland and the Carolinas imported from England many horses and mares of the best blood in the kingdom. The importations of others, as good, has been going on, in a degree, ever since. The thoroughbred blood has been kept unsullied by any other strain; and these are of it," said Sassafras, looking back at the bay and gray.

"It may be as you say; but I hardly believe that the thoroughbred horse of real high stamp can have maintained his excellence here."

"Why not?"

"Well, because things are so different. The country is vast, overwhelming! But it isn't like England, you know."

"Did you expect it to be like England—come, Tom?" said Sassafras.

"Well, not altogether, but in a measure I did."

"That's where all the trouble between Englishmen and Americans comes from," said Sassafras, earnestly. "Each wants to find the other country like his own, and the other people like his own people. And because God never made the countries alike, and in the nature of things the people can't be just alike, they pitch in and abuse one another."

Mr. Scarlet stared at the roving, racing philosopher for about a minute. He then said:

"I shall never speak ill of this country or of its people. I should be a fool or a very ungrateful man if I did; but there are things here I don't think I could put up with permanently."

"What may those things be?" said Sassafras.

"The heat has been intolerable for two or three months, and before we left the settlements and wooded land the mosquitoes were awful."

Sassafras laughed.

"You had a very light touch of the mosquitoes, considering."

"Considering what?"

"Considering the time of year," said Sassafras. "However, a few musquitoes are too many for strangers. Like the giant in the story book, they can smell the blood of an Englishman. I remember a boxer who had landed at Orleans, a stout, ruddy fellow, by the name of Bonnox, brought over from Hampshire by the sailor Cox. On the second morning after his arrival he looked as if he had lately had the small-pox, or had been having a turn-up with somebody and got the worst of it. His eyes were bunged up, and his nose was well-nigh as big as a champagne bottle. 'Halloo, Bonnox!' said I, 'have you been fighting here already?' 'Noa, master, noa!' says he. 'It's the d—d insecks as worrits me. Blast such a country as this, I say! Give me Old England, even if we're never able to bring off a civil fight there again.'"

When Tom had laughed, Sassafras continued:

"Such men as Bonnox, if it's summer time, generally go back home after a stay here of about a fortnight or three weeks. That time is spent, for the most part drunk, in expatiating upon the joys of life in England and swearing at every-thing in this benighted country. There is another class much more to blame, because they ought to know better than the poor ignorant fellows of the Bonnox stamp."

"And what say those?"

"O, it runs after this fashion: 'Having seen a great deal of the country, and given its people, institutions, climate, and so forth the most careful consideration, I have come to the im-partial conclusion that everything here is wrong. The State House at Albany is a wretched building. At Buffalo the houses are built of wood, and the people use it for fuel, which was once the wasteful and improvident practice of the lower classes in England. I admit that there is coal at Pittsburgh, but the lamentable truth is that it is nothing like as black as our English coal is. The country about the Ohio river is too hilly. About the Mississippi it is too flat. The Missouri is a muddy, turbulent stream, not at all like the Avon or the Thames. Finally, there's no ale anywhere, and the American water is unfit to drink.' "

After another laugh, Sassafras continued:

"This is the style of the people who after a few weeks in this country go home to England and write a book about it, or a few letters to the newspapers, in which this western land is rode over rough-shod. Now the men know no more about this country than a hen scratching on the top of a hill knows of the ores that lie beneath. But then in consequence of what one fool has published in England up jumps a bigger fool here and denounces England, lock, stock and barrel, for everything she has done since Julius Cæsar's time. So the game goes on —see-saw! you're another!—and it's carried on in the main by those who think themselves above their neighbors. The truth is that the prevailing notions in the Eastern cities about the people of the West are no more correct than those of the conceited English tourists. Some day they'll find out that there is a little of this country outside of Boston and New York."

"There is a great deal of misconception, no doubt. To understand things rightly, we must see them close and observe them carefully," Tom remarked.

"True, my friend. Look at that speck yonder in the sky," said Sassafras, pointing to the southeast. "What do you think that is?"

"I don't know. It looks like a skylark hovering high over a brown harvest field," replied Tom.

"That is an eagle, ten feet or thereabouts across the wings," said Sassafras. "But we must better the pace. The change in the weather I told you of will come at sundown or soon after, and we ought to be off the levels and to the leeward of a hill when the storm strikes."

To the untaught Englishman there was little or nothing in the aspect of the heavens to indicate the storm which Sassafras so confidently predicted as close at hand; but to the experienced eye of the latter, and those of the Frenchmen, the signs were unmistakable. The cloud, no bigger than a man's hand, had appeared upon the western horizon, and they knew what would speedily follow. They held a brief consultation. Then the course of their journey was slightly changed and its rate increased. The mules, stimulated by the whips and loud cries of the negroes, were put to their best pace wherever the ground was good. The party held straight for the nearest of the bold ridges which bounded the prairie. It was still at some distance, but had taken form and substance to the eye—a rough, sharp slope, with a few stunted, twisted trees and straggling bushes on its northwestern front. Sassafras now looked over his right shoulder frequently and called to the negroes to hasten. They, in turn, shouted to the mules lustily, calling them by name, sometimes with coaxing and entreaty, and again with loud yells and vituperative epithets. The sun was still tolerably high in the heavens, and the heat was even greater than at his meridian. The light eastern breeze had almost died away to a close, sultry calm. In the western board there appeard a large bank of pale, woolly-looking clouds, with here and there a white, rounded dome rising above it. Gradually, and as if inflated by some vast power within, these domes swelled upwards and outwards, and threw forth other and loftier domes of the like shape and color. Great snowy mountains seemed to be heaped one on another in the west, with other mountains, many and huge, struggling and pushing from below, in all that quarter of the sky. It was as if the powers of the air were gathering their forces on the confines of the earth to try and overwhelm it. Slowly, and with the calm grandeur of nature before a great convulsion, these white aerial mountains, half earth, half cloud to the erring sight, rose to meet the declining sun. He sank in their eclipse, gilding the edges and domes of the moving mountains for a few moments with rims of burning gold. Then a sombre shade fell upon the western world from the towering clouds, whose bases had become as black as night. The ravens flew to the left. There was a low moan over the land, as if the earth drew breath for the coming struggle in one last flutter of the eastern breeze.

The travellers reached the ridge, and with shoulders to the wheels and loud shouts to the mules, forced the wagons up it. They crossed hastily, and descended into a low bottom, among trees of some size and thick underbrush. Here Sassafras soon found the refuge in which he intended to pass the night. It was a rude, half-ruined structure of logs, bark and saplings, built in the centre of a group of the largest trees. It took the work of about an hour to stop its holes and brace its sides, against the rapidly coming storm. The men worked with a will. Buffalo robes were stretched over the top and down the windward side. The provisions, feed and fodder were carried into the place. The wagons were drawn up as close to its sides as might be, so as to break, in a measure, the stroke of the wind. The latter would come from the west, but Sassafras knew that it might chop to the north or south. The mules were hobbled, fed and turned to leeward. The horses were led in and fastened in close array to the sides of the hut. Then the fire was built and kindled, and while the dusk of the coming night caught a deeper, darker shade from the advancing storm, the party sat down to their evening meal. It is a wise provision of nature that while a man is in bodily health he will eat. Sickness may abate the appetite, but imminent peril, or the near approach of certain death, does not. The forlorn wretch whose feet are almost upon the steps of the scaffold, eats heartily in the very presence of the hangman. The sailor in a sinking ship, with boats stove by the raging sea, and the crags of an iron-bound coast grinning in his face, takes his last meal unsparingly. The men under the shelter of the poles and bark, beneath trees already groaning and sighing, were not at all likely to neglect their fare. They ate and cracked their jokes. Some told of storms they had formerly experienced in that region until the war of elements had actually begun.

Meantime the black and ponderous sky, to the seeming almost as solid as the earth itself, came towering on. Cloudy mountains, like Alps on Alps, and Teneriffe on lofty Andes piled, bearing the red pennons of the forked lightning, and the chariots of the thunder! Before the storm really began there was darkness for a few minutes. Then lightning split the black arch that hung like a pall over the troubled earth; the thunder crashed and rolled away to the eastward; torrents of rain came beating down; and the fierce winds rushed in to complete the uproar. Half the night the tempest raged. Towards the last, by the flashes of the spent lightning, beasts of chase, elk or deer, might be seen mingled with the mules of the travellers.

CHAPTER XIV.

> " Upon the banks where panthers steal along,
>   And the dread Indian chants a dismal song,
>   Where human fiends on midnight errands walk,
>   And bathe in brains the murderous tomahawk,
>   There shall the flocks on thymy pastures stray,
>   And shepherds dance at Summer's opening day."

ON the morning after the storm the sky was clear to the westward, but in the East masses of black-blue cloud hung about, as if threatening to return and renew the wild tumult of the night. Most of those in the camp slept soundly towards the morning hours, lulled as it seemed by the low rumble of the then distant thunder. The French hunters were more wakeful. They arose at dawn, renewed the fire, lit their pipes, and made a pot of coffee, the fragrant and favorite beverage of the frontier. Having partaken of this, the Frenchmen woke the negroes, then took their rifles and went upon a little scout. Not far from the camp they came upon the tracks of elk ; whereupon François, the elder of the two, told his companion to beat through the underbrush of the swale along the banks of the creek running from a spring beneath the ridge, while he would mount the ridge towards the prairie, and lie in wait for a shot at any animal which might pass. The elk, however, had gone on through the wooded valley to the higher hills which lay to the southeast of it, and François waited in vain. After some time he passed down the declivity up which the wagons had been forced the previous evening, and, looking out upon the prairie, suddenly drew back to the edge of the cover and crouched down among the stunted bushes. He was motionless and silent, but his quick and searching glances swept the swells of the prairie far and near, and he looked keenly along the broken outline and ragged scrub of the ridge. He laid down with his ear near the ground, and listened intently, but heard no sound save the rustle of the mules behind him. A low, peculiar call, like the plaintive cry of some wild animal, brought Jules to his side in a few minutes. François, with a gesture, indicated the necessity for silence. He then pointed to the prairie, and exchanged a few words with Jules. Thereupon the latter moved with the crouching action and silent, stealthy step of a panther, along the ridge towards the south, while François advanced with like craft and caution in the opposite direction. About an hour elapsed before the two men met again at the point from which they started. Their search had been ineffectual, and François, stooping low, went swiftly out upon the prairie for a short distance. He soon returned, and then they went down to the camp. When they reached it the other men had fed the horses and mules, and got their own breakfasts.

Sassafras was seated on a bale of fodder, smoking and pondering.

"Any game about?" said he

"We came upon the tracks of elk," said François, "but found that they had gone off to the higher hills. I think they left as soon as the storm abated."

"And no wonder, mon Dieu!" said Jules; "for there have been other visitors about since we went into camp. Sassafras, there are moccasin prints about the ridge, and a band of Indians dismounted upon the prairie last night."

At this relation Sassafras exhibited no alarm, and scarcely any surprise. The Frenchmen, too, went at their breakfast in a very matter-of-fact sort of way. The former watched the smoke as it curled upwards from his pipe, as if waiting for the guides to satisfy their appetites before questioning them further. He, however, ordered the negroes to load the wagons, and then said to the Frenchmen:

"Boys, we are no more alone. We must have been watched yesterday for many a mile, as nobody could follow our trail after the storm fairly loomed up. Either the Indians were close upon us before the storm broke, or knew where to find us when it was over."

François and Jules looked up as though about to speak, but one appeared to wait for the other, and both remained silent. Sassafras then added:

"This is what I propose: we will be in no hurry to move until we have tried to find out something about these newcomers. What say you, François?"

"I say the plan is good, so far as it goes," replied François; "but, Sassafras, we shall hardly learn much about this party while we stay here. This much I can tell already—the band is small. There are six Indians and six horses, no more. They did not come to the ridge until after the rain had fallen; the tracks showed it. When they dismounted and climbed the ridge, they walked wide, and some of them slipped."

"Which shows that they are Indians of the plains, and almost always on horseback," said Sassafras, quietly. "But if there were but six here, they know where to find six more—ch, Jules? But which way do you think they have gone?"

"It is not easy to say," replied François. "They set off to the north of west, and the tracks show that they galloped fast. But they may have doubled back, for all we know, and be behind the ridge to the south and east of us."

"I hardly think they have done so," said Sassafras. "The Indians of the plains like to keep on the backs of their horses, and being but a small party, they would not be likely to leave the prairie for the hills and the timber. Besides, they may be a part of Cinnamon's band upon the scout to meet us."

"Is it not too soon for their arrival?" said Jules. "The South Fork of the Solomon is a long way off."

"I know it," returned Sassafras, "and did not expect to see or hear anything of him and his men so soon. Still, the Indians travel fast and far, and Cinnamon is not the man to loiter by the way when a friend calls for him."

"Ay, but Indians must eat though, and so must their horses," remarked François. "It may be that the chief got your message a long way east of his usual hunting-grounds. News travels fast over the plains, when it is of a party bearing presents and going to have a talk."

"But as Cinnamon is a chief, if he heard of coming presents and a talk, would he not stay to get his share?" said Tom Scarlet.

"The question is well put," replied Sassafras; "but I do not think he would, after my message was carried to him. Cinnamon is a young and active chief, more renowned for hunts, forages and marches than for council with the whites. The talks are mostly left to the elder men; and as for the presents, the share of himself and the braves of his band would be kept for them. I have good reason to know that he will be here soon, if he is not already in the neighborhood, and I think these men may belong to his band. But they may be none of his and we must move warily. Whatever the Indians may be, who were here last night, and who are certainly not far off this morning, they know our strength. They are aware that no six or sixteen, for that matter, can make a raid on us with impunity. We are eight, three of us tried frontier men. We have the best of arms and the Indians know it. And though they may not belong to Cinnamon's band themselves, they will be apt to know that the red riders of the Horse-head from the Forks of the Solomon have come far east on the plains. This little party will not attack."

"They may know where to find a bigger one," said Jules.

"What does 'red riders of the Horse-head' mean?" said Tom Scarlet to François.

"It means the Cheyennes. Their totem is a horse-head; and unless I'm mistaken, Sassafras carries it of right, as one of the tribe."

Sassafras looked at his pistols and examined the lock of his rifle, a heavy weapon of soft metal, with the Kentucky gaining twist. The guides finished their meal, and by this time the wagons were loaded.

"Hitch up, boys," said the leader to the negroes. "François, Jules, I have settled in my own head upon our plan of action. If you have any objection to make when you hear it, speak your minds. Jules shall take charge of the train, snake the wagons along the ridge to the nearest place to the west of this, and then cut across the bend of the prairie towards the southwest bluff, which is visible from the top of the ridge above us. You and I, François and Tom, will make our way on horseback inside the ridges and hills and round the bight of the bend out of sight. Before Jules gets to the bluff we shall know a little more about our neighbors than we do now, unless they have gone right off towards the west, which is not at all likely. They are within eyeshot from a tall tree, no doubt."

"The plan is good," said the guides.

"Ay, I think it'll do! Jules, if you reach within half a

mile of the bluff without seeing or hearing of us, halt there," said Sassafras.

"The train will be so weak that the Indians may make a rush and carry off the race-horses," said Tom Scarlet.

"To some, if they knew the quality of Virginia and the Young Chief, the temptation would hardly be resistible," replied Sassafras. "But these Indians number but six. They'll know there are rifles in the train, of long range and true, especially when fired from the rest of a wagon rail by a man stretched upon his breast. Besides they'll know that the three horsemen out of sight are scouting them, and ready to come in unawares. Come! we three shall have far to go, and there will be no riding fast upon this route. Boys, take care of the racers."

With this he mounted his horse, and followed by Tom Scarlet and François, rode away into the timber and underbrush of the bottom, and crossed the creek which meandered along it.

The ridge of hills which ran out to the bluff spoken of as its westernmost elevation, swept round in the section of a circle, so that the teams upon the prairie would travel by a straight and comparatively short line, while Sassafras and his party would go round the bend. This he deemed necessary in order to be able to survey the plain unseen from time to time, and to reach the bluff unknown to the Indian band, which, beyond all doubt, was prowling in the neighborhood. This route was impracticable to the wagons, and therefore the separation was made. Threading his way among such obstacles as ravines, fallen timber, and the thickest growths of vines and brambles, Sassafras led François and Tom Scarlet along the rough and devious route. At intervals, when they were upon the high ground, they could see the wagons with their teams and drivers, following the lead of Jules, upon the prairie. No Indians appeared, nor could Sassafras detect any signs by which it might be inferred that they had approached the ridge at any other place than the one above the last night's camp. He knew their stealthy character so well, however, that he and François remitted no vigilance, and watched warily as they made progress over the rough and woody ground. The sun was now lofty and triumphant in the heavens, like a monarch who has subdued and driven away the legions of a formidable rebellion. The effects of the storm were seen, however, in the branches strewn upon the soil, and here and there in the trunk and top of a large tree, which, loaded with wet, and stricken by the furious assault of the wind, had come down with a sough and a mighty crash. It was high noon, and upon the banks of a swollen creek in a grassy bottom the party halted to bait and water their horses. When they remounted they ascended the ridge and saw the teams slowly moving across the prairie at the distance of four or five miles. Nothing was discovered of the Indians. Two or three miles further was travelled in solitude and silence, for neither beast, bird nor man appeared. Then Sassafras dismounted and again ascended the ridge. Upon its crest he laid down his rifle, and climbed the tallest tree he could find. From amongst its topmost boughs the frontier man, with an eye trained for ranging over a great space, like that of a sailor who sees the far-off land while it is still invisible to his passengers, and nothing but sea and sky appear to their untaught vision, surveyed the country for many miles around. For a time he made no discovery. At length, however, his roving gaze was fixed upon the southwest, beyond the western bluff, and upon the prairie. Swinging himself from bough to branch, and from branch to lower arm, he slid down the trunk, rejoined his companions, mounted his horse, and led the way.

"Any signs of the Indians?" said François.

"Yes, but they are at a smart distance and in ambush," replied Sassafras. "They have made their horses lie down in a hollow, and are watching the train as it moves towards them."

"Indians of the West?" said François.

"Ay, no doubt of it, for they keep on the prairie, and use what little cover it affords with much craft and skill. They forget, however, that where trees grow a tree can be clomb," replied Sassafras; and then he hummed:

> "O, the oak and the ash and the bonny hick'ry tree,
> They do all flourish best in the West country."

"Do you think them part of Cinnamon's band?" said François, anxiously.

"I think it probable they are," returned Sassafras; "but I

shall be more able to judge when we reach the head of the bluff. They lie in a bunch to the sou'west of it, and within a couple of miles. From a tree-top on it I shall be able to look down upon their *caché* and make them out."

"It would seem from their lying in wait, near the route of the train, that they mean to attack, and are none of Cinnamon's men," said Tom Scarlet.

"Not so," replied Sassafras. "If they intended to raid upon the wagons they would lie behind the knoll and pretty close to it, so as to come out with a sudden rush and a yell, and close before the rifles could be brought to bear. As it is, they would have to ride about a couple of miles in plain sight before they could strike a blow."

"That's it," said François; "they are only scouting."

"Only scouting," repeated Sassafras. "They are now observing the train, believing that it belongs to friends of their chief. They do this in Indian fashion, wary-like, and ready to go off without parley, and without letting us know what they are and what they came for, if they conclude that we are not the men. Besides, they go upon the certainty, that while they are watching the wagons they may be watched themselves by another band. Then, again, they know that three horsemen who were with the wagons yesterday are with them no longer. They want to account for that before they come near and show themselves. I reckon they expect us to be doing just about what we are doing, and think that we shall appear upon the route before another camp is made."

"That is it," said François. "They lie hidden, as they think, out on the prairie, because they are uncertain where we shall debouch."

No more was said, but the pace was increased so far as the nature of the bushy, broken ground would allow. Still the progress was slow, so that the sun was sinking towards the west, like a great orb of red gold in the deep azure sky, when they reached the west knoll and dismounted. Standing upon his horse's croup, Sassafras grasped a branch of a tree above his head, and swung himself upon it. Climbing to a lofty fork, his lookout commanded the prairie for a vast distance, all lit up and mellowed by the beams of the sinking sun. The wagons were halted half a mile north and east of the bluff on which he was. The Indians yet lay close in the hollow way, and made no move. It seemed that they still thought themselves unobserved, and were yet uncertain whether to advance or retreat. The frontier man looked long and fixedly, but at length descended to the ground and rejoined his anxious companions.

"Well," said Tom Scarlet, "what do you make out?"

"Some of Cinnamon's young men," said Sassafras, confidently. "You two wait here while I ride out to where they are, and have a talk."

"May it not be dangerous?" said Tom Scarlet. "I see not how you can be certain of their character and tribe from a mere glance at a group of men and horses lying down two miles off."

Sassafras and the Frenchman laughed.

"Well, now," said the former, "it seemed as certain to me that these Indians were part of Cinnamon's band as it would if I had seen the chief, armed and mounted, at the head of them. But then I was the 'man up a tree.' However, you remain here. Ten minutes will settle the business." With this he mounted and rode down the western slope of the bluff.

"I cannot understand it," said Tom Scarlet to the guide. The latter had seated himself snugly in his saddle, had filled his pipe with much deliberation, struck fire from knife and flint, caught the spark with well-dried punk, and was now puffing away with much content.

"I say, François, I cannot understand it," repeated Mr. Scarlet, with some perplexity.

"Very likely not; I couldn't myself once, but that was long ago. I can now," replied François.

"And you say that, partially seen, the character of Indians could be made out two miles off?"

"Yes, four miles off, by Sassafras, when he is well acquent with the tribe they belong to," said François, positively.

Sassafras had now reached the prairie. Tom Scarlet and François saw him canter off towards the Indians. As soon as they perceived his approach the braves rose to their feet, got up their horses and mounted them. Then one rode forward to meet the white man, each carrying his rifle across his horse's withers. They met. Some words and signs were exchanged.   The Indian pointed with his gun towards wooded heights lying away in the southeast and dim in the distance. The savage then returned to his silent band, and the six rode rapidly away.   Skirting the bluff and making a signal to Scarlet and François, Sassafras rode towards Jules and the wagons.   Half an hour later the camp was formed and supper eaten.   Afterwards, by the camp-fire, Sassafras informed his friends that the Cheyenne chief was near at hand with a band of hunters and braves.

This intelligence was received by the Frenchmen without emotion, but the negroes appeared to be excited and disturbed. A sort of natural antipathy existed between the red and black races, such as is found between the domesticated dog and the wolf.   The Indians, hunters and warriors almost from the cradle, disdaining steady work, barbarian in all their tastes, and without knowledge of any of the arts of civilized life, looked down upon the blacks as a people made by the Creator expressly for labor and bondage.   The blacks, while secretly holding the Indians in contempt, as ignorant savages, good for nothing but to be scalped, yet feared and hated them, as their ancestors on the banks of the Niger feared and hated the lion of the great woods and the crocodile of the reedy mud-banks.   But the certain intelligence that the band of Indians from the western side of the plains and the spurs of the Rocky Mountains had arrived, wrought most effect upon the young Englishman.   In all probability, he had never seen an Indian before that day.   A fellow had, indeed, been exhibited at a country fair, in company with a giant and a dwarf, as an Indian.   He ate raw beef and performed strange antics; but some thought that though he might be savage enough for any-thing, he never came from the tribes of North America.   This was afterwards confirmed by the worthy landlord of the Seven Bells.   He declared that, going to his back door in answer to a summons late at night, he there found the proprietor of the caravan and the Indian; when the latter swore at the show-man in round English, with a rich brogue, and drank the greater part of three pots of beer with exceeding relish.

CHAPTER XV.

"Loud rush the torrent floods
The Western wilds among,
And free, in green Columbia's woods,
The hunter's bow is strung."

INSTEAD of proceeding to join his Indian friends and allies in the morning, as Tom Scarlet and perhaps the Frenchmen expected he would do, Sassafras remained in camp all day, chiefly devoting himself to the exercise, grooming and feeding of the gray mare Virginia, and the bay horse, the Young Chief. The negroes slept for the most part. The Frenchmen smoked much, and cleaned their guns and pistols. The Englishman walked uneasily about, with a dejected air. The region in which he now was seemed even more wild and threatening than the melancholy expanse of the great prairies itself. The hills were rocky, broken and uncouth, and to the southeast were dominated by higher hills, where huge precipices might be perceived, frowning over chasms which broke the forest with which the hills were mainly clothed. At that day those parts were seldom visited by white men. The passes in the mountains were known to but few, and these were mostly adventurers of the stamp of Sassafras and his French companions. Time has changed all that. This region has become common enough, like other tracts which were savage and remote two score years ago. Commerce, the pursuit of mining, and the desire of exploration penetrate everywhere, and when foiled return again and again.

"The Hyrcanian deserts, and the vasty wilds
Of wide Arabia, are but as thoroughfares now!"

In the evening Sassafras left his camp in the charge of Jules, and set out with Tom Scarlet and François upon a projected expedition. Perhaps he had thought it best to appear in no hurry; perhaps he knew that he would not be expected at the Indian camp until night had set in. However this may be, the sun had set when he mounted his horse and rode

briskly away to the southeast. The moon had just risen over
the eastern highlands when they turned towards the wooded
slope, and rode cautiously up it. The night was still and
calm, the air and earth fresh from the recent rain. As they
reach·d the highest point of the ridge, and the glimmer of
fires, in a sheltered, grassy bottom below, was visible through
the brush, the figure of an Indian rose from the grass. He
appeared so silently and suddenly that Tom Scarlet uttered a
startled exclamation. The man was naked to the waist, for
the blanket belted around him had fallen from his shoulders,
and he held a rifle in his hand. He spoke a few words in an
Indian tongue, with a sign to Sassafras to follow him a little
apart. He was tall, straight and well-built, but not stout.
The shade of his complexion could not be determined by that
uncertain light, but it was dark even for a native of the western wilds; in fact, its hue was a rich brown, befitting one who
lived, like the eagle, "close to the sun, in lonely lands." His
manner was grave and collected, and he was, indeed, Cinnamon, a young but famous chief, renowned from the Rocky
Mountains to the settlements of the whites for his success in
hunting and his exploits in war.

After a short conversation between him and Sassafras, they
returned to the others, and the chief bade Tom Scarlet welcome in a few words of broken English. He seemed to speak
it with difficulty and unwillingly, for he addressed the Frenchman in the Indian tongue. Cinnamon then led the way
towards the camp of his people, who were soon seen sitting
and reclining round the fires in the valley below. The wild
appearance of the Indians, seen by the red glare of blazing
logs and brush, with their picketed horses and rude tents, mere
blankets and skins on sticks, was strange and striking to the
Englishman. Sassafras and François had no doubt seen the
like of it many times before, for they followed the chief down
into the valley without pause or remark. Cinnamon passed
on to the fire in front of his own scanty tent, around which
was a group of his young men. The Indians appeared to
know Sassafras well, for they came up one after the other and
greeted him in a few words, their gaze being meanwhile fixed
upon the ornament of a horse's head, cunningly carved in red
stone, which he now wore upon his breast. The costume of

the Cheyennes was sparse to a degree, consisting mainly of moccasins and leggings, with here and there a scrap of blanket. But if their wardrobe was scanty, there was no lack of rude ornament among Cinnamon's men; and the glare of the fire showed a profusion of paint upon their faces and bodies. Their heads were uncovered save by their shaggy black hair, with which were intermixed the plumes of eagles, hawks and perhaps other birds of prey. One figure there was whose outfit presented a striking contrast to those of the chief and his men. It was that of a youth of perhaps seventeen years old. His form was handsome, and his features may have been good, but they were obscured by much paint. He wore scarlet leggings, with a sort of tunic of the same color, belted at the waist. A white blanket, trimmed with scarlet, lay across his shoulder in the manner of a Highland plaid. Braid and trinkets were plentifully disposed over his apparel; his hair was plaited, twisted round the top of his head, like a coronet, and bedecked with eagles' plumes. Upon this boy the gaze of Sassafras was soon fixed. The lad returned it with a haughty air, and then seemed to be wholly interested with the appearance of Tom Scarlet. He stood aloof. At the earliest opportunity, Sassafras addressed the chief.

"Cinnamon," said he, in a low voice, "you have a stranger in the band—one of another tribe. Who and what is he that my friend has brought here?"

"Indian from the southwest. Young Kiowa, son of a great chief I have sometimes hunted with," replied the Cheyenne.

Then seeing that Sassafras was hardly content, he added:

"Brought here from down the great river by my brother. I will answer for the boy."

"Very good," said Sassafras. "And so your brother has come up from his plantation, has he?"

"He has," replied the Indian.

Cinnamon's brother was, in fact, an elder half-brother, being a son of his mother and a wealthy French trader. He was settled on a plantation near the mouth of the Arkansas river, but sometimes made trips to its upper waters, where, as Sassafras knew, he might often meet roving bands of the great predatory tribes of the southwest branches of the Arkansas, the Kiowas and the Comanches. This brother of the chief, being a man of substance, liberality and enterprise, as well as of part Indian blood, had reputation and influence with many bands and tribes. A conversation, weighty in matter, but comparatively brief, ensued between Sassafras and Cinnamon, at the close of which the former rejoined Tom Scarlet and François. The wary Western man threw a keen glance around before he recited to Tom Scarlet in English what had passed between himself and the chief. A discussion followed, in which Sassafras became earnest, and enforced his view of the case with a louder voice and much force. When he finished and looked up, he was surprised to find the painted Kiowa near at hand. He seemed, however, to be lost in revery, thinking of things and scenes far away, for his piercing eye appeared to look beyond the fires and tents and figures of the camp, and to penetrate the darkness which hung heavy on the hills and woods around. And yet Sassafras was not altogether satisfied. As he threw himself upon a pile of brush, pipe in mouth, and weighty thought in brain, he muttered:

"Cinnamon will answer for the boy. Cinnamon is good, but the boy is none of his tribe, and has been with him but a few days. Safe bind, safe find! François shall watch him!"

Almost worn out by the fatigue of the last sleepless night, and by the anxiety of the day just past, the Englishman, in spite of the novelty of his situation, soon slumbered heavily by the side of the Western man. When he was fast asleep the latter drew a blanket carefully over him, and sat some time in thought. He then aroused François, and led him to the verge of the valley, where they sat down on an old log. The camp was nearly still, the moonlight mingling its white rays with the fitful, dying glare of the fading fires. An Indian, however, might now and then be seen stalking out of the shade of a pile of brush or a clump of bushes, and getting a brand to light his pipe. The horses had eaten their fill of the fresh grass of the valley, and lay here and there all around the camp. At times the hoot of the owl was heard from the timber of the hill above, and the long howl of the wolf resounded from the ravines. The Frenchman filled his pipe with much deliberation, and having lighted it, signified by an inclination of his head that he was ready to hear what Sassafras might have to communicate. The latter, looking around cautiously, spoke in a low voice.

" François, there is a boy in there," pointing to the tent of the chief, " for whose presence here I can't account. You, no doubt, saw him when we first arrived, if not since."

" I did, and I cannot make him out any better than yourself," replied the Frenchman. " I asked one of the Cheyennes if he was of their tribe. He said no, but partly of their blood, being a son of Cinnamon's half-brother, Pierre Langlois. Pierre is now at the trading post, and having brought up his son from below, has suffered him to join his uncle in camp here."

" That cock cannot fight in this main," said Sassafras, quickly. " The story don't agree at all with what Cinnamon told me two hours ago. He says that lad is the son of a chief of the Kiowas, intrusted to Pierre Langlois by his father, when he was up in the mountains near the head-waters of the Arkansas, over towards the Spanish line."

" It may be so and the Indian not know it," said François.

" Devil a bit!" said Sassafras. " If the boy was a Kiowa every Indian in this camp would know it. You've seen Kiowas —did you ever see one painted like this boy?"

" I have seen their warriors—this lad is none."

" Ay, but he's of age to be a warrior," returned Sassafras. " Besides, though he looks a little like a dandy Indian, he don't walk like an Indian ; and his blanket and other fixings ain't a month old, instead of being five or six."

" Sassafras, we have always said that you were the keenest man on the frontier, and you are," said François, " but I think you take too much note of this lad."

" It may be so," replied Sassafras, "but I tell you I have got no use for that boy here until I know more about him."

" And this may make trouble, as he is with Cinnamon himself," said François. " You don't doubt the chief?"

" Surely not, for I wear this, won by his side in a hard-fought tussle with the Sioux," said Sassafras, laying his hand on the ornament which hung upon his breast. " But you see this stripling is really as little known to Cinnamon as he is to you and me. The chief may be imposed upon. Pierre Langlois brings the boy here from a quarter whence I expect an enemy, and he is a neighbor of Staples."

" Yes, but hates him worse than he hates a snake—I know it well," said François.

" For the matter of that, everybody hates him that ever had anything to do with him," said Sassafras; " but he manages to get many to go in with him for all that. But no matter! I spoke to this bedizened boy in as good Indian as I could muster for the occasion, and no answer did I get."

" Well, he may not understand Cheyenne," said François.

" Then I want to know how he understands Cinnamon, who can speak but precious little else, though he can understand my English," remarked Sassafras, with a little impatience.

" There's some difference between Cinnamon's Cheyenne and yours," said François, with a smile. " Of all the people that have to do with the Indians, you and the English speak their tongues the worst. Now, we French and the Spanish of Mexico soon learn to speak them well. That is, well for white men."

" You may speak them as well as you like, but d—n me if I think you can make this boy understand Indian of any sort. What do you say to that, now?" said Sassafras, with some heat.

" I don't know. To-morrow I'll try him with French, and with as good Kiowa and Comanche as I can command. If those fail, I'll at him in Spanish; for I'll bet a horn of powder he's Spanish if he's no Indian. His eyes and his hair show it, as well as the small size of his hands and feet."

" Do so, François; and watch him narrowly, without letting him know that you are doing so. You can stay here on some pretence, when I have gone back to our camp. We shall not move to the post for some days. I must give Virginia and the Young Chief work—sharp work."

" Good! the boy will be more off his guard, if he is now on it, when you have left the band again," said François. " If I can find out nothing from him, we must wait until we see Pierre. Pierre is a talkative as well as a prosperous man, and by getting him to drink three or four times I can learn almost all he knows." After a pause of a minute or so he added: " But as you know the chief to be true, why trouble yourself about this youngster? What can the boy do?"

" Why, no harm that I can see, just at present," replied Sassafras; " but the minute I laid eyes upon this gay bird it struck me that he was not what he seemed. When I find a blind at the beginning of a trail, I am never satisfied until I know what is at the other end."

"There's wisdom in that, and we will try to find out," returned François.

"One thing made me more suspicious than almost all that I have mentioned," said Sassafras, earnestly. "I noticed that when we came into camp to-night with Cinnamon, this boy looked straight at Tom Scarlet and gave you and me but just a glance. Now, I say that's not natural, if the boy is Indian, or even half or quarter blood, through Pierre Langlois. Would a young Kiowa, from the plains and mountains of the Southwest, take more note of a green Englishman than of men like you and me, François?"

"Hardly! though the Englishman is a fine-looking young man, a *very* fine-looking young man," replied François.

"I grant it—much better looking than you or I, so far as mere form and features go," said Sassafras; "but don't you see, he has none of the air and carriage of the West—of men who have hunted many a year, and fought in many a scrimmage—and I tell you that's what would have fixed the eye of this youngster, if he had been the son of a chief of the warlike Kiowas."

The Frenchman silently assented to this by an inclination of his head, and Sassafras went on:

"As for our mate from the island over the sea, he needs vigilant as well as staunch friends here. Good man, brave and true, he is no doubt in his own country; but here, François, he is little more than a baby—no experience, you see—and a self-willed and obstinate baby at that. Why, he sticks out for honesty and what he calls fair play, and what not, in our dealings with the men we must circumvent. As if honesty was of any use against Staples, three or four hundred miles west of the Mississippi river!"

The Frenchman nodded acquiescence once more, and Sassafras went on:

"If there was no one but you and Jules and me concerned, it would be different, and I should be less alert, knowing we could hold our own, whatever might turn up trumps. I never told you before the exact state of affairs. It is this: The man who stole the best horse in England, or one about as good as any, and a lot of money, from Tom Scarlet, will be at the post with Staples. My business is to make him fork over, one way or another. Do you see?"

"I see well enough—go on," said François.

"The fellow ran away with a lot of money belonging to other people, too; but that don't concern us," said Sassafras. He then continued, speaking very earnestly: "I met this young fellow, Tom, at Baltimore, as soon as he landed, and struck hands with him. I have brought him all this way west, and I'm bound to stick to him, come what may. 'He's here in double trust,' as Macbeth says of Duncan; for he has confided in me, and I like the man himself, François; while his talks of the girl he left behind him have made me like her, too. I swear I'm almost in love with her myself."

"And good reason," said the Frenchman. "I, too, have heard him talk of her, and, my faith! it reminded me of the little girl I was to marry twenty years ago, when we used to dance under the trees on the bank of the big river, half through the summer nights. But Louise died in her spring time, you see."

"Well, my true and trusty friend, remember to look close after that boy. Find out something about him somehow, and then ride straight over to our own camp. Now, we'll lie down and sleep, as well here as anywhere about, for the night is warm."

Midnight was some time past, and the dark, dead hour had come which precedes the first faint tinge of dawn. The camp was as still as though no living thing was in it. No breeze sighed among the branches of the lofty trees, and the moon had gone down over the vast silent prairie to the west, leaving the valley to the little light afforded by wasted brands of the waning fires among their own ashes. It was the time of night—

> "When the graves, all gaping wide,
>   Every one lets forth his sprite,
> In the churchway paths to glide;
>   And the fairies, that do run,
> By the triple Hecate's team,
>   From the presence of the sun,
> Follow darkness like a dream."

The deep, solemn sleep, so like pale death itself, into which Tom Scarlet had first fallen, was now changed into uneasy slumbers and swift-changing dreams. His home across the Atlantic, the scenes of his boyhood, the favorite haunts of her he loved, and many incidents of his life, long forgotten, flew through the chambers of the brain, faster than the sunbeam which chases night's black shadow round the revolving world. More uneasy the sleeper grew, for the sombre shadow of his brother's death, and the white face, upturned to the pale blue wintry sky, were again before him. Again he felt the stunning horrors of the gale which smote the brig, and almost overwhelmed her in the waves of the Atlantic. The fierce hissing scream of the wind; the thunder-clap of the topsail, when its chain-sheets parted and flew loose aloft; the calls of the captain and mate; the hoarse cries of the sailors; and the tumult of the raging waters, rang in his ears again. Then the noises subsided into the merry echoes of the village feast at eventide, and the rustle of summer winds among the hawthorn and the gorse. And then came music, to a soft air, and low, as of the hum of honey-bees about the fresh June flowers. After a space this was shaped into words, and the man, in the mysterious debatable land which lies between dead sleep and wakefulness, heard the following, like a faint but distinct and clear echo:

High the hawks fly in the dappled sky,
  And over the blackthorn stream
The partridge knows, while swift she goes,
  They float on the morning beam.
A maiden bright, at their foremost flight,
  Says, " Well! ah, well-a-day!"
The Scarlet and Gold, so lithe and bold,
  Is over the seas away!

Early and late, near the garden gate,
  The linnets sing love's song;
The sparrows hatch in the old barn thatch,
  And the ploughmen plod along;
And at morn and night the maid so bright
  Says, " Well! ah, well-a-day!"
The Scarlet and Gold, so lithe and bold,
  Is over the seas away!

There's a yeoman tried at Hawk'ell side
  In all the tales they tell,
And the hunting mare is grazing there,
  In the paddock by the well.
The throstle's note, from his golden throat,
  And the blackbirds seem to say,
The Scarlet and Gold, so lithe and bold,
  Is over the seas away!

The hawks fly, too, and the wolves pursue
  Where the wild buck leaps for life—
O! the beak and claw of the border law
  Are the tomahawk and knife.

Will the maid once gay e'er see the day
  When the sun shall clear the wrack?
Will the Scarlet and Gold, so lithe and bold,
  O'er the racing seas go back?

From first to last, while this strange chaunt was going on, the young man lay like one in a trance. Conscious he was, but partly unable and partly unwilling to stir and break the spell of the voice. When the song was finished he lay for the space of a minute. Then he rose and looked about him with a bewildered air. No one was in sight. He felt for Sassafras; but the Western man had long left that couch, and was now fast asleep with François upon the outer verge of the camp.

"This is like witchery," said Tom. "I must have been awake —somebody must have sung. It can't be Sassafras, for his voice is not so tuneful. It can't have been an Indian, for no Indian could master the words, to say nothing of the harmony. Can it have been François? I'll tax him with it in the morning."

Morning was now near. The sky was steel-gray in the eastern board, and soon one after another of the horses rose and shook his lariat. Tom Scarlet had no opportunity of speaking to François, for when the time came for the white men to return to their own camp the Frenchman was not to be found. An Indian briefly stated that he had gone, with two of the young men, to hunt the elk, which were to be found in the neighboring hills. Sassafras remarked that he could not wait, and bidding farewell, for the present, to Cinnamon and his braves, he and Tom Scarlet put boot in stirrup and rode away. The young Kiowa was not to be seen.

CHAPTER XVI.

"Good people all, I pray give ear,
  And a doleful story you shall hear;
'Tis of as stout a rogue as ever
  Bade a true man stand and deliver."

ABOUT two weeks had elapsed since the meeting between Sassafras and Cinnamon, and both had moved their camps to the near vicinity of the trading-post. The interval had been mainly spent by the former and Tom Scarlet in training

Virginia and the Young Chief for the races they expected. The Indians had passed their time in hunting excursions, and in much eating and sleeping. Game was abundant. The young men brought in elk and deer. François and Jules shot many turkeys. The former found no opportunity to sound the young Kiowa, for when he returned from his first hunt the youth had left Cinnamon, and the Frenchman was told that he had returned to Pierre Langlois at the post. Nor was he to be seen at that place when Sassafras reached it; and Cinnamon then said that he was gone on a hunt with some of his young men. The Western man was too much occupied with his horses and in settling the preliminaries of a race or two with his old antagonist, Captain Staples, to make further quest just then.

The trading-post alluded to was situated among the hills, but on a flat prairie some two miles long and a mile and a half wide. The hills were bold but not high, and bushy valleys ran up between them from the open ground. The grass of the prairie was short, more like that of a meadow in the valley of the Ohio than the coarse but nutritious buffalo grass upon which herds of bisons fed on the great plains further west. Often camped upon, trampled, and fed off close, it had lost much of its wild character, and become tame pasture. This change had, perhaps, been aided by the mixture of other grasses, from seed which had been scattered by such wayfarers as Sassafras and Staples at their periodical visits. The main structure was a square log-building, standing on the north side of the prairie. It was of considerable extent, part being used as a depot for the goods of the company who were the nominal owners of the land, and part for the residence of their factor and his men. On each side of it, at the distance of a few rods, there were shanties of slight poles, roofed with bark; while in some of the valleys between the hills, rude log-houses had been built at some time, which could be hastily repaired. The prairie sloped very gradually inward to a slough or pond, in which there was nearly always tolerable water. It was fringed with low bushes of cottonwood and alder, and the surface of the water was overgrown with lilies then in flower. A rude sort of race-course, called a mile, but probably more, for the vast ranges of the Western country belittled measured spaces in the eyes of the adventurers who had laid it out, and now resorted to it, ran around the pond. It had once been ploughed up and harrowed by the men of the post, who, cultivating a few acres of corn and potatoes, had the implements of simple husbandry; but it was now overgrown with short grass, very good to gallop over. At the foot of the hills, in various places, small bands of Indians were encamped. In some of the shanties near the main building there were a few white men, with blood-like horses and negroes. The traders had done a good business with the Indians, considering the rate of profit, buying buffalo robes, skins and furs for next to nothing, in whiskey, powder, lead and blankets. The Cheyennes of Cinnamon's band had bartered away in this manner the furs and skins they had brought on the backs of their horses. For two or three days there was high revelry, and some danger of an outbreak and resort to arms between them and some of the other bands. But it was prevented by the vigilance of their chief. Cinnamon had pitched his camp in the bight of a narrow valley, between two of the largest hills on the south side. Further on it opened out and became the bottom lands of a creek, one of the head-waters of the Neosho, which is itself, in turn, one of the almost innumerable streams which contribute to the volume of the Arkansas without apparently increasing it. Such is the thirsty nature of the soil, and so great the evaporation in summer time, that the river is nearly as large five hundred miles from its mouth as it is within sight of the Mississippi, into which it falls. In the next little valley on the south side lay the camp of Sassafras; but this was a mere branch of the prairie, running up into the wooded hills, but not piercing them through. It had good grass and fine water. A living spring, small but constant, gushed out at the foot of a lofty rock near the head of it. Pierre Langlois, a small partner in the trading company, lodged in the post. The young Kiowa may have been there also, but if so he kept very secluded, and made no visits to Cinnamon's camp.

It was the evening of the fourth day after the arrival of Sassafras at the post, and he sat at the entrance of his log-hut, expecting a visitor. He had not long to wait after he had sent the Frenchman and Tom Scarlet away, for the man soon approached, and addressed him with a familiar air. He might be nearly sixty years old, and much weather-beaten, but plainly very tough and vigorous for his years. He was not tall and sparse, as most white men in that region were, but below the middle height, with a broad, deep chest, and massive, round shoulders. His dark hair was shaggy, and a little sprinkled with gray. His eye was red and lowering, like that of a sulky bull, and upon his face there were the scars of several wounds. Such, in appearance, was the redoubtable Captain Staples, a man of uncommon shrewdness and cunning; bold and unscrupulous to the last degree. Subject to the laws of Arkansas when within her boundaries, and to those of the Federal Government when to the westward, he had, to use his own expression, no use for either of them.

> "For why? The good old rule
> Sufficed him; the simple plan
> That they should take who had **the power,**
> And they shall keep who **can.**"

Sassafras preceded the captain into the shanty, and without much ado they sat down facing each other, with a barrel between them, which served the purpose of a table. A stone jug, and a tin cup, were soon put in requisition, and they each took a drink of whiskey. Sassafras lighted his pipe, while the captain renewed the enormous quid of negro-head tobacco, which he had removed when he drank. With some people Captain Staples enjoyed a reputation which was very rare in the West and Southwest in those days. It was thought that he drank no liquor. This was an error; he drank none in company, save when the latter was very select, but a great deal in private. Why he had adopted such a rule nobody knew. It could not be because he was afraid of being over-reached in his dealings, if he drank in the rude society to which he was accustomed, for liquor had no effect upon his muscles and nerves, and abated none of his singular resolution and craft. A town pump might have been made drunk as soon as he. He was now, however, aware that by pretending he never drank he should merely excite the disgust of Sassafras, which might have interfered with the object he had in view. Therefore, the worthy captain tossed off about a third of a pint of whiskey, and praised the quality of the liquor. The two men looked each other full in the eye for a few moments. The captain then placed his hands squarely on his brawny thighs, and said:

"Sassafras, we have been acquainted a long time; I believe we know each other pretty well."

"I shouldn't wonder if we do," returned Sassafras. "It ain't been your fault, if I don't know you."

"No, it has not! And yet I believe you don't know me through and through, Sassafras," said the captain, with much complaisance. "The fact is," he added, "there have been at times words between us, and perhaps hard feelings on your part. Now, in spite of all that, I have always had the highest opinion of you, and am the best friend you've got, from the Missouri to the Red river. I think you didn't know this," concluded the captain, coolly.

"I'm d—d if I did, until you told me!" said Sassafras, pouring out more liquor, and handing it to his best friend to drink first.

"Well, you know it now. Here's to you, Sassafras," said the captain, drinking with a relish. "The last time we raced against each other, I beat you——stop! hear me out! Something was said at the time; but if anything was done wrong, it was without my knowledge and against my wish. That's what it was. You've got the gray mare here now, and she'll beat me."

"I don't intend to let her be dosed before she starts," said Sassafras, bluntly.

The old man was unmoved. "That's right," said he. "It's always well to look out. There's generally a lot of loafing fellows and half-breeds hanging about these posts, and they'll do anything for a few Mexican dollars and a jug of whiskey. I see you've got the mare in good condition, and she's sure to win."

"Well, you haven't come here a-purpose to tell me that?" said Sassafras. "Come, now! Why did you ask me to send my men away, and meet you here alone soon after sundown? It isn't your way to take much trouble for nothing, captain."

"It is not. You're quite right, Sassafras. I meant, by coming, to do *you* some good. That ain't nothing."

"How much good, in regard to what good you mean to do

yourself?" said Sassafras, knocking the ashes out of his pipe preparatory to filling it again. He probably thought that this question would lead to an explanation from the captain, and he was not wrong.

The fine old gentleman gave his quid a twist, and said:

"Sassafras, I've got a betting man up here with me, a gentleman—an English gentleman—a man with plenty of knowledge and plenty of money. Now, this gentleman is inclined to lay some of his money against your mare. He'll do so, if I let him alone; and I, out of friendship for you, feel inclined to let you win some of his sovereigns. In short, we could go halves, you know."

"But why don't you let Keeps or Kirby lay against him for you, and go it all yourself?" said Sassafras.

"It don't suit me to trust Keeps or Kirby," said the captain. "Besides, they are greedy and unprincipled, and have a hankering after the gentleman's money themselves. You'd hardly believe it, but it's been all I could do to prevent Kirby and Keeps, especially Keeps, from cheating the gentleman at poker. I declare to you that these fellows had a cold deck all ready, and would have got his money out of him by downright cheating. That, you know, I could not stand."

"Of course not," returned Sassafras; "the money is not for them. They might as well undertake to rob *you* at once. You have a large interest in this English gentleman."

"I think I have," said the captain. "I reckon it *is* a large interest, present and contingent."

"And in order to make pretty sure of the contingent interest you are willing to share the present interest with me. Ain't that it?"

"I don't think it is altogether," said the captain. "Of the bets we win on the first race you shall have half. But after that comes the heft of the undertaking. Listen now, for I mean real business. It won't do to cut deep at first for fear of exciting the gentleman's suspicions. He's a very nice man—fine specimen of what I've heard a good deal about in my time, the English gentleman. But I can't say that I find him quite perfect. Sassafras, he's mistrustful of most people, and I sometimes think that he suspects even me."

"O, the villain!" cried Sassafras. "What's his name, and
10

what brought him here, so far from the settlements? Come, tell us a little about the stranger."

"His name is Reginald Grosvernor," replied the captain, with readiness and composure. "That's his private travelling name."

"He's got two or three, has he? Staples, I think you had better begin to suspect *him*, and not make sure of your buck while he's running in the woods."

"That's all right! you leave that to me," replied the captain confidently. "This gentleman is a kind of lord, what you call viscount, but has dropped the title for a time, which is right and proper, being on a tour in this land of republican liberty and free institutions, where titles——"

"That'll do! I've heard enough about that. You ain't on the stump addressing the people down the river. Come to this business. What brought this stranger to these parts?"

"Friendship, and a desire to see the world," replied the captain. "He was on his travels, and I brought him here, where he can see the works of natur' on a stupendious scale."

Sassafras was about to interrupt him, when the captain changed his tone, and continued.

"He is owner of a plantation in the West Indies and mines on the Spanish Main. Having been to visit those properties, he came back by way of the Crooked Island Passage. You don't know where that is, but I do, having been on an expedition to an island thereabouts, on which the buccaneers buried a mighty treasure. Lord! Sassafras, if we could only find it! Well, he lands in Cuba, and comes on to Orleans, to make a tour in this country before he goes home."

"Then your contingent interest is in the sugar plantation and the——"

"Coffee—coffee plantation, Sassafras! It's coffee grounds he owns, and the quality of the berry is beautiful. He brought a sample and we tried it at Orleans. He had offers for the crop, but had contracted it in England."

"Well, coffee, then. The contingent interest is in the coffee plantation and the mines on the Spanish Main, is it?" said Sassafras.

"No," replied the captain. "If it was it would not be easy to realize it. It is in certain money he has deposited in the

Bank of Louisiana. I tell you this because I feel certain you'll want to know what induces me to divide with you in the mattter of the ready money."

"All right. I don't care a picayune what the contingency is in. That's your affair. The present interest in the ready money is to be equally divided between us, when we have bagged it."

"No, it ain't; only the money won on the first race is to be divided that way. When we come to the main stakes, I must have two-thirds," said the captain.

"Then I can tell you," said Sassafras, decisively, "that your interest, present and prospective, is worth just about as much as a share in the treasure buried by the buccaneers on the island near the Grand Cayman. I know what that's worth. Man alive! I've been there, too. Do you think that I, who must be the actual winner of the money, am to be put off with less than half?"

"Not so loud! Hear reason, and don't be hasty. If you have a fault, Sassafras, it is going off at half-cock. Listen to me—not a dollar of Ja—of Mr. Grosvernor's money can be handled except through me. Not a dollar! If you agree to that which I propose, your third, with the half of the first winnings, will amount to five hundred guineas—five hundred guineas!" the old man repeated with slow and round emphasis.

"Your'n will amount to about a thousand," said Sassafras, curtly.

"Ay; but I must give Kirby and Keeps each a share, recollect that. Besides, consider the risk and unpleasantness of taking the gentleman down the river broke. That will fall on me, while you will go north to St. Jo., as rich as a Jew and happy as a king. I wish I was in your place and you were in mine, I do," said the captain.

"Now, look here," said Sassafras, "the contingent interest will pay well for taking the man down the river. If it wouldn't, you would leave him to get down as he might. As to Kirby and Keeps, you won't give 'em more than two hundred silver dollars a-piece, when you strike the Arkansas, and you'll win that back before they see Little Rock. They won't ring in any cold decks on you."

"I don't think they will," said the captain, dryly. "But

considering that I have in a manner got this money already in hand, and that the five hundred guineas will be the same as a gift to you, don't you think that you are in conscience and duty bound to be content with one-third of the main stakes?"

"No, I don't. I must have half or as good as half," replied Sassafras. "I'll take the Englishman's white stud, and allow two hundred dollars for him in the settlement between you and me."

"Two hundred! he thinks him worth two thousand," said the captain. "But never mind his horse for the present. The thing to go for first is his money. Since we are old friends, and I may never have such another opportunity to oblige a friend, I will agree that you shall have four hundred dollars out of every thousand won by us from Grosvernor after the first race—there!" he exclaimed, as if amazed at his own generosity. "Your shares together will reach eight hundred guineas—eight hundred guineas!" he repeated, slowly, and with round, dwelling emphasis. "There ain't another man west of the Mississippi that I would do it for."

"No, nor east of it either," said Sassafras; "but suppose I should come into your plan on these terms, how is it to be carried out?"

"You say agreed, I'll find the way; and after the little business of the first race, we'll go for blood—meaning big money, you know."

"Very well! I say agreed. Now let's hear how this man is to be corralled in, so that he'll lay pretty nigh two thousand guineas on a second race, after having lost on the first. He isn't altogether a fool in such matters, I suppose!"

"A fool! oh, no! he knows more about such matters than you and I put together. The Derby, the Leger, Newmarket, and what not—he knows it all, Sassafras; knows it all!" said the old gentleman, with a chuckle. "I said he was suspicious; he's conceited as well, and reckons his own judgment better than mine. He contradicts my opinions, and rejects my advice—thinks very little of it, and will think less, when the first race is over. Now," continued the captain, leaning forward over the barrel, in such a manner as to endanger the whiskey jug, which Sassafras thereupon removed, "after your mare has beat my horse in the match now made, we can make another. He'll back your mare at strong odds, and all we have to do is to stretch out our hands and grasp 'em!"

"We shall never grasp them in that way," said Sassafras. "The plan won't work. The Indians will back the mare, and I daren't pull her. There was nearly a bloody fight when Virginia was beat by you last year."

"Never mind their small amount of silver—we can make it up to them through the traders."

"Ay! but we had better mind their lead. The end of it might be a bullet in my head and another in yours, and what would be the use of the Englishman's gold then? The thing would be too plain, Staples. If it was the Englishman's white stud now that run against her, *he* might win. He's a very fine-looking horse, and ought to beat her."

"You think he could beat her, eh?" said the captain, with another chuckle. In a moment, however, his merriment ceased, and he added, "but the money couldn't be laid right in that case. He conceits that horse mightily. The best way will be to run my horse and let him beat Virginia. The Indians can be squared, and the Cheyenne band can overawe the others. The chief is your friend."

"His band couldn't overawe a marksman in a bush, and I tell you that plan won't work," said Sassafras. "Besides, there's a little coolness between me and Cinnamon just now, caused by the interference of Pierre Langlois."

"I see! something has been said," returned the captain. "I have been all my life trying to get people to mind their own business, and let that of other folks alone, but I can't effect it. But now to come back to our business. Suppose you were to run the Young Chief against my horse and got him beat. It's true there would be no odds laid against him, and we should have hard work to raise enough to stake against the Englishman's guineas, at even bets."

"I don't know about that. You've got some money, I've got some. We reckon upon winning some on the first race. And then the traders will cash a bill on Orleans for me, on good security. Young Campau comes from St. Jo., and knows my plantation. Still, I am of the belief that it can't be worked that way, for the Young Chief is lame, and the Eng-

lishman would see it with half an eye.   Better leave the
shaping of the main matter until after the first race is run.
To make sure work, let the Englishman lay plenty of money
on that.   Meantime, I'll make his acquaintance, and don't you
come mixing in when we are talking together."

After Sassafras concluded, the old man sat in thought.   He
was considering whether he could not contrive some means by
which Sassafras and his mare Virginia might be beaten in the
first race.   That would have been a coup after his own heart,
but he could not see how he could win the money of the Englishman, after having deceived Sassafras, without jeopardizing
his chance and contingent interest in the Bank of England
notes and sundry securities deposited in the Bank of Louisiana.
Jagger, as bold and unscrupulous, in his way, as the worthy
old captain himself, had led him to believe that the amount
was about ten times as great as it was in reality.   By this
means he had acquired a strong influence on Staples to insure
his personal safety.   The old man was virtually bound over
in the amount deposited in the bank, to bring Jagger safe
back to New Orleans.   Moreover, the captain had a saving
conviction that a repetition of the strategy by which he had
been enabled to defeat Virginia the year before, in the Territory of the Cherokee Nation, would be dangerous.   He rose
and said :

" Well, we understand each other.   Don't let your mare
look too well, for Mr. Grosvernor will scan her general appearance, and if she shows racing like, may take a notion to
bet on her, or not bet at all."

" Leave it to me to manage his lordship on that point," said
Sassafras, going out with the captain.   " She shall go in the
balance of her work in such a way, and look so queer, up to
within ten minutes of the start, that he'll reckon she can't beat
a bull."

CHAPTER XVII.

"Away, and mock the time with fairest show;
For the false face must hide what the false heart doth know."

WHEN Captain Staples and Sassafras parted after their interview, the mental exclamation of each in regard to the other was, "Here's a pretty rascal!" It was the more emphatic on the part of Staples, who had expected Sassafras to make some remonstrance before coming into the fraudulent scheme by which the intended victim was to be despoiled. On the other hand, Sassafras knew that Staples was an unscrupulous rogue just as well before the latter unfolded his plan as he did after he had announced it. The captain walked out into the night, like a hardy robber, to whom darkness is a familiar and welcome cloak, or a wolf who prowls, watchful and confident, in his haunts of chase and prey. He had gone some eight or ten rods into the prairie, when he halted, and seemed to deliberate as to whether he should not return and renew the conversation with his partner in the conspiracy he had planned and was bent upon carrying out. But after brooding for a minute or two, he said:

"No, I'll see him no more to-night. He's so very ready to go into this business that I must beware of him. The fellow bears me no good will. He has threatened me once or twice. He has kept up a sort of character for honesty, and all that sort of thing, a good deal too expensive for my means, and for that I always hated him. But see, now, how he jumps at the golden bait as soon as the stakes are big enough. He's as great a rogue as I am. As great did I say?—much greater; for this money, as I look at it, is mine by a sort of right. I steered it safe through New Orleans, where Jagger would not have had sense enough to keep it twenty-four hours. I have protected it all the way from Kirby and Keeps and others, who would have got the Englishman roped in long ago. Besides, Sassafras is a young man, without a family to provide for, and with a good plantation on the Missouri, close to St.

Jo. Beyond all doubt, the fellow shows himself to be a much bigger rogue than I am. But I hate him now almost or quite as much as I did before. He's fallen out with the Cheyenne and Pierre Langlois! That's what makes him afraid to throw a race in my favor, between the gray mare and my horse. A rogue, and afraid, too! What a world it's got to be since I was a boy! I didn't think this villain would have been afraid of the d—l himself. He's afraid of these Indians, however. Now, if I could get them on my side, it would be a strong stroke of policy, and might be the means, by and by, of making Sassafras disgorge some of this money of mine that he greedily insists upon having for his trifling share in the business. How to manage it is the thing. Go to the chief in the first place I can't, for he's a sulky sort of redskin, and does not like me. Prejudiced by the rascal Sassafras, no doubt. Pierre Langlois doesn't like me either; but I can manage him. Pierre's the man, and I'll go to him right away."

With this the captain strode rapidly on, passed the bushes by the pond at the east end, and on up to the traders' fort, as it was called. He was soon admitted, and inquiring for Langlois, was shown into an apartment partitioned off with rough boards, at one end of which were rows of sleeping-berths, like those on the beam deck of a ship. Pierre Langlois, a man of forty years, with the figure of an Indian and the yellowish complexion of a French half-breed, was seated at a table with the acquaintance of Sassafras, young Campau, whose father was the principal man in the company of traders, and two other men belonging to the fort. They were playing cards. It is very likely that Pierre was on the winning side, and that he had been taking a drink or two of the fine old whiskey in the company's store, a much superior article to that sold by its factors at enormous rates to the Indians and hunters who were almost the sole customers at the fort, for his reception of Staples was not ungracious, and in his talk with the other players he was loud and voluble. There was another person in the room besides those of the card party when Staples entered, but he was so situated as to be unobserved. It was the young Kiowa. He lay in one of the berths, so shaded from the light and so still that the captain did not notice his presence. At the conclusion of the game then pending, Campau

and the other men of the fort retired from the room. Up to
this time the conversation between Langlois and Staples had
been of that broken, interjectory order which may be held between the fall of cards and during the dealing of them. It
was not to be thought that Staples would bring on his motion,
in re Sassafras, while Campau was present; but now that he
and the other man were gone, he improved his opportunity.
He began by assuring his neighbor, Langlois, of his sincere
regard, and went on to lament that so good a man should be
in a difficulty with a desperate character such as Sassafras.
He, Staples, had had several differences with Sassafras himself, in all of which the young man had been wholly to blame.
Langlois might have heard of this, and of the moderation and
mildness by means of which Staples had avoided the shedding
of blood. Sassafras was quarrelsome, violent and vindictive—
bull-headed as an old, solitary buffalo. He had a very bitter
tongue; had said hard things of him, Staples, and when a
man would do that, what was not to be expected? He had
said many hard things of Langlois, and the captain was not
surprised at it. He then very glibly repeated some of these
sayings, for the information and satisfaction of the object of
them. There were such as Sassafras had never uttered, but
the captain did not invent them for the occasion. They mainly
consisted of what Staples himself had said of Langlois on
various occasions.

At the close of an address of some length, the captain
paused to hear what his neighbor had to say to it. At first
the latter had been eager to put in, and had tried to interrupt
the steady flow of the captain's narrative once or twice, but
on the last of these occasions something had happened which
made him change his mind. He was in front of the berths,
before mentioned; Staples sat with his back to them. All at
once, Pierre's manner changed from that of the eager, excited
Frenchman, to that of the stolid Indian, determined to maintain dogged silence at any cost. Perhaps the captain attributed this result to his own eloquence. He had just then recited some of the bitterest things, which he alleged were said
of Langlois by Sassafras. However that may be, when the
captain came to his pause, Pierre remained silent and smoked
away with the obstinacy and grave assiduity of the most

ponderous Dutchman. Thereupon the captain opened the second head of his discourse, to the following effect: It would be a very bad job if Sassafras made trouble between Langlois and his brother, the chief. He, Staples, was afraid he would try to do so, and Langlois ought to take measures to head him off in time. He ought to see the chief and put him on his guard against this vindictive and dangerous man. The Indians were easily misled, and this Sassafras was of all men the very one to do it. He, Staples, would advise Langlois to go to the chief in the morning, and enlighten him as to the true character of his pretended friend from Missouri. Sassafras was no friend to the Indians at all, but a greedy adventurer, ready to plunder and betray friend and foe alike. Langlois might be sure of this, for he, Staples, had had proof of the greed and treachery of Sassafras that very night; and of all things in the world between man and man, Staples most hated treachery and greed, especially where Indians were the victims of them. Much more to the same effect the old man said; but he extracted nothing from Langlois, whose replies were very brief and indistinct, from his speaking with his pipe in his mouth. When he thought he had well primed his man, so that the quarrel between Sassafras and the chief was sure to be fomented, and the breach between them certain to be widened, the captain rose and left the room. Langlois, perhaps, might have followed, but the door was no sooner shut upon the retreating figure of the former, than the young Kiowa sprang lightly to the floor, and putting one hand on Pierre's shoulder, laid the other on his mouth. They listened warily for a few moments, then they sat down together, and talked in whispers.

Meantime, Sassafras left his camp, and, gun in hand (he was seldom without his rifle when on foot), began leisurely to climb the wooded hill, between his camp and the valley, in which the tents of the Cheyennes were pitched. Although it was nearly dark, he made his way between the trees and bushes, and over the fallen, rotting trunks, as if guided by a sort of instinct. "A nice man is Staples," said Sassafras, "especially for an old man. The saying is 'No fool like an old fool;' it ought to be 'No rogue like an old rogue.' And the old humbug thought to come it over me with his tough yarn about a lord in disguise, coffee plantation in the Leeward Islands, and mines on the Spanish Main. The mine is the Englishman's guineas, and it's all fair to work it. These men are villains! anything is fair to beat them—that is, anything in reason." He reached the top of the hill, and saw the fires of the Indians glowing and sparkling in the valley below. Sometimes, as they blazed up, the forms of the warriors might be perceived reclining near them. " I wonder, now, whether that boy has been to see the chief again," said Sassafras, " or whether he is up at the fort with Pierre Langlois. He may be out on a hunt with some of the men, but I doubt it. He wa'nt rigged in hunting gear to my eye. But never mind! I'll see Cinnamon." With this he strode down the slope, and saluting the Indians who were upon the verge of the camp, moved in towards the centre, where Cinnamon's tent was pitched. The chief was at some little distance, leaning against a sapling which grew in the glade, within the circle of light cast by one of the fires. He was very grave, and so still that in that ruddy light he looked more like a grand, severe statue of a warrior of his tribe, than a living man ; and yet if one had caught a glimpse of his deep, dark eye, as it received the rays of the fire, and flashed it back again, he might have seen a world of life and power in the brain beyond. As Sassafras approached, the Indian made a step forward, and put forth his open hand, while his countenance, before so sombre, glowed with pleasure. "Sassafras is welcome to Cinnamon's camp," said he, leading the way to his own tent. They sat down together, smoked the usual pipe, and then conversed for some time, in short, sentient phrases. Sassafras carried on the conversation for the most part, the chief listening attentively, and occasionally making an observation. When they rose the Indian walked with the white man to the foot of the hill.

Sassafras had crossed it, and entered the little valley in which his own camp was placed, when his quick eye, farreaching almost as that of a tiger by night, caught sight of a form half crouching in some straggling bushes. The ominous click of the lock of the Western rifle, as Sassafras cocked it, sounded in the still night upon the ear of him who was half in hiding, and, straightening up, he stepped clear of the brush.

" Halloo, Joe! What brings you skulking here? I had

almost put a bullet through you!" said Sassafras, addressing
a half-breed lad belonging to the fort.

"No skulk—not at all," said the boy; "only wait for you."

"Well, here I am," said Sassafras, as they entered the edge
of the flickering light of the fire, from the dark void beyond.
"Now what is it, Joe?"

"You to read alone," said the boy, putting a piece of folded
paper into the man's hand.

"From the fort, is it?"

The boy nodded, and was about to turn away.

"Stop!" exclaimed Sassafras, laying his hand upon his
shoulder and detaining him. "Who sent it?"

"Say that inside; you read alone," said Joe.

"That is, nobody else must read, eh?"

"Nobody see you read—you read alone, I was to say,"
replied the boy.

"Ay, I am to read it when I'm alone. Very good. Do
you know what is in it?"

"Writing in it. You read alone, Sassafras."

"Maybe you have read it alone—eh, Joe?" said Sassafras,
with a half-laugh.

"No, I can't read," said the boy.

"Can't read! I thought you had been east to the mission
to school?" returned the Western man.

"I was, but I read not writing; only read book. You read
alone, Sassafras. Friend say to me, 'Tell Sassafras to read
alone.'"

"What friend?"

"Campau. He say: 'Joe, you take this to Sassafras.
Nobody see you but Sassafras, and Sassafras read alone.'
Nobody see me. I see Kirby and Englishman at Staples's
shanty, both drunk."

"You are a good boy, Joe. I like you, Joe. If I win a
race here, as I'm sure to do, you shall have something to remember it by."

When Sassafras had said this, he made a pause. He might
have resolved much of which he had asked the boy, by opening the paper, going to the fire, and reading it; but he had
held the youth in parley for another purpose.

"Joe," said he, in a confidential sort of tone, "there was a
young Kiowa at the fort; is he there now?"

"He is," replied the boy.

"What do you know about him?" asked Sassafras.

"Nothing," replied the boy, in a sulky tone. "I like not the Kiowas. They kill my fader on the Arkansas, above the great bend."

"Ah! I remember hearing of it," said Sassafras. "Well, Joe, what does that boy do at the fort?"

"Notting that I know of," said the half-breed.

"Nothing! why don't he practise with the bow and arrows and his rifle at a mark?"

"He's got no bow and arrow and no rifle, but he does practise at a mark, and it's wonderful."

"Tell me how, Joe; I'm somewhat anxious about that boy. Of course he is an Indian?"

"Kiowa! bad Indian! son of war chief beyond the Arkansas, way up in mountains. I don't like 'um. His practice is with a knife. Sassafras, he can stand twenty feet off from a mark the size of a dollar and stick the point of his knife into it every throw."

"The d——l he can! That beats the fellow in the calaboose, after we left the Grand Cayman. Joe, have you heard this boy talk?"

"Very little; only to himself when he thought he was alone."

"Did you understand him? What was his tongue?"

"I don't know. It was not English, nor French, nor any Indian that I understand, but they say nobody can understand the Kiowas."

Sassafras pondered a few minutes and then said:

"Joe, do you understand Spanish?"

"I don't think I do," replied the boy, "if the Mexicans speak Spanish."

"Well, Joe, keep your eye on that boy and take care of his knife. I say—did you see any name on that knife? Describe the knife."

"Ivory haft, two-edged blade, five inches long, tapering to a point. On the blade these letters in gold, 'T O L E D O.'"

"And that spells Toledo! Well, Joe, come and see me again."

The boy sprang forward towards the prairie, with his head

low, and footsteps soft and agile as those of a panther. Sassafras went to the fire, threw on a handful of brush, and as it blazed up, read the following note :—

"Staples was here trying to get Langlois to make a difficulty between you and Cinnamon. Beware of him. Be secret and be shrewd. Fear nothing from the young Kiowa. Send Tom Scarlet to the hills on a hunt with François.   CAMPAU."

Sassafras re-read the note, commenting as he proceeded :—

"'Staples trying to make difficulty'—d—l doubt him! He's always trying to do that. 'Beware of him!' all right! unnecessary advice! 'Fear nothing from the young Kiowa.' Now, that's the kernel of this nut, if I could crack it. There's no Kiowa about him, I'll bet a hundred to one on it. 'Send Tom Scarlet on a hunt with François.' That piece of advice is good, for if he and Staples and Jagger should meet he would betray himself—he couldn't help it, and the fat would be in the fire in no time. 'Campau!' very good name is Campau, especially on a note promising to pay money at bank, but if Campau wrote this I'll eat it. I know his hand-write, and this ain't a bit like it. Let me see! I'm not much of a scholar, but when I see a thing once, of any moment, I generally know when I see it again, and I'll swear I have seen this handwrite before."

Sassafras sat and pondered. Suddenly he gave a start, and said :

"The letters from New Orleans to Tom Scarlet and me! That's where I saw it before ; and the same hand that wrote them wrote this. I wish we had those letters here! 'Fear nothing from the young Kiowa!' Fear! I should think not. But I am curious concerning that boy, especially after hearing of his doings with a knife. It's my opinion that he knows another trick or two with it besides casting it at a mark. No rifle! That shows he is no French creole from below. No bow and arrows! That shows he's no Indian from the southwest. Besides, he doesn't ride much, and he is not in-toed when he's afoot! Let me see! The little hands and feet which François observed! And the eye which is neither French nor Indian, but deeper, and brighter in its fire, than either of them. I have it! He's a Spanish creole from the islands; that's what he is! And what he is doing here I'll find out yet. I'll just catch him alive some of these nights, knife or no knife."

He went softly to the wagon under which the Frenchmen were sleeping, and awoke François.

"François," said he, "take Tom Scarlet on a hunt to the hills to-morrow. He's eager to go for a day or two."

"My faith! Sassafras, there's no deer in the near hills. The Indians have driven them away by so much hunting."

"All the better. Take him to the farther hills, where the deer are, and elk, too, and keep him there a week. I want to get him out of sight of Staples. Propose the hunt to him forthwith—he'll readily agree. Fill your saddle-bags, and start soon after daylight—' over the hills and far away!' I should like to go on a good hunt myself, but have much to do here. Staples tries to make a difficulty between me and the Indians; but his scheme will fail. By the time you return I shall have all ready for our great stroke."

CHAPTER XVIII.

"Though in the trade of war I have slain men,
Yet do I hold it very stuff o' the conscience
To do no contrived murder."

IT was the break of day, and the air came fresh and cool, with the gray tints of dawn, from the tops of the eastern mountains. The clarion of the cock at the fort, and the answering challenge of others at Captain Staples's quarters, valorously ushered in the morn. In the vale of Sassafras's camp the grass was heavy and dank with dew; the horses rising one after another, and shaking their manes, began to crop it. The active leader of the little band was early on foot, and now there was bustle all around in getting ready for the hunting expedition of François and Tom Scarlet. By the blazing fire, the negro cook, a master of his art in regard to frying steaks and making corn cakes, was busy preparing the breakfast. The boiling coffee spread its fragrant essence through the fresh morning air, while collops of venison and slices of fat salt pork hissed and spluttered in the frying-pans, one of which the cook dexterously held in each hand. Proud was the cook of his skill, fully appreciating the importance of his art to sojourners in the wilderness. Behind the tents and wagons two other men of his race were equipping the horses of François and Tom Scarlet, while they ate from feed-boxes of the rare dainty, to them, of sound, bright oats, mixed with Indian corn. Further to the rear another negro, perhaps a man, perhaps but a youth, for his appearance gave little indication of his age, was rubbing down the gray race-mare, Virginia. This personage paid but little regard to the proceedings of his mates with the other horses; and though his wide nostril expanded as it owned the savory scent from the frying-pans, he seemed to look upon the cook even with a supercilious air. It must have been the dignity of his station and occupation which inspired him, for of natural advantages he had few to boast. He was black as night, when the thunder clouds fill the vast arch of the sky and shut up the stars. His form was spare and ungainly, especially when he was on foot, for in the saddle he displayed a sort of rough readiness and ease which almost amounted to grace. His bullet head was covered with close, crisp hair of the woolly order. His features were hard. One bright eye, which fairly glowed when he was animated, was all he had. His mouth, enormous in its width, was garnished with very white and even teeth. At a little distance stood Sassafras, with Tom Scarlet and François, to whom he was making rapid explanations and giving instructions. Where the valley and the prairie met the form of Jules was just visible as he brushed the dew away with long strides, carolling gaily on his way to the fort with a message to Pierre Langlois.

Breakfast over, the hunters mounted, and with a hearty shake of the hand, Sassafras said:

"Good-by, Tom, and good luck. I know you'll have sport, and should like to see you enjoy it. But that can't be this time. You have with you one of the best men that ever tracked a buck or shot an elk upon the frontier. François, within six days return, and come in secretly by night."

The hunters rode away up the hill, so as to strike the valley of the Cheyenne camp below the bend at which it lay. Sassafras looked after them until they entered the thick timber and underbrush of the saddle between the two hills. Then he turned to his favorite mare Virginia, and his true and trusty rider, Black Dick.

"Dick, I shall not be on the track this morning. I have another matter to look after," said Sassafras.

"Berry well. Massa tell what I do," returned the negro, with his hand on the crest of the mare.

"The boys will go with you when Jules gets back. He must be breakfasting at the fort, and will be here by the time you have finished your own."

As Sassafras said this the lips of the negro parted, so as to display his formidable teeth, all ready for their matin meal. His master continued:

"Walk the mare a bit, then canter a couple of miles; then strip and take her a mile at above half speed. Scrape, then, if she will scrape, and wind up with a good brushing gallop, twice round. You understand?"

"I understand," replied Dick; "but must hab 'e Young Chief to gallop with her. Dis ar mar' nebber go at all alone, and 'e Chief sound enuff."

"Never you mind the Chief, he'll stay where he is until almost noontime, when you can walk him. Do just what I say—no more, no less."

"I brieve I allus do what massa say," replied the black in a sulky tone, with his eye lowering and dull. "But massa better tell 'e more too. Dis ar mar' nebber go a bit alone."

"Give her a touch with the spur."

"Spur!" said Dick, with a faint tinge of contempt, "'e mar' fight agen 'e spur; and nebber go a good sharp lick alone."

"I don't want her to go a good sharp lick, but only to seem as if she was doing nearly her best," said Sassafras. Then he continued to his pupil, and, in part, his confidant: "And mind this, if the Englishman over there says she is tired after her gallop don't you contradict a gentleman of experience and high degree from the old country—a man that can buy us all. D'ye mind, Dick?"

The negro looked at his master for a moment, as if unable to comprehend his drift; but as Sassafras looked steadily and significantly at him, awakening intelligence began to spread over the hard ebony face. The bright eye lighted up, and

11

opening the capacious mouth so that the white walls and red lining yawned like a cavern, the black laughed till he shook again.

"Come, that'll do, Dick. You understand how to work after breakfast?"

"Brieve I do. Dat ar mar' allus pull up tired," said the negro, with another powerful laugh. "I nebber contradict a gemman of high degree, 'cause 'e mar' allus pull up tired, berry tired indeed! Ho! ho! yah! berry tired!"

Sassafras walked off, rifle in hand, and the negro went to breakfast with his mates. For some time, seated on a feed-box, he put his great mouth and beautiful teeth to exceeding good use. Then looking at the gray mare for a long time with the one bright eye, he suddenly burst out with such a roar of laughter that, rocking himself to and fro, he slipped off the box, and rolled and roared with ecstasy upon the grass.

"What ail dat nigga Dick?" cried the others.

"Nebber contradict a gemman of high degree in all 'e life," said Dick; then sitting up and wiping his o'erflowing eye, he exclaimed, "Dat ar mar' allus pull up tired! berry tired! ho! ho! ha!"

Sassafras, whistling as he went, proceeded to the Cheyenne camp. Pierre Langlois, in compliance with the message delivered to him by Jules, was already there, and the chief sat grave and still near the brands and ashes of the morning fire. A few words from Sassafras were sufficient to inform the Indian and his half-brother that the border man had come to hold a sort of council with them. Cinnamon rose, and passing by the men of his band who lounged about the camp, led the way into the wood on the hill. The three men sat down on a mossy log, the chief in the centre. The latter filled the pipe of ceremony with the choicest tobacco, mixed with some other dried and fragrant herbs, and lighted it. A puff or two were taken in turn by Sassafras and Pierre, as a matter of established form, after which they produced their own pipes, and all three smoked steadily in silence. When the pipes were finished Sassafras opened his business by a few terse sentences in the Cheyenne tongue, and concluded by requesting Langlois to relate what had fallen from Staples in the night interview at the fort. Pierre readily complied, and as he hated Staples with a vivacious hatred, and there was nothing to check his volubility, the story lost nothing in the telling, and Pierre's comments upon the facts were vigorous. Sassafras said nothing. The chief sat very grave and still, with eyes cast down, until his half-brother had finished. Then Cinnamon arose, and facing the white man, laid his hand upon the ornament, the horse's head, the latter wore upon his breast.

"Sassafras," said he, "is a warrior of my tribe. Together we went out against the Sioux of the north, and their young men fell like leaves from trees when the west wind blows. The skin of Sassafras, clothed from the sun and wind, is pale, but his blood is red as that of the Indians of the plains and western mountains. He has an enemy. The wolverine is hated by the hunter and the warrior, and every man slays the cunning beast when he can. Sassafras is a man! His gun is true, his hand is strong, and his knife is keen. Let my friend kill his enemy, and leave him to the ravens of the woods."

Cinnamon's friends appeared to be somewhat unprepared for this decisive counsel, though not much startled by the cool ferocity with which the summary taking off of Staples was proposed. They looked at each other, as if each was waiting for his neighbor to speak. Meantime the red man of the immense plains and stupendous mountains played with his tomahawk, and felt its keen edge with an air of abstraction. After a silence which lasted from five to ten minutes, Sassafras laid his hand upon the rich-brown arm of the chief, and said:

"Cinnamon, you mean well. The thing might easily be done, and very few would go into mourning because the ravens and wolves had cleaned the bones of Staples. In you it would be human nature to take him unawares; but I, you see, cannot do it. I cannot kill a man in cold blood; neither can I get up a passion, and contrive a quarrel for the purpose of fixing him in that."

"Sassafras had no quarrel with the Sioux; he was cool when we went into ambush, and shot their young men," said the chief, with a smile.

"Ah, but circumstances alter cases, Cinnamon," said Sassafras, in reply. "It's true I had no quarrel with the Sioux, but you had; and they were a bloody set that we fought against. It was a state of war, which makes all the difference. That Staples and I shall have a fight in the end, is very likely. I shall neither bring it on, nor try to avoid it. When it happens, his time is come, and I shall kill him. For why? Because he will kill me, if I do not kill him."

The chief said no more, and Langlois looked relieved. Sassafras adverted to the note sent to him the night before from the fort, but Pierre made no observation. Nor could the chief or his half-brother be drawn on to talk of the young Kiowa; so Sassafras, changing the subject, spoke of the match between the gray mare and the horse brought from the South by Staples. The Indian listened with interest to the praises bestowed by her master on Virginia; and before the three men separated the sun was high in the heavens.

The meridian heat was past, and a tinge of crimson had begun to flush the light clouds in the western sky, when Sassafras sauntered carelessly down to the race-track. Jagger, alias Reginald Grosvernor, was already there, mounted upon the White Horse. This man was about forty years old, lathy in figure, about the middle height, and far from prepossessing in countenance. His face was thin and blotchy. His nose was very red and somewhat swollen, having been scorched and peeled, instead of tanned, by the fervid western sun. His eye was small and uncertain, stealing furtive glances from under the drooping lid; and his scanty hair and whiskers were sandy in color. In his attire and general get-up there was a mixture of finery, soiled and worn, instead of the rough but serviceable garments adapted to the prairie and the woods. A figured satin stock did not altogether hide the breast of a dirty shirt. His pearl-colored doeskin trousers were strapped down over much-worn boots; his coat of the Newmarket cut, once bright-green, but now faded, showed many a soil; and his Panama hat was bruised, broken and begrimed. But with all this he wore a profusion of jewelry, and looked like a member of the swell mob in adverse circumstances. In external points the horse he rode seemed much the nobler animal of the two. The eye of Sassafras ranged over him from his muzzle to his hoofs, and dwelt with delight upon his excellent proportions. But he soon directed his attention to the man, and addressing him with such familiarity as their presence in the wilds and their occupations might justify, began by complimenting him upon his riding and evident general knowledge of horsemanship. The gudgeon eagerly snapped at the bait. Feeling pleased with the admiration bestowed upon him, and the modest deference so artfully paid to him, Reginald decided to patronize the young fellow before him in so much as to give him the benefit of some of his knowledge and experience in racing matters.

Jagger was, in truth, but a poor horseman; his knowledge of the turf was mostly confined to rascalities, practised by the few who believe them to be universal, in connection therewith. Sassafras had already taken the measure of his man, but although his breast swelled with alternate emotions of anger and amusement, as Jagger held forth and instructed him in the mysteries of breeding, training and riding, there was no sign in his hard, dark, hickory face. It was long since Jagger had enjoyed the enlightening of a man who suited him, and who seemed so thoroughly the slave of his humor. Staples was too opinionated to listen, and had too much experience of racing himself to hear patiently the romances related by Jagger of his own wonderful exploits. Kirby and Keeps knew of no better horses than the hardy and clever animals on which they had been accustomed to hunt the buffalo. They were willing enough to drink with Jagger from dark to dawn; but whenever he began to feel the effects of his deep potations, and commenced the account of the way in which he won the Derby with an outsider, and brought about the defeat of the three favorites for the St. Leger, the burly hunter summarily desired him to "shet up." As for Tom of Lincoln, he had no sooner found himself in America, and consequently out of the purview of a warrant from an English magistrate, than he quarrelled with his patron, knocked him down in a drunken spree, and went off on his own hook, after extorting a considerable sum of money from him. Jagger galloped his horse, and Sassafras was profuse in his professions of admiration and delight. His intended victim talked long and learnedly, and after going to the fort to drink, talked long again. Once more, twice more, they went to the fort for liquor, and Jagger treated Staples's negro boys. The Western man made feints, as if about to leave, but Jagger detained him, and talked on and on. To the fort again, where Jagger, seated on a barrel, and thrashing his legs with his whip, harangued and drank, and declaimed and drank again, until his eyes were red and watery, his voice was thick, and he forgot, from time to time, the thread of his discourse. Finally his docile and admiring friend flatly contradicted him touching the merits and condition of the gray mare, Virginia. Jagger declared that she was no race-horse. He had noticed her frame, and no horse made in that form could run fast, or stay for more than a mile. And then he hiccoughed out that he had seen her pull up tired, after a moderate gallop of two miles, and that the black chap who rode her would confirm what he said. To all appearance Sassafras was in high dudgeon, and the end of a long, rambling discussion between them was a bet of five hundred dollars, Sassafras backing the gray mare, and Jagger taking the chestnut horse belonging to his earnest and sincere friend, Captain Staples. It ought to be stated that this result was not finally brought about until the captain himself had arrived, and had heard Jagger relate, in a corner, with the cunning leer of intoxication and with owlish gravity, the distressed condition of the mare after her morning gallop.

"Are you sure of that?" said Staples.

"Sure as heggs is heggs. Ask the blackamoor who rode her," said Jagger, with a reel.

"What, Black Dick? O, if he said she was tired, or allowed she was tired when you made the observation, it's all right. Make the bet, and don't let Sassafras back out. Make the bet at once," said the venerable and disinterested Staples.

The bet was made, play or pay, as Staples in a whisper suggested, and Jagger obstinately insisted. The money was staked in Campau's hands, and was by him handed over to the manager of the company for safe-keeping. More drink and more hubbub followed. At length the parties separated. Staples followed Sassafras into the dark shade, and exchanged a few sentences with him. Jagger was dragged off to the shanty between Kirby and Keeps, and awoke the next morning with a headache and an intense longing for soda-water, of which there was none within about a thousand miles. Two days after the match was run, a dash twice round the course. The chestnut horse led for a mile and three-quarters, and

Jagger oracularly announced that it was all over. It is possible that if Black Dick had heard him he might have been loath to contradict, in fact, a "gemman of high degree;" but as it was, he brought Virginia to the front in the last quarter of a mile, and won by a length.

CHAPTER XIX.

"Haste still pays haste, and leisure answers leisure,
Like doth quit like, and Measure still for Measure."

IT was night, and the store at the fort was almost full of rough and noisy men. Indians, hunters, traders, and a few negroes were there, talking and drinking. Sassafras was, for the present, king of the company. He had received the stakes of the race, and had liberally treated all who chose to partake at his expense. Everybody did choose, except the manager, and one or two of his clerks; and one jug of whiskey after another was consumed by the seasoned and thirsty rovers who composed the throng. Jagger was in the crowd, at least half drunk. The liquor had not, however, allayed the bitterness which had possessed him ever since the gray mare collared the chestnut horse, and ran home a winner. Everybody and everything was to blame, except himself; and he distributed his blame with such plentiful impartiality, that nothing but the prospect of more whiskey, and perhaps a row, prevented Kirby and Keeps from leaving him to "paddle his own canoe," as the former expressed it. He was loud and severe against Staples as a trainer. The clamor of his complaints and upbraidings had driven the old man to leave his company. In default of a better, he now seized upon Sassafras as a listener, and declaimed, with droning vehemence and ludicrous sentiment, upon his own knowledge and experience, and the stupidity and obstinacy of Staples and his men. If his own suggestions had been followed, the horse could hardly have lost, though the riding of him was wretched, and simply disgusting to one who knew what riding was.

"What you say is true in the main," said Sassafras, with apparent candor; "but you could hardly expect science and skill here, such as you have picked up, year after year, at Epsom, Newmarket, and where not. I say you look for too much, and try us by too high a standard. We are well enough in our way."

"Ay! but it's a d——d bad way!" cried Jagger. "Was there ever a race thrown away like this before? No condition, no management, no riding, no nothing. I protest to you, Sassafras, that you are the only man in these parts with a bit of sense. You appreciate my abilities and acquirements, and you are the only one, unless it be the red man at your elbow, who seems to be interested in what I say."

"Yes, Cinnamon is interested in your remarks—deeply interested, considering that he can hardly understand the language. But fill up, and let us drink all round: To the turf and the races thereof—may the best horses always win!"

"And that's what they never can do, as long as ignorance and folly have charge of them," said Jagger, after doing justice to the toast. "Staples isn't fit to train a plough-horse, to say nothing of a racer. I could teach you a good deal, Sassafras. You are tractable, and not above learning from a man like me. In six months I could make a man of you. But you overestimate that gray mare—you do indeed!"

"It may be so," returned Sassafras. "I raised her myself, and it is but natural that I should think well of her. She isn't Flying Childers nor Eclipse; but for the wooden country she was bred in and the sort of races we run out here the mare is a good one."

"Good one! You mean that there's nothing but very bad 'uns to try her with," said Jagger, with a snarl. "Why, she couldn't win a hunter's plate in any county in England; and if she ran for a saddle and bridle at Barnet Fair, I doubt whether she could pull it off. There's better than her in stage coaches and doctors' gigs where I came from."

"Very likely!" cried Sassafras, "but she can beat any horse west of the big river (save one) two or three-mile heats, weight for age." With this he rose and struck the table with his fist.

Jagger rose too, and their loud voices in opposition to each other stilled the brawling in other parts of the store, and drew the men around them. Hunters and Indians, half drunk, ready with the knife and pistol on small occasions, hemmed them in. The broad-shouldered Kirby and the lithe, snaky Keeps ranged themselves with Jagger. Cinnamon and Pierre Langlois stood with Sassafras, and young Campau was close behind him.

"I say, and mean no offence, only a fair race, if anybody wants to take it up and make it, that she can beat any horse save one west of the big river, weight for age, two or three-mile heats. Is that fair?" said Sassafras.

"It is good," replied Cinnamon.

"Then if anybody wants it, I'll make the match for a thousand dollars a side."

"Say save none! You might as well, for there is not one can beat Virginia, the flower of St. Jo.!" said young Campau.

"Was there ever such stuff as this talked before?" said Jagger, with much disgust. "Why, a winner of the Oaks could not be more highly spoken of."

"There have been some not half as good," replied Sassafras.

"I've been mistaken in this man," said Jagger to Kirby. "He's a bigger fool than you, or Staples."

The hunter was about to make a rough and rude reply, when Keeps interfered:

"Listen! listen! Sassafras is going to speak. Hear all and say nothing."

"The challenge is made, coupled with the exception. What I said I'll stand to. Any horse west of the Mississippi river except one," said Sassafras.

"And what one may the excepted horse be?" asked Jagger.

"Well, sir! your own—the White Horse. I have a high opinion of him, and cannot tell how good he may be," replied Sassafras. "Besides, with the science and skill of Epsom and Newmarket against her in the way of training, Virginia would be under another great disadvantage. Therefore the exception holds."

"Keeps, this man is no fool!" said Jagger. He then exclaimed: "Sassafras, you are a good fellow, and fairly wise for your limited experience. I'll treat all hands upon it."

There was a hum of applause, and the butts of several rifles fell upon the floor, testifying the emphatic approbation of their owners at this announcement. They drank, and drank deeply.

Jagger began to brag of the races he had won and the feats he had performed with the White Horse in England.

"He is responsible for the deaths of two noblemen, and was the cause of the breaking up of the ministry," said Jagger. "They couldn't pay their losses when he won the Ascot Cup. One of 'em took prussic acid, and the other blowed his brains out at the Lord Mayor's dinner-table. Sassafras had better not match him, I can tell you."

"You're right, Mr. Grosvernor," said Sassafras. "Prussic acid wouldn't agree with me, and I've a notion it's better to blow out another man's brains than my own. If I was to match Virginia against your horse I should want a heap of odds in the weights as well as the stakes. He looks like a grand horse, and I reckon you have got him into fine condition."

"I have, by following my own method. I have refused to listen to Staples, and have got the horse in better order than you ever saw a racer before. I was my own trainer in England."

"I told Black Dick how it was," said Sassafras. "I said this horse has had the grand preparation by the English method." (He had really said: "Dick, there's a horse that looks well outwardly, but he's fat inside, and couldn't last in a good race.") "However," continued Sassafras, "next to winning with a right good horse is being beaten by one. Since the horse is so famous, and has come so far, it would be a pity to let him go away without running against him once. We are up here in the woods and out on the prairies, and few of us may ever see one of his stamp again. Now, if you'll give me forty pounds the best of the weights, and bet me two to one in the stakes, I'll run Virginia against him, two-mile heats."

"I could beat her easily enough," said Jagger, "for I should ride him myself; but I'll make no match of that sort."

"I have another proviso to mention," said Sassafras. "If I lose, as no doubt I shall, you shall tell me all about your method of training. Give us some more whiskey here, and we'll have a match somehow."

Jagger drank again, and then held a whispering consultation with Kirby and Keeps. These worthies strongly advised the making of another match, seeing in it the probable source of much whiskey and some money. But Keeps protested against acceding to the terms mentioned by Sassafras. " Let us," said he, " hold out for even weights. The odds in money is nothing. It makes no difference what you lay when you are dead sure to win. Sassafras will refuse to strike hands for even weights, but you can afford to stand out as long as he can. The night is young yet, and we're in no hurry."

" That's it !" said Kirby. " I'll stay here all night before anybody shall get the better of Mr. Grosvernor in anything. Meantime there's plenty of whiskey in the store, and by calling for it often we can make Sassafras drunk. Once get him drunk, and he'll agree to anything you may choose to stand out for. Eh, Keeps ?"

The latter made no reply, but his look seemed to intimate that in a drinking match between Jagger and Sassafras, the former would be drunk first. Returning to the group in the centre of the room, Jagger said : " I will make this race on the condition that each horse shall carry the weights for The Whip at Newmarket, ten stun, which is one hundred and forty pounds, you know. My horse holds The Whip now. I challenged for it, named him, and it was resigned by the Duke of Grafton without a race. I was sorry for the Duchess," continued the veracious Jagger, "as an old friend, I may say relative. She was much vexed at their having to give up the trophy. In fact, I brought the White Horse from England in order that, he being out of the way, the Duke may have a chance to win the prize again. He had none whatever while I was there."

" I should think not ! but what has that got to do with a race between us, four thousand miles away ?" said Sassafras.

" It has this to do," replied Jagger, pompously : " I should lose standing in the Jockey Club, if I ran the winner of The Whip with less than ten stun."

" I don't ask you to carry less," said Sassafras ; " but I reckon the Jockey Club won't care what an old gray mare, owned on the outskirts of the American settlements, and run in the Indian country, carries. Let the horse carry one hundred and forty pounds, and the mare one hundred pounds. That will be the fair thing!"

" I will make no match if it be not even weights, ten stun each," replied Jagger. " I don't care about running here at all, especially heats. There's a sort of barbarity in it, and it'll be positive cruelty to the mare in this instance."

" Well, she may save her bacon by cooking mine, and get clean distanced in the first heat," said Sassafras.

" I may choose to distance her, or I may not," said Jagger, complacently. " If I make a waiting race, she will not be distanced; if the horse comes away with the running, she will be. But it would be an inglorious conquest for me, and I do not care about running the horse at all. I have trained him for amusement merely, and would not match him at home for less than a thousand guineas a side."

" There must be a heap of money in your country; we are poor folks here," returned the border man. " Still, if we can agree about weights, I'll try to make it worth your while, by consenting that the winner shall have both horses, as well as the stakes. Now you will give me the forty pounds?"

" I'll give nothing! nothing! I hate giving!" cried Jagger. " Nobody proposes to give anything to me."

" Ain't there though?" said Kirby, aside. " I've promised you a h—l of a licking, for cheating me at cribbage, and then blackguarding me to the old man."

" Look here!" said Keeps to Jagger, " split the difference, and give him twenty pounds in weight. What's the odds, when you are sure to win?"

" Why, certainly it matters but little, for a ton would not bring the horses together, under the different methods of training," replied Jagger. " But I concede nothing in the way of weight. It is a condescension in me, which Sassafras don't deserve, to make a race with him at all, and if I do it, I'll have my way."

The Western man heard the latter part of Jagger's remarks, and a biting reply had almost escaped him. He controlled his rising anger, however, and said, " Why! I thought it was altogether different in your country. We have heard that there, if a man was passably well behaved, and had the horse to do it, he could run and win against the very best in the land. They have told us that Eclipse himself, though bred by a royal duke, was owned and run by a butcher; and I have heard say that the prize-fighter who licked Gregson has often in races beat George the King."

"Not in matches, young man!" returned Jagger, snappishly. "A gentleman of my rank and standing in the country would hardly condescend to make a match with you in England."

"I reckon that's so!" replied Sassafras, significantly. "But here we are in America, four or five thousand miles from England, and well on towards the heart of the continent. If it comes to rank and standing here, Cinnamon is the greatest man among us. But that's neither here nor there. What you propose as to weights is hardly reasonable. Virginia would have to carry thirty or forty pounds of dead weight, enough to beat almost any horse."

"Ride her yourself, and she need carry none. I intend to ride the White Horse," replied Jagger.

"I reckon it would be hardly wise for me to ride against you, from what I have seen of you in the saddle. Newmarket against St. Jo. is too steep, unless it was in a buffalo hunt. I ought, by rights, to have another Englishman to ride against you, but I'll warrant you can't tell me where to get one who is qualified just now. Therefore, you ought to give twenty pounds in weight, as against Black Dick, to say nothing of the difference between our horses. Come here, Dick!"

The one eye of the negro had flashed from Sassafras to Jagger, and from the latter to Sassafras, like a dancing jack-o'-lantern in a dark night, during the latter part of the discussion. He stood on the outer circle of the listeners, but his master now stretched forth his hand and hauled him into the centre of the throng, saying:

"Do you think I ought to run Virginia against the White Horse at less than thirty or forty pounds, Dick?"

"I think I nebber run 'e mar' agen 'e White Horse at all. A darkey knows beans when de bag is open!" replied Dick.

"Good, ebony, good! Give the blackamoor a drink, there!" cried Jagger.

"Who 'e call blackamoor?" said Dick, in his sulkiest tone. "Don't raise 'e blackamoor in Ole Virginia, I reckon."

"Never mind!" said Sassafras. "Drink to Mr. Grosvernor and the White Horse! And never contradict a gentleman of high degree from the old country, if he should be pleased to call you the d—l himself."

"De debbel hisself no fool!" said the black; "'e nebber run agen 'e White Horse!"

There was a laugh as Dick said this, and Jagger was especially merry.

"You hear what the boy says—how can you insist on even weights?" said Sassafras.

"For the same reason that you desire to run heats—it's my fancy; and I'll have the match no other way," replied Jagger.

"Wait a few minutes, and I'll decide," said Sassafras.

He took aside Cinnamon, Campau and Black Dick, to hold a consultation in his turn. Campau talked rapidly in whispers. The Indian delivered his opinion in just six words: "Virginia beat the Snake-Eye's horse!" Black Dick was understood by the by-standers to urge objections and remonstrances to the end, but they were overruled by Campau. Sasfras looked grave. He weighed the reasons advanced by his followers, and, as usual with great men and commanders, found none sufficient to set aside the resolution he had come to before he asked his friends and subordinates for their advice. He passed into the centre of the eager throng and said:

"Mr. Grosvernor, I accept the conditions—Virginia against the White Horse at even weights, one hundred and forty pounds each, one thousand dollars a side in money, and the winner to take both horses. To run this day week; two-mile heats."

"Very well!" said Jagger, after having been whispered to by Keeps and Kirby; "but the match shall be play or pay, and the money shall be put up now."

This was agreed to. The minute was made and the money staked with the manager.

"What a fool he is!" said Jagger, as Sassafras left the place with Black Dick.

As they passed along towards their own camp they came suddenly upon Cinnamon, Pierre Langlois and the young Kiowa. Sassafras was about to seize the latter, but thought better of it. He said good-night to the chief and went on towards his own camp. As they neared it the one-eyed black spoke:

"Massa, I don't know 'bout dis yere match. The folks away down in Ole Virginia allus say de good English horse can beat de good horse of de States. Dey say dat in King George."

"I know it," said Sassafras, "and we are in deep water now. But it's to be heats, Dick; and that fellow can neither train nor ride. You can outride him."

"Ay, but de dead weight—forty pounds. Besides, I brieve dat White Horse to be a good 'un. I see him run through dat stretch faster than a buck. I brieve he outrun de mar' anywhere."

"But it's heats, and he'll be in no condition."

"De mar' 'll be in no condition when she's carried me and forty pounds dead weight two miles."

"Hush! I hear a man in the bushes. Say nothing to anybody, especially as to their horse's want of condition."

The man in the bushes was Captain Staples. He was not in an amiable frame of mind. Jagger's talk had enraged him; he was suspicious of Sassafras, and he was irritated because he had been waiting long. The Western man dismissed the negro and said:

"Well, captain, what's the word to-night?"

"The first word is that I want two hundred and fifty dollars of you," said Staples. "You have drawn the money, and short settlements make long friends."

"Drawn the money—yes! but I have staked it again, and as much more, to make up your part in a match for a thousand a side."

"My part! Who gave you authority to make matches for me?" said Staples.

"You did. Are we not partners in this little scheme to relieve Reginald What-you-may-call of some of his ready money?"

"That's as may turn out. I doubt whether your old mare can beat that White Horse the race you've made."

"You know what it is, then?" said Sassafras.

"Ay, I heard of it as soon as you agreed, and have been in the brush on the hill, like a fox prowling round a camp-fire, ever since. The Cheyennes came near where I lay once; it was well they didn't stumble on me."

"It was, captain," said Sassafras; "for if they had, your scalp would have been at one of their belts by this time, in the event of your bringing on a fight."

" It might. They're here in numbers, and the chief is as sassy as if the continent was owned by him. But what a fool you were to agree to carry a hundred and forty pounds! The old mare will be licked into fits, unless something is done."

" I don't say she isn't beatable, but I couldn't stand the bragging of that English lord. I am an American—a man raised in Old Virginia—and nobody shall overcrow me without being called to show his hand."

" I honor them sentiments," said Captain Staples. " My patriotism is well known, too, and I'll show it by keeping as much of this British gold in the country as I can. But what possessed you to make such a fool's match as this? You've got nobody to ride."

" There's lead enough at the fort to make Black Dick the weight," said Sassafras.

" Black Dick—black devil! The Englishman has ridden in matches for thousands of guineas—at least he says so— and shall Black Dick, with forty pounds of dead weight, be put up against him?"

" What can I do?"

" Pay forfeit. The Englishman will then be so full of conceit that he'll make another match on better terms for you, and for twice as much, I say, pay forfeit."

" There is no forfeit. The match is, play or pay. The money up."

" Then the Englishman has got you," said Staples, with a show of disgust. " I'm d——d if you ain't damaged the Western turf and disgraced the country worse nor Old Hull when he surrendered to the British and that red devil Tecumseh. I ain't in it, and I must have my money before it comes off."

" I might very well dispute that, and the forty Cheyennes would stand by me," said Sassafras; " but take your own way. You always undervalued the mare. Suit yourself as to whether you'll go in or not. You musn't play fast and loose up to the race though. In three days I must have your answer—ay or no. If you say no, I shall be able to carry it on alone; and then, sink or swim, let the hardest fend off."

" But you've no right to carry it on alone, if you can carry it on to win," said Staples. " I brought the Englishman and his money up into this country, and have got a lien upon 'em. Nobody must disregard my rights."

"Nobody wants to."

"They had better not want to. No race will come off, if I tell the Englishman not to run."

"Perhaps not," said Sassafras. "But in that case a thousand dollars of his gold and his White Horse will come off. Keeps advised the making of it play or pay, and the gentleman insisted upon it."

"Keeps is a villain and Kirby is a bull-head; I tell you that in confidence, though I dare say you have suspected as much yourself," said the old man. After a pause, he added: "I'd sooner be in with you than anybody, Sassafras. In deep —and safe, safe! You work the mare three or four days, and then I'll tell you what I propose to do. Work her good and strong four days."

"I said I wanted your answer in three days—four will not do," said Sassafras.

"Well, well! You young men are so suspicious of your elders, not to say betters—I mean in wisdom and virtue. You might trust to my honor for six days, I should think, if it came to that. But you young men lack faith and confidence in other people. It's a great misfortune. When I was your age, I was the confidingest mortal that ever was. But the world has growed worse fast since then."

"Looking at what you are now, I should think it has," said Sassafras. "But never mind, captain! We will endeavor to recoup ourselves for the degeneracy of all, by winning this man's thousands, and a good deal more."

"Out of each thousand won, I am to have six hundred," said Staples. "That is the agreement, you know."

"Ay! and I know you are to have the Englishman's horse in your stable," said Sassafras. "But, Staples, I'm opposed on principle to dosing."

"Dosing be d——d! who said anything about dosing?" said Staples. "I hate to hear the thing mentioned, especially when a bucket of water or the accidental slipping of the muzzle may do just as well. Work the mare—work her good and strong! I begin to think she may win. Good-night!"

As the old man moved off rapidly, Sassafras stood and looked

12

after him, until his form was lost in the dusky light and mist that hung over the prairie. The slight rustle of leaves and boughs in the bushes close at hand caught the Western man's ear, and he saw the young Kiowa stealing swiftly but cautiously away. With a bound like the spring of a panther, Sassafras went through the underbrush, and took after him. The youth was swift of foot, but not so swift as the powerful frontier man, especially over the broken ground and through the bushes. The latter gained on the boy, whose hard breathing he could already hear. His hand was ready to be stretched out to grasp the flying youth, when another figure suddenly started up, and caught Sassafras in its arms. It was the Indian chief.

CHAPTER XX.

"Kingly his crest, and towards-the West,
With his battle-axe he pointed."

IT was the golden evening of the western day towards the fall of the year, and the foliage of the woods was rich with varied tints, and full of gorgeous colors. The sun touched the horizon in the west, and fell upon a slope of wooded land which declined into a thickly-timbered valley. Some of the trees, without having lost their freshness, seemed to have caught the rich hues of the sky. The great white-oaks, however, retained their glossy green. In the large black-walnut trees the squirrels were busy, as if preparing for and rejoicing over the harvest which was ripening on the wide-spreading branches. A light breeze played among the boughs of the loftiest trees and rustled the crimson leaves of the gigantic creepers which had twined and wreathed to the tops of the monarchs of the wood. It did not reach the young saplings which had sprung up thick from the rich mould of so many generations of their ancestors. Here at once went on the shoot of infancy, the rise of aspiring youth, the strength of middle life, the ripening of autumn, the wither of age, and the rot, mould and decay from which sprang the resurrection. And thus, saith the great poet of antiquity, it was with the human species :

" Like leaves on trees the race of man is found,
    Now green in youth, now withering on the ground."

Upon this wooded slope François and Tom Scarlet had lit
their camp-fire at the close of the first day's hunt. It had
been successful. Several turkeys had fallen to the buckshot
from the smooth-bore of the young Englishman, and a small
ball from the heavy rifle of the Frenchman had brought a
fat buck down. Their kettle had sung merrily over the crack-
ling fire, the venison steaks had been toasted, the evening meal
was done. The sun had gone down over the hills and woods
which stretched away like the dark billows of a great green
sea towards the west. The stars came out in the clear sky
unveiled by cloud or mist. Upon the still air of the open
places of the woods the scent of wild flowers and fragrant
shrubs was quickened by the falling dew. A drowsy hum of
insects was heard in the low leaves ; the owl swept by on noiseless wing and disappeared again like a spectre among the silvery trunks of the trees. Once the long howl of the wolf
came from the rugged ground of the pass above. The plaintive cry of whip-poor-will was often heard from the depths
of the forest, as in warning or lament over the sojourners in
the waste.

"How beautiful the night is, François! How grand and
solemn these great woods seem in which we are alone—all, all
alone!" said Tom Scarlet. "It was worth the voyage from
England and the journey from the sea-coast to be in such a
scene. It seems as though we, of all men, had been admitted
by nature into one of her secret, solitary places to see and feel
her truths. François, the Druids and the old Scandinavian
races did well to make the deep oak woods their solemn temples."

"It may be so," replied the Frenchman, " but you may find
some things here natural, withal, but not pleasant. Throw a
blanket over your shoulders, and then draw into the curl of
the smoke and heat of the fire as I do. The calmness and
beauty of the night are hardly greater than its danger to one
unacclimated like you. These still, beautiful nights in the
early fall sow the poison which ferments in the blood to bring
on the deadly chill and the consuming fever."

"So I have heard you say before. Yet it seems hardly possible that, under such a sky, and in such a scene, glorious but now with the splendor of the dying day, danger can lurk. We are upon the upland."

"And therefore more exposed to the breath which breeds the fever than if we were in the valley, or on a bit of dry ground in the middle of a swamp. The places and the hours most beautiful are here, like the tiger and the painted snake, the most dangerous. In a night of storm you would run no risk."

"But for all that, I cannot but admire the beauty of the star-lit sky, as I see it from beneath the arms of the mighty oak under which we rest, and feel the influence of the time and scene."

"Tom," said François, with decision, "we cannot afford to have you laid up with the bilious fever, or even with the ague, active or dumb; therefore, a cup of whiskey, well-flavored with the snake-root and the bitter bark of the wauhu, thence to bed upon the green brush, wrapped in a horseman's blanket, and with your feet to the glowing fire."

"The dose is very unpalatable, François, but I owe it to Sassafras and you to be careful, so I'll take it."

The still night wore on. Tired by the exertions of the day, satisfied by a full meal of venison, and all alone, as they believed, the Englishman and the Frenchman, born of the civilization of the west of Europe, where commerce, the sciences, and the arts had made their home, while the owls and foxes inherited the temples and palaces of the east, slept side by side in the land of the stranger. It was past the hour of twelve, the dead time of the night. The fire had burned low; there was no longer a blaze to cast its cheerful glare abroad into the bushes. The slumber of the Englishman was less profound, and through the restless brain there were visions swiftly passing. He dreamed of home and some vague calamity; of fire on shipboard—"'twixt the green sea and the azur'd vault,"—of Indian raids and midnight massacres; he heard the war-whoop ringing through the arches of the forest—saw the wild riders rushing like a whirlwind over the prairie to swoop down upon their prey. At length he awoke, and turned upon his back. Looking down upon him as he lay there stood a tall Indian, leaning on his gun. The young man sprang up with a cry to François. The Indian, without moving, said in broken English :

"What fears the Golden Bough? The Cheyenne is his friend. He looked upon the faces of those who slept, and they were safe."

"Cinnamon," said François, "as a friend we know you ; but what brings you here to-night?"

"The friend of Sassafras from the great river and the Golden Bough shall hear," replied the Indian. "But I will call my companion."

He put his hand to his mouth, and uttered a peculiar cry. An answer was heard at no great distance. In a few moments there was a rustling of the bushes, and the young Kiowa, painted as a brave upon his first war-path, came into the circle of light. François started, and said :

"Has the chief of the Cheyennes made ready the battle-axe, and prepared to loosen the arrow from the string of the bone bow?"

"No," replied the Indian, pointing to the youth ; "but the Young Eagle of the Kiowas, who live among the lofty mountains, whose horses drink above the Great Bend and of the sweet waters of the great river of the South, was pursued by Sassafras. The chief of the Cheyennes stayed the white man's hand, and kept the Young Eagle from his grasp. Was it good, François? Say, O! Golden Bough, was it good?"

"It was ; for Cinnamon is wise and just," said François. "Sassafras is his friend. They struck the Sioux together, and they mingled with the dark waters of the river the blood of the Blackfeet warriors."

"It is true," said the Indian. "In the morning François and the Golden Bough shall turn upon their trail, and rejoin Sassafras. The Wolverine and the Snake-Eyes have put a cloud between Sassafras and the Cheyennes. With the Young Eagle of the Kiowas I will rest by your fire till the sun has risen over the great river, and touched the hill-tops. Is Cinnamon welcome?"

"He is," replied François, while Tom Scarlet took the hand of the chief. The Frenchman added to Tom, "Mischief is brewing through the acts of Staples. But that Sassafras, knowing the man, should have listened to him, passes my comprehension."

" Ay, and Jagger too!" said Tom Scarlet. " The chief calls him the Snake-Eyes, and mentioned him also."

" If Sassafras has allowed them to bring him into feud with Cinnamon, he has gone crazy," said François. " But I cannot believe it; I will not, unless he says so himself."

" The cloud will pass away," said the proud Cheyenne, " and the dark shadow of the night give place to the brightness of the ripening day. Let the Golden Bough tell me of his country beyond the great salt water; of the home of his fathers, and of the fair maiden of his love. Let the Indian of the wide plains and lofty mountains hear of the island of the sea." With this he filled his pipe and began to smoke, while the young Kiowa, who had hitherto stood rather aloof, advanced and seated himself by his side.

" Tom, do you amuse the chief!" said François. " He will understand almost all you say. He has come, you see, to stop the breeding of bad blood between himself and Sassafras. We will all start back soon after it is light. While you interest the chief, I will talk to the Young Eagle of the Kiowas."

" François," said Cinnamon, " the eagle understands not the cry of the hawk, or the call of the swan in the morning mist, when the snow lies on the mountain tops. No white man, and but few Indians of other tribes, have learned the tongue of the Kiowas. Those you have heard talked the language of the Comanches. The Young Eagle speaks only as his fathers spoke; his ears are open to no other tongue."

" That's true enough, as far as it goes," said François. " I have always heard that mortal man, whether red, white or black, could never master the lingo spoken by the Kiowas as their own. Go on, Tom."

The young Englishman was always ready to talk of his country and his friends. He now spoke of such things as he believed to be most likely to interest the Indian and the white hunter who heard him. The little island in the stormy seas, with its white cliffs gleaming through the mist; the beauties of its hills and dales, its woods and pleasant homes; its vast population and inestimable wealth; the stately buildings of London; the hoary edifices of Oxford, solemn and grand in their venerable antiquity; the princely country-houses and parks, Blenheim and Stowe. And then he told of the enormous commerce and possessions of vast extent all over the globe; of England's powerful fleets; of Waterloo, and the Irish major, a friend of his own, who had lost an arm and won a medal there; of Sir Jerry and Lady Snaffle, and her father, the fine old Admiral, who had sailed and fought all his life; of John Bullfinch, and his daughter May, and all the pleasant walks about Hawkwell; of his own home, the lone Grange, near the wild heath; of the green lanes and shady nooks, where the gypsies camped, and he had often lingered by the tents to play with the young children and laugh with the dark-eyed maidens just come from the copse a-nutting. And thus his tale and talk went on, as such do in many a hut and tent in distant lands, and on the decks of many ships in far-off waters, until the young Kiowa rose abruptly and broke up the narrative by throwing a pile of brush on the fire.

When Sassafras found on the preceding night that it was Cinnamon who held him in his grasp, and prevented him from further pursuit of the Kiowa youth, he was surprised and a little indignant. When the chief released him he demanded an explanation, which was what the Indian could not give. He pointed to the route the boy had taken, and said, with a low voice:

" The son of the great chief of the Kiowas is the guest and friend of the Cheyennes. He must be as safe as at his father's side, with five hundred horsemen of his tribe around him. Cinnamon must keep him from harm at the hand of Sassafras."

" Harm !" replied the latter; " who wants to harm him ? I think he should be made to mind his own business, that's all. I wish he was safe enough with his father, whoever that may be. I saw the great chief of the Kiowas, when he watered his horses in the Red river, and I do not believe this sprig of maple to be his son. Cinnamon, you are deceived in him! The boy is not what he seems, and I conceive that he is some sort of a spy. He was lurking about to hear what passed between Staples and me, not a quarter of an hour ago."

"Cinnamon is not deceived," replied the chief. " I will answer for this boy. My life is the pledge for his truth. Why should you think he was there to listen ? The young Kiowa understands no English."

"And I say this boy understands English as well as, if not

better than, you do. He was hid in the brush, like a fox, while I was talking with Staples, and it was not until the old man had gone that he tried to steal in silence away."

"It was near your camp! Sassafras, I think he wanted to look upon the guest of my friend. He likes to see the Golden Bough, the first Englishman he ever met, except the Snake-Eyes, whom he despises. I will find out."

The chief went up the hill. Sassafras, somewhat angry, and much perplexed, sought his tent for repose.

It was night again. After a busy day spent with Jules, Black Dick and the favorite gray mare Virginia, the border man sat by the fire in front of his tent. The night was clear and star-lit, the air brisk and chilly. The half-breed boy from the fort was at the shoulder of Sassafras, as the latter read and re-read a brief note he had brought.

"You say Campau gave you this, Joe? Did he send any message about it, or about anybody?"

"He say, 'Take this to Sassafras. Let him read alone and do what is said.'"

"It is in the same hand, and comes from the same person as the other letter you brought here, Joe."

"Yes, from Campau—he give it to me."

"Joe, is the young Kiowa with Campau?" said Sassafras.

"He is not. I have not to-day seen him—nor yesterday. I like not the Kiowa. His tribe killed my fader above the Big Bend, because he was a white man, like you."

"Well, you'll be man enough to get even some of these days," replied Sassafras. "The note makes a good suggestion—one that I ought to have thought of before, whoever the writer may be. I may take it, and better the instruction. Joe, good-night. Tell no one you were here or that anybody sent a letter from the fort."

The boy nodded and went silently off into the darkness, with the footfall of a cat, and an eye as capable of seeing at such times as those of the feline tribes, the night wanderers. By the large but fading fire, Sassafras sat smoking and musing until it was near midnight. He was about to rise and enter his tent, when his quick ear caught the tread of horses on the saddle which joined the two hills, and formed the background of the valley in which he had made his camp.

It was a sound he never mistook, for from his earliest boy-hood the step of the horse had been music in his ears. He seized his rifle, withdrew into the shade, and awaited the new-comers. As they approached, he found from the voices with which they conversed in low and guarded tones, that the horsemen were François and Tom Scarlet.

"Hail, friends! why so soon returned? Are there no deer in the woods? Does no track of elk point for the Neosho?"

"There were deer, there were turkeys—the hunting would have been good," replied François, as they dismounted, "but, Sassafras, we came back at the bidding of Cinnamon, who reached us last night, after the turning of the time well to-wards the coming day."

"Yes, we were sleeping by our fire," said Tom Scarlet. "I had dreamed bad dreams, and when I awoke the Cheyenne chief was looking down upon me as I lay."

"Ay!" exclaimed Sassafras. "But that I know the chief, I might have thought such dreams would have been no worse than the awakening by brand and beneath glittering steel. François, how was it that you let an Indian come upon your camp in such a manner that he might have lifted your scalps and gone again, unheard, unseen, as the light wind of the night goeth?"

"I knew you would say that," replied the Frenchman. "It is provoking, and I do not think any one but Cinnamon could have found our fire and come upon us unheard. I am a light sleeper, and the rustle of the leaves by anything other than the wind will awaken me. The truth is, we were tired by our fast journey and a long hunt afterwards. I had no thought that there was Indian or white man within many miles of us when we laid down to rest."

"And Cinnamon brought you back? For what purpose?"

"Speak, Tom; you know what he said," replied François.

"I will," said Tom Scarlet. "He thought we ought to return here, Sassafras, to remove a difference—a sort of mis-understanding—which has arisen between you and him. He says the Wolverine and the Snake-Eyes have put a cloud before the eyes of his friend, and evil may come of it."

"The cloud is before his own eyes," said Sassafras. "I too have been like one from whom things were hid by mist, but I now see the light through the breaks and rifts. Look here! This note, received by me a short time ago—two or three hours—is signed by the name of Campau, but the hand is that of the writer who sent us letters from New Orleans. This letter-writer I believe to be the boy now masquerading here, as if it was *Mardi-gras*, in the form of a young Kiowa. He raised the cloud between Cinnamon and me."

"Sassafras, it cannot be," said François. "The young Kiowa came with Cinnamon to our camp last night, and has but now returned. We left them behind yonder hill, and I doubt whether they have reached their own camp yet."

"Then I am again at sea," replied Sassafras. "I thought I had it all clear before you came back, although I was told the Kiowa had not been seen at the fort these two days. I am now like the justice, when the last witness had involved the case in contradiction and confusion. 'It was,' said his honor, 'plain enough until you thrust your spoke into the wheel to bother the court and everybody else. I've a great mind to fine and commit you for contempt.' But you must be tired and hungry. Call the boys to look to your horses. Eat, drink and rest. I will see the chief myself to-night. It grows late,

> "'But, notwithstanding, haste, make no delay :
> We may complete this business yet ere day.'"

With this quotation on his lips, the borderer arose and walked away. Tom Scarlet would have stopped him, but the Frenchman interposed to prevent, saying it was better Sassafras and the chief should meet speedily, and alone. He ascended the hill with long strides, and overlooking from the summit the fires of the Indians in the valley below he saw two horsemen alight near the centre of the camp. Putting his forefingers into his mouth, Sassafras whistled so loud and shrill that the Cheyennes started from their slumbers, and the echoes awoke among the neighboring hills.

"He comes!" said Cinnamon to the Kiowa youth. "It is good. Let the Young Eagle go into the tent, and see not the white warrior of the great river and the chief of the Cheyennes until the cloud between them has passed away!"

The youth made no reply, save by a pressure of the hand. He moved off to another tent, and entered it, before Sassafras came up to the one near which Cinnamon stood. When these two met they were both grave, it may be said dignified, for the white man moved and spoke with conscious courage and integrity; while the Indian, with friendship and devotion unimpaired, had also the sense of power.

"Sassafras is welcome to the camp of the Cheyennes," said the chief. "It is his home—the home of his brother, whose life he saved when the hatchet of the Sioux was swung."

"For the matter of that, Cinnamon, I owe my life twice over to you," replied Sassafras. "But for your timely aid, when my gun missed fire and the knife fell from my wounded hand, my bones had been ground in the den of the great grizzly bear in the Rocky Mountains. And again, but for you my scalp had been drying long ago in the smoke of a Blackfoot lodge, t'other side of Hell Gate Pass and the British line."

"It's enough! We are friends! We are brothers!" replied Cinnamon. "I have said it, and sworn it by the head of the Red Horse. The cloud has passed away. Sassafras has seen the Golden Bough, for whose affairs the Cheyennes followed their chief from the Fork of the Salmon. His enemies are bad men. They are the enemies of Cinnamon and his young men, and of Sassafras. Why should I not kill the Wolverine and the Snake-Eyes before the sun comes up from the hills near the great river to look again upon his lands in the golden west? We could then follow in his course."

It was not the first time Sassafras had heard something like this proposition, but the Indian had never before come out so "flat-footed," as the former called it. The truth was, the chief was getting tired of inaction. A few sharp blows would have pleased him much, and he could then have mustered his band and turned their horses' heads toward the West with great satisfaction. Sassafras, however, could not accede to this method of settling the affair. As to Staples and Jagger, if it became necessary to do so, Sassafras was fully resolved to "deal with them in steel," as honest Touchstone hath it; but his present aim was to "overrun them with policy, and bandy with them in treason."

"Cinnamon, it will not do; that is, not at present," said he. "The work goes well. In four or five days we shall see the end. I think I shall win our whole venture. If Staples then chooses to draw and fight, he may. But he will not do so. He fears you, and he fears me. His hope was to raise a misunderstanding between us. That is futile. Those who might venture to back him in some cases, will not do so here. They are cowed by the presence of your band. The best of them would wilt at the whoop of the wild Cheyennes when your young men had their war-paint on."

The eye of the chief glowed proudly in the red light of the fire, and yet he seemed to be a little disappointed that there was no immediate chance of dealing with the Wolverine and the Snake-Eyes, after his own summary plan.

"Sassafras loves the Golden Bough as one of his own blood," said he, after a pause.

"You may well think so, yet he is no kin to me, and five months ago I had not seen him. But we met. He was a stranger, in a strange land; come over the great salt waters which are wider than all the plains. He was open-hearted and free-spoken. Wrong had been done him in his own country. The Golden Bough had been rifled and robbed of fair fruit by the Snake-Eyes, and had followed him to this land. To prevent more wrong and utter failure, I took upon myself the guiding of this business, and sent to you to meet us here."

"It is good," said the .Indian.

"It is. You came, the best and boldest of the chiefs who hunt upon the plains between the great river and the lofty mountains of the Rocky range."

"I say that it is good," replied Cinnamon. "When the Wolverine and the Snake-Eyes are beaten, and the Golden Bough goes with his own again to the great salt water, let Sassafras ride with me and my young men towards the West. The buffalo in autumn are plenty on my plains as the leaves on the trees. The elk of my hills are big and fat; their antlers are tall. The evening sky is very red when the sun goes over the tops of the great mountains. When the snow lies upon the plains there is grass for our horses in the parks. My tent is very warm in the frosty days of the winter. Let my friend send his Frenchmen and his black men to Missouri with the Golden Bough, and ride with me to my home in the West."

"Cinnamon, I should like it of all things, and next year I

will try to arrange my affairs so that I can spend the winter with you," replied Sassafras. " We will hunt the grizzly bears again, just before they retire to their inaccessible holds to lie and sleep through the cold weather."

" My friend shall be welcome as the melting of the snows in spring, when the sun shines warm and large," said the Indian.

" Then here good-night. We meet to-morrow," said Sassafras, as he left the chief.

CHAPTER XXI.

" Go, make thyself like a nymph o' the sea; be subject
To no sight but mine and thine."

THE plans of Sassafras had been changed in reference to the race between the White Horse and the mare Virginia by the note he received at night from the fort, and by the unexpected but opportune return of Tom Scarlet and François. Although it was very late when he returned from the Indian camp, he was up soon after break of day, and arousing Tom Scarlet and François, he called them to a council in his tent.

' " It is," said he, " a good thing that you have returned, for though there was no need of any pacificators between Cinnamon and me, there will be use for Tom that I did not think of. You must, however, be still unknown to Jagger, Staples, and all their set."

" Then your interview with the chief was satisfactory to you both !" said Tom Scarlet.

" Entirely so ; in fact, there has been no trouble between the chief and me, except a little difference of opinion as to that boy. We have been friends so long, and stood together in such dangers and difficulties, that no little matter would bring us to a quarrel, or even to a coolness."

" Did you see the Kiowa last night ?" said François.

" No. Tell me, what did he say or do—how did he look and act when at your camp ?"

" He said nothing. He talks neither English nor Cheyenne, you know," replied Tom Scarlet.

" I know it is so said, but I don't believe a word of it," said Sassafras. " How did he look and act ?"

"He looked the same as before, but François says he was in war-paint."

"War-paint! What foolery is this? I know that Cinna mon isn't going to let him make war with me. I've a good mind to arm young Joe, whose father was killed by the Kiowas above the Great Bend, and let these two cockerells fight it out!"

"It would be dangerous," said François.

"It would," replied Sassafras. "If blood were once drawn here, there is no knowing where the slaughter might stop. Cinnamon himself proposed the killing of Staples and Jagger last night. But why was the boy taken to your camp at all, if he cannot understand what Cinnamon or anybody else says, and nobody can understand him?"

"We don't know," replied Tom Scarlet. "For my part, I rather like the lad, and wish he could understand what I might say to him. I have seen a smile under his paint and a grati-fied look in his eye when I have made a kindly sign to him. Last night, when I was talking about England, and my part of the country, and friends at home, he sat by the side of Cin-namon, muffled up in his blanket. But he was not asleep, for I could see his eyes at times glowing like live coals as I told my tale."

"Which he couldn't understand! Bah!" said Sassafras. "But no more of him. Cinnamon says he's honest, and that's enough for the present. As he has left the fort for the camp, you may enjoy more of his acquaintance, and commune to-gether as the deaf and dumb do; for you must abide with Cin-namon until the race comes off. You have heard all about it from the chief?"

"Yes; that it is the mare against the White Horse, the winner to have the two horses as well as the stakes. Sassa-fras, I fear you have overmatched her. You don't know how good the horse is."

"And you don't know how good the mare is, especially in a second or third heat. Why, Tom, she'll win it easy. I don't see how she can lose it, in the condition the horse will be. When it is over, as your hunt has been cut short with Fran-çois, I'll take you on a hunt myself; and if we do not find elk on this side of the Neosho, we will cross to the left bank.

You shall have a set of antlers for Sir Jerry Snaffle's ball such as was hardly ever seen in England, and another for the parlor of John Bullfinch, that your lady-love may see the game we sometimes follow in the West. Now to our immediate business. I want you to answer me a few questions."

"As many as you please," said Tom.

"This Jagger gives out that he was a great turfman in England. Is that so?"

"Of course not. He laid a little money, as many men do who can hardly tell a race-horse from a circus nag, and indeed think the latter the better of the two. He was what we call 'a leg;' that is, a rogue who cheats everybody he can, and is himself the fool and dupe of touts."

"Then he never won the Derby, running his horse under another man's name; never challenged for the Whip with this White Horse, and had it resigned to him by the Duke of Grafton, to the imminent danger of the life of the Duchess, through sheer vexation?"

"Derby! Whip! Does the villain say that?"

"Ay, does he! and a great deal more. For instance, he was sorry for the Duchess, a family connection of his own, and brought the White Horse from England as a delicate way of letting the Duke get possession of the Whip again. Now, tell us what this Jagger really is."

"The biggest liar in all this land, for one thing," replied Tom. "He was no horseman at home, and of no more use to the turf than a rat is to a granary."

"Then he is not even a good rider—I mean in a race."

"*He* ride a race—the humbug!"

"Just what I thought, Tom; but he means to ride the White Horse in this match."

"I wish it was a steeple-chase, so that he would have a fine chance to break his neck."

"That might save the hangman some trouble one of these days," said Sassafras, "unless he should hear the war-whoop of the Cheyennes some fine night, and get frightened to death while his neck is whole. Did he ever ride a race in England of any sort?"

"Certainly not! No trainer would let such a muff get on a race-horse, even if it was but to run for a saddle and bridle on

some common at a country fair. He may have been in the
hunting-field a few times, for all sorts of people go out with
the hounds.   But I'll bet a hundred to ten that May Bullfinch
would 'pound' him in ten minutes over our grass lands and
stiff fences.   He is an arrant imposter—that sort of bragging,
vaporing fellow who disgraces Old England in foreign lands."

"In the minds of the inconsiderate only," said Sassafras;
"for reasonable men do not impute the follies of a blockhead
and the lies of a false knave to his country, whatever his
country may be.   I have heard some Americans go on in the
West Indies in such a way that I was almost mad enough to
pistol 'em, or at least to knock 'em in the head and silence
'em for a while; but I never thought the worse of my country,
or my countrymen, on account of the braying of such native
jackasses as these.   Therefore do not mind Jagger.   He may
disgrace himself—England never.   How did the man get
hold of such a stallion as the White Horse?"

"By some transaction with a party who was hard up, and
about to sponge out accounts by going through the insolvent
debtors' court.   I don't believe he was ever on his back in
England.   He can't ride a bit.   Let me ride the mare, Sassafras.   It'll be the richest go that ever was for me to ride Virginia; for I'll manage it so that the White Horse shall run
away with Jagger, and perhaps bolt the course and get distanced."

"What's your weight?"

"I can ride ten stone five with my saddle, to-day, just as I
stand."

"Very well!   You must toddle up and down the hill at the
back of Cinnamon's camp and get that five pounds off.   The
mare carried a hundred and thirty pounds yesterday in her
work and went like a bird.   Nobody knows what she had up
but me and Black Dick besides yourselves, and of course
nobody is to know.   Dick was cased in lead, a Black Knight
in armor.   The mare, though alone, was very free—went
right up to the bit.   In fact she was almost too free, considering that she is a slack goer when there is nothing with her.   I
watch changes of that sort.   When a horse has not done well,
and there is an alteration in his way of going, I like it.   It
indicates improvement.   But when a known good one, that is

in fair condition, changes the style of running, I have my doubts. It may indicate an improvement, but it may be a sign of the reverse. However, the mare always went more freely after she had a race in her; and she knows as well as I do that there is another soon to come off."

"I'll see her gallop to-morrow," said Tom Scarlet.

"You may, but it must be from a tree-top," replied Sassafras. "If Jagger should see you now and recognise you, all our plans might fail. It is true the match is play or pay, but we will avoid all dispute, or wrangle, until it is run. To that end I shall let them believe that they have got the best of it, and avoid showing my own hand until the start. You see, the people at the fort have behaved very well, and the manager and Campau are my friends. A row and a fight would be against their interests; and, as I said before, there is no knowing how red the tomahawks of the Cheyennes would be before it ended, if it once began. Therefore, you must go to the Indian camp within an hour, and stay there as an Indian until I send for you."

"I can see no need for it; I can keep close here, and then you know I can look over the mare every time she gallops. I have had experience, and am a fair judge of condition as work goes on."

"I am sure you are; but nevertheless it is necessary that you leave the mare to me, and just reduce your weight five pounds," said Sassafras. "I have a presentiment that Staples or Jagger, perhaps both, will pay me a visit to-morrow; besides which, that fellow Keeps lurks and pries about here as if he suspected something. Now, he will take good care not to go near Cinnamon's camp; so you must become an Indian."

"That is not possible. I can be no Indian, even in outward appearance. But I have no objection to stay with the chief if he will give me his hospitality. I consider disguise unnecessary."

"And I say it is altogether necessary to the success of my plans, and a proper precaution. I shall want you here just before the race, and in the guise and paint of an Indian, you can visit the fort as well with Cinnamon. Campau knows something of the scheme, and so does Pierre Langlois. Come, François, get you paints and dyes and razor. Red enough he

is already, but not of the real coppery tinge of the Indians of
the plains and mountains. Scarlet by name, scarlet by nature!
Perhaps descended from Robin Hood's bold bowman, Will of
Sherwood Forest. An ancestor to be proud of! Tom, I had
as lieve be descended from one of Robin's merry men as 'fetch
my life and being from men of royal siege.' Go to work,
François. Off with those whiskers. Get your walnut dye
for his hands and arms, neck and face, and your pigment for
his hair. You can make him an Indian good enough for our
use in half an hour."

"I don't fancy this notion," said Tom. "I would much
rather go as I am. Besides, I shall never be able to impose
upon the Indians, and they may take it ill. I may find it
easier to go into their camp in disguise, than to get out again.
The chief himself sometimes has the look of a bloodhound
asleep with his eyes half open, and then again there shoot
such lightning glances from under his brows, that they almost
seem to scorch what they fall upon. He is a good man, no
doubt, but his virtues are those of a savage. You say he proposed to kill Staples and Jagger last night, as a ready, simple,
natural way of settling affairs?"

"So he did! What then?"

"He has not been consulted in this matter, and it may offend
him."

"Nothing of the kind. Your appearance in the paint of
the tribe will please the chief and all his band instead of of-
fending them. Man alive! you don't know the Indians. They
all like the Golden Bough, and will take it as a compliment.
Besides, it will please the young Kiowa from the Southwest,
and most likely get you an invitation to visit his father in the
mountains. That's a smart boy, Kiowa or no Kiowa, and I'll
bet a trifle he don't go from here until we are better acquainted."

François confirmed what Sassafras said in regard to the reception by the Cheyennes, and then Tom Scarlet put on leggings
and moccasins and a hunting-shirt, and suffered the Frenchman to do as he would. François was an expert artist. He
had taste and skill, and in half an hour he had effected such
a change in the appearance of the young Englishman that
there was no probability of his recognition by Jagger or any
one else who might meet him by accident. While the meta-

morphosis was in progress, Sassafras sat in front of Tom and gave François such hints and advice as a connoisseur may offer to a painter when he is putting the last finishing touches to a picture. The transformation completed, Sassafras rose and surveyed his plumed and painted friend with much care and gravity.

"I believe it will do," said he. "The skin is a leetle too dark, to my mind, and the hair a leetle too shiny, but there are worse-looking Indians about here by a mighty sight. The paint is beautiful! beautiful! The Cheyennes will be delighted. On the whole, Tom makes a good Indian of the Western plains, having the proper bow in the legs, the result of being a fine horseman. Taken altogether, the get-up is like the acting of the fellows who play the fool in the circusses which travel the States—too natural. But it will do. Come along now, and we will breakfast with the chief and his young friend from the Southwest."

When they reached the Cheyenne camp, it was easily perceived that the Indians knew who the man in the paint and feathers of their tribe was. This partly arose from his arrival in company with Sassafras and François. The red men seemed pleased, and a little amused. Tom Scarlet immediately declared that the disguise was futile, as everybody seemed to know him.

"Every Cheyenne, you mean," said Sassafras, "which is natural. They know you are not one of themselves well enough; but neither Jagger nor any other stranger would easily discover that fact. They see you with us, too, and that accounts for their actually and readily identifying you."

By this time they had reached the tent of the chief. Cinnamon came out, and welcomed them, taking Tom Scarlet by the hand, and laying his palm upon his shoulder. The young Kiowa avoided them, going off as they came up, with his head down, towards a clump of bushes which was near at hand. Tom Scarlet thought the youth was shy, and had therefore gone away to evade a meeting with a strange Indian, or that he had perhaps left the tent through dislike of Sassafras. The latter had no such idea. He looked keenly at the youth as he walked away, and was convinced that he was merely seeking a place in which to give vent to laughter he was almost unable to suppress where he was.

CHAPTER XXII.

"——Now, whether he kill Cassio,
Or Cassio him, or each do kill the other,
Every way makes my gain."

MORNING came again, lighting up the woods and shedding a golden lustre in the dells and nooks which opened towards the east. Sassafras was early afoot, meditating an important move in the game of strategy he had begun to play against Staples and Jagger. He called for Black Dick, and taking him apart from the other men, gave him such directions, in a few brief, emphatic sentences, as raised the kinks upon the darkey's bullet head, and caused his one eye to assume dimensions approaching that of a Cyclops, while the white of it, in strong contrast with the sooty-black hue of his face, indicated alarm, or enterprise of pith and moment. The other negroes were all ready for duty, and leaving François and Jules in charge of the camp, Sassafras proceeded with the gray mare and her sable train to the race-course. She was prepared for her work, and with a countenance of more than usual gravity, a face which might have been likened to one carved upon a block of ebony, Black Dick mounted. After her canter, she went a mile and a half at three-quarter speed. This was done in the most satisfactory manner; and then she was sent a rattling two-mile gallop at nearly her best rate.

A group of men stood in front of the fort while all this was going on. They took great interest in the proceedings. Some remarked that Sassafrass worked his horses very hard, and took almost too much out of them before the race. The general verdict, however, was to the effect that the mare was very fit, and never went better. But when she was pulled up on the back-stretch of the course, where Sassafras and her attendants were standing, it was plain that something out of the ordinary course had occurred. There was a running to and fro by the negroes. The mare's saddle was hastily taken off, and waving back the man who proffered the bucket and sponge to him, Sassafras went upon his knee and passed his hand several times down over the back tendon of her off fore leg. The spectators at the fort saw all this plainly enough; but when she was blanketed and led away towards her owner's camp by Black Dick, they were unable to see whether she was lame, as Sassafras and the negroes followed her in close array. Ominous nods and whispers were, however, exchanged by these on-lookers, those who had previously mentioned the hard-working system followed by Sassafras saying to the others: "I told you so!" Before the mare had been gone from the course ten minutes Staples had been informed of what had happened, with the usual embellishments and exaggerations, and had sent for Keeps. That worthy was not far off. He and the captain had a consultation, in which the latter delivered certain instructions to his man. In pursuance of these the latter set out for the camp of Sassafras by a roundabout route, taking care to avoid the tents of the Cheyennes and the woods in which they were strolling and shooting at marks. Arrived near the camp of the Western man, Keeps lurked about, concealed by the bushes, for some time, but at last got speech with one of the negroes. The latter was a stout fellow, with a wooden look and a vacant stare. He was commonly regarded as a very thick-headed darkey, with little or none of the cunning and acuteness so often possessed by his race and hidden under a stolid exterior. From this apparently dull and obtuse negro Keeps extracted the intelligence, given with much circumlocution and digression, that the mare had pulled up lame at the end of her two-mile gallop, and that Sassafras, François and Black Dick were fomenting her off fore leg. On receipt of this important piece of news the captain's henchman swore an oath or two of some force, whether expressive of satisfaction or of disappointment and regret was uncertain, for Keeps was accustomed to mark any and every sentiment in this manner. Leaving the dull darkey without ceremony, he set off at his best rate to communicate with his employer. The venerable captain, having heard Keeps to the end, seemed to be involved in doubt and unprepared to come to any decision in this crisis. He wanted time for consideration, and perhaps for the gathering of more facts touching the nature and extent of the injury the mare had suffered.

"Keeps," said he, "say nothing of this at present. There

are plenty of people to do the talking, Keeps—too many ; for the world grows more given to gabbling and spouting every day. You and I are men of action. You had better not mention what you and I know to Mr. Grosvernor. He is now upon the course with his White Horse, and will hear nothing but what you can represent as a vague rumor, most likely started by Sassafras himself to get long odds. If he should once find that the mare is broke down, the Englishman will get so uncommon bumptious that we shall be able to do nothing with him—nothing at all."

The worthy captain then took Keeps into his shanty, and produced a large demijohn of old Bourbon whiskey, which having been taken from the beautiful blue-grass lands of Kentucky, down the Ohio and the Mississippi to New Orleans, and up again to the Arkansas, and along that stream, had acquired such excellence and flavor that it was kept for its owner's private use and entertainment. Of this golden and oily but potent spirit the captain treated his henchman to a cup before he dismissed him. When Keeps was gone, the veteran sat upon a barrel, in the midst of old horse-clothes, saddles, bridles, rusty bits, and empty kegs, smelling strongly of the distilled juice of Indian corn, and pondered over the change which had suddenly come about in the state of affairs. At first he was cheerful, not to say gay. Pouring out a large dram, he quaffed it with a relish, and with a sense of congratulation on the fact that he had carefully avoided committing himself to a partnership with Sassafras in the pending match. "I look before I leap," said he. "Sassafras, and the fools and blackguards of that age, may go it with a rush—the whole hog, as they say at Cincinnati—but none of that for the old man !"

But in the midst of his satisfaction over the fact that he was not "in" with Sassafras, he recollected that he was not "in" with Jagger either. As things were likely to turn out this was a manifest matter of regret ; and besides, the domineering, boasting spirit of the latter was sure to be augmented and inflamed if his horse beat the mare from whom the captain's best racer had lately suffered defeat. Of late these worthies had begun to discuss politics, and had as often quarrelled over the institutions of their respective countries. The captain was

all for republican government, and very dogmatic in his assertions, which he called his reasons. Jagger was voluble in
praise of monarchical institutions. He took under his pro-
tection the king, the aristocracy, and the church, especially
the last, and the bishops, one of whom, he said, was his brother-
in-law. The captain did not like bishops, had "no use for
'em," and his opinion of brothers-in-law was not high, but the
reverse. So the captain saw the almost absolute necessity of
getting "in" with Jagger; but with all his fertility of invention and unscrupulousness he was at fault as to the means.
If he could hit upon a plan whereby Sassafras and Jagger
might both be brought to grief he would be happy. The
former was a villain, bold and desperate, who ought to be
undone. The latter was a minion of the crown, who ought to
be despoiled, and his money employed by a good republican
for the public benefit. But no expedient, even for the bringing
about of a partnership with Jagger, presented itself just then
to the captain's mind, and he felt like one about to be defrauded
of his rights and deprived of his substance. Should such
things be? The venerable captain thought not, if he could
help it. The mare was lame! The fate of the horse was in
his own hands, for he could enter his stable at any moment.
Yet he was about to lose the bountiful harvest springing from
seed scattered by two fools by the way, for want of a device
by which to reap and bind it. The captain felt that he was
an injured man, and was highly disgusted with the situation.
There was, however, no apparent remedy, since it was not in
the nature of things that the fools and rogues who had made
the match and carried it on without consulting him could both
lose it.

In the middle of the forenoon, having brought his fruitless
cogitations to a close, the captain determined to pay a visit
to the camp of the Western man. He walked across the
prairie and up the little valley in which it lay. Sassafras was
nowhere to be seen, but Black Dick was seated on a rock at
the base of the eastern hill, looking more glum, more solemn
and more black, if that were possible, than usual. Over to
him the captain walked, and when within a few paces, said:

"Halloo, you Dick! what are you all about here? Where's
Sassafras, you black rascal?"

"Ober dar," replied Dick, pointing to the stable of the mare.

"And what's the matter with you?" said Staples. "You look as sulky as a lone bull driven from the herd."

"T'ink I ought, when I get licked for nothing," replied Dick, in his sulkiest tone. "'Cause 'e mar' slip and pull up lame, Sassafras git mad and lick 'e darkey like eberyting."

"Ah! he whipped you on account of the accident to the mare. Now, that was wrong, very wrong, Dick. It was unjust and I hate injustice. I never whip my boys without good reason, as I tell 'em; but there's very few such masters as me. In fact, my only fault as regards them boys is, that I am too indulgent. Sassafras is different. I'm sure this wasn't your fault, Dick. I have always said you were the best rider in the country, and a pattern for other boys. Is this matter serious, and how did it happen? Is she broke down?"

"Can't tell," replied Dick, looking down. "Felt her falter at de t'ree-quarter pole. Jest afo' de gallop was finish felt her let down. I t'ink she break down in de off fo' leg. Sassafras got mad 'cause I didn't pull up afo', and gave me an awful lickin'."

"It's jest like Sassafras, but all wrong," replied the captain. "I shall tell him so. He was wrong to lick you."

"He lick somebody else afo' long," said Dick, with an ominous look. "'Fore God, captain, I nebber see him so mad as he is now since dat ar' time when he kill de t'ree men what murdered his father and brother!"

"I've heard of that. It was a bad and bloody business. You think he feels like that now, eh?"

"Am berry sure he does," replied Dick.

"Well, I must see him, for all that," said Staples, walking slowly away towards the light log-stable of the unfortunate gray mare.

The black looked after him, but furtively, seeming to think that he might turn around. Once the wide mouth of the negro was opened so as to display all the white teeth which guarded the red cavern within, but he closed his lips again firmly, and the single bright eye was again dropped to the grass at his feet.

The old man neared the stable, and glanced around. Entering without notice to whoever might be inside, he found Sassafras leaning against the side of the building, and watching his favorite mare as she ate a feed of oats and hominy wetted down into a cold mash. Whatever injury there might be to what her owner called "the running tackle," it was plain that Virginia had not suffered any to her constitutional appetite; for she was feeding with a relish which bordered on voracity. Her fore legs were in red-flannel bandages, and it was plain to the captain that in the off one there was an enlargement between the knee and the ankle joint. Sassafras took no notice of his visitor. The old man glanced from the mare to her master, and his eye fell upon the rifle which stood against the logs, ready to the hand of the borderer. It was a time for caution. The venerable captain knew that whenever his young friend was in an ugly mood he always had that formidable weapon with him, together with a brace of pistols and a long knife. It was a trait of the man that whenever things went wrong, and friends, horses and luck seemed to fail him, he straightway took to his arms, and hugged them close, as if drawing composure of mind and strength of resolution from the steel of which they were composed. Another minute or two passed, when Sassafras, without turning to look at Staples, said:

"You have come now when the mischief is done, like a raven to a dying horse. I fear the jig is up for the present. The music has got to be paid for; and we must get out of the hobble the best way we can."

"We, Sassafras! who is we?" said the captain. "I ain't in with you in this business, you know."

"What d'ye mean by that?" replied Sassafras. "You were to give your answer in three days, if you declined to take a hand, and the fifth is now half gone."

"You mistook the matter," said the captain. "I was to let you know if I *would* go in, not if I wouldn't. I certainly am not '*in*' at present, but I may be after all. Let me have a look at the mare's leg. This may be a trifle."

"Look away! I shall not take the bandage off for anybody; but you may see her walk, if you like."

The captain did like, since he could see no more. In a few

minutes, when Virginia had finished her feed, Sassafras put a bridle on her and taking her outside led her up and down before the stable.

" What do you think of it ?" said he.

" She walks quite lame. I could form a better opinion if I saw her leg with the bandage off. The best way will be to gallop her a mile to-morrow morning, and see whether she stands up or not. We shall then know the worst."

" Ay ! and the Englishman would know the worst too, and insist upon the full stake. She will gallop no more until she strips for the race, if she ever runs it."

"Suit yourself," replied Staples. " You asked for my opinion : you have had it. The business is on your sole account. I ain't in it in any shape or form."

" You said, suit yourself," returned Sassafras, as he led the mare back into her stable. " Now I say, you suit yourself. The case is far from desperate, though it might be made so if I galloped her to-morrow morning. She has had plenty of strong work, and the let-up of a day will do more good than harm to her condition. I have two things to try. By means of one I may yet win ; for that horse can't repeat, if the pace is strong in the first heat. He's too fat inside."

" He may be a little fat inwards," said the captain, who knew that Sassafras was the best judge of condition of all the racing men he knew.

" By the other," said Sassafras, " I shall avoid much loss, even if I conclude not to start her."

" And what may these things be ?" said Staples.

" The first is a kind of liniment and spell confided to me by Black Dick's great-grandmother, who was a Voodhoo woman raised in Africa, and one of mighty power. She warranted it to cure anything less than a broken leg in twenty-four hours, with rest. It's on the mare's back tendon now, and I have great faith in it."

" It might be of some avail, if she was a real Voodhoo 'oman ; but, Sassafras, you know as well as I do that most of 'em are impostors, and have no power for good or harm—only the ignorant and superstitious darkeys think they have. Now I am neither superstitious nor credulous, and I ain't going to believe that Dick's great-grandmother was a real Voodhoo 'oman, having established dealings with the African devil, because she said so. What proof is there that she had power?"

"This liniment," replied Sassafras, "which has never failed, and it will not fail now. Don't you know that as long as I have had race-horses none of mine ever broke down?"

"Well, I have heard as much," said Staples. "But if it was the Voodhoo liniment that kept 'em up, you'd better have had 'em break down as often as I have, Sassafras. I call it irreligious to use the African things and Voodhoo spells; by G—d, I wouldn't do it, if I was you."

"But I will, though. If the devil himself was to rise, and show me how to save a good race-horse from the misery and fatality of a breakdown, I think I would follow his instructions."

"Well! well! never mind the Voodhoo. I know you'll have your own way. What is the other thing you mentioned?"

"It is this," replied Sassafras. "If I find at the end of the next twenty-four hours that the leg is no better, I will go to Mr. Grosvernor, and propose to pay a moderate forfeit, stating that though Virginia may be able to run, I do not want to expose her to the risk of a breakdown."

"A good idea this," said Staples, with a sarcastic grin. "As it's a play-or-pay match, he's sure to agree to the proposition, when he knows that your mare is on three legs."

"Why, a gentleman of England," said Sassafras, "connected with the nobility, a man of great wealth and high degree, with no end of money, and mines and coffee plantations in the Leeward Islands and on the Spanish Main, is sure to do so. Don't you see, it's in character?"

"To be sure it is!" replied Staples. "And, this being the case, and everything so satisfactory, you needn't want me ' in,' and I ain't *in*. Try out the Voodhoo spell and liniment, and, if the mare is not as sound as a Mexican dollar to-morrow, rely upon the generosity of the English gentleman. I'm so convinced of his having that quality in abundance that I've a good mind to go and ask him to give *me* five or six hundred dollars." With this the captain left.

It seemed probable the next day that the Voodhoo charm had failed. In fact, the horseshoes in and about the stables may have destroyed its efficacy; for it is well known that spells and incantations are rendered of no avail by the exhibition of such articles; and it is admitted that the Voodhoo rites are intended to propitiate the evil one, and secure a grant of power from him to be exercised on earth. Be this as it may, Keeps succeeded in learning from the thick-headed darkey, in a brief, stolen interview, such news that he hastened to give Captain Staples the benefit of it. It was to the effect that the gray mare was no better; that Black Dick had been compelled to hide in the woods for fear of serious injury from Sassafras; that the latter was savage as a mad bull, or a baited bear; that he had picked a quarrel with the Cheyenne chief, which would have been fought out upon the spot but for the intervention of Campau and Pierre Langlois, who had been sent for by François when he found that mischief was brewing. The last item of the news in catalogue was that the whole party had gone to the fort at nightfall, and were there drinking deeply.

The good old man was somewhat surprised and a little moved by this intelligence. When he had left Sassafras the day before he had seemed rather hopeful than desperate—rather pacific than furious. He saw the probability that if he met him at the fort while he was inflamed with rage and whiskey a broil would be brought on; and, remembering the sharp and sudden fate which overtook the three men who killed the father and brother of Sassafras, the captain sagely determined to keep away.

"Keeps," said he, "the fit comes on him now and again, as it does on a mad dog. It will be better for you and me and Kirby to steer clear of him to-night. He is a bloody-minded man when he takes these fits. Double dangerous, as them insurance people called it, who never paid when my property was burned up down the river, and, indeed, said it was done a-purpose. He's desperate and a villain, with no love of God and no fear of the devil. Practising of the Voodhoo, which you know is irreligious, when not a cheat and fraud."

"Captain," said Keeps, "if I was you I would not mention the Voodhoo just at present, if there's any chance of blood-letting about here."

"Why, you don't believe in it, Keeps?"

"I'm d—d if I don't then, to a certain extent; and if you want to talk about it at all, it'll be a good deal better to speak well of it."

"Dou you believe it can do any good—to the mare's leg, for instance?"

"I don't think it can, but it may do a sight of harm to somebody before long. All Sassafras's niggers agree that Black Dick's great-grandmother was a real Voodhoo 'oman, and we will let that pass."

"Well, you see, if we go where he is, he is sure to raise a row, and it will not pay expenses to fight him here. We will let him alone. In default of anybody else to quarrel with, he may have another difficulty with the Cheyenne chief. If he should fight Cinnamon and get killed, it would be a pleasant thing for all good people. If he should kill the Indian it would be better still, for a redskin I have no use for would be out of the way, and the other Cheyennes would have the scalp of the slayer before to-morrow sundown, as sure as your name is Keeps. That is how the thing stands."

"That is how it seems to stand; but still I should like to know what goes on among them yonder; and I think it would be of some service," replied Keeps. "Campau, coming from St. Jo., has much influence with Sassafras, and may quiet him so as to hatch up some sort of a plot. They have these western Indians under their control, and there is no telling what they may contrive before to-morrow."

"I will take care to learn a little of what goes on," said Staples. "We will stay away. But I will get Mr. Grosvernor, who is my partner in the match, to go in and mingle with them."

"Then you are not afraid of *his* being killed," said Keeps, with significant emphasis.

"Not much," replied the captain. "He is not a fighting man. Sassafras could offer no excuse for such a thing."

"Besides which, all his money and effects would be left in your hands," said Keeps; "and then again, as he is a gentleman of high family and station, with noble connections among the dukes, bishops and what not, the British might take it up and bring on the next war, if anything of that sort happened to him."

The venerable captain did not altogether like the tone of irony with which his henchman delivered this.

" You take this drink of the old particular," said he, handing Keeps a cup of whiskey, " and then go and send Mr. Grosvernor and Kirby to me. That fellow is too smart by half," he added, when Keeps had left the shanty. " He knows too much, which I have noticed is not a sign of long life in these parts. He don't take what I say upon trust, and he believes Jagger is not the man he holds himself out to be. Now, Kirby, honest fellow, is easily satisfied ; but he is so bull-headed, that, for anything other than main strength and stupidness, I have to employ this cunning fox, Keeps. However, the fellow is useful ; and having been well-blooded in fights on the river, and sent three or four to their last accounts, he will not be apt to stick at trifles, if real, thorough work is called for." With this, the captain poured out and drank a good dose of his especial medicine.

It might have been an hour after this when Jagger strutted into the large store-room of the fort, in which Sassafras, Cinnamon, and others were drinking. The former had been informed by the captain that Virginia was broken down, and literally standing on three legs. He had also received many cautions and instructions from the old man as to what he should do, but all these Jagger was determined to disregard. Treating with contempt the assurance that it might be dangerous to exasperate Sassafras in his present state of mind, he gave full swing to his domineering disposition and love of vulgar triumph. A coward at heart, but a fool in head, and well primed with liquor, he was rash to a degree ; and the taunts he inflicted on his opponent were such that most of the friends of the latter were surprised at the forbearance with which he suffered them. In fact, the Indian, Cinnamon, although apparently unmoved, was more excited than Sassafras himself ; and, after Jagger's most offensive boasts, looked at him with such a concentrated gleam of white light as is seen in the eye of the royal tiger when he is about to spring. Had Jagger seen the Indian's face at these times, it might have subdued his vaunting spirit, and caused him to moderate his insolent manifestations of superiority ; for there was something in its savage ferocity which would have appalled him. But he looked at

Sassafras alone—talked only to him, and drank deeply from time to time of the fiery whiskey which the traders dispensed to the rude hunters and Indians at the fort. The Western man remained silent during most of Jagger's long harangue. He looked down, and his foolish opponent believed that he had lost heart, and was cowed and broken by the misfortune which had befallen him. To Jagger this was a reason for ostentatious triumph and unbridled exultation. It may be doubted whether the barbarous forefathers of the Indian chief ever tortured a captive at the stake with more zest and less feeling than Jagger displayed in taunting Sassafras, and accusing him of ignorance and stupid presumption, amounting to moral insanity, in pitting himself against one experienced and renowned upon the English turf. At last the border man made a sort of faint reply, or rather protest.

"Mr. Grosvernor," said he, "did you overcrow your noble relatives, the Duke and Duchess of Grafton, in this way, when they were compelled to give up the Whip?"

"There is some difference between my relatives and you, I take it," replied Jagger. "Every man to his proper place and tools. I believe yours are the spade and hoe."

"It is, in some measure, true," said Sassafras, "for I have dug men's graves in my time, and may do so again. You are said to be an English gentleman——"

"Said to be—said to be?" cried Jagger.

"Ay, sir, said to be. I have met other Englishmen who were said to be gentlemen, and were so called by the consuls of Great Britain; these men were not a bit like you. But that is nothing to the purpose. If you had resembled them, I might have requested you to take a moderate sum as forfeit, and declare the match off. As it is, I would not accept anything like a favor at your hands. I shall run the mare if she is in anything like a state to make use of her leg under the heavy weight, and, win or lose, it is the sole race I shall ever have with you. The transactions of the turf ought always to be between men whose principles are honorable, no matter what their wealth and station in life may be. You are no such man."

With this Sassafras turned away, leaving Jagger somewhat confounded by the words and the stern, emphatic manner of their delivery. He first had recourse to the whiskey, and then addressed himself to Campau :

"Your friend from Missouri is out of his mind," said he. "It's lunacy—sheer lunacy, to talk in that manner to me, or to think of starting his mare. I'll lay a hundred to one on my own horse."

That observation was overheard, and there were offers to take the bet, but Jagger would not stand to it. At last, however, after much altercation and banter, he retired into the back room and made a bet of a thousand guineas to two hundred and fifty with Sassafras, and produced the gold from two large belts worn round his body. It thus appeared that while Staples thought the money was in a brass-bound box, double-locked and committed to him for safe-keeping, it was really being borne, night and day, by Jagger himself, at great inconvenience. Sassafras was furnished with money by the manager, from an amount deposited by Tom Scarlet, but in Campau's name, and the stakes were made good on both sides. After this Mr. Jagger returned to the outer store, and in company with Indians, half-breeds, hunters and trappers, got so drunk that Kirby and Keeps were sent for at midnight to take him away.

CHAPTER XXIII.

"Virginia was a noble steed;
  Gray, and of the Medley breed—
  Full of fire, and full of bone,
  All her lineage tried and known.
  Muzzle fine and nostrils thin,
  But blown abroad by the pride within."

THE morning of the day named for the race was clear, bright and beautiful. The sun rose without a cloud on the eastern horizon, and the haze which lay upon the lowlands soon disappeared, while the rich tints of the forest foliage showed all their varied hues in the autumn rays, as the god of day topped the eastern hills. There was great anxiety in the minds of the immediate parties to the race, and some uncertainty in those of the men not immediately concerned, as to whether it would come off at all. The prevailing impression was that, at the last moment, Sassafras would refuse to run his mare. The numbers about the fort had been somewhat increased. The news of the race had been spread far and wide throughout all that wild region by hunters and runners. Indians had come in, as well as some roving white men from the frontier parts of Arkansas, Missouri, the Cherokee territory, and the Indian territory to the west, which is now the populous and thriving state of Kansas. Keeps was very early a-foot and in a restless state of mind. He had a devouring curiosity to hear more about Virginia. Neither he nor his worthy principal, Captain Staples, knew of the last large bet made by Jagger with Sassafras, for as soon as the former got sober his heart began to fail him on account of the amount of money he had upon the event, and he resolved to say nothing about it until after the race was run. Still, Keeps could not altogether suppress the suspicion that Sassafras meditated a secret, sudden and staggering blow of some sort, and that his strategy was to be watched and feared. In his assertions Keeps put little faith, and scarcely more in his admissions to Staples. Keeps knew what his own were worth in such emergencies, and determined to see all he could for himself. From a close cover he saw the mare very early in the morning led out for a walk, and she went lame in the off fore leg, but, so far as he could perceive from a distance, not very lame. After that she was taken back to her stable, into which no man had since entered save Sassafras, Black Dick, and an Indian Keeps did not know.

Whether these parties were engaged in making another trial of the Voodhoo charm, in which Keeps was somewhat of an unwilling believer, as many were who had mixed much with the negroes of the southwest, he was unable to determine. Ignorant and incredulous in regard to many things, and without much fear of the white man's particular devil, Keeps was superstitious, and had more present fear of the African devil, whose proceedings he had always heard were much more summary than those of the evil one of the Scriptures. If Jagger had not been silent about his last large bet with Sassafras, Keeps would have feared the worst, and might have conjectured the truth. But he now thought that, in his desperate strait, Sassafras was relying upon the enchantments of the

14

Voodhoo. From what he had been able to observe at a distance, the man of the border had the air of a necromancer, while Black Dick was not unlike a familiar, bound to work his master's will. Keeps silently rejoiced in the conclusion that the Voodhoo power inherited by Dick could not amount to much. Even admitting that his great-grandmother possessed it in all its native force, fresh from her African home on the banks of the Niger, there were two generations between him and her, both of which had been born in America. After lurking about for some time, and making many signals, he at last succeeded in attracting the attention of the thick-headed negro. and got him to come into the cover where he lay concealed. Keeps hastily questioned him, asseverating his warm friendship, and his determination to pay him well for information—"truthful and useful information, Calabash," said he.

The result was rather unsatisfactory at first. The man seemed to be more addle-headed than ever. In a daze of amazement and fright, and with a stare of downright vacuity, he shook his large head and helplessly muttered:

"Somet'iug in haud, I t'ink."

"Well, I know, and it ain't unreasonable on your part. But, Calabash, I got nothing myself just now. After the race I shall have a great deal of money, and you'll see that I will divide with you. Now, just tell me who is down there, and what they are doing."

"'Fo' God, Massa Keeps, I brieve dey makin' preparations to raise de debbil. Dere Sassafras and Black Dick, de Frenchmen, Cinnamon, and a strauge Indian nobody know. I hab reason to brieve him Medicine Man from de Rocky Mountains. Den dere come last night, after dark, two more Indian. One a horrid-looking sabage, wid big gash all down de face."

"Ay, ay. Three Scalps. A bloody-minded redskin that, Calabash. What of the other?"

"De oder was de young Kiowa. Dat limb of Satan swagger about round de fire, swingin' knife and tomahawk, and make signs dat he mean to scalp me. Keeps," said the negro, in solemn tones and with a portentous look, "last night I hab a dream. In dat dream I see de debbil, Keeps, plain. He stretch out his orful claws for me, and I wake. What you t'ink I see next?"

"Why, Black Dick, of course," replied Keeps.

"No, sah! Ober me stood de Kiowa. In his eye malice ob de fiend; in his hand de scalping-knife, which he flourish round my head, and say, in his barbarous tongue, 'Wool-isriz!' I know not de meaning ob de sabage, but from his gestures 'spect some frightful 'lusion to my top ha'r. De fact is, Keeps, de mar', lame or not lame, dese parties say dey jest raise de very debbil hisself but what dey make her win."

"And I say that Sassafras will never raise anything worse than himself. The devil don't come at the call of such a vil-lain; that is, not the right and proper devil."

"I dunno! I dunno! but I's in mortal dread. Sassafras is a Voodhoo man," said Calabash, in an ominous voice and with another portentous look.

"That's all nonsense. The whites never have the power. Besides, it's a female gift. There is no such thing as a Vood-hoo man," said Keeps.

"Ain't dere?" said Calabash, with some contempt in his tone. "So de ignorant t'ink, but I hab 'sperience. Keeps, dere is but one man on dis Western continent wid more know-ledge and 'sperience of de Voodhoo practice dan me—dat man is Sassafras. I admit de Voodhoo men to be more scase, but dey hab most power, Keeps. I seen it, being what you call inwoluntary spectator ob de horrid rites. Black Dick's great-grandmoder, dying at de age of 'bout a hundred and fifty, at de plantation near St. Jo., gib Sassafras all her power, and mo', too, befo' she take lebe ob de world, and go back, as she say, to Africa."

"Calabash," said Keeps, "is this actually true?"

"True as de Voodhoo itself, and dat you know is true as gospel—de adepts in de sorcery say great deal truer. Keeps, I brieve you to be my true friend."

"You may bet your life on that!" replid Keeps, with ardor. "Not my own brother, much as I love him—I'll go further than him, for we have not been on good terms lately, all his fault. Calabash, you got no other sich friend as me on earth. Hear me swear——"

"Nebber mind now—time presses! Besides, I hab heerd you do dat once or twice afo'. Now, listen to me. Dere is more'n life and deaf involved in de secret I gwine to tell. I hab long been anxious to tell it, but didn't dare. When de ole African got very feeble, I was sent to wait upon her. She lib in a hut, solitary, all alone, 'cept a porcupine and a rattle-snake—wouldn't let de oder women come near her. De night she died she started up at dusk and say, 'Dere Sassafras! I hear tread of his horse. Fetch him heah.' Keeps, I did so, and when he came, wid his rifle and knife—he was returned from a hunt—de ole African 'oman send me away. Now, what passed between dem after I left was dis——"

"By what means did you find out what passed? I reckon Sassafras didn't tell you?"

"Massa Keeps, he did not," said Calabash. "I found out by de same means which hab enable me to gib you various information. I just crawl up to de back of de hut, and looked and listened t'roo a chink in de clapboard."

"Ah! all right. Go on, Calabash."

"Well, sah, de ole African say, 'Sassafras, you good man, only you nebber whip dat boy Dick enough. If you jest whip him strong once a week, you make man ob him.' Now, Keeps, what you t'ink of ole 'oman on de brink ob de grave wanting her own flesh and blood whipped once a week? It is bery well for some folks to talk 'bout whipping, but it is a t'ing I hab strong objection to. De ole African went on: 'Sassafras, chile, I gwine dead to-night—gwine back to Africa, I brieve. 'Fo' I start I gib you de power ob de spirits, de Voodhoo and de fetish; what I bring a hundred years ago from de land ob de lion and de elephant, de crocodile and de serpent. I get up now. Sassafras, chile, you de only man fit to hab de gift. No black man heah brave enough. Draw your knife and look upon de edge. Now open vein in your left arm, and I catch blood in the gourd. Must drink blood ob de brave 'fo' I got strength to face de Voodhoo power, Prince ob de jungle on de Niger. When he comes he will say: "White man, thou art my subject." You say, "Not so, dark Prince; thou art *my* subject. As Heir of the Woman and Master of the Steel, I will compel?" Now, Sassafras, stand fast; be all-brave! If coward hear or see what is now to come, it is certain and sudden death to him.'"

"And what came next?" said Keeps, with eager and impatient curiosity. "What next?"

"Well, Keeps, I next cl'ar out away from dat chink in a hurry, habbing no reason to t'ink de Voodhoo secrets do me much good, if I gone struck dead certain and sudden de next minute. After long time and prayers twice ober, I crawl back agen. De ole African lay still. Sassafras, bery pale, paler dan you, Keeps, now, sat by her side. She lay a-dying. Sights were seen and voices heard round de hut whar' de ole Queen ob de Voodhoo lay a-dying. At de first faint tinge ob dawn she raise up and look awful—white ha'r, black skin and bone, and fiery eyes! She say, 'Sassafras, chile! one last little gift. All who possess de Voodhoo power must hab it. Take dis bottle. If you got enemy, bad man, ten drops in coffee or in water make him good; dat is, good 'nuff! Ten drops plenty for de worst and strongest man dat lives; but, Sassafras, chile, if you eber 'spect Calabash ob treachery and treason, gib *him* eleben!' O, Keeps, eleben! and with dat she died. What you t'ink now, Keeps?"

"Think! I don't know what to think, except this: Ten drops in coffee or in water, the old sorceress said. I'll drink nothing but whiskey in the infernal company of Sassafras."

"You don't want to be made good, eh?"

"Not by them unlawful and diabolical means," said Keeps, as he stole hastily away.

It was nearly three o'clock in the afternoon of the day in question, and the time of the race was near at hand. Considering the remote situation of the place of action, a large crowd was assembled in front of the fort. Every Indian, every hunter, and every trapper about those parts had come to see the event, and to bet his money if he could. There were three distinct races of men, as well as the half-breeds. The aborigines of North America were in the majority, the white men were next in number, the negroes were the smallest body, and, in fact, slaves, for the most part, to the whites. The Indians, the whites, and the half-breeds were already engaged in gaming, a practice for which the first have a notable passion; and it was surprising to see the quantity of silver dollars of Mexico these roving borderers produced with which to play and bet. Some, indeed, gambled for stakes of gold, and put up their ounces and doubloons with as much nonchalance as grandees of New Spain or planters of Louisiana. The White

Horse was brought on to the course first, attended by Staples, Jagger, Keeps, Kirby, and the negroes belonging to the party. He was taken to the edge of the track, and his rider, Jagger, alias Mr. Grosvernor, went into the fort to be weighed. The manager of the trading company had been selected to act as judge of the race, and had reluctantly consented to do so. He found that Jagger was the stipulated weight, 140 lbs. The latter was nervous and shaky, the result, for the most part, of his previous carousals, but also in some degree from the near approach of the time when he must undertake a task for which he knew himself to be unfit—the riding of a race. He requested to be supplied with a stimulant, and having taken two doses, by way of medicine, as the captain would have said, he found himself much better.

The arrival of the gray mare was so much delayed, that some began to think she would not be brought out at all, and large odds were offered against her. Still the oldest and most wary of the borderers. the men who had the doubloons, and were prepared to stake them, hesitated about making the White Horse their favorite. The air of mystery, which had been kept up about the mare all the morning had caused them to doubt, had perplexed Keeps, and had mightily provoked the venerable captain. Of those who had seen her during her .morning walk, some said she was quite lame forward, while others declared that she was apparently sound, but it was agreed on all hands that in bodily condition she was as near perfect as possible. It had been remarked that she was bright in the eye, blooming in the coat, lean but muscular, with flesh as hard as brass. The patience of some in the crowd was nearly exhausted, and the manager had been spoken to concerning the delay, when there was a murmur of "Here they come!" and a sort of procession was seen emerging from the little valley on the other side of the prairie. It was headed by the famous gray mare, always a prime favorite, in her palmy days, with the Indians and borderers who knew her. She was led by Black Dick, and Sassafras walked on the off side at her shoulder. The Frenchmen and the negro attendants followed. The Indian chief, the young Kiowa and a party of Cheyennes brought up the rear. There was something portentous in the ebony-like face of Black Dick, and in the set stare of his one eye. As they approached the back-stretch of the course, some of the men in front of the fort crossed over to look at Virginia. Sassafras was questioned, but his replies were of the Delphic order, which is commonly and naturally the case with the answers of **trainers** to questions put concerning their horses just before a race. While the bystanders were making their observations, the thick-headed negro approached Black Dick, and whispered a proposition to him. The steady, stony stare of Dick did not relax, and he shook his head, muttering, "Go 'way, niggah!"

The thick-headed darkey turned to Jules, and informing him in his maundering way that there was no fun in horse-racing without betting, produced a greasy rag from the inside of his shirt. From this he took twenty Mexican dollars, and re-quested the Frenchman to bet them on Virginia for him at odds of three to one. Looking at the wooden-headed darkey with amazement, the Frenchman protested with volubility, and not without some show of reason, against the venture. But the wooden-headed darkey would not be denied. He forced the money upon Jules, and when the latter said he did not know whom to bet with, desired him to lay it with Keeps, and make Campau the stakeholder. The Frenchman sought his man. With the wager in view, Keeps borrowed thirty dollars from Jagger, extorted thirty more from Captain Sta-ples, and staked it with Campau against that of his muddle-headed confidant who had predicted in the morning the "Rais-ing ob de debil, Massa Keeps!"

Just at this time somebody made the discovery that Black Dick had not been weighed. The negro moved never a mus-cle, but kept his one eye fixed on his master. The man then said, "Here's Dick not weighed!"

"I know it. Here comes my rider," said Sassafras, as a dark, tall, lithe man, with a saddle on his arm, came up, ac-companied by Campau. He was a man not known to any there save Sassafras and his confidential friends.

"You're the right weight?" said Sassafras.

"A pound more," replied Campau.

"Here goes, then," said Sassafras. With great quickness, but with care, he saddled the mare, drawing the girths tight with ease and a display of power in the exercise of which the

perfection of his sinewy frame and build were displayed.
Meantime the dark man threw off a woollen shirt, exposed his
jacket of the Sassafras blue, and put on the jockey cap of the
same color.   He vaulted into the saddle.   Sassafras went
down upon his knee, and in a moment removed the bandage
from Virginia's off fore leg.   The thick-headed darkey, deft
where horses were concerned, stripped her near one.   Black
Dick let loose her head, and away she went at an easy, springy
canter towards the quarter-pole.   These proceedings, so quickly
and quietly effected, opened the eyes of the border men on that
side of the course.   Without words, but with meaning looks
at each other, they hurried across to take some of the odds
which were being freely offered near the fort.

Sassafras and his immediate friends and assistants followed
them.   Among the crowd near the starting-place much noise
and confusion now prevailed, and sometimes there was a wild
border whoop followed by a yell which was caught up and
echoed by the neighboring hills.   All this tended to shake the
nerves of Jagger, while it excited the spirit and chafed the
temper of his fiery horse, as he cantered him up and down.
It was already apparent to those who were good judges and
who watched the horse and rider that the latter was afraid of
the racer on whose back he had incautiously ventured at such
a time.   The horse moved with free and powerful action,
fighting against the bit, while Jagger, pale and apprehensive,
kept a desperate pull upon the bridle, as if his life depended
upon not letting the former have his head.   The mare had
been turned at the quarter-pole, so as to have a breathing gallop of three-quarters of a mile to the starting-place.   She now
came sweeping by at fair speed without any signs of lameness
or infirmity.   Astonishment made the crowd silent as they saw
with what ease and gaiety the supposed cripple skimmed along.
Jagger was too much occupied with his own fiery and impatient horse to notice her.   Kirby had been drinking, and was
better capable of seeing many things all at once than of mark-
ing a single matter in particular.   But Captain Staples and
Keeps were at no loss to perceive the nature of the stratagem
which had been employed, and what they didn't say, as they
stared helplessly at each other, was very eloquent.   Keeps
was the first to recover, and having done so, he expressed his

feelings by a strong volley of oaths. The venerable captain exclaimed:

"Here's villainy! here's roguery! here's iniquity for a man that's young! I'm d——d if this world'll be worth living in when Sassafras and his partners in rascality and audacity have come to be as old as I be."

The bell was loudly rung and the gray mare was brought back to the starting-post. Tom Scarlet displayed the ease and mastery of practised and noble horsemanship, so that Black Dick and the wooden-headed darkey exchanged looks, and the young Kiowa, standing at Cinnamon's side, uttered an exclamation of delight.

A start was soon made, in spite of the inability of Jagger to control his horse. On the other hand, the mare had the steady air of an old practitioner who knew what was wanted as well as her experienced and accomplished rider. The White Horse was a little in the lead when the start was given, and at the shout which followed it, he got the better of Jagger at once, and dashed away in front at a great rate. At the quarter-pole he led ten lengths, and at the half-mile as much as twenty, whereat the unwary ones and those of the Indians who were not of Cinnamon's tribe, set up a great shout in anticipation of an easy victory. For the next quarter of a mile the mare held her own, and when they reached the starting-post again the lead of the White Horse was much diminished. The mare was going with an easy, level stroke, and under a good pull, while the White Horse was without support, under no control, and, as Sassafras remarked to Campau, "running all over the course." But his speed and resolution were such that with any one of even moderate capacity to ride him he must have won the heat. With a good pull in the first half of the second mile he could not have lost it. He was still leading at the end of a mile and a half, but the mare had stolen forward inch by inch, and was within three lengths of him. Another furlong and Tom Scarlet shot her up to his girths all at once. The horse was not beaten, but Jagger was. As he saw the mare's head opposite his knee he uttered an exclamation. Letting go the off rein to ply the whip, he pulled upon the near one. In went the spurs unconsciously. With a furious kick, and then a mighty lunge and leap, the White

Horse cleared the fence, ran away in the infield, and pitched his rider off into the mud on the margin of the pond in the centre. The mare went on, distanced her antagonist as a matter of course, and won amidst the shouts of the majority, but the bitter execrations of Staples and Keeps.

"You rode like a captain—a master of the art !" said Sassafras to Tom Scarlet, as he ungirthed the saddle. "By Jove, at the critical instant you shot her up alongside of him like an arrow from the bow. It is well enough he acted as you predicted he would, and bolted out of the course, for otherwise, with a change of riders after the heat, it might have been a tough job to beat him."

"Ay, Sassafras. You can see what a horse he would be in slap-up good condition, with a horseman on his back, for a steeple-chase. You know he's fat as a bullock fit to kill inside, and had the worst rider that ever crossed a horse."

"It is all true, Tom. By the gods, what a jumper he is ! When he took Jagger over the fence it was with a leap as though he would clear the Rocky Mountains. I wonder Jagger didn't fall off then. But get weighed, and let us clinch this business."

The dark man was found to be the proper weight. The manager pronounced the mare the winner, and in the midst of the clamor which followed, her rider, to escape further notice, went off to the fort with Campau. Sassafras became so popular that he received an ovation, and if the scene of the race had been in one of the States, a proposition would probably have been made to nominate and run him for Congress. It was astonishing to find out how many there were who had expected and even predicted the result of the match and the method by which Sassafras would achieve his victory, all along. Even those who had laid their money the other way declared that they were not disappointed in the least. They had always thought it would be just about as it had turned out. They had lost their money, which was really a very small matter, and could be made up another day, as their judgment was confirmed and their expectations were verified. Another time they should follow the dictates of their own knowledge and common sense. On this occasion they had been misled by Staples, who was getting advanced in years,

poor old man ! and by the English gentleman, who was a d—d
fool, and no doubt always had been. This was pronounced with
emphasis, within hearing of the man himself; and it was sad.
He had scrambled out of the mud in wretched plight and
much crestfallen; and here was he, the man of wealth and
station, the relative of noblemen and bishops—for all the
crowd knew to the contrary, as it had been so announced—
here was he, an object of contempt and derision to fellows in
buckskin shirts and moccasins, whose possessions consisted of
a horse, a rifle, and a knife. Here was a fall, my masters!
Staples was not there just then, and for this Jagger was pro-
foundly thankful. He feared the vindictive old man so much
that he even felt a flash of gratitude to Sassafras because his
stratagem in regard to the reputed lameness of the mare would
divert attention in some measure from his own inefficiency as
a rider.

Meanwhile the captain, assisted by his darkies, was engaged
in chasing the White Horse in vain, and in devoting Sassafras, Jagger, and nearly everybody else to the infernal gods.
Keeps, too cunning to waste his wind in running after another
man's horse, had sought and found his confidential friend, the
wooden-headed darkey. Catching him by the throat, the
exasperated henchman cried, "What's the meaning of this,
you black villain? What the devil does it mean?"

"You mean why de Englishman let go de horse's head and
ram in de spurs, Massa Keeps? Why, I was just going to ax
you what dat mean, sah!"

"The mare, you black rascal! what does that mean?"

"Oh, de mar'!" replied the black, with a vacant stare.
"Well, 'bout de mar', I tell you afo' I believe dey raise de
berry debbil. Dere was Sassafras, and de Medicine Man, and
Black Dick, and Black Dick's great-grandmother, Massa
Keeps; and I was satisfied they cure de mar', if dey hab to
raise de debbil."

"None of your humbug!" cried Keeps. "I'll choke you if
you don't tell me something better than this. I have lost a
heap of money to the Frenchman—Jules."

"Why, Massa Keeps, hab Jules lay money wid you?"

"He has, and won it," replied Keeps.

"I b'lieve den de debbil not only raised, but still above

ground and hab power. I didn't t'ink Jules would have beat you, Massa Keeps. It's too bad!"

"Sassafras himself comes this way. I'm off," said Keeps; "but before I go tell me who was the fellow that rode the mare!"

"Massa Keeps," replied the wooden-headed darkey, with a profound and solemn look, not unmixed with a sort of satisfaction and veneration, "I verily b'lieve he was de berry debbil what dey raise; for de Medicine Man——" .

Before he could conclude Keeps menaced him with his fist, and went off to avoid the man of the Missouri border.

But if he was unable to conclude his tale then, the thick-headed black was able to tell it to the end many another time. As he grew older his skull seemed to grow thicker, and he looked more hopelessly vacant than ever. But as he was a man of tried fidelity he became the trusty favorite of Sassafras, and had charge of many good horses. He proclaimed his firm belief in the mysteries of the Voodhoo and the sorceries of the medicine men of the wild tribes of Indians. To many a listening group at the stables he would tell how Sassafras and the Great Medicine Man of the Cheyennes raised the devil to cure Virginia's leg, which Satan refused to do until Sassafras bound himself to let him ride her.

The White Horse led Captain Staples and his men a weary dance, and was at last caught by Black Dick. The old man walked up to receive the bridle, but Sassafras took it, saying:

"This is my horse, captain, and I'll take care of him. The beaten horse goes, with the stakes, to me."

The captain grew pale, but not with fear. Under some circumstances he would have resisted and tried an appeal to force; but that was out of the question there and then. There were next to none to take part with him. The border men and hunters declared that the best horse and the best man had won the race. The Indians and half-breeds had no incentive to take up his quarrel, but a very great motive to remain quiet, inasmuch as the Cheyenne chief and his Western braves would cry their war-cry and strike for Sassafras until the prairie ran red with blood if a quarrel began. Swelling with hate and rage, and eager to visit his wrath upon somebody, the captain retired to his shanty. He sought out Jagger and took him with him, much against the will of that forlorn and discomfited rogue. The latter would have preferred any other company to that of the captain just then, but he had not the resolution to leave him. The vindictive old man covered him with reproaches, which were mainly deserved, and with ridicule of his pretensions as a rider. From time to time he changed that topic to another hardly less disagreeable at the moment to Jagger, viz.: the combined good fortune and villainy of Sassafras, which was, he said, clean against the old proverb, "A fool for luck," according to which Jagger certainly ought to have won. For some time the latter made no reply. At length, however, he was goaded to desperation, and being a proficient in the slang which was cultivated to perfection in the gin-shops near Seven Dials and the slums of Drury Lane, he turned upon his venerable friend with such force and variety of vituperation that the old man was silenced. There they sat in the fast gathering gloom, each cursing the other in his heart. The captain, ignorant of the loss of the thousand guineas staked the night before, was revolving other schemes by means of which to come at the supposed contents of Jagger's brass-bound box, while that individual was considering whether it would not be better for him to shake Staples off and make a friend of Sassafras. There was, however, this difficulty: he had not much money left, except that which was in the Bank of Louisiana.

CHAPTER XXIV.

"I dreamed a doleful dream yest'reen;
    I fear there will be sorrow!
I dreamed I pu'd the heather green,
    Wi' my true love on Yarrow."

"Captain of our fairy band,
    Helena is here at hand;
And the youth mistook by me
Pleading for a lover's fee:
Shall we their fond pageant see?
Lord, what fools these mortals be!"

THE various parties gathered at and about the post had prepared to break up and leave its vicinity. Some, indeed, had already gone. Captain Staples, devoured by rage

and by the pangs of disappointed avarice, had left the scene
of his discomfiture.   On the second day after the race he had
set his train in motion towards the East, revolving schemes of
revenge against Sassafras, but not quite clear as to how he
should endeavor to put them in execution.   The unhappy
Jagger, sorely tried by his losses, was with him, more like a
captive than a free agent.   He had not then told Staples of
the loss of the thousand guineas, but it was a secret which
could not long be kept.   Keeps had suspicions before they
left the post that there had been some secret transaction between Sassafras and Jagger, but he was at a loss to guess the
nature of it.   He waited for an opportunity to worm the matter out of Jagger, hoping to establish a hold upon him which
might be useful in the future.   At first he was inclined to
think that the race had been sold to Sassafras by Jagger.
The idea was, however, soon discarded, as Keeps was unable
to see how the rider, in such case, could have cheated any one
except himself.   He considered it certain that in the course
of their lonely journey of many days he would have ample
opportunities to get the truth from Jagger, and he said nothing of his suspicions to the captain, whose temper was morose
and irritable to a degree of savage sullenness.   They had
taken a difficult route, one leading into the rugged hills lying
to the eastward, and never travelled save by Indians, or the
roaming border hunters on horseback.   Its obstructions and
inconveniences had been pointed out to Staples by Keeps and
Kirby, but the old man had chosen it for purposes of his own,
after diligent but cautious inquiries respecting the intentions
of Sassafras ; and silencing objections and remonstrances in a
peremptory manner, he struck into the eastern hills with his
train.

The Indians were also on the move, mostly to the southward.   The Cheyennes were divided into three parties.   The
chief with ten of his men remained at the camp near the fort.
The others, in two bands, rode away to the west, to hunt the
buffalo on the plains, until Cinnamon should come up, when
the whole party would begin their march toward the South
Fork of the Solomon.   Sassafras and his Missouri band were
preparing to leave.   His business at the fort was settled up,
though the gold remained in the safe of the manager, and

what he called his "frolic," with the border men and hunters of the post, was now ended after several days and nights of conviviality. It was just break of day, and all hands in the camp were astir, when he and Tom Scarlet strolled up the little valley to its head, and drank of the spring which gushed out from beneath the rock. The paint and dye had been removed from the person of the young Englishman, by François, and, in appearance, Tom was almost himself again.

"We shall drink little more of this water," said Sassafras. "Our sojourn here is about ended, for when we return from the hunt we shall stop but a few hours. The equestrian games are over! There will be no time to train Danger, as you say you will remain but a few days with me at St. Jo. I shall be sorry when we have to part, and have half a mind to go on to New York or Baltimore with you, and see you on the ship which will take you to the little island over the main."

"Do so, Sassafras!" replied Tom Scarlet. "I am for ever bound to you. You must keep Danger as a small token of my gratitude. He is a good horse, and no man is as well able to manage him as you are."

"I accept the gift as freely as you make it," said Sassafras; "and if he wins when I train and run him, I will write and let you know. I would you could stay much longer, and see other parts of America. However, you can come back. Your visit has not been fruitless. You have recovered the White Horse, and got back the money Jagger defrauded you and the gypsy of—that is, you will get it when we reach St. Jo."

"And solely by your means, Sassafras."

"Not solely! We all did our work well, and I like your way of riding. The White Horse would not have been an easy customer, even for Virginia, if he had been well trained and ridden. The rush upset Jagger, and took the little horse-sense he ever had out of him. It wasn't the horse we beat, but the man. What a game it was, when he chucked him over his head into the mud!"

"I didn't see that!" said Tom. "It must have been good."

"It was good! and then to see old Staples running after the loose horse, knowing they were beat, and swearing two curses to every step—that was rich! Well, it's over, and we have one thing more before us—the grand hunt beyond the Neosho.

You'll say it equals anything you have taken part in here. If we have the luck I anticipate, we'll be back here short of a week, and bring the heads and horns of two or three elks with us. I shall strike right for the Neosho, and never pause long enough to pull a trigger on the way, unless a big buck crosses our bridles, and stops to see who rides so far in the hills and woods."

" I should hardly have expected you to select thoroughbred horses for service in this hunt. Many think them ill-fitted for four or five days' riding and wild fare," said Tom.

" A gross error!" replied Sassafras, decisively; " my experience proves it. The sound, stout-bred blood-horse will stand more than any other that goes on four legs. He is the best for nearly everything, except slow, heavy draught, when mere bulk tells."

" But the young chief was lame, and he and the White Horse are both very full in flesh," said Tom.

" All the better for our present purpose! They are not going to run against Virginia, but to carry us at a moderate stiff pace in the woods. When we reach our hunting-grounds, they will have plenty of time to crop the grass and to eat the wild-pea vine, which is the best green feed I know of, next to blue grass. I'll answer for the horses; and we shall take a third to pack the hides and horns we may get."

" But the lameness of the Young Chief?"

" Is cured," said Sassafras. " The fact is he never was very lame. In my plan there was no use for him sound. But he was nothing like as lame as the gray mare," he added, with a laugh.

" I should like to know how that lameness was produced and so suddenly cured," said Tom.

" It was a very simple matter. I may tell you before you leave the country; but it is a thing only to be practised in an emergency, to defeat a rogue. It is like putting one of a man's feet in a very tight boot. The cure is like ripping it off."

" It was, then, the bandage!"

" No! but what was beneath the bandage. But come! we will eat breakfast; and then for the saddle—off and away! Before sundown to-morrow we shall be on the left bank of the Neosho, and the morning after we will seek the elk. You don't seem to be as eager for the grand hunt as you were."

"I am eager enough for the hunt, but there is a drag upon my spirits," replied Tom. "I dreamed a dream last night of home and May Bullfinch. We were together in her flower-garden at Hawk'ell, plucking the roses, pinks and sprigs of the sweetbriar. Then again in the wood among the primroses."

"Ay, ay!" said Sassafras, "among the hazel and the haw-thorn thickets. 'I know a bank where the wild thyme grows!' But why should such a dream as this dash your spirits? Pluck-ing flowers like this with the maiden you love should rather forebode joy, and be a token of a coming bridal."

"Dreams, they say, go by contraries, and I feel disturbed— unkid, as it is called in our parts."

"More fool you then," said Sassafras. "Plucking roses in dreams a sign of sorrow! Pluck up your native sense and resolution! Let us eat and mount!"

Two hours had passed. The bright sun rising in the clear, rejoicing sky, over the fair face of the goodly earth, lit up the spangles of the morning dew beneath the variegated bushes. The young Kiowa sat on a rock just below the crest of the hill to the southward of the Cheyenne camp. He leaned his head upon his hand, and with the sunlight glancing on the beads and glossy hair, which hung over his cheek, looked to the southward over the far-reaching prospect. It extended many a mile. Hills and vales and rocky dells, virgin from Nature's hand, covered with forest trees, among whose foliage of green were the rich autumn tints of crimson and gold, all bright in the morning sun of the unclouded west. The land-scape was wild, but it was beautiful in its very loneliness. The horsemen of the hunt had just disappeared over the sum-mit of a lower hill to the southward, and the youth suffered his eyes to wander from the course they had taken. There was a grand sweep of country around him. To the right he could see the termination of the broken timbered land, and perceive the shimmer of the mist, not yet dispelled on the edge of the great and distant plains, like the sunlit surface of a silvery sea. To the left, far in the east, over a vast ex-panse of hill and forest, were the tops of the mountains, their westward slopes in shade. For awhile the boy was silent, but

15

at the end of some minutes, passed, apparently, in deep reflection, he sang with a low, but full and rich voice, these words:

> In the old days when the world was young,
> And there lingered strains of the anthem sung
> On creation day by the woods and rills;
> The laughing rivers and the glad, green hills,
> Our fathers lived o'er the Eastern deep,
> On the crown of the regal Indian steep;
> Fair was their lot as the pearl unstrung,
> In the old days when the world was young.
>
> God's fair young earth had a gladsome face,
> Joy was His gift to our Aryan race—
> Sorrow and guilt had not left us their scars;
> Of all in the world we were nearest the stars.
> Loving we roved, like the wild birds at wing,
> In the meadow-gales of the flowery spring;
> Peace was among us—no anger nor strife—
> Love ruled this earth in its morning of life.
> Sweetly and blithely our gay songs were sung,
> In the old days when the world was young.

The singer ceased, and Sassafras burst through the bushes of the crest above, saying: "At last! I knew from the first moment I laid eyes on you that there was somebody other than a Kiowa, or any other Indian, under your paint and clothes. Who and what are you? There needs no further mystery. Speak to me as a friend. As a friend I will serve you. You are not young Bullfinch, eh?"

"Young Jack! No, I am not Young Jack. But my part must have been poorly played."

"Not so, lad. It imposed upon François for a time, and it has imposed upon Tom Scarlet all the time."

"Poor Tom! What a horrid fright you made of him as a Cheyenne. I thought I should have died with laughing."

"Well, now," said Sassafras, "I thought that was a very pretty piece of work for our means. We had not the appliances that made you up so fine and gay. You surpassed for handsomeness, but not for an Indian. Boy, I have been too much among them to be deceived, and Cinnamon shunned an explanation. Tell me who you are."

"I am not of Indian blood, and yet I am. I am not of white blood, and yet I am," replied the youth, looking down. "Our people are called gypsies by those who build towns and live in them. We love the heaths and the woods."

"That is not strange," said Sassafras. "I myself soon grow

tired of being corralled in a sort of 'canyon' among houses, and make for the woods and prairies again. The gypsies came first from Egypt, I believe."

"No. The dwellers in the tents, now called gypsies, came, as our traditions tell, a long and weary way, always trending towards the West, from the Highlands of India, Asia. We have nothing in common with the Egytians but a sound. We never had."

"It was then to the people of that old and remote land that the song you sung referred?"

"Ay, to the ancient race who peopled the Hindu Koosh and lived nearest the stars. From them we descended, and our blood, after so many centuries and so many wanderings, is still unmixed. Sassafras, the oldest families of Europe are people of yesterday to us; and we follow the habits our fathers followed in the old days when the world was young."

"From your English, I reckon you were born over there," said the Western man, indicating Britain by a wave of his hand towards the rising sun.

"Yes, I was born in England, amid the bushes of a hazel copse, in the merry spring-time, when the young lambs frisk in the meadows, when the throstle sings in the grove, and the hedge-sparrow, silly bird, sits on a great egg with foolish pride and hatches out a cuckoo."

"And your name?" said Sassafras.

"Was Cotswold in the Midland vales of England. Now I am called the Singing Bird of the Cheyennes."

"Well, young Master Cotswold!" said Sassafras, seating himself beside the youth; "although time presses, and François will wonder why I tarry, instead of joining Tom Scarlet and riding on, I should like to hear what brought you here so far. I think you have been trending a good deal towards the West since you left the place your Aryan people landed at, when they struck this shore of the Atlantic ocean. Besides, I want to know where you are going to when we leave the post to its traders, hunters and Indian hangers-on!"

The youth looked down, and, avoiding the eye of Sassafras, said: "You may have heard Tom Scarlet speak of us Cotswolds. Many a time we pitched our tents in the green lanes and sheltered nooks which lie about the Grange, in his father's and his brother's time, and, since they died, in his own."

"I have heard him speak of Jack, and I think Cotswold was the surname he called him by; he was one of the men Jagger owed money to."

"He was, and he is my uncle."

"And he spoke of Jack's nephew, the boy Ike," said Sassafras.

"I am not the boy Ike!" said the youth, with a merry glance of the eye, which quickly fell again.

"Tom mentioned no other boy of the name," said Sassafras. After a pause, he added quickly: "he mentioned a girl, though. Let me see, what was her name?"

"Do you think it was Miriam?" replied the youth, drawing off a little from the reaching hand of the hunter.

"I think I was a blinking owl by daylight!" cried Sassafras. "I knew you were no Kiowa, nor Indian of any tribe; but I got on a regular false trail, I own. You are——"

"The Singing Bird of the wild Cheyennes here!" replied the youth, with a burst of mirth.

"Ay! but about the tents in the green lanes, and under the hawthorn bushes, you were Miriam. When Tom Scarlet set out in chase of Jagger, the White Horse, and the stolen money, you followed in another ship. I see it all now, as clear as if I had been there myself," said Sassafras gravely.

"Not quite all, I think, though you are marvellously acute," replied Miriam.

"I'll be bound you are in love with Tom Scarlet and followed him for love."

"I'll be bound I didn't," returned Miriam sharply. "Why, what do you know about love?" she added gaily.

"Precious little, except love for a good horse and a true rifle, and a little frolic now and then, ending perhaps in a free fight once in a while. But you need not tell me that you came for nothing."

"Listen, and you shall hear no lies," said Miriam. "You need not come any nearer. I never heard that you were deaf. I like Tom Scarlet; he has often been kind to me and my people. But a lass of his own country folk loves him, and he loves her. O, Sassafras! the sweetest maid in the fairest vale of England! the Rose of Hawk'll! Jocund as the morning lark in summer time! precious as the twilight hours of eventide in spring! And then the only daughter of one of the best men that rides to market and a-field in all the broad midland counties."

"I have heard of this maiden. *She* was left behind, you know, when you followed Tom to America."

"I followed my own chase, most likely like a wild goose as I was. Remember, I am a gypsy!" replied Miriam. "I had a purpose in what I did. It was to see that the rascal Jagger should not get clear away with his plunder if I could help it. At New Orleans I found out men who had been sheltered in our tents when the Bow street runners were hot after them. By their means I kept watch and ward over Jagger. Chance, a lucky chance, threw Pierre Langlois in my way. He is a good man, and has been like a father to me. I saw how I might follow Jagger and Staples in disguise, unknown and unsuspected. I wrote to Tom Scarlet and to you. I had been taught by May Bullfinch's mother, a kind and gracious lady, laid long ago under the boughs of the great elms in the old churchyard. You know the rest! I have done but little; still, that little was to let you know where to meet your man, and I don't regret the adventure. All the trouble and fatigue of it have been paid for twice over by meeting with the Cheyenne chief—a noble fellow! a king among men of common stamp!"

"Ay, ay! Pierre Langlois was like a father. What may Cinnamon have been like?" said Sassafras.

"Like a brother! like what I think a brother ought to be. I never had one," replied Miriam, frankly.

"Hem!" uttered Sassafras, after a pause; "you don't love Tom Scarlet, but the chief may love you, eh?"

"Lord! Sassafras! you question one as you would look a horse in the mouth!" returned Miriam. "Do you think I am to be wooed like a beggar under a bush?"

"The chief is a very fine fellow! A better man after scalps nobody would wish to see," said Sassafras, with deliberate emphasis. "But to my knowledge he has already four or five wives, each calculated to make her own ground good against a new one with a paler face; and, therefore, Miriam, when I return from the grand hunt, instead of going with Cinnamon to the Rocky Mountains, you shall 'trend to the Northeast,' and go to St. Jo. with me."

"I never thought of going near the mountains with Cinnamon, or anybody else," returned the gypsy. "You talk as if you had the command and disposal of one."

"Now, girl, you look at me!" said Sassafras. "I am a plain man. I live, when at home, on the Missouri river, near St. Jo., where I have a plantation. I own five or six race-horses; I know the use of the rifle; I love sport and have seen a good deal of it. You are hundreds of miles from any man more disposed or better able to be your friend than I am. I never was in love—I don't pretend to be now; but it seems to me that I may *fall* in some day, and prove tender and true; where acquaintance and friendship are, love may come at a racing pace. Miriam, I have made up my mind that you shall go to St. Jo., when we return from this hunt. When you see my horse's head coming over yonder hill, wash the paint away and be yourself."

"There is a certain impediment to my doing so," said she.

"And what may that be?"

"The lack of suitable petticoats and other things that you know nothing about," she replied with a laugh. "But seriously, Sassafras, you should waste no more time here now. When you return I shall be glad to see you, and then we will decide as to which road I shall travel. I suppose it may be left undecided until then. You seem rather slack for a hunting morning."

"No, I am not slack," he replied; "but I have come upon a sort of game I never thought of. Keep close to the chief until I return, or to Pierre Langlois. However, as you are known to be with them, and seem to be a spirited boy, there is no fear of any rudeness being shown. But that throwing of the knife young Joe told of. How about that?"

"A mere juggler's trick, taught me by a mountebank. All sorts of people used to come to our tents at times."

"Well, Miriam, good-by—good-by for the present."

With this the border rover sought his horse, and having mounted rode away. "Strange," said he, "that I should be so deceived. The paint and the breeches done it, especially the last. Yet I was an owl not to see that the boy was no boy, but a girl. I never heard her speak before. The voice would have informed me, even though it was the gypsy language, which may be the same as Kiowa, for all anybody can tell. Her face must be handsome, for even under the paint I can see that its lineaments are good, and her eyes are beautiful. She has a voice like the fall of water on a summer's day; and no young doe is more graceful in movement and figure. 'Tis a comely maiden, without doubt. What a wife she'll make for somebody! For the matter of that, why not for me? I want no pale-faced doll, with weak nerves and headaches, but one of tact and spirit, able to keep the roof overhead while I am away. Perhaps to ride and shoot upon occasions. She may suit me, and it would be a blessed thing for the people on the plantation to have such a mistress. I have no one to please but myself. My sister and my cousin Elizabeth, being of the Old Dominion blood, might object to the gypsy. But, what then? I'll have my way! They need not know it at first. She might pass for a Spanish creole, and, as she says, the oldest families of British descent are but people of yesterday to hers. It may come about."

Now here was a shocking instance of disregard of the beautiful principles of woman's rights. The man partly settles the matter in his own mind, as though whatever he desired must govern; and this has always been the way with the male tyrant, against whom America and Britain now afford some prospects of successful rebellion. Perhaps Miriam was not to be overborne in this off-hand manner. She had already put the —— on, and might assert her "rights." Meantime, she remained near the rock, and watched Sassafras until his form and horse were hid as he dashed into the bushes on the slope of the further hill. Then, O lamentable truth! it appeared that she had not the spirit to assert her "rights." In spite of her descent and independent habits, in spite of her arms, her paint and feathers, and her very handsome trousers, she proved as ready to meekly meet the half-advances of the "horrid man," as any maiden of Anglo-Saxon lineage.

"Heigho!" she exclaimed. "He is well-born and well-to-do. Bold, brave and honest. Far from bad-looking, to my mind. Much better than the youth of cream-and-strawberry complexions in England. This is a man! No gypsy can compare with him. Besides, I don't want a gypsy husband, sleeping in the tents or the fern all day, and poaching all night.

The ties that bind me to the tribe are thin and worn. I love the pleasant fields and thick overhanging woods of dear Old England, and their green glades in the gloaming, when the leverets play. Her kindly people have done well by me. I love the scent of violets in the spring, of rich bean blossoms in the summer days, the cuckoo's quaint and distant call, the coo of cushats to their nesting mates, the songs of birds from every bush and brake, the carol of the lark, unseen in the bright, blue sky, and the sweet sound of bells upon the breeze. Heigho! 'It was a lover and his lass that thro' the green corn-fields did pass.' "

CHAPTER XXV.

"Full moon, high sea,
Great man shalt thou be!
Red dawning, stormy sky,
Bloody death shalt thou die."

IN the wild section of country to the southeast of the trading post, and in a rough gorge between the broken hills, Captain Staples had made his camp for a short but indefinite time. Instead of going south, or a little to the westward of south, as he would have done had he sought the best route homeward from the fort, he had travelled due east for many miles, and then abruptly southeast by south through a sort of pass in the broken ridges. In the rocky gorge which now contained his wagons and animals, he had halted a night and a day. Another night was coming on apace. The sun nearly touched the tops of the trees which crowned the ridges to the westward, and the clouds in that quarter of the sky were edged with crimson and gold, like tents with royal fringe, for the reception of the retiring day. A cool breeze blowing from the northwest gave some tokens of freshening into a gale as the darkness came on.

The captain moved about his encampment with an air of dogged resolution mixed with impatience. He spoke neither to Keeps nor Kirby, and regarded Jagger with glances which indicated anger and contempt. As the shades fell and the loom of the hills was cloaked with the approaching darkness, a mounted Indian came into the camp. The man looked fresh and able to stand much greater fatigue than he had undergone, but his horse had evidently been ridden fast and far since the dawn of day. The captain took the Indian aside, and they held a brief conference, partly in English and partly in the Choctaw tongue. The first part appeared to be very satisfactory to Captain Staples, but not the last. The Indian either gave a dogged denial to some assertion made by the old man, or met some proposition of his with a flat rejection.

The captain retired to his tent and called for Keeps, who was close at hand. He found Staples seated on a bundle of horse-clothes and buffalo robes. His elbows were upon his knees, his head rested on his hands, and with his hard, dark face he looked like some ugly idol of the heathen. The demijohn containing his "medicine" was between his legs. He first invited Keeps to drink, and even told him to pour out for himself. The henchman speedily made avail of this unusual liberality and confidence by securing about half a pint of the liquor before the demijohn left his hands. It may be doubted whether, in any of the brawls and rough-and-tumble fights in which he had been engaged, this worthy had ever gripped a throat with more resolution and tenacity than he clasped the neck of the huge bottle on this occasion. But, although the captain saw the dimensions of the dram his man was pouring out, he made no effort to check him. Thereupon Keeps made up his mind that his services would soon be in request for some extraordinary purpose. After smacking his lips with much satisfaction, he lit his pipe, and took a seat opposite his chief, inwardly determined to make a good bargain before he consented to go beyond the terms of his engagement. The captain looked at Keeps some time before he spoke. The henchman looked at him in turn, as much as to say : " We understand one another. Out with it !"

" Keeps," said Staples, "I believe there is confidence between you and me. I think each of us knows the other means fair, between man and man, eh ?"

" Ay, ay ! That's all right, but come to the p'int. What is a-going to put this confidence on trial ?"

" You don't like the idea of being robbed by Sassafras. I think you've no confidence in him, and his way of grabbing everything, eh, Keeps?" said the old man, feeling his way.

" As to grabbing, I never had the good fortune to meet any of them excellent people what don't grab when they have a chance, and, speaking in a general way, I've got no confidence in anybody but myself.   You come to the p'int at once."

" Very well! the point is this—shall we sit down, robbed and swindled as we are by Sassafras, or shall we act in confidence, and take our own again ?"

" Who do you call *we ?*" said Keeps.

" You and **me**—nobody else!   The Englishman is a fool and coward," returned Staples.

" We found that out some time ago," returned Keeps.

" I believe we did," said Staples.   " I have now, however, found something else out, quite as much to the purpose.   This idiot, going upon his own conceit, and keeping his doings secret from me—I say from *me*, Keeps."

" I hear you.   Some would have thought he could not have deceived *you* easily."

" They might have thought so; but he did it," replied Staples.   " Concealing his operations from me, he walks right into the trap set for him by Sassafras.   He lays a bet with this villain at four to one on his White Horse, by which he lost a thousand guineas to the villain, and these golden guineas Sassafras has got.   Think of it!   A thousand guineas in gold —coined gold—*British gold!*   Ain't you astounished ?"

" No, I ain't," replied Keeps.   " I knew all about it before you spoke a word."

" You knew all about it!   Shall I hear next that you were *in* with Sassafras, and helped the villain to deceive and plunder this—this——"

" Fool and idiot!" said Keeps.   " No, you won't hear that. I knew nothing of it until your friend, the *gentleman*, told me all about it soon after we reached this camping-ground."

The old man paused in thought.   He desired Keeps to take another drink.   Staples then said : " Perhaps this *gentleman* also told you who he really is ?"

" He did.   I assured him I must know everything before I could do him any good.   The truth is, captain, that he is mortally afraid of you, and will turn on you at the first opportunity.   But for the money he has at New Orleans, and the fear that somebody from England will lay an embargo on it, he would have left our party and gone off with Sassafras to St. Jo."

Captain Staples relieved his feelings by a few round oaths and some remarks touching the ingratitude of mankind in general, and that part of it with whom it was his misfortune to come in contact in particular. He then said:

"With all his foolishness, this fellow is as big a rogue as Sassafras himself. But for all that, we must get back his money from the villain."

The henchman looked at his chief with a cunning and an eager eye, one in which insatiable greed, with cruel resolution and abundant craft, shone deadly and red.

"Yes, we must get back this gold for him." The henchman's countenance fell. "And for *ourselves*, Keeps. In a venture like this we shall be entitled to keep about three-fourths of what is recovered."

"I'll be d—d if we shan't be fully entitled to keep it all. I go in for Keeps, and nothing else," said Keeps in reply. "This man is useless—not able to get a dollar of it, or to help us in any way. Then why should he have any of it?"

"For two reasons," replied Staples. "He has money and means at Orleans, and he might make trouble when he gets there. We have enemies at Orleans, Keeps."

"He may never get there. I got no use for him there, if we are to lose a pot of money by his going there."

"But hear the other reason. There is another very strong reason why we must treat him as a partner. It is this: Sassafras is not the man to give up the gold quietly, or to rest easy under the loss after it has been recovered. He'll raise h—ll from St. Anthony's Falls to the passes of the river below Orleans, and from St. Jo. to the Rocky Mountains. The villain has many friends. Most of them are villains of his own stamp! Now, by acting in the name of Grosvernor, Jagger, or whatever it may please him to call himself next, and taking the money as his property—property he has been swindled out of—we shall do a right and justifiable thing, and public opinion, when we reach the part where there is any uncorrupted by Sassafras and villains of his character, will sustain us."

"Yes, but what will public opinion say about our giving this man the money back?" said Keeps.

"That is altogether another matter. Don't you see that Jagger, being what he is, dare not make trouble with us, if we but have the *name* of a little law and right on our side? You leave him to me!"

Keeps was silent. The old man watched his face, and at last caught the cold glitter of his eye.

"Sassafras will be hard to deal with, hard as the steel of this knife," said Keeps. "Besides, he may not have the gold with him upon this hunt. It may be left in the fort or hid in a safe *caché*."

"He will—he will have it!" replied Staples. "Leave it at the fort! why, Keeps, what are you thinking of? Do you think that I or that you would leave such a sum at the fort, or anywhere else about these parts, when we could carry it with us? Why the fool who brought it from England had sense enough to keep it on his person, although he had *me* to trust to. Sassafras has the money with him, and I know whereabouts he will be to-morrow, a couple of hours after noonday."

"And I know he'll fight like ten tigers, if we are to meet him when he is on horseback with his arms in his hands. That plan will never do. I'm no more afraid of being killed than another, but Sassafras is a dead shot and quick as lightning. Besides, he will not be alone."

"You had better hear the plan before you condemn it," said Staples. "I do not propose the meeting of him when he has his arms in his hands. By striking his trail an hour after he has passed to-morrow, we may follow and find out where he will camp. We'll take him when he's asleep. If he chooses to fight, rather than give up the man's gold, let him do it. If he is killed, the border will be rid of a villain; justice and law will be on our side, and what is quite as much to the purpose, we shall have the money. Now there's the plan, and I doubt whether anybody can propose a better one as matters stand."

"This'll be a tough job," said Keeps, seizing the demijohn uninvited, and pouring out a strong dose of the medicine.

"Not so tough as you imagine," replied Staples. "Our measures will be well considered. I have intelligence from the Indian, that Sassafras started this morning, with no more than one man in his company, and he a fellow of no account. I can guess whereabouts they will camp to-night. To-morrow we can strike their trail at the camp, and follow it cautiously until we find where they leave their horses to begin their hunt. There or thereabouts they will camp to-morrow night. That being known, we can come up near their camp-fire towards the dead time of night, when they are fast asleep, and—and possess ourselves of this money without any trouble."

" Not till we have knocked Sassafras square on the head, or put the steel through his heart—to say nothing of the other man," replied Keeps. " Who goes in this business besides us and the Englishman ?"

" Kirby—we must have Kirby. Not that he'll be wanted to do anything more than be in reserve, in case of accidents," replied Staples.

" Why not the Indian ? He could do more, and would come cheaper than Kirby. Kirby is not the man for this quiet midnight work, where the rustle of a leaf might spoil all. His tread is like that of a bull-buffalo upon hard ground. Take the Indian."

" The Indian refuses to do more than he has done," replied the captain, with some disgust. " He is like all the rest—he must ask his questions, and talk of Sassafras as if he was the only white man worth much on the border. The times are upside down," added the old man, feelingly. " I have seen the day when that Indian would have helped to do anything I proposed, no questions asked." After a few minutes, probably spent in silent regret over the degeneracy of the age from the customs of the good old times, the captain said, " Kirby will not earn, and must not have, much of the money. He cannot in conscience ask more than one, or at most two, hundred dollars. There will be nothing for him to do, but to keep ward, while you and I settle the business."

" The main part of which settlement," said Keeps, " will depend upon me. Now, it is a transaction that ought to be well paid for. It ain't like killing an Indian or two, or making use of a pistol or knife in a fight or a frolic. It requires talents of a particular sort, and nerves of a peculiar order. Them talents and nerves, I may say without boasting, I have got ; but I shall not use 'em for nothing. Besides, look at the strain it puts upon the conscience to crawl in like a wolf at night and kill a good man asleep upon his back. You'll allow Sassafras to be a real good man of his heft and inches?"

There was a sort of low growl from the chest of Staples, who saw what this prelude, especially the allusion of Keeps to the strain upon his conscience, was tending to. He made a motion to the henchman, signifying that he should go on.

" Well, then," said Keeps, " I'll come to the p'int! After the Englishman's and Kirby's shares have been set off, there will be about seven hundred sovereigns left. That is to be equally divided between you and me."

" I don't see it in that light," said Staples, with some show of alarm and discontent. " Consider the trouble and expense I have been put to. Consider that I have planned the thing, and that you are to help in the execution of it only—a mere trifle! a mere trifle, Keeps! I could do it all myself!"

" You couldn't do it at all, and you know it," replied the henchman. " In the first place, you are a little afeared of Sassafras, and, asleep or awake, I shall have to deal with him. Then, again, you are getting old and stiff, and would be sure to rouse him, with pistol in one hand and knife in the other, and get sent to kingdom-come instead of touching the money. You can't get the first piece of this gold except through me, and I'm resolved that the work which can only be done by my ability, and with wear and tear upon my conscience, shall be well paid for, if it is done at all !"

" Your conscience!" cried Staples, in a rage. " How many men have you killed in your time, conscience or no conscience ?"

" I don't know as I could exactly say, because I have always thought that two who were shot by me, in difficulties, would have recovered if the doctors hadn't killed 'em, so they ought not to be counted," replied Keeps. " But this I do say, that I never killed a man when he was asleep to get hold of money, and as I think that likely to be a very different thing upon the conscience to using pistol or knife in a promiscuous and general way, I'm determined not to do it for nothing. If half the seven hundred isn't enough for you, fix the matter yourself, and count me out."

The old man was furious at what he considered the unconscionable greed of his accomplice, but as he could discover no means of getting anything without the active aid of Keeps he suppressed his rage. He made, however, a mental resolution to secure the lion's share by some means or other, if it was possible, before they reached the settlements. He signified his assent to the arrangement named by Keeps, and again recited his plan of action, going over the details in a slow, methodical way, as though the business was nothing out of the common order of things. Yet they both knew and felt that it was. Staples had, in all probability, been at midnight massacres, but it was in Indian warfare, and sanctioned in the minds of such as he, as reprisals. Keeps had slain more than three or four men, but it was when they were upon their legs, and *not for money.* They did not attempt to disguise from themselves the atrocity of the contemplated deed, but the magnitude of the prize to be obtained overbore it, and the younger, but, at that day, hardier villain of the two, " bent up each corporal agent to the terrible feat."

The mode of operations being settled, Keeps, while still appearing to defer to the captain as his leader, virtually took the ordering of affairs into his own hands. He wished Staples to say nothing to Kirby or to Jagger. The less said the better. With any knowledge of the plan in hand Jagger would cause much trouble, and by his fears and foolishness might do something which would bring about its defeat. It was bad enough to have to pay him, without letting him know of the scheme. As for Kirby, if he was told, he would be sure to interfere with the carrying out of the project when the crisis of action came; besides which, he would claim a larger share of the money than they designed he should have if they took him into their confidence.

" There is," said he, " no call to let them know how much we get when it is over."

Soon after it was day the four men mounted their horses and rode from the camp. Kirby did not care to ask where they were going or the object of the expedition. Jagger was afraid to do so. The old man led the way, winding among the hills, but holding a course as straight as was practicable to the west of south. On they went, Staples never speaking and Keeps cutting Jagger short when the latter attempted to open a conversation with him. It was past the hour of noon and their steeds were becoming jaded, when they struck the trail Sassafras and Tom Scarlet had made in the morning. Keeps gave it but a glance before spurring hastily to the side of Staples.

"Trouble is ahead," said he in a whisper, wherein surprise and ferocity were blended. "Three horses have passed here instead of two. That devilish Indian has played you false. He went off before day; he has joined them, and Sassafras knows that we are upon his trail. It'll come to a fight, and we are but three to three, for I count Jagger less than nobody. Besides, they'll have the first fire, for Sassafras will ambush us. What's to be done?"

"It can't be!" said Staples. "It ain't possible! But if the Indian has done this, then there's no more honesty, no more faith between man and man, in this world, and the sooner it goes to blazes the better. What I have done for that Indian nobody knows but me, and it's past telling, for my feelings is such that I can't tell it. I paid him well for this service. That is, I promised in case of success to——"

"That's it," said Keeps, savagely. "You're so infernal stingy. Why didn't you give him a matter of twenty or thirty dollars in hand, and whiskey enough to get drunk upon last night, and to keep drunk upon to-day? Wait here till I come back."

With this Keeps dismounted, threw his bridle-rein to Staples and entered the bushes. He carefully examined the trail for some minutes, passing along by the side of it for several rods. When he returned to Staples his face had brightened up, and he re-inspired the old man's confidence in the world, and the stability of things in general, by informing him that one of the tracks had been made by a led horse.

They now pricked ahead, following the trail, and keeping a good lookout, expecting to come upon some signs that Sassafras and his companion had dismounted and hobbled their horses, to begin the hunt. But hours passed, and the trail still led them direct, as in that country might be, for the Neosho river. They came to a place where Keeps and the captain could see that Sassafras and his companion had dismounted and halted to bait their horses and refresh themselves, but beyond that the trail again led due south. Staples was puzzled.

It was a good hunting country, with plenty of grass and fine water. Deer had been seen from time to time, and with difficulty Keeps had prevented Kirby from firing at a fine buck which presented the mark behind the shoulder at less than fifty yards. The henchman, after some thought, reached a conclusion, and spurred forward to tell the old man what he believed.

"Captain," said he, "we are on a stern chase. Sassafras means to camp to-night over the water. He is bound right for the Neosho, and will not pull bridle until his horses go down the face of the bluff into the river to swim across That's how it is."

"It looks like it. O, he's a crooked-minded villain, and always the cause of no end of trouble to whoever has any transactions with him! Any other man would have camped on this side, and matters would have been, in a measure, easy. What do you think we ought to do now, Keeps, to get even with him?"

"There is but one thing to do," replied Keeps. "We must cross ourselves before night sets in. We can't swim it in the dark hours. The bluffs are bold and high. The river is narrow, swift and deep, and may be in fresh, for it has looked as though there had been rain about its head-waters. The man and horse who once get below the landing-place on the other side will be in the rapids, and never reach the east bank alive. We must ride as fast as we can, to get to the stream by sundown. Once over, I'll undertake to find the camp-fire of Sassafras, which will be pretty near the crossing!"

"Enough!" said the old man. "Let us go ahead!"

"One thing more," returned Keeps. "If Jagger swims his horse over, and lands, it will be more by luck than judgment, the river being high."

"A terrible peril!" replied Staples; "for when he finds he's lost, the fool, instead of taking it as a man ought to do, will screech before the water stops his mouth, and Sassafras may hear his cry. This comes of acting with a chicken-hearted fellow. I tell you, Keeps, when this thing is over, I'll have no concern with anybody but men like you."

"As to his screeching, it is nothing," said Keeps. "He may screech as loud as a panther, and nobody will hear him

16

over the roar of the lower rapids, so as to know where the cry comes from, or what it is. Besides, he'll be too frightened to screech, when he finds that he's a-going down the river towards the roar of the broken water below. His heart will be in his mouth, and all he'll do will be to hang on like grim death 'round his horse's neck."

"So it will—so it will, Keeps! Let us go ahead," said the old man, cheerfully.

"I thought you said it was necessary that he should reach Orleans," said Keeps.

"So it is in one way," replied Staples. "The money in the bank will not be paid over without him, or without his order."

"Which you can get, knowing men skilful in write of hand," replied Keeps.

"I don't know about that. Still, if anything should happen to him in a providential sort of way, we shall have the money from Sassafras all to ourselves. It might be best for us, and would be different from what you proposed."

"I proposed nothing," said Keeps, "except that, as he is useless in the recovery of the money, it would be throwing it away to give him any. However, let him take his chance. It will be a poor one if we linger longer, and have to take the stream between daylight and dark. Go ahead! I could wish he was mounted on a better horse; but in that case a good one might be lost! Go ahead!"

While this hurried conversation was proceeding, the subject of it, ignorant of the probable impending fate which had been so coolly and heartlessly discussed, had endeavored to ascertain from Kirby the object of the expedition. He was hungry, weary and miserable. The burly border man, revolving his tobacco in his cheek, did not reply. In fact, Kirby was mentally proposing the same question to himself, and being unable to find any answer, made up his mind to require Keeps to speak out when they should again go on. But he had no opportunity to do this, as the henchman led the way when they started, and rode rapidly, in spite of obstacles, while Kirby himself had to bring up the rear in Indian file. But fast as they now travelled, the sun set while they were yet a mile from the river. The ground now rose in a slope, thickly timbered, to the top of the bluff above the fast-flowing stream.

Keeps and Staples were now convinced that Sassafras had crossed, and was in the bottom land on the other side of the bluffs which formed the left bank. There he would make his camp for the night—the night they meant to be his last. The crossing of the river before darkness set in was their only aim. Considering that to be equivalent to success, Keeps cried, "Come on! There is no time to lose! Come on! The d—l take the hindmost; for the crossing is bad enough by day! Spur on, man!" he added to Jagger; "keep at my horse's girths! Mind how you go down the face of the bluff, which is steep; and when in the water don't, for your life, let your horse get his head down stream!" As he rode on he muttered complacently, "I've done my duty by you, whatever happens, and more than many would have done under the circumstances; for if by following my advice you save your bacon and get safe over, I shall lose about a hundred and fifty sovereigns by the operation."

Through brush and tangled vines, over the trunks and arms of fallen trees, in the deep vegetable mold of the primeval forest, they forced their reeking horses, and at length reached the top of the bluff, high over the swollen river. Then broke upon the sight of Keeps and Staples that which made them feel their scheme of midnight murder to be abortive. In the gray twilight which hung over the waters, they saw the men they had pursued and were themselves seen. Upon a shelf of gravel, three parts of the way up the opposite bluff, stood Tom Scarlet, holding the White Horse by the rein. Further up, on the crown of it, was Sassafras, between the other two horses, and with his face to the river. As Staples and his men appeared in sight, the young Englishman hallooed and stretched out his arm, while the more wary and practised border man wheeled one of the horses quickly, so as to cover his own person. But for that, the rifle of Staples would have had another mark. As it was, the furious old man, shooting from the back of his horse, hit Tom Scarlet in the head and tumbled him into the river. The White Horse bounded up the bluff. At the shot, Staples, Keeps and Kirby threw themselves from their saddles and dodged behind the nearest trees. Jagger, agape with fear and astonishment, remained gazing on the opposite bank for a moment. In that moment there was a flash, and before the report reached the nearest of the echoing hills, he fell from his horse dead.   Sassafras had shot him through the brain.

CHAPTER XXVI.

> "Like one that on a lonesome road
>   Doth walk in fear and dread,
> And, having once turned round, walks on
>   And turns no more his head,
> Because he knows a frightful fiend
>   Doth close behind him tread."

DARKNESS had nearly fallen, a welcome cloak to the living, and a pall over the ghastly dead, in that solitary place, before there was any movement made on either side of the river.   No sound had been heard from the left bank after the tramp of the White Horse and the other two on that side, as they galloped away when Sassafras fired.   Whether the latter had gone after them, or remained upon the bluff, was uncertain to the three men in cover on the right bank.   The silence was profound, for the beasts of chase and prey had fled at the sharp cracks of the two rifles.   Keeps and Kirby had taken cover near each other, while the hiding-place of Staples was at a little distance.   The former, perceiving, as though by intuition, that the state of parties, as statesmen and politicians have it, was likely to be much changed by the late events, determined to be beforehand with the old man, and strike up a close alliance with the stalwart, but slow-witted Kirby. With a view to that end he wired himself silently to the side of the latter, and whispered to him such information concerning the expedition as he deemed most likely to forward his own purpose and prejudice him against Staples.   At length the latter believed that it was safe to move.   Coming from his cover, and calling to Keeps in a low voice, he stood near the corpse of the fallen man, and waited for his henchman to rise. The latter had now communicated to Kirby what he called the facts of the matter, true enough in the main, but so glossed as to conceal the truth, that he had himself been just as eager to make a blind tool of his companion as Staples was.   They joined the old man, and all three bent over the dead body, which lay with the pale face—a small red hole in the centre of the forehead—turned up towards the sky.

"He's as dead as mutton," said Keeps, with no more emotion than he would have displayed over the carcass of a sheep. "It was a good shot and true—killed clean, which is a sort of consolation, for I hate to see 'em writhing about in agony, and trying to speak after they are mortally hit. If I ain't killed clean and dead when my time comes, I shall be obliged to anybody as will put his knife through my heart. This, under the circumstances, was a splendid shot. I always knowed Sassafras was a master of his weapon. If there was anybody here who had curiosity on the p'int, and a small-toothed saw, he might find the bullet flattened against the back of the skull inside. As for the other man, if anybody looked for him, which nobody is likely to do, he might be found fifteen or twenty mile below, down among the catfish. And I'll bet anybody two to one he wasn't killed as neat and nice by the shot as this one here. When Sassafras kills with a rifle he does it artistic, and I have heard say that he is very quick and judgmatical with his knife, too."

"Hold your infernal tongue," said Staples, gruffly. "To hear you gabbling on about it, anybody might think you was preaching a funeral sermon. It was a cursed chance! just such as nobody but Sassafras would have brought about. If I had shot the villain himself there would be some satisfaction."

"Ay! but Sassafras is not going to be shot so easy," said Keeps. "He wheeled a horse before him quicker than wink; and must have shot under the throttle when he tumbled Jagger out of the saddle. As you couldn't kill *him*, you had no right to shoot at all. We might have kept on their trail, and got a chance to do something or another that would have paid. Sassafras might finally have been settled, and then we could have grabbed the money."

This seemed to remind the old man that something of that sort might be done upon a small scale then, and had better be set about as soon as possible. Muttering to himself, he went down upon his knees as though about to pray. But Keeps knew better than this, and watched him with tiger-like interest. Undoing the coat and shirt of the dead man, Staples quickly removed that which was round the body. He probably thought that in the dim light the belt would be unobserved, but in this he was mistaken. Weighing it for an instant in his hand, as if to estimate the quantity of the contents, he proceeded to secure it round his own stout loins. The performance did not meet the approbation of Keeps. Nudging Kirby to second him, he said :

"The belt which you have grabbed, according to what I was told by the owner, contains a certain amount of gold. That gold must be turned out and counted, so that it may be accounted for. It must be held in charge of all three, not of one; and we must each have a third to take care of—eh, Kirby?"

"It is in charge now, and will remain there," replied Staples, rising rather hurriedly. "I'll take care of it. You needn't trouble yourselves at all. What you have got to do is to look out for this desperate and dangerous villain, Sassafras!"

"I think I had better look out a little for the carrying out of the bargain we made at the camp," said Keeps.

"O, the bargain!" replied Staples. "Of course we must stick to the bargain when we get the money Sassafras holds. It may not be very soon, lads, for the villain has three horses, a rifle, plenty of powder and ball, and knows the country we are in like a book. This trifle of money I have taken into possession don't come into the bargain at all."

"Don't it!" replied Keeps with an ominous voice. "Then it must be counted over, and taken charge of for the man's friends."

"The man's nearest and dearest friend has got it," said Staples. "He owed me a sight of money, and what I do is lawful and right. I'm his administrator, executor *de bonis non,* if you know what that means!"

"I can't say that I do," said Kirby.

"Nor I," said Keeps, "unless it means the good of nobody but himself. I want to know more about this."

"Bring up the horses, Kirby," said Staples.

"Don't be in a hurry, captain," said Keeps. "When the horses are brought up we may ride different roads; for if you are going to collar everything, and never say 'turkey' once to us, here we part!"

"If you want this gold, or any part of it, you can't have it," replied Staples, with firmness and decision.

"We don't want the gold," said the veracious Keeps. "Being as it belongs to a dead man, and blood on every piece of it, we wouldn't touch it, to keep it, on any account. It is not the gold, my venerable friend, as I heard the preacher say when he chiseled you at seven-up, with aces hid in his boots, but the principle of the thing! We want fair dealing between man and man, and if we can't have that, here we part! We split upon the p'int of honor! D—n the gold! Eh, Kirby?"

"Certainly, I say so!" replied Kirby.

"Now, was the like ever heard?" said Staples, as if appealing to an audience. "Honor! I'm the soul of honor! as everybody knows with whom I ever had dealings. I don't think even Sassafras could deny that. If ever I seem to depart from the strictest principles of honor in my dealings, it is when I'm bothered and pestered by rogues and fools."

"Who do you call rogues and fools?" cried Keeps, with some heat. "Who put up a double cross against Sassafras and this man who lies dead here, and then got 'coppered' by Sassafras, and was beat at every point of the game? You ride away, and we will take our way."

"Who is to bury this man?" said Kirby. "You ought to do it, captain, if you keep his money."

"Let Sassafras bury him—he killed him," replied Staples. "There's another thing," he added: "If I go alone I shall take all of these horses; they all belong to me."

"Perhaps you would like to take this, too," said Keeps, advancing the muzzle of his gun until it was close to the old man's breast. "I told you I had scruples about killing a sleeping man, when you proposed this business to me. I now tell you that I shall have none at all about killing you, if you *will* bring on a fight."

"It will not come to a fight," said Kirby. "The captain will go away and leave us to hoe our own row."

"The captain might be followed," said Staples.

He felt that it might be a good deal better and safer to have Keeps before rather than behind him.

"Besides, you can't get out of this country without my help.

I brought you in, and I only can take you out. You dare not go near the fort."

"We dare go anywhere," replied Keeps. "As to the country, I know it about as well as you do. You might try to make it hot for us, if you dared stay in these parts, but you don't. Every minute you remain here is worth a drop of blood out of your heart. The mules won't be in your wagons before Sassafras and the Indians are after you, and they'll never leave your trail until your scalp swings at Cinnamon's belt. Go your way, old man! We shall be much safer anywhere than in your company. Sassafras and the chief are a brace of true bloodhounds. When they come upon you, hand over hand, see whether that gold will stop a ball like the one that killed Jagger. No wonder you want us to go with you."

The truth of this was so obvious, as well as dispiriting, that the captain was unable to reply. He looked at the moon, which had just risen over the mountains to the eastward, and now threw a shimmering light among the leafy boughs of the tree-tops. It was, in one sense, welcome, for it would help him to pick the best paths through his rugged way ; but in another it might bring danger and death upon him, even before the morning. There was no knowing what so bold and active a man as Sassafras might undertake in a pressing emergency. The river was a very formidable obstacle to any immediate pursuit by him, but, aided by the light of the moon, he might cross it. Should he do so, the captain would be well pleased that Keeps and Kirby would be on the bank to delay, if not to kill him. If they had left before he crossed, their tracks might divert his attention from the captain's own, and in this way give him valuable time.

"It would be a blessed thing," muttered Staples, "if these three unmitigated villains would meet, fight a Welsh main right here, and kill one another!"

With this he mounted his horse and rode down the slope, not without misgivings that something hot and swift might be sent whistling after him before he was out of sight. He plunged at once into the thick brush among the largest trees. The dim, retreating figure of the old man was still visible to the practised, cat-like eyes of the men behind, when Keeps dropped on his right knee, and levelled his rifle. His left elbow was on his left knee, the hand supporting and steadying the heavy barrel like a rest. His finger was upon the trigger.

" He is yet in sight," said Keeps, in a hissing whisper. " I have him in line by two trees, and can break his backbone at a single shot."

" Hold on !" said Kirby, catching him by the shoulder.

The rifle was fired, but the bullet flew wide of the mark Keeps would no doubt have hit, had he fired without interference from Kirby, and the old man spurred rapidly on without looking round, but turning short to the right. Keeps loaded his rifle, and seating himself on the ground, produced dried buffalo meat from his scrip, and desired Kirby to sit down and eat.

" You should not have grabbed hold of me," said Keeps. " I don't think I should have fired, for, barring the money in that belt, the old rascal is worth more to us alive than dead. It is him that Sassafras will be after in the first place. He has heard that shot, though, and is just now considering what it can mean. But no matter ! When he crosses the river he will do one of two things—go northwest with all speed to the fort and bring up his Indians, or strike the trail Staples is now making, and follow it. In either case the old man is a gone captain, and we shall be safe for the present. You'll owe me another life, Kirby. This is three times I have saved your bacon."

" I don't see that it *is* saved yet," said the giant.

" Yes, it is ! We shall jog along down the river while the hunt goes on up it. If we determine to go into the fort we shall have a clear road from below ; or we can keep to the woods until from some Indian or hunter belonging to the post we hear when, where, and how Sassafras comes up with Staples and kills him. He's sure to do so within four or five days."

" And what then, when we have heard it ?"

" What then ! why then we will send him word that we have kind of been on his side all along ; that after Staples murdered his friend in that cowardly manner, and committed a sort of highway robbery upon the man as Sassafras killed himself, we could stand it no longer, and fired upon him."

" We can tell him that in the morning, when he crosses," said Kirby. " That will seem the most straightforward."

"It might, but I don't think it will be best to be about here when the morning breaks. Before we could get speech of Sassafras, to make this little explanation, his rifle would go off and tumble one of us over. I would not give much in that case for the chance of the other. I don't mean to be within a mile of Sassafras, from this out, until he sends me word to come. Let us mount and ride away."

"We must bury this man somehow before we go," said Kirby.

"Not a bit of it. It was well enough to talk of it, but it would be useless to do it. We might put him in a crevice of the rocks and cover him with stones if we had time and daylight, but what would be the good? The wolves and ravens would have him out piece by piece. Take all the tobacco and powder he has on him, and let him lie. I'll have his pistols, and hide his gun. What use a gun ever was to such a man I could never make out, for he couldn't have hit a standing drove of cattle if there was another man within half a mile who might be likely to shoot at him."

With this Keeps mounted his horse and rode slowly away, followed by Kirby, the latter leading the horse which had been ridden by the unfortunate Jagger.

While these events were passing on the right bank of the Neosho, Sassafras had not been inactive, though cautious and silent, on the left bank. As soon as he had fired the shot which slew Jagger, he threw himself down and reloaded, letting the horses run. He then crawled to the top of the bluff again, and surveyed the other bank through the fast-gathering gloom of the coming night. All was still, and he could discover nothing. He sighed as he glanced at the spot where Tom Scarlet had last stood, and a low sound escaped from his lips as the roar of the rapids below, borne upon the wind of the evening, murmured in his ears. After a few minutes spent in bitter reflection, plans for a swift and terrible revenge occupied his mind. Rising cautiously and passing down the slope with swift but noiseless strides, he soon came to the horses, quietly grazing. His low whistle brought them to his side. The Young Chief and the spare horse were quickly stripped of their saddles and bridles, and turned loose. The White Horse was hobbled, his bridle removed and a blanket strapped round him over the saddle. Sassafras then placed the spare saddles among the boughs of a sapling, and giving the White Horse a good feed of oats from the saddle-bags, sat down and ate his own supper while the steed consumed his feed. He then ascended the slope, and lay down upon the bluff. Sassafras had not been long there when his quick ear caught the sharp voice of Keeps, raised in the altercation with Staples. The silvery moon rose over the ridge of the dark mountains, and Sussafras slid down to the level on which Tom Scarlet had stood when he was shot. The report of the rifle followed. "They have quarrelled, and there goes one," said the border man to himself. "That was Keeps's rifle. If he has killed old Staples he has cheated me, before his own accursed time has come!" He listened intently, but there was no further sound that he could catch. "Nobody hit! there was no return; no screech or imprecation; no movement to signify of the other two. This may be a plan to draw me over, but I shall wait." He rolled his blanket round him, and, half-seated, half-reclining, fell asleep.

Before the dawning of the day Sassafras awoke. His first thought was of the fate of his lost friend, whose body had gone down the river into the furious rapids of the rocky pass below. "Grief," said he, "is unavailing, but there remains revenge! I could almost wish that I had been the man to fall, only in that case I should not have been left to bring these two-legged wolves to their assured and bloody end." He strode silently to the top of the bluff and waited until it was light, listening for a movement or sign on the opposite bank. For another hour Sassafras lay upon his breast, his eyes scanning the bluff on the other side, and his ears alert to catch any sound from that quarter. The sun rose red in the eastern board, above the tops of the blue mountains. The man turned to look at it, and said, "Red dawning! there will be a storm. Ah!" he exclaimed, after a pause, "here comes a scout, who will tell me what there is on that bank besides the dead man."

Far in the eastern sky Sassafras had seen what seemed but a mere speck, but which was, in fact, a large bird of the vulture tribe, in full flight for the river, coming with eager wings towards the body which lay with face upturned upon the bluff. No very long time elapsed before the bird swept over Sassafras, circled round once or twice above the tree-tops on the other side, and settled slowly down, with wings half spread, upon the dead man's breast.

"They have gone! the way is clear for me," said Sassafras. He caught the White Horse and prepared him quickly for a long and rapid journey. The river was soon crossed. As Sassafras led his horse up the steep face of the bluff, the huge bird with horny beak and long, sharp talons was loath to leave its prey, and screamed defiance. It rose lazily, however, to the lower limb of a tree, while Sassafras passed hastily down the slope without looking on the horrid banquet to which it again descended. The single track made by Staples was readily found. The mark of the bullet jointly fired by Keeps and Kirby, as it were, was noted on the bark of a sapling. The wary borderer made a wide circuit from the beginning of the trail towards the north, round into the woods, and back to the starting-place. He saw that Staples had turned to the right after having been shot at, but discovered no sign that the other men had pursued him. He found, however, the tracks of three horses going down the river, just beneath the high bluff—that is to say, on the slope between it and the forest. One of these he saw, from the way it had planted its feet, was in leading reins, and kept close to the hip of the ridden horse.

"They have quarrelled and parted," said Sassafras. "The old man has hurried away for his camp, which must be to the north. The others have gone down the river. I must get the chief and two or three of his braves to hunt down Keeps and Kirby. Staples shall be my point. No man but me shall touch a hair of his head. Of the three not one shall escape!"

CHAPTER XXVII.

" ———————————— Let the great gods
That keep this dreadful pudder o'er our heads,
Find out their enemies now!"

ONE of the heavy storms which sometimes sweep over the great plains from the lofty mountain tops of the northwest had come booming down upon the neighborhood of the trading fort. It blew great guns! The sky was wild and ragged, as though torn by a convulsion, and at intervals rain and hail were pelted down in thick sheets, whose violence could scarcely be withstood by those who were exposed to it. The gale had set in before the going down of the sun. It had freshened hour after hour, and now, as midnight approached, it raged with increase and excess of fury. Betimes Antoine and Jules had sheltered the negroes and horses of their party in the shanties near the fort, and taken refuge in the post itself. Cinnamon and his Cheyennes, after providing for their hardy horses as best they might, had betaken themselves to the same building. A large log fire blazed upon the hearth of the largest room, and some twenty-five men sat around it, some on chairs and benches, some on the floor. The shelter of the place, the heat of the large fire, and the flavor of good tobacco, and a little whiskey, were grateful to all. The enjoyment of these comforts was heightened by the howling of the wind and beating of the hail and rain outside. At times the men conversed in low tones, as though unwilling to be heard by the spirits of the air who seemed to carry on howling war without. Once there was a laugh among some of them, but it was shortly hushed, as it seemed to be taken up and repeated in mocking tones and with ten thousand times more power, by the wild wind which swept over the roof and along the walls of the stout building.

" A real nor'wester, this. The first of the fall. It gives warning that the pleasant days are over, except the short Indian summer that lights winter in," said Jules.

" 'Tis a gale that sweeps over a wide extent of country—all the great plains," said Antoine. " What say you, Cinnamon ? Does this begin west of the Solomon's Fork ?"

" The storm," replied the chief, " was born about the Hell Gate Pass of the Rocky Mountains, in the country of the Blackfeet, the Crows and the Sioux. It sweeps around the tall peaks which keep sentinel over the parks, and gathers force as it crosses the plains, until it strikes the sides of the Ozarks. My people have gone to the mountain hollows, but the wind and hail smite my young men, who were here upon the prairies. Let it blow. The Indian is not a child that cannot endure the weather."

" That is true," said Jules ; " but they'll have a rough time of it, to my mind; and so will Sassafras and his companion on the other side of the Neosho."

"Sassafras is a man of the plains and woods," replied the chief. "He knows how to provide against the storm and to withstand it. He is in the timber land. The axe hung at his saddle-bow. The trees will fall, and he will make a wigwam among the branches. The Golden Bough may suffer, but he is strong."

"For all that, I wish they were here with us, before the fire," said Miriam Cotswold, who, still attired and painted as a young Kiowa, sat between Cinnamon and Antoine, and a little further back than either of them. She had spoken so as not to be heard by most of the company, and soon added: "It is a fearful night. There are howls and shrieks and moans in the air, as if the fiends had broken loose and flown up to rage between the earth and sky. I wish our friends were here!"

A silence followed, broken only from time to time by a word or two among the men and the flare of the fire as the logs blazed on the hearth.

"Hark!" said Miriam, placing her hands on the shoulders of Cinnamon and Antoine. "Did you hear anything? I thought there was a voice in the uproar of the elements."

"I hear the wolves howl in the gulches to windward, nothing more," replied the Frenchman.

"Antoine, the Singing Bird is right!" said the chief. "There again is the voice of a man. Sassafras is at hand. Unbar the door, and let my friend tell us what brings him back."

Campau and Antoine sprang to the door, while the other men rose to their feet. As soon as the fastenings were undone the door was thrown back by a strong gust, and the rain and hail came beating in. Another moment and Sassafras entered, leading the White Horse. Their appearance denoted the hardship of the journey they had made. The man's countenance was dark, haggard, and streaked with blood from cuts upon his cheeks and forehead, made by the boughs of trees and tall underbrush through which he had ridden at a great rate. His garments were torn almost to tatters, and the water streamed from them. The horse was covered with mud, bleeding from cuts and scratches, and evidently very tired. His nostrils flared out like the mouths of trumpets, and he blew hard at each beat of his powerful heart and each contraction of his muscular chest. Still his eye was bright, and he moved his lips and ears as Sassafras removed his saddle and bridle and sponged his mouth and eyes. Until he had done this the man said not a word. He then exclaimed:

"Jules and Antoine, let this horse be looked to, and well cared for. He is a good one—the best I ever rode for a whole day and half a night of storm."

His eye fell upon Miriam Cotswold, and making a sign for the Cheyenne chief and Campau to follow, he led her into an inner room. Here, too, a bright fire blazed upon the hearth, and everything was made snug, as if to defy the storm, and enable people to enjoy gently the warmth and shelter of a place impregnable to the elements. It was Campau's own apartment. Cards had been played earlier in the night, for the pack lay scattered over the rough table, and a stone jug of whiskey was at the head of the bunk bed. Sassafras seized the liquor, and pouring out about half a pint, drank it neat at a draught.

"A little of that will do the White Horse good as well as me," said he. "Campau, let Antoine have about a pint, and give it to the horse in as much water."

"The horse is here and will do well. You are here, somewhat weather-beaten, it is true, but that is well. Now, where is Tom Scarlet?" said Miriam Cotswold.

Sassafras shrunk within himself for a moment, and there was a contraction of his face, as if a pang had struck his heart. His countenance then became firm, his mouth was set, and his dark eyes flashed in the light of the fire. He answered with a stern but troubled voice: "I left him in the Neosho river. He is dead!"

"O, Sassafras! the fine young fellow from the dear old land! You do not, you cannot mean it?"

"I would to God it was not so," replied the border man; "but why try to conceal the truth, even for a few brief hours? He is dead, and I have come to tell it. Staples killed him at sundown of the day after we left here."

"Has my friend got the scalp of the Wolverine?" said the Indian, seizing the handle of his knife.

"Not yet, but he will have it before the moon is three nights older," replied Sassafras. "This is how it happened: We had just swum our horses across the river, which was well up, nearly in flood. I was on the bluff, with two of the bridles in my hands. Tom was on a shelf half-way down, with the White Horse. All at once four men rode up to the top of the bluff on the other side. I just saw they were Staples, Keeps, Kirby and Jagger. Tom uttered a cry, Staples fired, and down our friend fell into the river. At the shot Staples and the Western men took cover. I fired and killed Jagger."

"The Snake-Eyes was no more than a squaw," said the chief. "He cannot pay for the life of the friend of Sassafras and the Cheyennes. His scalp is too little. It is no good! I will go upon the war-path, while Sassafras comforts the Singing Bird, and revenge the Golden Bough."

"You will, Cinnamon, and so will I," said Sassafras. "The Singing Bird knows that our friend must be avenged. That is all the good we can do for the satisfaction of those to whom he was dear, and it shall be done well. Miriam, for every tear the Rose of Hawk'll will shed for poor Tom, a hundred drops of blood shall follow the bullets and blades of Cinnamon and myself. Chief, we will take horse in the morning, with four or five of your young men, and of the three who went alive from the crossing when it was dark, not one shall escape. Presently, I will tell you which way they took, and where they may be found."

The face of the chief worked with exultation he made no effort to suppress, and his eyes glowed like the live coals on the hearth. Whatever regret he felt at the untimely fate of Tom Scarlet was as nothing to the ferocious and exceeding joy with which he he heard the ban of extermination pronounced by Sassafras against Staples and his accomplices. Indeed, Cinnamon was ready enough to make the doom much more sweeping than Sassafras meant it to be.

"True, my friend," said the savage warrior, with unbridled ferocity. "My knife and the tomahawks of the Cheyennes have been dull—they shall now be sharp. Let Sassafras eat and rest. My young men know where the Wolverine hid his wagons in the hills. Longwind shall start at break of day, and we will follow. The Golden Bough was as one of the

Cheyennes, and my friend. We will avenge him—slay the slayer, and all that belong to his party. We can come up with Longwind to-morrow night. The camp of the Wolverine we will then surprise, and put every man in it to the edge of the knife and axe. The blacks being disposed of, we will follow the trail of the three whites, take their scalps and those of any other men who cross the war-path. Let Longwind and Three Scalps come into this council."

"Hold!" said Miriam Cotswold. "What have the negroes done? Why are they to suffer, poor fellows?"

"Done?" said the chief; "they live in the tents of the Wolverine; they saddle his horses, cook his food, and clean his guns. They must die! as the cubs of the wolf, which never did damage, die. Shall Sassafras and the Cheyennes fail to take full revenge? Shall the fair maiden over the sea be cheated of her dues? No! when the scalps of the three whites are at the pole of my tent those of the blacks shall hang in the smoke of the pale-face fire at her father's house. I would there were more of them, that she might say 'It is good!'"

Miriam would have remonstrated further, but Sassafras told her quietly that it was useless to argue with an Indian on such a point as this. He either could not, or would not, make the distinctions which were obvious to all but savages in arms. Food was then partaken of by Sassafras, and he related at greater length all his proceedings after the firing of the fatal shot. The Indian rose and left the place of the conversation to rejoin his braves in the other room, despatch Longwind at once, and prepare four or five noted for courage, wariness, and skill for the expedition. Before he lay down in front of the fire to sleep, Sassafras gave his word to Miriam Cotswold that none of the negroes should be hurt, unless they took arms and joined in a fight.

The storm roared on through the latter part of the night, but in the morning the shrill whistling of the wind indicated that the heart of the gale, as the sailors say, was broken. At break of day there was a lull; the rain ceased. A few pieces of pale blue appeared through breaks in the thin clouds and flying scud. The wind, however, still blew freshly, shaking showers of large drops from the overhanging boughs of the trees. A group of men and horses at a very early hour stood

17

at the back of the shanties near the fort. Four armed Indians were already mounted. Two others held Indian horses, while Campau, Pierre Langlois, Miriam Cotswold, Antoine, Jules and Black Dick stood by the side of the gray mare, Virginia. She was caparisoned for service. The eyes of Miriam Cotswold and the men were cast from time to time towards one of the shanties in which it was understood the chief of the Cheyennes with Sassafras and Three Scalps, one of the most daring and crafty warriors of the band, were holding a sort of council. At length the buffalo robe which hung before the entrance was pushed aside and the men came forth. The chief led the van with a stately carriage, and an unsparing glitter in his hard, dark eye. He was in his war-paint, vermilion and black, nearly bare to the waist, and a necklace composed of the huge claws of the grizzly bear hung down upon his breast. The lineaments of his countenance were stern, and his stature seemed to be increased by the near prospect of battle and of blood as he strode, rifle in hand, to his horse. Three Scalps, the warrior who followed him, was neither as tall nor as powerful as Cinnamon, but his frame was singularly well-balanced, and his limbs were all bone and sinew. The scars he bore, and now showed with pride, indicated that he had been in some desperate fights. He was painted much as Cinnamon was, and though his face was stern and composed, there was no mistaking the exulting eagerness for blood which glowed in his eye. The borderman followed the Indians with an air of perfect resolution somewhat tinged with sadness. When he reached the group of his friends he took Miriam Cotswold by the hand and led her aside.

"Miriam," said he, "I start upon this expedition to avenge the murder, bloody and unprovoked, of your friend and mine. Before I go I have some words for your ear, and, I hope, for your heart. To some it might seem an ill-chosen time to tell you I love, and that you are the object of my love; but the moment to me is fitting enough. In the stormy and fitful hours, when my heart was torn with grief, and my mind tossed with schemes for a swift and terrible revenge, in all their wanderings they came again to you at last. Why then, when I am about to do the last duty by the dead, should I not declare my love for the living? Can you accept my vow and return one to me?"

"Sassafras," she replied, with much feeling in her voice, "this is sudden. But I see that it is earnest, and I will be plain. It is no time for dissimulation, nor have I a mind to it. This hour chosen for interchange of troth, while the wing of the Angel of Death casts its dread shadow upon us, and you are about to go forth to take other lives, might seem ominous of evil instead of happiness; but I am a daughter of the dwellers in the tents, and you are a hunter and armed rover of the frontier. We may not woo as the wrens woo among the early rose-leaves, nor coo like the ring-doves in the bosky copse. All we can ask from each other is truth. Mine I pledge till death, by the great God who sees our hearts, and from his starry throne rules all the races of the world, the children of men!"

"Thanks, Miriam! I will be true to you, as the sun to the west from his rising in the east, whether under clear and pleasant skies, or in cloud and storm!" said Sassafras. "My mind now springs again, and my heart leaps to meet the duty of the hour. The Indians are ready. We go, and it is done! I shall strike harder, quicker and surer now than ever before. Love and revenge will inspire and guide the blows!"

"But, Sassafras," said the girl, earnestly and hastily, "as you love me, and we honor the dead whose loss we deplore, see to it that none but the guilty fall. The negroes of Staples's camp are clear of the deed, and you must save them. The chief, once mild and kind, is now all the savage; and in the fearful battle-paint of his tribe has no more feeling of mercy nor reason than the tiger who scents blood on the wind of the jungle. Sassafras, I do not ask you to spare Staples or Keeps, but when the frightful war-whoops ring in the night, see that the guiltless negroes are unharmed."

"I have provided for it. There will be no night attack, and I will bring them off harmless," he replied.

"Further, Sassafras, husband and lord that is to be! until you are certain that he deserves the doom, let not Kirby die. He had probably no hand in the murder, no knowledge of the plot. Antoine and Campau and Pierre Langlois say so. Therefore, spare him!"

"It may not be!" said Sassafras, firmly. "Miriam, he was *there*, art and part with the others! The negroes shall be saved. Not a hair of their heads shall be touched, unless they take arms to fight for one who has been a hard task-master to them. Staples will be my mark. The warrior who was with me and Cinnamon in the hut, and another Cheyenne, will go with me, while the chief and the other three Indians will make for the Neosho. We shall find Staples in his camp or on the move with his train, and then——"

"What then?" said she, as he paused.

"Then he dies on sight!" he exclaimed, while his color rose and his eye dilated. "This, Miriam, is the doom and justice of the border. He is already as one of the dead."

"The man is old. I could wish some other hand than yours might send him to his long and last account."

"Miriam Cotswold," said Sassafras, "if he lives to be much older, they shall call me liar and coward. I and no other will execute justice on him who treacherously slew my friend. I must shoot the fatal shot or strike the blow! To what end should I leave this to either of the two Indians, who will be with me? If there were no other reason—and there is one that is all-powerful—the safety of the negroes demands this from me. The Cheyennes, both tried warriors, will be like blood-hounds in the slips. If either kills Staples, and swings his reeking scalp, with the whoop of the tribe, I shall not be able to hold the hand of the other; and there will be carnage while one of Staples's men remains alive. To guard against some such thing as this, I have persuaded Cinnamon to go south after Keeps and Kirby, for in that quarter there is no one else to kill. And now, Miriam, wife and part of my life that is to be! farewell for a while. The Indians look towards us."

"Yet stay! another word! Is there no hope that poor Tom may be wounded, but yet alive?"

"There is none. If there had been, think you that I would have left the river? He fell headlong, no doubt, shot through the brain, and so unconscious of what killed him. Besides, if he touched the water alive, he was swept down into the rapids and there an end! Had there been one chance in a thousand for his life, I had not been here now."

"I feel it! I know it!" she said. "But, oh! if the remains could be recovered and decently interred, it would be a consolation to us in after times and to his friends at home. The Indians, hot for blood, caring nothing for what lies cold in the river, will make no search until their ire is glutted. Shall nothing be done?"

"There is reason in what you say, though the hope of finding his body is vain, I fear. Still, the last slight chance shall not be thrown away. Antoine shall go with Cinnamon and his men to the Neosho, and make the searching of the rocks and shallows his special object. Tell him to saddle the best horse and ride after us. He may easily overtake us ere I and Cinnamon part. Miriam, good-by!"

With this Sassafras folded her in his arms, and held her for a moment to his brawny breast. In another instant he sprang to the saddle of the stout gray mare, and the party rode away.

"Haste, haste, Antoine!" said the gypsy. "Saddle your horse and overtake them. You are to go, too. Nay, Antoine, Jules! saddle two horses. I will go myself with Antoine."

CHAPTER XXVIII.

"Heigh, ho! sing heigh, ho! unto the green holly:
Most friendship is feigning, most loving mere folly.
Then heigh, ho! the holly!"

IT was the day before Christmas, and preparations for the proper celebration of the great Christmas festival were being made in all the hamlets, mansions, farm-houses and cottages about Wootton, Ridingcumstoke and the Vale of Aylesbury. "Store's no sore," was the motto of the neighborhood, as well as of Justice Greedy, and much provision of substance and luxury was being laid in. At a shop in the nearest market town there was a small assemblage, at once grave, critical and jovial, examining the stock of the tradesman who owned and kept it. Now, it was a butcher's shop—a place certain to be esteemed low, if not vulgar, by those who affect artificial perfumes and drink absinthe. The butcher, however, is a man whose calling is held in some esteem by the nations who keep Christmas in the Scandinavian and Anglo-Saxon manner. Besides, neither Sir Jerry Snaffle, John Bullfinch, nor the other worthies who looked on while the butcher bustled about, whistling, "O, the Roast Beef of Old England!" cared for any perfumes but such as came from bunches of violets, rosebuds, lavender, bean blossoms and the like. As for absinthe, none of them had ever heard of it, and all of them would have repudiated it as a beverage if they had tasted it.

The butcher's shop was in truth a very clean, fresh, wholesome place, and the joints of beef and mutton, artistically cut by the butcher, and trimmed with holly and ivy by his wife, looked as handsome, and more eatable, than so many clever pictures. The butcher's round, red face shone like the berries on the holly boughs as he slapped the joints with his long knife, and related the history of each ox and wether which had contributed to his Christmas show. Mr. Cleaver spoke of the animals as he might have done of old friends, and no wonder, for while the Christmas beasts he intended to purchase were in the course of feeding on the farms of their owners, it was his custom to visit them about once a fortnight, to handle them and report progress to his wife, his journeymen, and his principal customers. A few of these last had been invited to look in that morning, chief among whom were Sir Jerry, John Bullfinch, and another good man and true, who had not yet arrived. The butcher was bustling and important, often looking down the street, as if rather impatient for the coming of the other man. The baronet ventured a remark upon the beef and the Cotswold mutton, to which Mr. Cleaver replied by saying:

"They was all good, Sir Jerry, this year—all excellent good. They all died well, full of fat, and they have cut up well. My Christmas beasts always do. But there's one extro'nary animal. He died better and has cut up better than any fat beast I ever had before. I mean the red ox fed by Mr. Southdown, who ought to have been here before now. Here he comes, however. He's a pictur'."

It was never exactly settled whether this last sentence referred to the ox or the yeoman who fed him, for the greeting extended to the man was so hearty and noisy, that no opportunity for explanation offered, and the ox was momentarily forgotten by all but his best friend and ardent admirer, the butcher.

Mr. Southdown was a man of great stature and bulk, nearly

as big himself as a moderate-sized ox of the Highland blood.
He strode along with ponderous tread, vast but not fat, in a
blue coat, drab breeches, leather leggings, and a low-crowned
hat. Instead of a riding-whip he carried a stick of tough
ground-ash. Mr. Southdown was a man of mark in those
parts. A man of many acres, arable and pasture. A man
of money. Crisp bank-notes carried in a bulky pocket-book
and bright sovereigns in a yellow canvas bag. A man of
strong opinions and few words. He was as great a stickler for
the landed interest, and Church and King, as Sir Jerry Snaffle
and John Bullfinch themselves, but it was in his own way, not
in theirs. Sir Jerry Snaffle was sometimes eloquent in his de-
clamations on these topics, from sheer force and plain sense.
John Bullfinch was apt to be disputatious. Mr. Southdown
was neither eloquent nor disputatious. It was not, as he said,
worth his while. His mind was made up! He cared nothing
for radicals or revolutionists! "Argeyment" was of no use
in such matters—nothing but a waste of words! Could the
radicals argey the elm trees out of his pastures? or the oaks
out of his spinneys? That was what he wanted to know!
Being of a solid temper, and with a voice like the boatswain
of a line-of-battle ship, Mr. Southdown usually succeeded in
putting down the radical bagmen and tradesmen he encountered. The only people who ventured to argue with him were
his youngest daughter, Margery, and her particular friend
Young Jack.

"Servant all, gentlemen," said he. "This looks like Christmas. I left my missus and daaters making plum-puddings
and mince-pies, as is but reason. Well, Cleaver, what's said
to this here beef? If anybody says there's better beef in
Lunnon, or in Windsor Castle, or anywhere else, he's wrong.
I shan't argey the question with him, but he's wrong!"

"Cleaver never had a better show," said Sir Jerry. "And
he says your red ox is the best that ever was seen here, or
hereabouts. He ought to know!"

"If he says that, he don't know, Sir Jerry," replied Southdown. "In his father's time there was a bullock killed by
him, called the Great Ox of Hawk'ell, which was fed by John
Bullfinch, and it was the biggest ever seen in England, except
the Durham Ox. We must knock under to the Durham Ox,

though I have my doubts whether the northcountrymen didn't give short weight when they made up the report."

"Gentlemen all!" said the butcher, "I remember the Great Ox of Hawk'ell well. He was bigger than this one, but this one was riper, and died better."

"I shan't argey the p'int," Mr. Southdown roared. "You can't get rid of the Hawk'ell ox by argeyment. My counsel was took by John about feeding him towards the last, and we made him the greatest ox ever seen, as well as the best, if the northcountrymen gave in short weight. Cleaver, you're wrong. That settles it."

"I ought to be heard about this," said the butcher. "Being in the trade, I have the right to an opinion."

"Sir, you have no right to argey from opinions. I fed the red ox, and I won't argey the p'int at all. I, being correct, decline to argey. You, being wrong, have no right to argey!"

"O," said the butcher, "you haven't seen the prime parts of the red ox at all."

Mr. Southdown was about to interpose another protest, but the butcher bawled, "Now, missus!" and missus entered. It was the butcher's wife, comely and rosy, deft at curtseys and pleasant smiles, and with red ribbons among the laces of her cap. Together they drew a white sheet from something it covered, and there lay the sirloins and prime ribs of the red ox in all their massive beauty. On one sirloin the name of Sir Jerry Snaffle appeared in red holly berries on the rich, yellow fat of the back. The other bore that of John Bullfinch. One side of the mighty ribs was marked, in like manner, Richard Southdown.

"Now," said the butcher, "I call that a pictur'!"

"I know but little about pictur's," replied Mr. Southdown, except pictur's of live cattle. You may see the pictur' of the great ox in John Bullfinch's parlor at Hawk'ell, done by a man who needed but a little knowledge of the p'ints and beauties of a bullock or a horse to make him the finest painter that ever was seen in England. He done the Black Horse at Aylesbury. I don't mean done the landlord out of his score for drink, but done the pictur' of the horse on the sign. As to this beef, I call it capital beef, as good beef as ever was in England, save the beef of the great ox of Hawk'ell."

The baronet, John Bullfinch, and the others complimented Mr. Cleaver and his wife—the former upon the appearance of the beef, and the latter upon her own. The conversation was still going on in loud tones when Young Jack drove up with a spring cart, which seemed to be already well laden with divers boxes and hampers. The sirloin, together with many pieces of beef of about ten pounds each—cut by the knife of Cleaver at Christmas time for a man like John Bullfinch— a ten-pound piece always weighed from twelve to fourteen, and this was so much the better for the laborers and widows with families, to whom they would be given at Hawkwell. The beef being loaded, the cart went down upon the springs. Young Jack, touching his hat to Sir Jerry and Mr. Southdown, and favoring the butcher's wife with an agreeable nod, resumed the reins.

"Drat that boy!" said Mrs. Cleaver, as she retired smiling, while John Bullfinch said:

"Hold on! what have you got?"

"Everything!" replied his son.

"Everything means nothing, sir. You give straightforra'd answers when gentlemen are in company. Mention what you've got."

"Well!" said Jack, "there's change for a five-pound note in shillings—one apiece for the children on Boxing Day. Change for another in half-crowns—one apiece for the lassies and lads. A lot of tea and sugar for the old women. Tobacco for the old men. A box with a sight of toys, and a hamper from the confectioner's, ordered by May. A saddle and bridle, ordered by May and me."

"A saddle and bridle! and who's that for? Sir Jerry, my daater and son do nearly as they like at Christmas time, and for a man of my means, they are good givers."

Sir Jerry nodded and smiled. Mr. Southdown gave a portentous wink, and shook his stick at Young Jack.

"Who's that saddle and bridle for?" said John. Seeing that his son hesitated, he added: "Come! you needn't be afraid to speak out. I insist upon being told."

"Then don't you tell him!" said Mr. Southdown. "I mean to encourage in my godson no disrespect to his father, but 'I insist upon being told' is a species of argeyment not to be tolerated.   It's like what goes on at the Fox and Grapes, when one of the fellows that spout against the Land and the Constitution, winding up with an impertinent question, says, 'I insist upon being told.'"

Sir Jerry laughed and John Bullfinch laughed.   He then said, "Well, I believe you have named everything and forgot nothing—go on.   Stay! by George! you've forgot the brandy.   We should be ruined at twelve to-night past remedy without the brandy!"

"The brandy!" replied Jack, "I declare I had forgot the brandy.   I'll stop for it as I go by.   It was Parkins put it clean out of my head, with a story that Tom Scarlet was killed in America."

"Tom Scarlet killed!   Sir Jerry—Southdown—did you ever hear the like of this?"

"An idle tale, no doubt," said Sir Jerry Snaffle.   "Parkins could have no news, good or bad, of Tom Scarlet before I had.   I took measures to get news of him three months ago."

"That settles the p'int!   Parkins knows nothing," said Mr. Southdown.

"Ay! but, gentlemen, Sir Jerry has been unable to get any news of Tom, and that looks bad," said Young Jack.

"Jack," said Mr. Southdown, doggedly, "when you was a baby being christened, I stood godfeyther.   I shan't argey with you.   Lady Snaffle stood May's godmother—she may argey the p'int with her, if she pleases.   I say it's all settled. Sir Jerry is right.   Parkins is a conceited fellow and knows nothing!"

"Give me leave for a moment," said Sir Jerry.   "Now, Master Jack, who is said to have killed Tom Scarlet?"

"The Indians, Sir Jerry."

"What for?" cried John Bullfinch.

"To eat him, Parkins says."

"Parkins is a fool," cried John.   "Eat him! why, it's unnatural.   And besides, haven't we heard that there's millions of buffaloes in that country?   Who would prefer Tom Scarlet to beef?"

Mr. Southdown shook his head.   He had no faith in buffalo beef.   No faith in American beef of any sort.   No faith in any beef but that of the cattle bred and fed in and about the pastures of the Vale of Aylesbury. The Indians might have had buffalo beef, but still wanted a change. " I've heerd tell of such things," said he.

" Master Jack," said Sir Jerry, " I believe nothing of this story which you have heard from Parkins, and I charge you to say nothing of it to your sister. John Bullfinch, my old neighbor and *friend !* if such a thing had happened I should have heard of it before Parkins. Three months ago there came a brief notice to me from America—that if, I accepted the steeple-chase match offered by the Duke for any horse hunted in the midland counties last year, gentlemen riders. I could win it. The match was made. Tom Scarlet was in the Indian country when he sent that message to me, but he was on good terms with the Indians, and his business there was ended. The message was one in trust, and faithfully brought to me by the purser of an American ship."

" That's good news, Sir Jerry!" said Young Jack. " And besides, if your honor pleases, we should have heard from the American who took Tom into the Indian country, if anything had happened to him. Everybody who knows that American says he is a good man."

" The suggestion is good, Jack ; but who does know him ?" said the baronet.

" Well, sir, the sailor Cox and Gypsy Jack. Jack says that the American is a first-rate man. But Parkins says he knows better, having had it from a sure hand."

" I'd give a pound if Gypsy Jack was here," said John Bullfinch, in much perplexity. " He knows as much about this American business as anybody. Besides, he'd tell me what to say at home. It's nearly impossible for me to keep a secret from my daater, May, without help, and I fancy she isn't as hearty like as she was last spring-time."

" You must not mention it to her on any account," said Sir Jerry. " It's ten to one there is no truth in it. I'll give anybody a sovereign to lay me ten to a hundred on it. Parkins always has evil tidings to tell of somebody. Where did he get this, Jack ?"

" From three tramping sailors who were in the lock-up at Aylesbury yesterday evening."

"These men were discharged, no doubt, this morning, on account of their being sailors," said Sir Jerry. "Which way were they travelling?"

"Towards London. They had come from Liverpool, and told Parkins they should join a King's ship at the Nore."

"Ay, ay!" said Sir Jerry. "Very few of those fellows ever reach the fleet, though. Now, John Bullfinch, these sailors I'll overtake before night, and hear what their story really is, and upon what it was founded. I'll send word to Lady Snaffle that business calls me away to-day. Ride over to the Hall after your Christmas dinner to-morrow, and I'll tell you all about it. Not a word to your daughter on any account until after I return."

With this the baronet mounted his horse and was about to set off at a great pace. But Mr. Southdown interposed.

"One word," said he. "In questioning these sailors, keep it dark that you be a magistrate. You may as well burke the baronet, too. But let 'm know that her ladyship, your honor's wife, is daughter of an admiral—one of Nelson's fighting captains at the Nile and Trafalgar. Sir Jerry, you'll find th' of more use than any amount of argeyment. Sailors don't like argeyment. My mind's made up on the main p'int. Tom Scarlet's alive and well. But as you're going to overhaul these sailors, Sir Jerry, keep the magistrate and the baronet in the background, and bring forward the admiral's daughter."

Mr. Southdown delivered this in his most impressive manner, and accompanied it by some heavy blows from his stick upon the butcher's horse-block. Then Sir Jerry rode away.

When John Bullfinch reached home he found that his son had got there before him. The Christmas presents had been unloaded and put away. May had finished the decorations of the rooms for the coming eve. The last sprig of ivy and the last bunch of holly had been put up, and the bough of the mistletoe of the oak had been hung in the centre of the ceiling of the largest room. By the hearth lay the great oak log which was to be burned that Yule, and which might keep aglow for about a week in its own ashes. May Bullfinch was paler and thinner, and her expression more thoughtful and subdued than before. Her father was ill at ease. He had agreed to ride with her to the Grange that afternoon, and the

rumor he had heard as to the fate of Tom Scarlet made it a
very unpleasant and embarrassing arrangement. He ordered
her horse, however, to be brought out, and after luncheon they
set off together. The day was raw and cloudy. The father,
in no mood for conversation just then, knew no better way of
avoiding it than by riding fast, and they cantered rapidly on,
almost without a word until the Grange and its farm buildings
were in sight. The strong, old stone house, with the dark yew
trees standing by it, as they had stood for two hundred years
and more, looked gloomy, but the reception within was cheerful.
A large fire had been lighted in the parlor, and the crimson
curtains at the old-fashioned, diamond-latticed windows relieved
the sombreness of the dark oak wainscoting and carved furni-
ture of antique pattern. The housekeeper, an old gentlewoman,
some distant relative of Tom Scarlet's father, placed cake and
wine upon the table, and invited them to partake of it. She
had hoped Tom himself would have been home again by
Christmas, but she had received no news of him.

"My dear Mrs. Ruth," said May, "we have not come to
eat, and news was scarcely to be expected here. Have your
men provided the holly and ivy?"

"Yes, miss, and a fine lot of it. Every room in the house
is trimmed with it but this. This, by your request, was left
for you."

"Thank you! A glass of wine, and then I'll begin work."

The boughs were brought into the room by a shock-headed
lad, who had often been threatened by Moleskin with imprison-
ment for trespassing, and by Parkins with the stocks for small
offences and disrespect to the "authorities." As he threw down
the ivy and the splendid holly boughs, thick with berries, very
large and very red, the shock-headed, yellow-haired youth
made a shy bow towards May and shot a glance of dubious
expression at her father. John Bullfinch did not perceive it.

"That's wonderful fine holly," said he. "It beats what we
have at Hawk'ell all hollow, and I saw none in town this
morning half as good. Where did you get it, Joe?"

There was no Joe to answer this question, for the shock-
headed youth had stepped on the mat, and gone out as softly
and quickly as could be. Well he might. That very morning the gardener of a rector in an adjacent parish, upon whose

lawn there were some holly bushes of uncommon beauty, was astounded at finding that the finest boughs had been cut in the night, and carried off.

May Bullfinch was soon busy with the decoration of the room.

"Father," said she, "if he should come home to-night or to-morrow, or any day before the new year begins, he will be glad to find this room prepared as it used to be. The bare walls would be cheerless welcome."

John groaned in spirit, and knew not what to reply. As she continued her task, he stood and looked on, making no remark, but wishing it was over. The last thing to be adorned was a picture of Tom Scarlet on a white pony, painted when he was a boy. The finest sprigs of holly, the ones with the largest and richest berries, were reserved for this. As May stood upon a chair to set the picture off with the little boughs, her father wore some such expression as he would have had at the dressing of a corpse. At last it was done. The old lady, Mrs. Ruth, declared that the room was beautiful, especially the picture. "But," said she, "you have put no ivy on his picture, Miss May."

"No; it is a plant of the damp and shade."

"Ay, it minds one of the cold churchyard," returned the old lady.

"While the bonny holly," said May, "glows like the fire of the Yule log upon the hearth, and the red Christmas wine."

"I must stop this," said John Bullfinch. Then aloud, "May, my dear, the way is long, and the day is almost done. Let us say good-by to Mrs. Ruth."

"Go, father, I will follow."

The farmer and the housekeeper went out of the room together, May knelt just under the picture and said the Lord's Prayer. Then she joined her father.

Mr. Bullfinch was unable to leave the Grange as soon as he expected. A turning movement was executed upon his flank, and his retreat was cut off, so to speak, by an old inmate of the Grange. It was the hunting groom, Straddles by name, who now accosted him, and made a request that he should visit the stables.

"What, is there something wrong, Straddles? Anything lame?"

" No, sir ; nothing of the kind. I only want you to see that things are in order," replied Straddles. " He'll find his hunters fit to go to the meet and take part in a hard run, if he comes home to-morrow. You come and see."

" Go, father. I should like to see myself," said May.

The horses were examined, and John pronounced them all right.

" So," said he to Straddles, " you look for Tom before the hunting season is over, do you ?"

" Of course I do ! My own opinion is he'll be here before another week is over ; but it ain't an event to bet upon. He's uncertain as to time, but sure in the end. I have lived at the Grange above fifty year, and I ought to know the Scarlets. Tom is a Scarlet all over. You can't say just when he'll come, but you can say that he *will* come."

" Straddles," said May, " perhaps you can say when you expect him."

" I can, miss," replied Straddles confidently. " I expect him every hour. He may come at any moment. There's a box kept done up for the horse he'll bring. There's hot water kept ready to make a bucket of gruel for him ; for ever since he was a boy, and even then, Tom has always been a hard rider."

The confidence of the old man infected May and her father. The evidence of the box kept in order, and the hot water ready to make gruel for the tired horse, seemed to John to outweigh anything which might have fallen from roving sailors, and had come through Parkins. Besides, the old man put the finishing stroke by an allusion to Sir Jerry Snaffle's great match.

" He may," said he, " be detained for a week or two more. The wind is east at present. But he's sure to be here to ride Sir Jerry's horse, in the match. That's the latest moment, and that's in March. Mr. Bullfinch, Tom will ride Sir Jerry's horse, and the duke will lose, as sure as his duchess wears strawberry leaves. We may not beat him in the horse, but we shall in the rider. They can't bring a man here that can ride over our stiff country like Tom Scarlet."

" I don't believe they can, Straddles," cried John. " By Jove, if this comes off, what a time we'll have at Hawk'ell !"

"I wish he had come, or that he will come this week," said Straddles, "not that it matters to the match, but Tom is a young man of a kind heart, and the poor will miss him this Christmas."

"Send the poor to me. Every mother's son and daater that could have had a gift from him, you send to Hawk'ell. Am I right, May?"

"To be sure, dear father. As to Tom, everybody likes him."

"My dear, everybody don't like him. Parkins don't like him. Sir Jerry made that remark this morning, and it accounts for—eh!—Straddles, he's sure to be here in time for the match, is he?"

"Sure to come, and sure to win. You put your money on as soon as Sir Jerry has got his on," said Straddles, assisting May to mount her horse.

"I'm so glad we came here. That Straddles is a sensible man," said May, as they cantered away, while the shock-headed lad was still looking intently at the half-crown she had left in his hand as he put the reins in hers.

"Ay! a knowing fellow," said John. "Sir Jerry will be glad to hear of this, May. I'll go over to the Hall to-morrow, after dinner, and tell him all about it. It's five o'clock, and that nag of yours is lazy—send him along!"

CHAPTER XXIX.

"Duncan Grey cam' here to woo,
    Ha, ha! the wooing o't,
On blithe Yule night, when we were fu',
    Ha, ha! the wooing o't."

"Ye gypsy gang that deal in glamour,
And you, deep read in hell's black grammar,
    Warlocks and witches."

JOHN BULLFINCH and his daughter had left Hawkwell on their way to the Grange but a short time, when a visitor arrived at the farm, who received a very cordial welcome from Young Jack. They had not been acquainted many weeks, but the visitor was in high favor with the lad, and not without some reason. In the first place, he was young; in the next, of high birth and station; third, he was very frank and courteous; and last, Young Jack had been able to do him a favor, and confer distinction upon him in the hunting field. He was tall, slender, with a high-bred look, and he was mounted on a superb gray hunter. The young man's complexion was fair, his hair was brown and curly, his eyes were a rich hazel, and he had not a shade of beard or whisker. His age was about two-and-twenty, but he looked much younger, and this was a matter of some annoyance to the heir of the Doomsdays, one of the wealthiest and most powerful of the noble families in the kingdom. Often, as Lord Doomsday surveyed his very handsome face and fine figure in the glass, he turned away with impatience, because of his boyish appearance. He commonly hunted in Leicestershire and Northamptonshire, in which counties his father possessed large estates, but this season he had given much of his time to the hounds of Sir Jerry Snaffle and those of the famous Heythrop Hunt. He had soon become passably well acquainted with John Bullfinch, whose sterling character and worth had been made known to him by Sir Jerry Snaffle, the major, and some other gentlemen of the neighborhood. Moreover, he had formed a habit of blushing and raising his hat to the farmer's daughter, May, whenever she appeared at the meet by her father's side, which was hardly as often now as it had been the season before. True it is, too, that Lord Doomsday's horses, somehow or another, got to know the road to Hawkwell, and took him there of their own accord, at times, when he was out for exercise on non-hunting days. When John was at home the young man talked with him on such subjects as hunting, shooting, the landed interests, and the turf—especially the last. The Doomsdays had been great breeders of thoroughbred horses ever since the time of Queen Anne, and the family was held in especial esteem by John Bullfinch, because, through the union of Waxy and Penelope, early in the nineteenth century, it had produced the ever-famous Whalebone blood. To these conversations May and Young Jack commonly listened with interest. Sometimes John Bullfinch was not at home when the young man called, and then Young Jack entertained him with his notions of hunters, hounds, race-horses, &c., to which

18

the young nobleman listened with courtesy, although he rather
preferred conversation with May Bullfinch upon the usual
topics of the country side at that season—the weather, parties,
balls, the coming Christmas, subscriptions to charities, &c.
The young man was, of course, well educated; he was well
informed on general subjects, and his abilities were good, as
those of the men of his house always had been. But his
youthful looks and his extreme diffidence, not to say bashful-
ness, kept him back in general society, and many mistook his
shyness and modest reserve for haughty pride of birth and
prospect of future succession to immense estates. He felt much
more at his ease in the presence of Farmer Bullfinch, his
daughter May and his son Jack, than in that of the gentry
of the provincial town where he kept his hunters. The ful-
some flatteries of some annoyed him. He drank but little,
and gambled none at all. He was too reserved to mingle
much in the general society of the place, and hated flirting
and gossips. John Bullfinch and his daughter treated the
young man with the greatest respect and some deference, but
no sycophantic observances. He stayed to tea sometimes, as
the long nights of the winter season set in. Once or twice,
when Lord Doomsday called at Hawkwell, neither John Bullfinch nor Young Jack was at home, and on being told this by
May, the young man appeared to be very little disappointed,
and declared that, as he had nothing else to do, he would
wait, if Miss Bullfinch would be kind enough to permit him
to do so. As a matter of course, John Bullfinch held that
Lord Doomsday's visits to Hawkwell were on his account.
Perhaps May Bullfinch doubted this. The young man himself could scarcely have told what the object of his visits was,
but he knew that he liked to make them, and thought that
was enough. Young Jack was sure that the young nobleman
came to see him, arguing in this way: "With all his talents,
his noble family, his good looks, his great estates, the Whalebone blood, his splendid hunters, and his beautiful horsemanship, he is bashful. Now, in my company he's got no more
call to be bashful than I have in his; besides, I put him
through in the great run from Fringford Gorse, when we beat
the whole field, and huntsmen and whippers-in to boot." The
fact was that Young Jack, one day after Lord Doomsday's

first visit to his father's house, had galloped to his side as the
fox went away from Fringford Gorse, and said, "This is a
noted fox, and we shall have a great run. If your lordship
pleases, you had better keep with me."

"But you are not taking the line of your father, Sir Jerry,
the major and the other gentlemen."

"No, my lord, I am not. I am taking another line. The
gentlemen would take it, too, if they could conveniently, but
they can't. They are heavy weights, and the old and middle-
aged don't care to tackle it. We are light weights and young."

"I say, young Bullfinch! I'm not as young as I look," said
Doomsday.

"My lord, that's the case with me. I don't get credit for
my real age. It's a disadvantage at the start, my lord, but by
and by we shall get over it. Take a strong pull, my lord.
Your horse, good as he is, will need all his power to go through
some of the bullfinches presently. They are every bit as big
and stout as those in Northamptonshire."

"You have been over this line before, but suppose the fox
heads away to the right—we shall be thrown out."

"But he won't head to the right, my lord. I know this fox.
He was hunted four times last season. After the last of the
four runs I was shown over this line by the best hand in the
Midland counties, and it's the one to take for those who are
light in the saddle and on good horses. Now, here's the first
of the raspers. Let me go first, please, my lord, and give your
horse a lead over."

Young Jack was on Young Cowslip, and soon she went driving through the upper part of the whitethorn and blackthorn
fence. Lord Doomsday followed, and then they went on across
another large pasture field, the dairy-ground of a great farm.
"Now, my lord," said Jack, "you can tell by the cry that the
hounds incline to the left all the time, and that our line is the
shortest. If the Fringford Gorse fox runs as usual, and his
time is come to-day, there'll be hardly anybody in at the death
but you and me. So much for knowing the country well, and
being able to negotiate it. I was shown this line by Tom
Scarlet, the best ten-stone man in England. He pounded
your lordship once, I have been told."

"He did; and, what is more, young Bullfinch, it was not
the fault of my horse, but my own."

"Ah, my lord! there are few like you. Most of the others that were pounded that day bore malice against Tom because he did it. Tom has told me, my lord, that you were not really pounded by him, but by the presence of the others. 'Jack,' said he, 'young Lord Doomsday will be one of the best riders in England some of these days. Mark my words, Jack. He comes of a riding family, and his only fault now is, that he's too modest.' Perhaps that's my fault, too, my lord. But here we are at another splitter. Let us take it side by side, with plenty room between."

The situation of affairs at the end of the run was this—the hounds pulled down the Fringford fox in the middle of a grass field, within a mile of Woodstock, in the Heythrop country. Lord Doomsday, Young Jack, and a shepherd boy were the only ones present to give the death-halloo. The huntsman and one of the whippers-in came through the gate soon after, their horses dead beat. After them Sir Jerry Snaffle, the Irish major, and John Bullfinch followed. The young nobleman almost blushed at their hearty congratulations. Not so Young Jack, for he exclaimed:

"Gentlemen, if you please, his lordship and I did it, by means of being light weights, young, well-mounted, and following Tom Scarlet's favorite line. If his lordship is too modest to have proper credit given him in the county paper when the account of this run appears, it'll be a great pity, and I think——"

"Hold your tongue!" roared John. "I wish you was half as modest as Lord Doomsday, I do. For cheek you are uncommon. What do you mean by haranguing the gentlemen in that style, eh?"

"O, well!" said Jack, "I only thought it wasn't the habit of the heavy weights in this hunt to begrudge the light weights —that is, begrudge a young nobleman—the proper praise when he was the only man in at the death. I know Sir Jerry's too much of a man to——"

A burst of laughter from Sir Jerry and the major, in which the huntsmen joined, cut short Young Jack's second harangue on behalf of Lord Doomsday, and prevented the reproof which rose to the lips of his father.

Therefore Jack had some reason to think that Lord Doomsday's visits to Hawkwell were made with a view to see him, and on the day in question he met his lordship with a bow, a smile, and a joyful exclamation. To Lord Doomsday's questions he replied that his father was out, his sister was out, too, and he should have been out himself if his lordship had been ten minutes later. He was going to ride to the sheepfold under the hill by the mill, on the outskirts of their land, and hoped Lord Doomsday would ride with him, as he could show him the holt of an otter and a plump or two of wild ducks. His lordship hesitated—he had come just to say good-by to Jack's father and his sister, as he was going home to Northamptonshire to spend the Christmas week at his father's. The earl made it a point that they should all be home for the Christmas dinner. He must be at Brackley that night, and ride home from thence in the morning. Very well! Jack would deliver his lordship's message to his father and sister, and would show him that the green lane by the fold under the hill was the nearest way to the Barleymow, from which he could take the Brackley road. As one of his men had gone to Brackley with a spare horse, Lord Doomsday agreed to this proposition, and they jogged merrily along, leaping the gates and fences instead of taking the roads. Suddenly, after a thoughtful silence, during which he had paid no attention to Jack's free and easy chatter, the young man exclaimed :

" I say, young Bullfinch, I take you to be the happiest boy in these parts."

" Well, my lord, I am tolerably well off for a boy, although I consider that I don't get full credit for my age and real experience. Besides, I should be more pleased if Tom Scarlet was home again. When he gets home, if he does get home, we shall have a jolly time."

" You say ' if he gets home.' Is there any doubt about it ?"

" Why, yes, my lord ; there is a report—a sort of a rumor —that he has been killed in America—the Western parts, above a thousand miles from New York. But I don't believe it. Neither does Sir Jerry, who has gone to overtake the sailors who reported it."

" Does your sister know of this report ?" said Lord Doomsday, earnestly.

" No, sir ; she does not, and she isn't to be told until we have found out that it's all a lie."

The young man was thoughtful. He pulled his horse to a slow trot, and then, looking down upon the hunter's mane and withers, he said: "There is another report. People say that this Mr. Scarlet is—not engaged to—but in love with your sister. Do you think he is the sort of man to make your sister May happy?"

"The very man, my lord. Why not?"

"I do not exactly know, and, at any rate, I need not tell until you have found out that his reported death is false. My opinion of your sister is that she is in mind, manners, disposition, and person a very superior young lady It is not every man who can ride well and pound people that is worthy of her."

It was now the turn of Young Jack to look at his horse's mane.

"I know that your lordship has no spite against Tom Scarlet because he pounded the field. You do not know Tom as well as I do," said he. "I have known him a great many years, young as I look. He taught me to ride before he came into the property. My lord, I know all about him; he's the best ten-stone—I mean he's as good a young man as there is in these Midland counties. Ask my father and Sir Jerry and the major when you come back. As for May, she is the best and dearest sister in the world, except, perhaps, your lordship's own sisters."

"You need not except them; they are married, young Bullfinch," said Lord Doomsday, "and, good as they are, I cannot say that I very much admire their husbands. You need not mention that we had any conversation about Mr. Scarlet. But in telling your father that I called, you may say that I have great regard and esteem for him and—and—your sister."

With this he pricked his horse with the spur, and after a few good strides leaped the fence into a lane. Jack followed, and at sight of a string of donkeys exclaimed: "Halloo! what now?"

It was the cavalcade of three or four families of gypsies, with terrier dogs and lurchers, women, girls and boys on foot, and children in the panniers of the asses.

"What now! young squire! You may well say what now! Why, here be we, Christmas eve a coming, turned out of the copse, where we was as snug as rabbits in their burrows, and made to move off, the Lord knows where, by Parkins, the constable. May the d—l fly away with him!"

The speaker was a handsome, bold-looking woman of the tribe. Hair thick and glossy, black as the wing of a raven. Eyes large and deep jet. Figure tall, but apparently very agile, with long sinewy arms. Her skirts were short, and she wore a scarlet cloak, as did all the other women and girls. She led the foremost donkey. In one pannier there was a chubby child some year and a half old, in the other a brace of twins of some six months, who sat up and put Lord Doomsday out of countenance by the steady stare of their four bright eyes as black and round as beads.

"Where are the men?" said Jack.

"Men! why where they always be when wanted. They're off down in Northamptonshire, Whittlebury Forest way."

"Not on a poaching expedition I hope, Rose?" said Jack.

"Poaching! Good Lord! young Bullfinch, who ever heard of any of our people poaching? I've three brothers in the King's service."

"Ay, but, Rose, one of them serves in a King's ship, and the others at Botany Bay."

"And the d—l take them that sent boys like them to the Bay. But the two have done well in New South Wales. They own more sheep than your father and Sir Jerry Snaffle to boot, and ride good horses, young Bullfinch, though it's I that say it in this green lane and not so much as a haulm-stack to lay the kinchins to the lee off."

"Well, Rose, I know my father would not have you wandering about this afternoon if he knew it. The lee side of a sheep-fold is as snug as any copse. Go into our field under the hill, and tell the shepherd and his boys that I sent you. Make yourself snug there for to-night and to-morrow, and send the boys with one of the donkeys to our house before dark. He shall bring back beef and things, and something for the kinchins, too."

"That's the speech of the young squire," said Rose. "Good luck to you, Master Jack, and to your father and sister. If my cousin, Jack Cotswold, and my fool of a husband——"

"Is Jack in Northamptonshire?" said Young Jack.

"No, in Lancashire. He's gone because of something about Miriam, his niece. He may go to America for all I know. She's there, and some say the Indians have carried her off. But what then? Some say the d—l's dead and buried in Cold Harbor. What business had she where the Indians were, and why did she follow Tom Scarlet and his horse?"

"Rose," said Jack, "this gentleman is from Northamptonshire. His father owns great estates there."

"I know his father better than you do, and the young gentleman himself as well," said Rose. "Many a time we camp on his honor's estate, and though the steward would send us packing, the earl let's us stay, and says: 'Good people, you are welcome to camping ground, but you musn't injure the plantations!' O, 'tis a bonny old earl! Would the young gentleman like to have his fortune told?"

"Or to buy a dog?" said the eldest boy.

"Or to see the twins?" said one of the girls.

"No, never mind," said Lord Doomsday. "Take these two guineas for the twins. I intended to give them half-crowns, but it seems you are known to my father."

"Please, my lord, I think it is rather that he is known to them," said Young Jack.

And then, as Rose tossed up the guineas with her thumb nail and caught them as they came down, there was a rush forward of all the women, girls, and boys, to assure Lord Doomsday that they knew his father, the earl, too.

"May your honor's luck never fail," said the gypsy, Rose. "May your horse never tire in the longest day. May the owl never hoot nor the black dog howl under the eaves of your hosts and friends, nor the red cock crow in the stack-yards of your tenants. And good for you, too, young squire, is the word of the gypsy wherever her people go—you and your father. And for your sister, say to her, I have it from them as knows, as well as by the winter stars, that she'll hear bad news of a busybody and a fool, may the devil fetch him! doubtful news of a sailor; good news of him who slew the man on horseback."

She said this with great rapidity and volubility. And Lord Doomsday, escaping a moment from the steady, stony stare of the twins, asked Jack what she meant.

"Well, my lord, no harm to us. The red cock means fire raising among barns and ricks."

"Ay, young Bullfinch!" said Rose, throwing back her tangled hair, "and my young brothers, that was transported before your time, never 'listed under 'Captain Swing,' but was sent for poaching. Poaching! Good lord! If a boy looks at a hare's run, or a mouse in a hedgerow, people says he is a poacher. I scorn 'em!"

"Ay! But, Rose, I've heard say that your brothers maimed two or three keepers in the fight at Wootton," said Jack.

"You've had that from Moleskin. I scorn him, too. Tell him I said so!"

With this she strode off, leading her donkey and her tribe towards the field, in which stood the sheepfold of furze and haulm, some eight feet high, and well calculated to shelter the low gypsy tents and carts. Lord Doomsday rode the other way, while Jack looked after the gypsies, and cogitated: "I don't much like this," said he; "Rose knows more than she delivers; but, one way or another, I'll have it out of her. Never mind about the winter stars—it is what she has had from those who know that I want to find out. Bad news of a fool! It's two to one that's Parkins—he musn't have speech of May. Doubtful news of a sailor—that means one of the sailors Sir Jerry rode after. Good news of him who slew the man on horseback! If that means that he slew Tom Scarlet, the best news of him will be that he's hung. I must see Rose again. Better day, better deed! To-morrow, at break of day, I'll be at her tent!"

CHAPTER XXX.

"Under a palm tree by the green old Nile,
  Lull'd on his mother's breast the fair Child lies,
With dove-like breathings, and a tender smile,
  Brooding above the slumber of his eyes,
While, through the stillness of the burning skies,
  Lo! the dread works of Egypt's buried kings
Temple and pyramid beyond him rise,
  Regal and still as everlasting things!"

AT five o'clock in the evening of the English midwinter it is about dark, unless there be light from the moon and stars. There was none as John Bullfinch and his daughter rode home from the Grange, loving and happy, side by side. The sky was overcast and snow was falling.

At first the farmer whistled, but it seemed a disrespect to the silence of the night, and he ceased his melody. A solemn stillness prevailed for the most part, though at times they could hear the baying of the distant watch dogs, while at other times there was a near rush of many wings, as flocks of widgeon and teal flew from the head springs, down the brooks to the open ponds. As they rode along they could see the dark forms of the hares and rabbits upon the thin snow, which half-covered the young wheat. Once an old fox came stealing across the road, and the farmer had a mind to stand in his stirrups, and give the view halloo. He did not do so, however, but pointed him out to May, as he loped along in the dusk, and observed that he was foraging for his Christmas dinner. Away in the distance they saw the light of the cottage fires gleaming through the windows under the thatch, reminding them of their own hearth. The horses quickened their steps, and soon the evening peal from the bells in the solid, square tower of the old Saxon church mingled with the rapid patter of their hoofs. Pleasant are the bells in the young time of the long winter night. Much gaiety there is in the morning marriage peals which ring in the triumph of love, but other sounds interrupt the harmony, which, in the stilly night, sounds unbroken. Merrily yet softly rang the evening peal, to be succeeded at midnight by one more rapid and joyful, the ringers being then partly primed with draughts from the cheerful spring of stout John Barleycorn, a favorite time out of mind through all the Midland counties of Merry England. The lights of the old farm-house at Hawkwell appeared in sight, and then John Bullfinch and his daughter were received by Young Jack and two of the men with sprigs of holly in their button holes.

"Hawk'ell farm is a more cheerful place than the Grange," said John Bullfinch, as he gave his reins to one of the men in waiting. "It's just the same as it was in my grandfather's time."

"Well, I don't know about that, father," said Young Jack, "for I've heard you say that you saw the elms planted that are big trees now, as high as the old house itself; but nothing has changed in my time, and I hope nothing will. But, father, there's a party at Hawk'ell Farm to-night," he added, as he followed his father and sister into the house.

" Well, he's welcome—who is he ?"

" It isn't a man, but a strong party of women and children. You see, Lord Doomsday, going home to keep Christmas at his father's—it's an observance the earl expects—rode over to see me, and left many respects and good wishes for you and May.

" Very good! I'm obliged to his lordship. I'm sorry I was not at home."

" O, it made no difference. I took him over to the lane by the Long Hill and the sheepfold ground, and there we met the gypsy women and children of Rose Tanner's band, twins and all, on the tramp. Parkins, taking advantage of the absence of the men, had bundled them, bag and baggage, out of the hazel copse hollow, pretending that he had authority from Sir Jerry, and there they were, on the hoof—night coming, and nowhere to go to, with Rose and her twins at the head."

" D—n Parkins!" said John. " May, my dear, that fellow's meddlesomeness is insufferable. So the people are here now, Jack ?"

" Why, no ; not here. It seems that they have often camped on Lord Doomsday's father's estates, and promised—honor bright !—never to damage the plantations. Besides, Rose offered to tell Lord Doomsday's fortune for nothing, and the upshot was that I gave her leave to enter our ground and make their camp for to-night and Christmas Day under the burrow-side of the fold. I knew you wouldn't have the women and children wandering about in the cold and snow on Christmas eve, if you could help it."

" Come and kiss me, dear Jack," said May. " It was quite right."

" I am not so sure of that," said John Bullfinch. " Jack has fallen short of what I should have expected, considering the time of the year and the bells we hear. Giving them leave to camp was well enough in its way, but it wasn't enough."

" O, Jack ! that is true," said May. " You should have provided for their wants, in remembrance of those who were this night lodged in the stable of an inn, and of Him who was lain in a manger, between an ox and an ass."

"Never mind, Jack," said his father ; " it can be remedied. After tea you shall drive the spring-cart over with some beef and bread and things, and, as it's Christmas eve, a little summut in the drinking line, to keep the wandering creeturs warm in their thin tents during the watches of this blessed night."

"Father, I went further than you and May think. I ordered up two of the boys with a donkey. Rose sent one boy and the oldest gal ; because, she said, as the girl reported, two boys would eat and stuff and go slow all the way, whereas the gal would hurry back to the twins with the best things untouched. She knows a thing or two, Rose does. The gypsies are now sitting round their fires, wishing good luck to this house and everybody belonging to it. The twins are an uncommon fine brace of kinchins."

"I wish I had been at home for the sake of the children," said May.

"Then you needn't, as you'll find when you see how many of the patty-pan mince-pies have walked off to the sheepfold on that donkey's four legs," said Jack.

"All right!" said John. "I remember Rose Tanner when she was a gal, and her three brothers were convicted and sentenced to transportation. Mere boys! it was hard. And I think I can see her now, as she stood at the ring side a month or two after her marriage, wearing her husband's colors in her bonnet, and cheering him on while he licked the Northcountry drover in a battle for 25*l.* a side. 'Twas a good fight, and the gypsy won. I know who found his battle money. Gypsy Jack and Rose's father seconded him ; and, after it was over, Sir Jerry observed that Rose would make a splendid bottle-holder. The Admiral got her youngest brother's sentence commuted on condition that he should serve seven years in a man-of-war, which is, he says, the best place for the education of boys in the world. He ought to know, for he went on one at ten years old. But the table is ready, and we'll take tea," said John, with an eye to the cold chine. He then added, briskly : "I have heard good news, Jack. That is to say, not news altogether strictly speaking, but tidings."

"What is the difference between news and tidings?" said Jack.

"Sir, if you don't know the difference between news and

tidings, after the education you've had, and welcome to more,
I shan't take the trouble to explain it," said John. "Parkins
is a fool, mind that!"

"O!" cried Young Jack, his father having trod very heavily
on his toes. "Gammoned, perhaps," he added, with a wince,
and backing away from the boot.

"Regularly gammoned!" replied his father.

About ten o'clock, the farmer and his children left their
own sitting-room for the great kitchen, or hall, of the house.
It was prepared for the due keeping of Christmas eve. The
walls were bedecked with holly and ivy—the mystic bough
of the mistletoe of the oak hung in the centre of the ceiling,
and the yule log blazed upon the wide hearth. The milkmaids, housemaid, the dairymaid and ploughboys, living in
the house, were already assembled, dressed in their best,
with their ruddy cheeks glowing in the light of the mighty
fire. At a wink from Young Jack, as he glanced up at the
mistletoe bough, the dairymaid got redder in the face than
ever. John Bullfinch and his daughter and son took their
seats. The farm and stable men were expected every minute.
Old Will Dean, the shepherd, was the first to come. When
he had seated himself in one of the chimney corners May filled
his pipe and handed it to him. "We be met agen! master!"
said the old fellow, after he had puff'd out clouds of smoke
for some time, "round this here Christmas fire. I was a-think-
ing as I come along how many years it is since I first saw the
blaze on this hearth on Christmas eve. I got up to sixty that
I can remember; but there must have been more, master, for
I was but a little shaver when I was first employed as bird-
keeper and such like, by your father—your grandfather, Miss
May and Master Jack! I dreamed last night that this here
fire had never gone out since I first saw it on Christmas eve,
about sixty years ago!"

"It's onlucky to talk of such thing, at this time," observed
Timms, the ploughman, who had just come in, and had caught
the latter part of what Dean said.

"To be sure!" said the dairymaid. "It ben't Christmas
until after twelve o'clock."

"I'll stand to it that it is!" said old Dean. "I say Christmas begins on Christmas eve; and Christmas eve begins when

the yule log has been laid on the fire and is well lighted. Why, I ought to know. I be the oldest man here, and have seen more Christmas eves than any of ye. Moreover, shepherds be set down in the Bible in what it says about this blessed night, and there's no mention made of ploughmen or dairymaids!"

Old Will looked around triumphantly and resumed his pipe. John Bullfinch, to cut off further discussion of this knotty point, cried:

" Eleven o'clock, Jack! everybody's here strictly belonging to Hawk'ell! pour out horns of last year's October. May, my dear! see to the punch. Your brother had almost forgot the brandy."

Young Jack poured out for all the men and young women from a mighty flagon of ale, and then his sister returned from the bakehouse, followed by the two stoutest of the milkmaids, buxom lasses who could swing a full pail of milk over their heads without spilling a drop, bearing a great bowl of punch. It was tightly tied over with a white cloth, but when set down upon the hearth the fragrant fumes of brandy and spices arose from it. A few furtive glances at the mistletoe bough, with suppressed giggles from the girls, succeeded the bringing in of the punch. It was a signal that the crisis of the night was coming on.

Half-past eleven by the tall old eight-day clock in the corner, and John Bullfinch began to look impatiently towards the door, as though he was in the mind to chide the tarrying of some expected guest. The dogs, following the example of the great mastiff bitch, raised themselves upon their haunches, and made a little stir. The door was thrown open, and, shaking the snow from his hat upon the threshold, Moleskin appeared. Grounding the but of his gun, he cried:

" I know what you're going to say! Don't mention such a thing. It's all a mistake. I'm not late. I'm never late on Christmas eve. Your clock is fast."

" Dick, you *are* late," said John Bullfinch, with decided emphasis, "but better late than never. The clock is not fast. My grandfather had that clock, and it stood there in all my father's time. That clock is none of your gilded, new-fashioned gimcracks. She has been gone by a hundred years in this family, and was never known to be a minute fast, or a minute slow, on Christmas eve. I'll back her against any clock in England on Christmas eve, barring the church clock. May, my dear, we are *all* here now. Proceed with the narrative of the first Christmas night."

Then May Bullfinch arose and with a sweet and low, but clear voice, related the history of the birth of Our Lord as it is given in the gospels. How the shepherds, watching their flocks by night on the lone hills of Judea, saw a bright star in the heavens, over Bethlehem, which had never been there before; how there came a vivid light, and the Angel of the Lord appeared to them with great glory, and they were sore afraid; how he bade them to be of good cheer, for the Saviour of the world was born of David's line; how the Mother, going up to Jerusalem, had taken refuge in a stable, where the Child was born, and laid in a manger, between an ox and an ass; how the wise men of the East saw His star in the heavens, and came to worship Him; how King Herod issued a decree to kill all the babies, that the One foretold by the prophets might be cut off; and how the Angel appeared to Mary and Joseph and told them to take the young Child and flee into Egypt.

As she finished, a deep silence followed the cadence of her soft voice, and all eyes were turned to the clock. Moment after moment was counted, as they listened for its striking, or the beginning of the Christmas peal from the strong old tower, whose bells had rung it out to the frosty air of the night for many centuries. It stood within a quarter of a minute of twelve, and Moleskin said, in a ghost of a whisper:

"I know she's fast!"

He would have been reproved afterwards for breaking the profound silence of the supreme moment, but at the instant the clock struck there came such a clang from all the bells at once as would have shaken any tower but the old Saxon church tower, and as proved that the ringers were indeed tuned up to concert pitch by the generous juice of stout John Barleycorn.

"Now, then! who said that clock was fast?" cried John Bullfinch, triumphantly. "May, give me the punch-ladle! Uncover the bowl!"

"Jest so!" said Young Jack, with a wink which comprehended all the maidens, and a glance overhead.

"Now, then," said John, when he had served them all, "men and maids, here's a Merry Christmas and a Happy New Year! Drink it, every one!"

They did drink it, and drank it once again. The glasses were then then set down, and there were more glances at the green bough with the white berries above, and a good deal more giggling. John Bullfinch led his daughter underneath, and kissed her. Moleskin, as an old friend of the family, followed suit. Then old Will Dean advanced and took May's hand. 'I have kissed this here beautiful lass and good daater," said he, "every Christmas eve since she was born. Her mother, the best 'oman as I ever knowed, or as ever lived (except the Mother of Our Lord), brings her to me the first time on Christmas eve, when she was three weeks old—for she was born just three weeks before Christmas—and, says she: 'Will Dean, here is the prettiest little lamb that ever was sent to bless a happy couple since the Great Shepherd was born unto the world.' Them's the words she said. Master, you can't deny it. Master Moleskin, you can't deny it. I'll stand to it—nobody can deny it! Then I kissed her."

"Very well!" cried Young Jack; "kiss her again, and let some of the rest of us have a chance under that bough!"

May and the old shepherd retired, when, amid much giggling and laughing, Young Jack led the youngest and prettiest of the milkmaids under the bough, and the regulation ceremony followed fast and free.

The immense punch-bowl was largely lightened of its contents before John Bullfinch said : "Your shawl, May. Come on, Moleskin! Come on, Jack! Tom is ready, with his lantern, and we'll pay the usual visit to Cowslip. She expects it, and would be put out if we didn't go. She knows when Christmas has come as well as we do."

"I'm rather dubersome about that," said Moleskin, as he followed John and his daughter out. "She's a very knowing mare, no doubt—almost as much so as my dogs, but as to her knowing this night from another night——"

"Your dogs!" said John Bullfinch, with some contempt; "I tell you Cowslip knows it is Christmas eve as well as we do, if not better. Eh, May?"

"She does indeed, father."

"It's a true bill, Moleskin : let me explain it," said Jack, detaining him a little. "It's all along of the bells. They never ring at midnight on any other night save the night of the New Year, and then, you know, they begin with a muffled chime, a quarter before twelve. Don't you see?"

"Don't I see! why, it's as plain as the sun at noontime, on a clear day, but I didn't see it before."

The hunting-mare was on foot, wide awake, with her head to the door of the box. She answered their salutation, "A Merry Christmas, Cowslip!" with a joyous neigh, and to May's pats and fond caresses she replied with whinnies of gratification.

"I told you so!" cried John. "She's fully aware of the season, and up to the time o' night. See seems unusually pleased this year. What is it, old gal?"

"If I might venture to answer for her—I don't suppose she can speak herself yet—it must be this," said Moleskin, pointing out the new saddle and bridle in her box.

"Eh!" cried John. "This is a plot, and Southdown was in it."

"No, father! it's a Christmas-gift to Cowslip from May and me. There was nobody but May and me in it ; but I happened to mention that we had it ordered to Meg Southdown, and the little lass couldn't help telling her father."

"Well, my children, you have made me and Cowslip very happy—very happy!" said John.

When they returned to the house there was the usual leave-taking. The men went home. The maids and boys went talking and giggling up-stairs. May and Jack bade their father and Moleskin good-night, and retired also. Then the cronies sat themselves down to a quiet pipe and a last glass of the punch. Neither spoke—their silent satisfaction was too intense for conversation—until the keeper rose to go. Then John remarked :

"Dick, the night has been passed as, on this hallowed occasion, it ever should be. To my thinking, there was nothing forgot."

"A small trifle I forgot myself," replied Moleskin. "There should be a small matter of a bag here. Ah! here it is!"

He drew a bag from under a side table, beneath which he

19

had thrown it as he entered, and, emptying it at one shake, out fell three brace of the very finest pheasants that ever flew in the coverts. "With the compliments of the Marquis of Chandos," said Moleskin, his cast-iron visage at its hardest set.

"None of your humbug, sir!" said John, sternly. "What do you mean by trying to humbug *me?* At this season, too! It's your gift—your own, Dick! And why wasn't it made while the people were here, so that they might see how you remember your old friend?"

"Not a word on that," said Moleskin. "The sight of pheasants outside of the preserves—*dead* pheasants—is a temptation to farmers' lads and men not proper to be put before 'em. If, through seeing these pheasants, any of your men had been led to venture into the coverts, the consequences might have been serious, for man-traps and spring-guns——"

"Hold your tongue, sir! drop your humbug! It's your present! The marquis has nothing to do with it, and you know it."

"I know nothing of the sort. I can prove by statement and by argument, time and place fitting——"

"I'll hear no statement! Argument has no more effect upon me than upon Southdown himself. Stop your gammon, or I'll call my daater down, and she'll make you take the pheasants away agen!"

"The marquis," said Moleskin, "directs me to shoot so many pheasants, and give 'em away to the tenants."

"I'm no tenant of the marquis, sir!"

"I know it. But the marquis added: 'Don't forget your old friend, John Bullfinch, and give him my compliments of the season.'"

"There, now! It's your own gift to your own friend—that's what this is!"

"Well, good-night!" said Moleskin.

"Good-night, Dick! Remember we dine at half-past one on Christmas day."

"All right. I'll be here to a minute, providing that clock ain't fast!"

CHAPTER XXXI.

"Mother of Empires! Daughter of Jails!
Hail to thee, New South Wales!"

MAY BULLFINCH and her brother sat awhile in her room that Christmas eve, after they went up-stairs. The boy thought once or twice that he would tell her what Lord Doomsday said, but he did not. May repeated to him what Old Straddles said at the Grange, but it did not much impress Jack, although he determined not to say so. He would not do anything to abate his sister's cheerfulness, and, though his mind still ran upon the words of the gypsy, he talked of Tom Scarlet. But while his sister sat with his hand in hers, and recalled the incidents of former Christmas eves, at which Tom Scarlet had been at Hawkwell, the boy resolved to see the gypsy Rose at a very early hour in the morning. They then talked of their father, and what a pleasure it was to see him enjoy himself; of old Will Dean, the shepherd; of the keeper, and of the Southdowns, especially the lassie Meg, who was a great favorite with them. At last, May being tired, and Jack affecting to be so, the sister and brother knelt side by side, as was their constant custom, and said their prayers in the good, old, confiding style of children to a loving and protecting God, "Our Father who art in Heaven."

Some time before the dawn of day the lad rose, dressed himself silently, and went softly down-stairs. He patted the great mastiff, Fury, as she lay before the yule fire, and then went to the stables and awakened Tom, the groom, telling him to clap the saddle on Young Cowslip.

"She ben't roughshod," said the sleepy groom. "Better take Black Hearty. But wheer be 'e going before day, Master Jack?"

"To the sheepfold at the long hill, Tom."

"Then if I was 'e I wouldn't. Ship be all right, I know. Shepherd Dean 'ull look out for them."

"Tom," said Young Jack, "the gypsies are there, and I want to see Rose Tanner on particular business. Say nothing of it."

"Well, you knows best, Master Jack, but have a keer of that Rose. She's a regular rum 'un, she is. If you want your fortin' tell'd, better get Dark Janet to do it; she's the 'oman for that theer sort of thing. Rose is too obstropulus, and folks say 'ull stick at nothing—nothing!"

"All right! Mum's the word! I'll be back before May and my father are up."

"Hold on! through the strawyard, if you must go. The step of a horse on hard ground 'ull wake master any time. Look out for that theer Rose. All them Coopers be rum 'uns, and theer's a mighty sight on 'em all through the Midlands. Her three brothers was transported in their teens. The young 'un warn't fifteen."

There was a "nipping and an eager air," a light wind from the northwest sweeping over the crisp snow, and the stars were paling and waning in the wintry sky, as Jack cantered on towards the camp at the sheepfold. John Bullfinch had not told his daughter and son all that he might have done in regard to Rose and her brothers on the preceding evening. The truth was, that when sentence was passed upon the boy and the two young men and the elder gypsy women raised a wail of woe, Rose stood up, threw back her bonnet, berated the judge, and made such predictions touching the homesteads and stackyards of the jury as made some of them turn pale with fear. The judge ordered her to be removed, but she fought the sheriff's men like a young tigress, and tripped two of them off their feet. Long before her strength and fury were spent Tanner, the gypsy, who afterwards married her, a very strong and active young fellow, caught her suddenly under the arms and carried her bodily out of court. When the convict ship lay in the Thames, bound to Australia, Rose trudged up to London, took farewell of her two brothers (the other was already aboard a man-of-war, at Portsmouth), and bespoke the favor of some of the young officers and sailors for them. She saw the ship under weigh at Deptford, and repeated to herself the words of an old ballad often chanted at fairs, feasts and races in the Midlands:

O, as we sailed down the river, boys,
  It was in the month of May,
And every ship that we passed by
  We heard the sailors say,
‘There goes a lot of clever young lads
  And they’re bound to Botany Bay.’”

The gypsies never lost their cheerfulness. They were looked upon with favor by the sailors, marines and petty officers. Poaching is, no doubt, a crime of extraordinary atrocity, but that class of people do not so regard it. Only once during the passage were Rose's brothers put in irons, and that was but for two or three days. Even in a convict ship there are classes and factions. The London convicts, led by some eminent but unfortunate members of the swell mob, treated the country party with high disdain, calling them chaw-bacons, joskins, bumpkins, yokels, &c. This was borne for some time; but one day, when rations were being served out, one of the swells, with much dignity and hauteur, ordered the gypsies to stand back. “Stan’ back be d——d! we’ve as much right here as you!” said the elder, and forthwith knocked the gentleman down, whereupon his brother floored a highly respectable and polished forger. In Australia, the gypsies were soon assigned to an old army officer, who owned tens of thousands of sheep. For three or four years they were shepherds on some of the wildest and most remote runs in the colony. The life suited them and they suited the life. They had a desperate battle with a tribe of wild blacks, and repulsed them, with two or three killed and several wounded. They stood high in favor with their employer, and with his consent, volunteered for an exploring expedition in the interior. There was no Melbourne and no colony of Victoria then. After months of sore privation and the loss of many men, the expedition, or what remained of it, limped back to New South Wales. For their services, the gypsies received tickets of leave at once. The old colonel furnished them with sheep on credit, and set them up on a distant run. The gypsies were soon on the way to wealth, and in a very few years possessed such land, flocks of sheep and droves of horses as constituted riches beyond the wildest dreams of their tribe at home. Behold, O rulers, philosophers and sages, the mockery of fate! Here was the one who had been “graciously pardoned,” a man before the

mast in a ship of war; and here were those who had crossed
the line, under the sign of bayonets and handcuffs, great
proprietors at the Antipodes, sure to be ranked among the
explorers and founders of the future mighty empire of the
Southeast. John Bullfinch did not know all this, but he did
know that the Coopers were now free men, their fourteen years
having expired, and that they were uncommonly well-to-do.
They had sent money to their sister Rose through him. The
first time it was twenty pounds, a draft drawn by a Sydney
bank, and there was a sensible injunction from the brothers to
keep it secret. The letter in which the draft was enclosed
read as follows:

"MISTER JOHN BULLFINCH: We writes this for you to read
to our sister Rose, having been larnt on the passage, a long 'un.
This is a fine country when you get used to it. We got a
sight of sheep and some land, also horses. Our run is a long
way from the coast. We are glad to hear that Rose is well
married. She was the handsomest gal of all the Coopers. A
Warwickshire cove, sent out here for nothing in pertickler, he
says, though the beaks called it highway robbery, tells us her
husband, one of the Tanner's, you may know him, is a good
two-handed man. He seen him fight Dick the drover, and
our Rose was there. We sends this money to you because we
know you to be a good man, real gentleman. The bankers
advised us to send it to the parson at Riding-Stoke, but we
have our doubts about his honesty. We was pulled afore him
and fined twice, when we never done it. So now no more,
only if you can buy a good thoroughbred horse cheap, fit for
a stallion, ship him to Sydney, consigned to Belcher & Buckle,
for us. We got plenty of money in the bank at Sydney, and
have left directions to pay all charges. So here's good luck
to all at Hawk'ell, and to Rose.

"From her brothers,   TOM AND ELIJAH COOPER."

The second remittance sent to John Bullfinch from Australia
for Rose was larger than the first, and with it came news that
her brothers were more and more prosperous. What she did
with the money John could not well make out. He offered to
put it in the bank for her, but Rose received the suggestion
with some contempt. Her husband got but little of it, and

that was doled out to him about half a crown at a time. The way of life of the family remained unchanged, but the brown bare-legged girls were sometimes ornamented with earrings and beads of gold. On one occasion the farmer asked the gypsy whether she would not like to remove to Australia with her husband and family.

"What!" said Rose, "leave my country, Old England? Never, never! Unless Jack Tanner should be fool enough to get transported."

As Young Jack drew near the fold he gave a low whistle, at which there was the barking of dogs, followed by the voice of Rose in low tones. The gypsy came from her tent, and made a gesture to the boy signifying that he should dismount. She then made a dive into the tent and returned with a Whitney blanket in which she and the lad enveloped the horse. He was then hitched to the gateway of the fold. "Well, young master, you're up betimes. I wonder if it betokens a merry Christmas. I wish you one. Come into the tent. There's no one there but the twins, with Jenny and her young 'un. Come in out of the cold."

The tent was tolerably spacious, and very snug. When the gypsy lit a lamp, Jack saw by its dull light that the twins lay on a bed or rather on a blanket, thrown over boughs of balsam fir. They were wide awake, and staring with all their might. Beyond them was a large brown mass, at which the lad looked with some surprise, when he could make out what it was.

"That's Jenny and her young 'un," said the gypsy, holding the lamp so that young Bullfinch could plainly see a she ass with her young foal. The latter, with its great, mild eyes, stared as hard at him as the twins did. "Young squire, you may talk as much as you like about racers and hunters, but give me Jenny for my money. If anything happened to me she would nurse them twins. They suck her sometimes as it is."

"It's a wonder to me that the twins don't catch cold, Rose; there's little or nothing on them," said Jack.

"I took the blanket for your horse," she replied. "But our people never catch cold. We leave that to you folks. You put up houses like jails, and it's my opinion that all sorts of ailments are built inside. Look at me! I was never sick a day in my life. Besides, the heat from Jenny keeps the twins warm. Sit you down on the panniers there, and tell me what you came for. Is it for me to tell your sister's fortune?"

"No, it is not. May don't believe in those things. She thinks it wicked, and says we should abide in faith and trust, inquiring no further," said he.

"That's what she says, is it?" replied the gypsy; "then why the nation don't she abide in faith and trust, instead of doubting and pining and saying prayers? Perhaps you want *your* fortin' tell'd?"

"No, I don't; I want the truth told. Besides, they say that you are not in that line. Dark Janet is the one for that, people say."

"Dark Janet! bah! young Bullfinch! She never tells nothing above the cut of servant wenches, ploughboys and cowboys. When I consults the stars it concerns the aristocracy and gentlemen's daaters. How would you like to have the young lord for your brother-in-law, young Bullfinch?"

"Not at all," said Jack, stoutly. "It's a thing not to be heard of. I'll stand for Tom Scarlet against the world. Besides, Lord Doomsday don't like brothers-in-law. He told me so!"

"You mean he don't like them he has got. Well, there's reasons for it. They want to come it over him, being older than he is, and a precious sight poorer. They'd like to win his money at blind hookey, and he won't let 'em, so no love is lost. Scarlet was all very well. Good fellow enough—the best rider in the Midlands. But he's running a race with the d—l, and it's neck and neck, if he isn't dead by this time."

"Rose," said the boy, "I love my sister; I have always loved her, and now I see her with trouble on her mind, I would give anything to help her. I am sure you know more about what the sailors said, or what somebody has said, than you have owned up to."

"Now, by the bright stars that shine over the eastern lands and above the southern seas, where my boys live—my brothers —you say well, Young Jack. If I consults the stars, I shall find out more about Tom Scarlet, and Miriam, and the other, and what not, than Sir Jerry would get out of them sailor chaps in a month of Sundays. Them fellows can hardly be called real sailors. Now, I have got a man-o'-war's man, who went aboard at fifteen, or a little less, and has been in the service eighteen years. Shall I consult the stars about Scarlet, and him, and the one who slew the man on horseback?"

"Never mind the stars now. Look here, Rose! Here are five guineas. Take them and tell me the news, good or bad. It seems to me that if Tom Scarlet is killed, my sister's heart will break and I shall never want any money any more," said Jack, with tears.

"Let me see that money!" said the gypsy, violently. "It's honestly come by, I'll swear. Boy, put that money up! You remind me of my young brother Jim, when he stood with Tom and Elijah at the bar and the judge pronounced the cruel sentence, 'transportation beyond the seas for the term of fourteen years.' Put that money up, I say! I have gold galore. Look here!"

She drew forth an old tea-caddy and poured out a stream of coined gold into her lap. The boy looked on amazed, but said nothing, and she returned the money to its hiding-place.

"Now, be secret about this money," she said. "Nobody knows of it but you and me and Tom and Elijah, who sent it from Australia to your father. I've hoarded it for years and years. What do you think it's for?"

"For the twins and the other children, I should think," he replied.

"The d—l a bit, Young Jack! The children's uncles in Australia have plenty for them. This is for their young brother, *my* young brother, Jim Cooper; the bonniest lad that ever snared a hare or took a duck's nest. O, Young Jack!" she exclaimed, seizing his hand, "'tis eighteen years since that boy stood at the bar. Eighteen years in men-of-war, all over the world, and now, for the first time, he's coming home again! I always knew the young one would come. I never thought the others would, especially after I found they had so much money."

"Rose, I'm very glad; and I'll say nothing about the gold," said Young Jack. "But now, since you feel so much joy over the near return of your brother, tell me all you know, or think, about Tom Scarlet. Let my sister and me rejoice too, if it is possible. You didn't find out about Jim's return from the stars."

"You're right, I did not. I had it from a person who knows; one who saw him at Halifax. His ship was about to sail for England, and ought to be, by this time, in the Channel, if not anchored off Portsmouth."

"And that man told you about doubtful news for my sister May from a sailor, and good news from the man who slew the man on horseback?"

"Nothing of the sort. It wasn't a man that told me at all, but a woman—a young woman who expects to be married to a man now at sea, but running in for the land, I think."

"Then there's no hope from that source," said Jack, despondingly.

"Jack, my boy! my good boy! I never said so. It may be a deal better than you think. Nay, I am sure it is. Go home and keep your spirits up. By that means you'll comfort your sister. Be of cheer! Look at them twins, and at Jenny's foal. Care killed a cat! I can't say any more, and I won't. When you see or hear of a sailor in this neighborhood—I mean the real thing—man-of-war's man, captain of the foretop, and well-beknown to the Admiral—jump on Black Hearty and ride to me as if the d—l was behind you."

"Thanks, Rose! Good-by!" said Young Jack. "I see by the light through the tent that the dawn is breaking. Shall I tell my father about that gold? As it came to him, I suppose I may?"

"Jack, the least said about that the better, until Jim arrives," said the gypsy. "My husband is very well content now, but he would worrit the life out of me if he knew how much money I have. Wait till Jim comes home. You may tell your father that he's coming."

"Ay, coming from Halifax!" said Jack. "Rose, it just strikes me this moment that I've heard of that place before."

"Very likely! There's a town of the name in Yorkshire."

"Ay, so there is," said Jack, "but there's another in Nova Scotia, Rose, and that's in America, as sure as my name is Bullfinch."

"Well, what of it? It's a thousand mile, very likely two thousand, from where the sailors sailed from that said the man was killed and Miriam carried off by the Indian."

" You don't believe she's carried off, do you ?"

" Well, to tell you the truth, I don't," said Rose. " Miriam is a spirited girl—cousin of mine, you know, and isn't likely to be carried far against her will. She's more likely to have carried the Indian off than he is to have carried her. Your sister will be up before you're home. Mount and ride. I'd give you the stirrup-cup if you ever drank. When you hear that my brother Jim is in the countryside, jump on your horse, and come to me fit to split the wind. Do it ! And look at these twins. When you be married to Meg Southdown she may have such a pair."

" I say, Rose, none o' that. We are both very young at present—at least, Meg is ; and I know that when we are married she will be satisfied with one at a time. Good-morning."

CHAPTER XXXII.

" O'er capon, heron-shaw, and crane,
  And princely peacock's gilded train,
  And o'er the boar's head garnished brave,
  And cygnet from St. Mary's wave ;
  O'er ptarmigan and venison,
  The priest had said his benison."

AMONG the notable discoveries of modern times in " Merrie England " there is one, announced by several writers, including Mr. Frank Buckland, to the effect that no Englishwoman can cook a dinner. It happened, about a year ago, that this lamentable fact was brought to the notice of a party of exiles of Albion, who were dining in New York— very well, as they ignorantly supposed, after the manner of their savage and uncultivated ancestors—upon roast beef, boiled mutton and caper sauce, ducks, capons, plum-pudding, mince-pie, apricot-tarts, etc. This repast, coarse and vulgar as it must have been according to Mr. Buckland, a perfidious Englishwoman had pretended to cook, and the benighted company actually ate it with relish. Indeed, they treated the discovery of Mr. Buckland with that sort of churlish contempt with which the precepts of the wise are commonly received by the vulgar. One old fellow, of some wealth and standing, but much brutality, proposed that the writings of the philosophers above mentioned should be searched, over the wine, for the necessary corollary to the statement, "No Englishwoman can cook a dinner," which, the old fellow in question declared, must be, "no Englishman can eat a dinner!" The books were sent for, at this suggestion, and gone through by the chairman, but somehow or another, probably from haste and carelessness, the necessary corollary was not found.

It may be that no Englishwoman can *now* cook a dinner; but in that case, what with normal schools, women's rights, fish museums and snug sinecures for diletante philosophers, the culinary art has been much neglected of late, in the little islands beyond the melancholy main. Forty years ago it was an article of faith with the gentlemen and fox-hunters of good appetite and renown that Englishwomen could cook a very good dinner. If anybody had made a statement to the contrary in the kitchen of the Barleymow, where in the first week of January the buxom landlady, and the portly cook who presided in the kitchen of Sir Jerry Snaffle, were engaged in the preparation of the Hunt Dinner, it would have been received with some contempt, to say nothing of hot water. But this result would only have reminded the philosophers of what Tim Moore called " the barbarism of the English, who peels their 'taters before they biles 'em."

The annual dinner of the hunt was always one of the greatest festivals in the riding. The wits of the Barleymow were yearly threshed, and all its retainers, from the fat landlord to the smallest waiting-maid, were annually inspired to venturesome enterprise and exertion, in order that it might be served with the profusion and excellence demanded by such an occasion. Among those never absent from the time-honored festival were John Bullfinch, Mr. Southdown, and about a score more of the opulent farmers of the Vale and its neighborhood, all good men after the hounds and before the trencher. On the day in question they had agreed to come together at Hawkwell, and ride in company to the Barleymow, where they would meet Sir Jerry Snaffle and other country gentlemen, the Rev. Mr. Jericho and other beneficed clergymen, Major Fitzgerald and other officers of the army and navy, Mr. Doublefee, and some other gentlemen of the learned professions from the neighboring towns. There might be expected also some gentlemen from Oxford, students at that renowned university, and ardent lovers of hunting the fox.

John Bullfinch was already dressed in his best; his daughter had surveyed his manly figure and comely face with pride and affection. He had kissed her twice, and was about to do so for the third time, when the stentorian voices of Southdown and the others who "stuck by the land" and followed the fox and hounds, summoned him to the gate. In spite of the color which glowed in her cheek and of the light which kindled in her clear blue eye, as she parted from her father, May Bullfinch looked anxious and careworn. The rumor started by the sailors and blown abroad far and wide by the indefatigable Parkins, had reached her and filled her mind with doubt and anxiety, which her father and Young Jack were unable to relieve. Sir Jerry had overtaken the sailors on the London road, and had heard all the information they were able to impart. They told what the baronet called "a cock-and-bull story" of a fight on the banks of a river in the far West, in which an Englishman had been killed. Two of them thought the man's name was Tom Scarlet, but the other said it was not. They had heard the story at New Orleans, where it was told them in a drinking place by an acquaintance of one who had been at the affray. The acquaintance was a "river man" —meaning one employed on the steamboats which navigate the Mississippi and the Arkansas—and his friend at the fight was "a gentleman by the name of Keeps," who had made heroic but unavailing efforts to save the Englishman's life. The third sailor maintained that the name of the man mentioned as killed was not Scarlet; but he said that three or four were killed, and Scarlet might be one of the others. He, the sailor, remembered the Admiral, Sir Jerry's father-in-law, very well, having had good reason to do so. This was true, if two or three dozen with a cat-o'-nine-tails is good reason. He would have been glad to give the yarn from end to end, "right off the reel and without a kink," and he should have been able to do so, having meant to return and question the river man at the grog-shop at leisure, but unfortunately he was that night put in the calaboose for knocking a Dutchman down, and never got out until he was taken to his ship by the police, just as her sails were loose and her anchor awash.

To John Bullfinch this was very unsatisfactory, while Mr. Southdown admitted that he could make nothing of it. Sir Jerry, in his opinion, had failed to keep the magistrate and the baronet in the background, and had not brought "for'ard" the Admiral's daughter as he ought to have done.

"However," said he to John, "the main p'int is settled. I don't care who was killed—Tom Scarlet is alive and well! You may say there's no evidence of it, but I don't care for that. My mind's made up. No argeyment will change it."

The great room at the Barleymow had never held a finer company than those who stood up while the Rev. Mr. Jericho said grace. The apartment was ornamented with pictures, emblems and trophies of the chase, mingled with boughs of holly and ivy and branches of the laurel green from Sir Jerry Snaffle's lawn. Here was the portrait of Gray Goose, the famous mare ridden by the baronet himself in so many long and hard runs. Here was that of Kilkenny, the favorite Irish hunter, which carried Major Fitzgerald so well. Here was the likeness of The Waler, the wonderful jumper from Botany Bay, sent over from New South Wales to Mr. Sidney by his son. Here was the huntsman, Old Tom, on a famous brown horse, the picture having been painted for the hunt, by a convivial artist who had run up a score at the Barleymow, which the fastest and stoutest of foxes might have envied for its length. Besides all these, there were pictures of John Bullfinch on Cowslip; of Mr. Southdown on his great weight-carrier, The Bullock; of Tom Scarlet on Danger.

Then there were portraits of famous hounds, the heroes, the favorites, the beauties of the pack—Rallywood, Ringwood, Ranter, Rover, and Ranger, Vengeance, Velocity, Virago, Veracity and Virtue. Nor were the exploits of the vulpine race forgotten. Over the chair of Sir Jerry Snaffle, as he presided, appeared the head and brush of that famous dog fox which had run twenty miles, at a racing pace, as the crow flies. Over that of the vice-president, Major Fitzgerald, an Irish veteran, with but one arm and the scar of a deep sabre cut on the cheek, were those of the celebrated vixen who had three times fooled the pack at the end of good runs, but was at last viewed effecting the usual entrance into the Rev. Mr. Jericho's church, through a broken window among the ivy, after which it was her custom to take sanctuary in the pulpit, and sleep as sound as any Christian did during the sermons of that learned and eloquent divine. In short, the decorations of the dining room were artistic and complete, quite in keeping with the occasion, in the opinion of everybody who saw it except Young Jack. On being shown it on the forenoon of the day in question, Young Jack was critical touching the paintings, and said :

"If Lord Doomsday had been taken on Blue Peter and I on Young Cowslip, just as we gave the death-halloo when the hounds pulled down the Fringford Gorse fox, this room would have looked much better than it does to-day."

The dinner proper was over, the knives and forks had been removed, the ability of the cook had been mentioned with approval, and the company had settled themselves for a course of that steady drinking, which was the custom of Englishmen at hunting dinners forty years ago. The usual and loyal toasts had been given and cordially received, and now there was a lull, during which conversation passed upon various topics at different places round the table. Mr. Doublefee took advantage of it to address his clients, John Bullfinch and Richard Southdown, who were seated opposite to him, and in the centre of the farming array.

"Gentlemen," said he, with a bland smile, "have you heard that there is soon to be a vacancy in the representation of our county in Parliament ?"

They had not heard of it. Southdown doubted it.

"It is unquestionably the case," said Mr. Doublefee. "I have it from the best authority. Our senior member, Sir Jasper Jericho, in consequence of age and growing infirmity, feels compelled to retire from public life."

"More's the pity!" said Mr. Southdown, solemnly.

"Sir, you may well say so. He has been an able and a conscientious member," replied Mr. Doublefee.

"He stuck to the land and defended the Constitution," said Southdown. "That's what is wanted in times like these here, when all sorts of doctrines meet us on every hand."

"So he did. Now, as to his successor," said Mr. Doublefee, in his most insinuating tone, with his right forefinger in the palm of his left hand, and leaning over towards them as far as the table would allow. "I think there will not be much difference of opinion among us here."

"So do I," replied Mr Southdown; and he added in his most positive manner, "Sir Jerry's the man."

"Eh! Sir Jerry!" Mr. Doublefee exclaimed, with evident surprise and some embarrassment. "Sir Jerry Snaffle is an excellent man—good landlord, patriotic in sentiment, highly respected, and all that sort of thing, but——"

"But what?" said Southdown, looking Mr. Doublefee in the eye.

"Why, my dear sir, and you, Mr. Bullfinch, both gentlemen of influence—of very great and deserved influence with the intelligent and patriotic gentlemen of your a—a—class—who cast five out of six of the votes for the counties, and whose knowledge and integrity form one of the strongest bulwarks of the glorious Constitution in Church and State—I say that you, gentlemen—I venture to say *to* you, gentleme——"

"Come to the p'int! We have heard all that before once or twice at the hustings. You come to the p'int," said Southdown.

"I am coming to it, my very dear sir and esteemed client," replied Mr. Doublefee, in a coaxing tone. "Don't you think that Sir Jerry's abilities and virtues are much more appreciated here than they would be in Parliament—that he is, in fact, much more in his element here, if I may so speak, than he would be before the—the—not the woolsack, but the Speaker's chair?"

"No, I don't!" replied Southdown, sternly.

"Lawyer," said John Bullfinch, "Sir Jerry Snaffle *is* in his proper element here—among his neighbors, his friends, his tenants, and the people in general of these parts. It would be very hard to get another country gentleman like Sir Jerry that is equal to him in every quality a country gentleman should have. It's easy enough to get a tolerable member of Parliament, so far as my experience goes. But it's my opinion that Sir Jerry in Parliament would tell the House a thing or two, now and then, which the House ought to know. Not this county alone, not our class alone, but all England, would be benefited in the most marked degree, by having Sir Jerry in Parliament. It would be like bringing in a strain of the old blood after two or three out-crosses."

" Jest so! my sentiments exactly. Just what I was a-going
to say myself!" cried Southdown with exultation, while the
other farmers, laughing with glee, nodded to each other and
took wine.

" Therefore," said John Bullfinch, "seeing that we could
still have Sir Jerry among us for about nine months in the
year, I say we ought to be willing to let the whole of the country have the benefit and assistance of his long experience and
uncommon fine talents the other three."

There was great applause around John as he finished. Mr.
Doublefee looked vexed and astounded at this amazing defection of the men he had considered certain to support his views
and the nice little plan he had cut and dried for the filling of
the expected vacancy. His temper was not improved by the
observation of Mr. Fallowfield, a farmer of great wealth, one
of his own clients, who after staring at him intently for a long
time, said, "Lawyer Doublefee, you be put down! John Bullfinch has laid 'e flat o' your back."

" Hem—the gentleman has argued well, but from mistaken
premises," replied Mr. Doublefee. " Sir Jerry will not stand
for the county."

" He will if we ask him; and we will ask him! eh, John?
eh, neighbor Fallowfield?" returned Southdown.

" Gentlemen, gentlemen, I beg of you to do nothing in
haste," said Mr. Doublefee, hurriedly. " The fact is, that a
candidate has been already selected and agreed upon."

" Who by?" asked Southdown, with a lowering, brindle-bull
sort of look at the lawyer.

" Who by! why, bless my soul, gentlemen, by the professional classes—the townsmen and constituents, represented by
the committee which agreed upon him."

" Then I say let the professional classes—townsmen and
what not—elect him," roared Mr. Southdown, " for I'll be
d——d if I put boot in stirrup to ride for any such purpose!
John Bullfinch and above five hundred more will say the same.
Sir Jerry's the man!" There was the hum of approval falling like a knell upon the ear of Mr. Doublefee from the score
of representative men who sat by John Bullfinch, Southdown
and old Fallowfield, and gloried in the force with which, as
they expressed it, Bullfinch and Southdown had floored the

20

lawyer. The latter, however, was determined not to give it
up.

"The time and place," said he, "are not suitable for the
dispassionate argument of the question, but allow me to——"

"I won't allow nobody to argey the question with me, sir,"
cried Southdown. "My mind's made up. Sir Jerry's the
man for me!"

"Exactly so!" cried the Irish major. "O, Sir Jerry is the
man for me!" It was the refrain of a hunting song, a great
favorite with the members of the hunt, composed by the convivial artist who had put up so long at the Barleymow, and who
had been unanimously voted "an out-and-out clever fellow!"

"But Mr. Southdown, Mr. Bullfinch, gentlemen!" said Mr.
Doublefee, pathetically, "allow me to state who it was that
the—the—constituents selected."

"It don't matter who, as it wasn't our man," replied Southdown. "Sir Jerry is the only man."

"But it was Lord Doomsday!" said Mr. Doublefee, impressively, and leaning back in his chair like one who had delivered a knock-down blow and fallen from the recoil.

The farmers, one and all, looked at Southdown to ascertain
what effect this *coup* might have upon their redoubtable champion. It was not such as Mr. Doublefee had confidently anti-
cipated.

"I don't care for Lord Doomsday—he's a sort of boy," said
he, doggedly. "None of us care for him. His father's land
is not in this county. He only comes here to hunt, and that
but seldom. Sir Jerry's the man!"

"To be sure he is!" said John Bullfinch. "Lord Doomsday's father owns a great deal more land than Sir Jerry does,
but it's nothing like such good land. And, besides, it lies a
long way from this county. Then, again, in regard to the
two gentlemen as hunting men, which must be considered as
having great weight, Sir Jerry is the best rider. The young
lord is a good one, for a light-weight and a young man of his
experience, but Sir Jerry is a man of ten thousand in a real
hunting run. My son Jack is the only one who dares to compare Lord Doomsday to him. Besides, Lord Doomsday says
he does not want to enter parliament for some years to come.
He told me so himself at Hawkwell. Sir Jerry is the man
for this county. If Tom Scarlet was here he would say so."

In grief and wrath, while the applause which followed John's remarks was yet humming, Mr. Doublefee turned to his right-hand neighbor, Doctor Dose, the gentleman with whom he had the colloquy respecting Tom Scarlet, mentioned in the early part of this history. The doctor's memory was refreshed by his hearing Tom Scarlet's name, and he said :

" Have you heard what has happened to that Scarlet, Mr. Doublefee ?"

" No good, I venture to say, if he has met with his deserts. What about him ?" said the lawyer.

" He's dead, that's all, and a good riddance."

" When and where, doctor ? and did he die intestate ? The Grange is a very snug property, and there's no knowing who may be the next in succession to the deceased."

Mr. Doublefee put these questions with a revival of cheer-fulness, and the learned gentlemen took wine together, as though toasting the next heir, whoever he might be.

" When and where he died, and what was the cause of death, I cannot exactly say," replied the doctor. " In all probability there was no post-mortem examination, perhaps no inquest ; for, though he died by violence, it was somewhere or another in America."

" Somewhere or another in America ! That's vague doctor ! The next of kin could hardly eject those in possession, without more definite evidence than that. The deceased may turn up again."

" I know he *may*," said Doctor Dose, "for the vitality of patients of that stamp is amazing. Nature seems to have formed their economy to show that she is more powerful than science. When Scarlet's crony, Belcher, was shot through the right lung, I attended him. You would have thought that would have killed him, if anything could, but he recovered, and refuses to pay the bill."

" What a villain ! Recover, and not pay the bill. Why not bring your action, doctor ?"

" He pretends," said Doctor Dose, " that I never treated him. If so, it was not my fault. Scarlet would not allow me to probe the wound. Belcher himself refused to take any medicine."

" And yet recovered—shocking—shocking !" said Double-fee.

"Scarlet, however," said the doctor, "will not be likely to turn up again. If he is dead or permanently detained abroad by other causes, it will be an excellent thing for this neighborhood and county. Pheasants will be more plentiful, poachers more scarce. The fellow was a poacher and a friend to poachers. Whenever one was in jail, his wife, sister or mother, as the case might be, always flew to the Grange for relief and encouragement. It will be a good thing if Scarlet never comes back."

Mr. Doublefee nodded approval, and took wine with the doctor. The farming interest opposite looked sullen and glum. Relief was at hand, however, from an unexpected quarter. Sir Jerry Snaffle had heard a great deal of the doctor's discourse and determined to interpose.

"Doctor Dose," said he, "were you speaking of one of your own patients, just now?"

The doctor looked confused, and with some hesitation, replied, "No patient of mine, Sir Jerry, but Tom Scarlet."

The baronet's eyes dilated like those of one of the feline tribe about to spring. The reddish brown whiskers seemed to curl at their ends. With a frown upon his brow, and a flush all over his handsome face, he rose, pushed back his chair, and stood erect before the company of which he seemed the king. His was a noble presence.

"Silence, gentlemen!" cried the Irish major, "silence, for Sir Jerry Snaffle, President of our hunt!"

"Gentlemen and friends," said Sir Jerry; I purpose to make a few remarks, and to conclude with a toast, which I hope and believe will not be unacceptable." ["Good; go on."] "At our annual dinners, as you are all well aware, the majority are hunting men. A few gentlemen, however, generally do us the honor to be our guests, who are not hunting men. They are none the less welcome. But they do not understand as we do the sentiments which bind us together—the feelings which grow up through fellowship in the hunting field, between good riders and keen sportsmen of whatever degree."

Major Fitzgerald.—"Hear! Hear! How should they?"

"To the want of this understanding of this fellow-feeling I attribute the remarks I heard made by Dr. Dose concerning one who is now absent, but who was seldom or never behind at the end of a hard run, if he was at the meet. I allude to Tom Scarlet!"

Great applause from everybody, except Mr. Doublefee and Doctor Dose; but especially from the major.

Sir Jerry continued: "Doctor Dose says Tom Scarlet is dead; that if he is not dead, it is to be hoped he will never come back here; that his death or permanent absence would be a good thing for this neighborhood and this county: that pheasants would be more plentiful; that he was a notorious poacher, and a friend to poachers and their families; that he was a bad fellow generally, and it is to be hoped we shall never see him again. Gentlemen, is that true?"

A "No!" which almost shook the pictures in their frames was the answer all around the room, and Mr. Southdown, in a voice like the bellow of one of his own bulls, cried: "All lies!"

"Gentlemen," said Sir Jerry, in a louder and more animated tone, as though he had got what the company would have called second wind, "Tom Scarlet is not dead. Neither his death nor his permanent absence is to be apprehended or desired. Gentlemen, we know the man! We have seen him go at many a thick bullfinch and sail over many a wide brook. A better rider never sat in pigskin." (Great cheers.)

The Major.—"A man of ten thousand, and always behaved like a gentleman. Picked me up before I was down, when me horse was knocked over by a tailor from Tooley street on a runaway black mare."

Sir Jerry continued: "Tom Scarlet may have a fault or two. I do not mean to say that he is quite perfect; but when he returns, if he should bring an action for defamation of character, it will be very difficult for Doctor Dose to prove to a jury of this country that he is a notorious poacher."

The doctor got pale and red by turns. He appealed to Mr. Doublefee by a look, but that gentleman resolved not to see it, and nodded to John Bullfinch, as though to signify, "Sir Jerry had him there—upon the legal points involved, Sir Jerry has the best of it."

The baronet continued: "Something has been said by Doctor Dose about pheasants. Pheasants are very good——"

The Major.—" Nothing better, roasted, with bread sauce and the right kind of gravy. That I ate of here was done to a turn !"

" But in a part of the country like ours," said Sir Jerry, " there are other things to be considered besides pheasants and pheasant-shooting. Need I say I mean fox-hunting and farming, hounds and foxes, horses and men ? Without fox-hunting your men will degenerate in pluck."

The Major.—" True for you ! 'Twas and is the opinion of the Duke. His best men at Waterloo were fox-hunters. I know it. 'Twas there I lost me arm and got this slash in the cheek from the sabre of a cuiraissier. (Hear, hear! from Mr. Doublefee.)

Sir Jerry resumed: " Without hunting your best breeds of riding-horses would soon be done for ; because there would be nobody to buy one worth more than twenty pounds."

The farmers looked at each other with alarm, and regarded Doctor Dose with displeasure, as if he was an enemy to fox-hunting ; whereas, some of his best cases had arisen through accidents in the hunting-field.

Sir Jerry went on : " The noble hounds, in which we take so much pride, would be replaced with sheep-killing mongrels. Your foxes, famed for swiftness, stoutness and craft, would become mere sneaks—robbers of henroosts round the homesteads—instead of bold outlyers in the gorses of the heaths. Shall the breed of men, horses, hounds and foxes degenerate in and about this famous vale ?" (" No !" from the company, with uncommon vigor, Mr. Doublefee joining in as loud as any one.)

" Very well, then, you will unite with me in the hope that Tom Scarlet will speedily return," said Sir Jerry.

Mr. Doublefee had now turned his back on the doctor and regarded Sir Jerry with a mixture of surprise and delight. It sprang from his admiration at the art of Sir Jerry in so presenting the case to the jury, as Mr. Doublefee said to himself, as to make Scarlet, fox-hunting, and the preservation of the superior breeds of men, horses, hounds and foxes seem all one. Perhaps the worthy baronet scarcely knew himself how well he had done this ; but Mr. Doublefee, accustomed to listen to barristers of much art and eloquence, upon the circuit, knew it very well, and appreciated it.

Sir Jerry continued: "I hope, then, that Tom Scarlet will soon come back. Instead of his permanent absence being a good thing for our neighborhood, it would be a very bad thing —great misfortune. His absence, so far, we have been able to bear; but if he is away much longer I do not know what the consequences may be. Gentlemen, what are the facts? You know, that to maintain the reputation and exalt the honor of our hunt, I made a steeple-chase match for a thousand guineas a side."

The Major.—"So he did, with the Juke of Jumpover. I was at the making of it, and it was a good thing to do."

Sir Jerry continued: "The conditions are, five miles through the Vale, gentlemen riders, horses that were hunted in the Midlands or the Vale of White Horse last year, weights ten stone ten. 'Tis to come off in March. Now, how stands this matter? At every meet in Northamptonshire, Leicestershire, and Warwickshire they lay odds on the Duke, when the real truth is, that my horse couldn't lose it if Tom Scarlet was here to ride him."

The Major.—"Be me soul 'tis truth, every word Sir Jerry says, and if the young man is dead or does not come, I am in for a hundred myself."

"Sir," said Mr. Southdown, with much volume and emphasis of voice, "the young man is not dead. He's alive and well. If you think he's dead, on account of what these here wandering sailors said, about the fight and the Dutchman and the calaboose, you can do so. I shan't argey the p'int. It aint worth while, because Tom's alive and well. You can't kill a man by argeyment, leastways not till he comes to be tried for his life."

"Gentlemen," said Sir Jerry, "I propose health and prosperity to Tom Scarlet, and may he speedily return to this country!"

The toast was drunk with a thundering hurrah. John Bullfinch blew his nose very hard with a red silk handkerchief, while Mr. Southdown, looking at his lawyer, said with great deliberation, "Sir Jerry is——"

"The man!" exclaimed Mr. Doublefee. "There is no doubt about it, sir. His eloquence will do honor to the county in Parliament, sir. At another time I will enlarge upon this. I have now something to say to Doctor Dose."

In the great applause and satisfaction which had prevailed
at the end of Sir Jerry's speech the doctor would probably have
escaped further observation, if Mr. Doublefee had been willing
to let him alone. But he was not. He had determined to go
over to the other side, bag and baggage, and to signalize his
change of front forthwith. The learned gentleman, indeed,
resolved to act like the Bavarian artillery, who not only deserted Napoleon in the heat of a great and decisive battle, but
halted half way between his lines and those of the Allied Powers, unlimbered their guns, and delivered a destructive fire
into his shattered and wavering ranks.

"Now, sir," said Mr. Doublefee, with a truculent air, as he
rose and faced Doctor Dose, "look at me, sir, and at the—the
honorable court and intelligent jury, I was about to say, but
this shall be reserved for a future and more impressive occasion, sir, and I will now say, the honorable chairman and
worthy company. What have you to say for yourself, sir?
What excuse do you mean to offer? What pretext will you
allege for the base, false and malicious attack you have made
upon the—the highly respectable and—and exemplary young
man, whose absence is so much to be deplored—Tom Scarlet?"

If the floor beneath the doctor had opened and disclosed a
yawning pit, he could scarcely have been more astounded than
he was by Doublefee's defection and address. He looked at
his assailant with dumb amazement for a few moments, and
faltered out, "Me! why it was you, you know, who said that
Scarlet——"

"Come, sir! come, come, sir! equivocation will not do; prevarication will hardly serve your turn here, sir, and neither
will avail when the case comes on for trial in the Common
Pleas, or King's Bench, or at the assizes. As Sir Jerry Snaffle so well observed in his forcible, eloquent and feeling speech,
the damages will be heavy—very heavy—when the action is
brought, and the case is tried by an enlightened jury who know
the value of an Englishman's character, sir. I shall no doubt
be attorney for the plaintiff, sir, and it will be my painful duty
to set forth in the brief I shall furnish, the express malice
which impelled your observations. You had better make a
clean breast of it, sir, and throw yourself upon the mercy of
the court—company, company, in order that Sir Jerry Snaffle,

and the other friends of Mr. Scarlet, may intercede with him, on your behalf, when he returns!"

Mr. Doublefee would have gone on at great length, but Sir Jerry and Major Fitzgerald interposed. The hilarity of the evening was resumed and continued to a late hour.

CHAPTER XXXIII.

"The day is cold and dark and dreary,
It rains, and the wind is never weary."

IT was a dark, damp and dreary morning when the Birmingham coach left the Saracen's Head, in the heart of London, for its daily journey through the Midland counties to the metropolis of the hardware manufacture and trade. The passengers were few, and they seemed to be rather depressed and disconsolate—an effect, perhaps, of the weather. Just before the coach started two sailors came hastily up, with a bag and a bundle. The shorter of the two, a broad-shouldered, pock-marked man, rushed into the booking office and then rushed out again, exclaiming, "Inside or outside?" "On deck! on deck! even if they charge more for it," was the reply of the other sailor. "We don't want to be stowed between decks on this uncommon lovely morning." The speaker was tall, graceful, and well-proportioned, without being stout. His complexion was very dark, and his eyes were black and bright. His luggage consisted only of a bundle tied up in a silk handkerchief. Yet he was well dressed. His monkey-jacket of pilot cloth was new, and the suit of blue he wore underneath was also new, and cut in the smartest and most natty nautical style. Any sailor would have seen at a glance that this was a man-of-war's man, though the landsmen would have perceived no difference between him and a sailor just paid off from an Indiaman at Blackwall. He wore a tarpaulin hat—that is, one so-called, for there was no tarpaulin about it. The superstructure was of the finest Bombay sinnet, covered with fine silk, and painted a glossy black. He was an active man, for with a mere touch of his fingers to the rail he vaulted to his seat, the one beside the guard. Cox, the man of the racecourse, and of the fight at Baltimore, sat opposite. Before they had left the pavements of the metropolis and the suburbs which lie beneath its vast smoky canopy, the rain began to fall sluggishly; and when they reached the open country to the north and west, it had set in for a regular rainy day. Everything appeared to be in soak. The earth, the air, the sky, seemed to be saturated with the ooze of the English and St. George's Channels, and that of the German Ocean. The sailors sat with the collars of their monkey-jackets up around their ears, and said but little. Even the guard was taciturn. Cox observed that the weather was not much like that in the Gulf, and the other replied, or in the Bay of Bengal or the Mediterranean. With this they relapsed into silence, and smoked their short pipes and Cavendish tobacco incessantly. Whenever the coach stopped to change horses, the sailors called for brandy, and treated the coachman and guard. Besides this, they had recourse, at intervals, to certain flat bottles extracted from the pockets of their monkey-jackets. The bottle of the man-of-war's man contained arrack; from that of Cox arose the rich flavor of fine old schnapps. Altogether it was a dreary ride, like a watch on the Grand Banks, they said, and when they descended from the Chiltern Hills into the vales below, the weather got worse rather than better. At Tring and at Aylesbury the rain was still falling fast, but it had held up a little when they reached the vicinity of Wootton and Ridingcumstoke. But the waters were out in the low meadows, and the brooks ran swift and turbid, full to the banks. In passing a heavy carrier's wagon, with its slow strong team of gigantic cart horses, the coach was pulled off the hard road and almost upset into the ditch to the left.

"There," said the dark sailor, "a little more and he would have brought her by the lee. I say, Cox, this is the place. I know it is, though the country seems changed. The fields are smaller, and the woods are not as big as the old woods were in my time."

"A natural consequence of following the sea," replied Cox. "When a man on the lookout, or what not, casts his eyes almost constantly over miles and miles of blue water, it improves their range, and the big expanse of the ocean makes the old things at home on the land appear to be very small. But, as you say, here we be."

Without more ado the men dismounted at a cross roads, and bade farewell to the coachman and guard.

" Now, Jim," said Cox, " you see there's a great advantage in getting down at a cross roads. If any inquisitive body tries to find out which road you took, it's two to one he can't do it."

" Well, which are we going to take?"

" Nar'a one," said Cox. " You give me that bag careful after I get through this hedge. Then come on yourself."

Thereupon that worthy forced his way through the fence, and having received his bag, struck across the sodden, soggy field towards a smoke which arose from a clump of trees at a distance. It was not from a gypsy camp, but from the chimney of a hedge ale-house, one of those places in which the landlord was, in the elegant and perspicuous language of the Act of Parliament, " Licensed to sell ale and beer by retail, and to be drunk on the premises." Just then, however, he was not drunk on the premises, for the sailors found no one present save the landlady, a comely woman, and four or five shock-headed children. The sailors took seats on a bench near the bright sea-coal fire, and called for ale. The landlady quickly brought a foaming quart, which Cox warmed by plunging a red-hot poker into it. Could the sailors have dinner? They could. Gammon of bacon and ducks' eggs fried. Nothing better for dinner at a roadside house on a rainy day in all the Midlands, unless, indeed, the landlady should happen to have in her larder chops off the loin of one of the great breed of Cotswold and Lincoln sheep, for which the vales were famous far and wide. The dinner was quickly and beautifully cooked, and forthwith served with the large country loaf of the neighborhood, and the fresh butter of the vale. Then the sailors ate, and the conversation began. Where was the missus' man? He had gone hunting afoot after the hounds the day before, and had not returned. Did missus miss him? In one way she did, but in another it was a relief to have him out of the way. Was there a gypsy camp in the neighborhood? There might be and there might not. Did the missus know Rose Tanner? She thought she did. Was Rose in the neighborhood? The missus considered. She looked hard at Cox and harder at the other sailor. She couldn't exactly say, unless she was sure that what she said would do Rose no harm.

"Harm!" said Cox; "why, we be her best friends. This mate o' mine here's her brother."

"Lord save us! Be this Rose's brother? I thought he was jest like her. But which on 'em!"

"Why, the sailor man, to be sure—Jim Cooper, the youngest of the brothers."

"I've always heard Rose speak of him as a boy, and this is a proper grown man," said the landlady.

"Well, missus, I was a boy when I went away, and Rose was but a gal. But boys and gals grow up, afloat or ashore. It's eighteen years since I saw Rose, or she saw me. Where is she? and is she well?"

"She was never better. She's got twins, as like as two peas, and she is in favor with the gentry, I hear. The shepherds and ploughmen who come here for their ale o' nights say that Lord Doomsday gave her twenty guineas for the twins on Christmas eve. Her husband, Jack Tanner, is off after the hounds with my man. Rose's camp is t'other side the woods, on the heath. It'll soon be dusk, and if you're a-going there to-night, you had best be moving."

"Ay, ay, missus, I'm thankful for the news," said Cooper. "We're going there, sure enough; but we will have a pot and a pipe before we start. I must consider things a minute. A man's feelings ain't many fathom deep when the lead is really hove for 'em. I say, Cox, you never mentioned them twins. I could have bought something for them in Lunnon. I saw a great many beautiful things for sale on Tower Hill."

"All infernal trash. Just as counterfeit as the money the coves make down here at Brummagem, and not half as useful. You give Rose the money you want to spend upon her children, and she will lay it out well."

"That she will," said the landlady. "Why, at the fairs and races her gals wears gold necklaces, the envy of some of the people of quality. Says I to a Jew peddler, says I, in this very room, 'Be them necklaces Rose Tanner's daughters wears gold?' 'Missus,' said he, 'they be, and fine gold at that.'"

She forgot to say that he added, "As fine as dese chains and earrings and brooches, vot I sells for half de walues."

After some further conversation the men left the house, regained the road, and turned up a lane on the other side of it, along which they strode in silence for a quarter of a mile. Then a small field only intervened between them and the boundaries of the great preserves. They looked through the leafless hedge, and saw hundreds of hares and pheasants out of the coverts upon the young wheat. As if fascinated by the sight, the sailors stood and gazed. They then looked each other in the face, and Cox said :

"Our nearest way is through this part of the woods. It's half an hour, plain and rapid sailing, and then we shall strike the heath just where we want to be to see the light of the camp-fire."

"Ay, ay, I know," replied Cooper. "But this is just about the place where they came down upon us that time, and we three got fourteen years apiece."

"Yes, Jim, but the job had been put up beforehand, and the keepers knew just where to look for you. From what I've heard since, Tom of Lincoln whistled on the plan. He turned against Jack Cotswold since, and cut and run along with Jagger. He's still enough now. A fellow settled his hash at Orleans with five inches of steel. The place is here as still and lonely as if foot had never trod it. Besides it's nothing but trespass anyhow—simple trespass, and we won't go round. Follow me !"

In another minute or two, they passed through the straggling fence into the woods and walked rapidly forward. At the edge of a sort of open glade Cox paused, and placed his bag upon the moss at the foot of a large and very old oak tree.

"Jim," said he, in a whisper, pointing to a tall larch which grew in the glade, "look up there !"

"I see 'em," said Cooper, "and it's very tempting; still, it's fourteen years if they grab us."

"Not at all. It's only three or six months in the daytime, and nobody can prove that it's night yet. Besides, there's nobody here to grab us. We shall be upon the heath before old Moleskin gets anywhere near here, and I'll have a brace if I die for it."

With this he drew the stock and short barrels of a handy little gun from among the clothes and contents of his dunnage bag, and quickly fitted the barrels.

" Very well, fire away, Flanigan !" said the gypsy, with all his ancient ardor for the old methods revived in full and over-powering force.

Bang ! bang ! went the gun, and down came two pheasants from their roost on the horizontal branches of the larch, while the others went whirring away among the tree-tops. The gun and the game were hastily placed in the bag, and the men, stooping low and walking rapidly, with caution approached the outside of the wood. They were about to congratulate each other on their success, when from the thick fern and briars of a swale up jumped two men with a big mastiff dog and collared them.

" Mind," said Cox, as Moleskin tightened his grip upon the collar of his jacket, " we offer no resistance. We're merely travellers that have lost our way, and it's nothing more than trespass, if it's that."

" That'll do, Cox," said Moleskin, at the voice. " Where's your gun? And where's yours, young fellow ?"

" Mine's in this bag," replied Cox, " and unloaded, which is perhaps lucky for somebody. This man never had one, and he is, I may say, a stranger to me. Never met before yester-day."

" We shall see," said the keeper. " What the d—l brings you sailors here anyhow ?"

" I think it was the d—l," said Cooper, " for we had no use for the birds, and if they had not come in our way we should have been out of this before now."

The keeper looked closely at him, but the light was now very dim, and the gypsy's collar was up. " Men," said Mole-skin, " I never was a hard man, though I have always done my duty. Will you go peaceably and quietly to my lodge and stay there until I see what is to be done ?"

" We will !" said Cooper.

" Then I can tell you that you'll be none the worse off for it. Come on !"

The keeper led the way. The sailors followed, and the un-der-keeper brought up the rear with the mastiff. It was a long walk, and thick darkness fell upon the woods before the lodge was reached. A fire was burning on the hearth, and Moleskin produced a lamp and stooped to light it.

" I say, keeper," cried Cox, "it wanted just about five minutes of sundown when that gun went off. I want that understood."

" Five minutes of sundown! Why the sun had set an hour, as the almanac and my watch will prove."

" No they won't. Your watch is always fast, and in respect to sunset you are always wrong. You don't allow for his declination. No landsman ever does."

" What does it matter?" said the gypsy, sharply.

The keeper had lit the lamp, and turning to look at him, he started with surprise. The man had thrown off his heavy jacket, and stood in the full light. There were the fine straight figure, the nut-brown face, with the red tinge of excitement on the cheeks, the very features, the glowing eyes, and the earrings of gold, so that had it not been for the close-cropped hair and the hard hands, Moleskin would have sworn that Rose Tanner stood before him disguised as a man.

" Now, I'm sorry for this," said the keeper. " Which is it, Tom or Elijah?"

" Neither; it's me—the young 'un—Jim the sailor."

" Ah, it was you that fetched me the clout with the butt of the gun after the others had mainly given up, when I was under-keeper."

" Well the jury said so, and there was an end. But this was a long while ago, Master Moleskin, and I've never been in these parts since. As Cox and I have run into shoal water without meaning it, what's to be done? He tells the truth when he says that we met for the first time yesterday morning."

" I must consider. Bill, I must consider!" said Moleskin to his man. " Go you the rounds to-night, and in the morning tell Parkins to come here. Don't you sailor chaps be two fools, and make bad worse by trying to get away. I have your words, I suppose?"

" You have, honor bright!"

" Well, then, sit down. We'll smoke a pipe and drink a glass, and I'll consider."

The keeper considered for some time—so long, indeed, that he replenished his pipe and refilled the glasses. Then, looking at the fire with the air of a man in a brown study, he soliloquized as follows, with intervals of silence between the sentences:

" A town magistrate wun't understand the true ins and outs and merits of this case. Sir Jerry Snaffle will." (Cox nudged Cooper with his elbow.) " My duty is to deliver these men to the constable, and I must do it. That's plain enough to the man-of-war's man. It rests with the constable to take his men before any magistrate in the neighborhood he pleases. He's fond of good ale, the constable is. Sir Jerry brews the best in the county, and the tap at the Hall is pretty much always a-running." (Cooper nudged Cox.) " There will be a matter of an hour or two in the morning before I can go with the constable anywhere. During that time he'll naturally want a glass or two. The constable likes gin as well as ale."

" What does he say to rum? I've got in the dunnage bag some as fine as ever left Port Royal Bay," said Cox.

" The constable is *very* fond of rum and milk in the morning. We shall have milk brought here about daylight. Sir Jerry may not be at home when we reach the Hall. It's a hunting morning, and I think he'll be gone when we get there." (Cooper and Cox looked blank.) " But her ladyship will be. As an Admiral's daughter, when informed by the constable that he has two sailors there for a *trifling offence,* her ladyship may wish to speak to the sailors. If them sailors make a good impression on her, the lady may ask a favor or two in their behalf. I've known her ladyship to ask favors that wasn't refused. Still I, Moleskin, keeper to the Marquis, must do my duty."

" Certainly! 'England expects every man to do his duty,' and in you and me she won't be disappointed," said Cooper, with much vivacity. " I will say that you'll be the means of saving one sailor to the King, and perhaps not the worst in his majesty's fleet."

" The constable," said Moleskin, coolly and dryly, " is a great man for king and constitution, likewise the church. The man-of-war's man is, of course, all right. If Cox has picked up any revolutionary, radical notions, he'd better keep them to himself."

" Me revolutionary! Me radical!" said Cox. " Why, d—n it, Moleskin, I've fought on the Tory side at every election there's been for fourteen or fifteen years, when I was ashore."

CHAPTER XXXIV.

"———Be not afear'd; the isle is full of noises,
Sounds and sweet airs that give delight and hurt not.
Sometimes a thousand twanging instruments
Will hum about mine ears; and sometimes voices
That, if I then had waked after long sleep,
Will make me sleep again."

THE winter season was passing rapidly away. The days grew longer and the gales grew stronger, for the stormy time of February was come. The sun was seldom seen except for a minute or two, when it shone from among dark, sweeping clouds, like the face of a beauty beaming for a brief space between jealous curtains. But for all that, the birds were already brisk and busy. The rooks cawed loudly and incessantly in the upper branches of the tall elms, and seemed to hold counsel and debate over the ways and means of repairing or rebuilding the last year's nests. The sparrows flew rapidly about, and saucily chattered on the ricks and thatch of the farm buildings, as if they owned them, or held them under a long lease. The shepherds of the Vale prepared for early lambing time, and now the ploughs of the husbandmen, with their teams of powerful horses, heavy in the shoulders and shaggy at the heels, were going early and late through the rich loam of the fertile land. The first blossoms of the young year, the snowdrops, might already be seen in the garden of May Bullfinch, and she was often busy there. The maiden was, however, restless and uneasy, and, as in the days of the last summer and autumn, glancing early and late from the garden gate. Hope deferred troubled and distressed her. To-morrow and to-morrow; but the truant never came. Tom Scarlet was still absent. Nothing had been heard of him since the roving sailors put afloat the rumor of his death. Mr. Southdown and John Bullfinch still talked confidently of his speedy return, but their anxious and impatient looks, when together, seemed to give the lie to their sanguine expressions before May. Straddles, however, was as positive now as he had been on Christmas eve, that the missing man would reach

21

the Vale before the day set for the great steeple-chase match between horses to be named by the Duke and Sir Jerry Snaffle. The box at the Grange was kept carefully done up.

It was morning, and having breakfasted, John Bullfinch was preparing to mount and ride to the cover side. The meet was to be at a noted and popular place, in a country of grasslands and small coverts, every one of which usually held a strong fox. Cowslip was at the door, arrayed in the new saddle and bridle, the Christmas gift of his children to John Bullfinch and his mare. Young Jack stood by the fire with an air of vexation and discontent upon his features, arising from the fact that his father had prohibited him from hunting that day. "It is not the place for boys; the field, when we meet at Stratton, is too large for boys; they are in the way," said John, as May tied his cravat. The farmer then slipped on his coat, kissed his daughter fondly, and held out his hand to his son. Young Jack took it warmly, though there was almost a tear of disappointment in his eye. But he suddenly looked up, dropped his father's hand, and cried, "Here's Sir Jerry, father! May, here's Sir Jerry! and I'm blest if he isn't on The Bagman!"

"This is an honor, my dear," said John. "You Jack!"

But his son was already outside, and at the baronet's stirrup. Dismounting, Sir Jerry Snaffle walked into the house, and taking the farmer aside, spoke to him in rapid, low tones, pointing through the window with his whip at the strong and beautiful horse held by Young Jack.

"I don't know about it," said John, looking very serious. "Work is well enough, and it is true that we can get no tidings of Tom and the horse he bragged about; but your weight, Sir Jerry, will be too much. The pace is always good, and the run commonly long, when we meet at Stratton and draw the copses; and you know, Sir Jerry, that you never pulled up in your life while the fox was afoot and the hounds were running."

"I have another horse out," said the baronet, "I shall change for him, and send The Bagman home at the first check. Besides, I feel confident that Tom Scarlet will yet come to time, and then he shall decide which horse to start. I thought you would like to ride with me to the cover. On the road we can talk."

"Greatest of pleasure!" said John Bullfinch. "A great honor, Sir Jerry, very great! May, my dear——"

The farmer looked round for his daughter, but in vain. The sudden appearance of Sir Jerry Snaffle at her father's house had surprised her, and it flashed across her mind that he came with some sad intelligence respecting her lover, and was then communicating it to her father, in order that he might break it to her. She ran to her sitting-room, and gave way to a flood of tears. She wiped them hurriedly away as she heard them coming along towards her room, but the heavy tread of the baronet and her father on the oak floor in their hunting-boots, sounded like a knell. As they entered she glanced timidly at Sir Jerry, as she curtsied, but instead of seeing the sad look of one who brought intelligence of a melancholy calamity, she beheld the genial smile which so well became his handsome face. A fine-looking man was Sir Jerry Snaffle, especially when he was in the uniform of the hunt—the well-fitting scarlet coat, the buff waistcoat, tight buckskin breeches, white as milk, and faultless top-boots with silver spurs. And as May blushed while he looked very kindly at her, and took her hand, she thought he was a marvellous proper man.

"I bring," said he, "an invitation from Lady Snaffle to you, Miss May. Her ladyship would be much pleased to see you at the Hall, and as there is no one there, I have no doubt you will pass a pleasant day."

"Oh, Sir Jerry!" said May, "I am sure I shall be delighted. It is always a pleasure to be allowed to wait upon her ladyship, she is so kind."

"Yes, yes! the truth is, Miss May, that Lady Snaffle is fond of you, which is nothing to wonder at," said he. "Therefore, as soon as we leave you, which must be now, you had better let your brother get your horse ready and ride over. He can go over in the afternoon and see you home, unless you remain all night."

"Thank you, Sir Jerry. My brother shall come for me in the afternoon, if you please, so that I may be home again as soon as father is," she replied.

"Be it so, then. Good-morning. Her ladyship must teach you to keep your spirits up until we get news of Tom Scarlet, which will no doubt be very soon. Come, John!"

The farmer, intensely gratified, kissed his daughter again and again, before he followed Sir Jerry. The latter, in a few words, told the lad that his sister was to set out for the Hall forthwith, and that he was to ride over and conduct her home in the evening. Young Jack heard this with great satisfaction. A visit to the Hall delighted him almost as much as a day in the hunting-field, as he not only had gracious notice and words of commendation from Lady Snaffle, but commonly managed to secure an interview with one or two gray-headed retainers of the family, whose large experience and long memories made them oracles in all matters of field sports. As Sir Jerry and John Bullfinch mounted and rode off they were followed by the admiring gaze of May Bullfinch, Young Jack, and Tom, the man of the lantern on Christmas eve.

"There goes the best two men I ever held a stirrup for," said the latter; "the very best!"

"Yes, good men!" replied Young Jack. "But Tom Scarlet for cross-country work, is, to my mind, the very best man we have in these parts."

"Why, young master, I warn't thinking of him. We don't have him in these parts now. He ain't come back, you see, and has been gone a'most a year. I don't think he'll come back; leastways, not for a good while."

"What do you mean?" said Young Jack.

"Well, a score of years or so," replied the man. "You see, nothing has been heard of him. Some think he is dead. I don't believe he is."

"What do you think then?"

"Master Jack," replied the man, "it's my belief he's 'listed for a soger; and, by George, what a sergeant in the dragoons he'll make! I think I should 'list myself if his regiment was to come along this way, with their helmets and sashes and long swords."

"Go and saddle May's horse," said Young Jack. "She is going to the Hall to visit Lady Snaffle. In the evening I shall be there to fetch her home. Be lively, Tom."

By the time Tom had the horse at the door May Bullfinch was dressed for her little journey. She was glad of the opportunity to reveal all her hopes and fears to Lady Snaffle. Indeed, she had been urged to do so by one of her best friends;

for, seeing how she pined, a prey to anxiety and doubt, Mr.
Southdown had recommended frequent visits to his wife and
daughters, and had insisted that she should no longer neglect
to consult with the Admiral's daughter. So, with an admoni-
tion and a kiss to Jack, May started.

The day was dark and bleak, as she rode between the leafless hedges of the lanes which were the shortest way to Sir
Jerry's house. At the top of the hill she paused and surveyed
the wide expanse of the dreary heath between her and the
woodlands which bounded Sir Jerry's park and shut in the
sheltered pastures of the vale. Far to the left, from among
clumps of gorse, in its winter suit, she saw the smoking rising
from a gypsy camp and drifting away before the wind. No
mark of settled habitation was to be seen upon the waste.
May had overheard what passed between her father's man and
her brother, and her mood was sad. The reins had fallen on
her horse's neck, and as he walked with measured tread, she
was absorbed in melancholy musing. She had almost forgotten
where she was, when a rich female voice aroused her attention,
and, as it were, stopped her on the way. It appeared to come
from a thick clump of gorse, brambles and dried fern, an acre
or more in extent. Its owner, unseen, sang as follows :

> O ! why does the Rose of the hamlet stray
>   On the lonesome verge of the windy heath ?
> Neither fern leaf nor flower is seen by the way,
>   The sward is as pale as a last summer's wreath.
> No note swells the brake where the wild thrush was loud,
>   No mirth-bearing carol comes up from the lea—
> The lark does not sing high above the rain cloud,
>   No bird sways a bough of the naked ash tree.
> The clustering gorse, that was once green and gold,
>   Is brown as the thatch on the oldest field barn ;
> No bleat from the flock in the snug haulmy fold,
>   No cry of the bittern is heard by the tarn.
> The earth seemeth dumb, and the sky dark and drear,
>   No music is borne on the dull laden air ;
> But the sad, gentle sigh, and the soft falling tear,
>   Lead the low, honey voice of the maiden in prayer.

There was a pause ; May Bullfinch thought the concealed
female had finished her song, but she continued with a deeper
voice and more animation :

> A horseman armed, of the wild West land,
>   Speeds fast as the drift of the screaming gale !
> The brown chief will ride at his red right hand ;
>   There are branches strewn over hill and dale.

His pale brow is stern as the night's dun cloud,
  His elf locks are flying, his raiment is dank!
What gleams in his eye—fierce, bloodshot, and proud—
  While the rowels are red in the White Horse's flank?
" Three more shall be slain!" were the words he said,
  As he shook to the sky his death-streaming gun,
" Ere the shaft that is loosened hath truthfully sped,
  Four lives must perish to answer for one.
I swear by the thunder thou bearest like fate!
  By the lightning which bursts from thy muzzle so blue!
Four grim, guilty ghosts, through the cold cloudy gate
  Shall follow the friend who was tender and true!"

O, Rose of the hamlet! oh, which thinkest thou,
  Were heard by the Father who loves us alway—
The wild, whirling words of the horseman's dark vow,
  Or the prayers of the maiden who fainteth to-day?

The voice died away in a long cadence. May Bullfinch
looked and listened, and had almost resolved to force her
horse through the gorse, when she saw a form in a dark cloak
pass swiftly from one clump to another, already far away in
the direction of the gypsy camp. Unsettled and agitated,
though scarcely alarmed, May touched her horse with the
whip. He struck into a steady hand-gallop, and in half an
hour she was at Sir Jerry Snaffle's. Her welcome was a warm
one. After some refreshment, Lady Snaffle took her to the
library, and there, seated by the lady's side before the fire,
May opened her heart and told her tale, including the purport
of the song she had heard on the heath. The sympathy and
tact of Lady Snaffle soon restored May's self-possession, and
inspired her with more confidence than she had lately felt.
The former treated her as she might have treated a daughter
or a young sister. She remembered that May had no mother;
and in close conversation they spent two hours, perhaps more,
very pleasantly. The lady's white, soft hand, with its dimple
and its jewelled rings, was upon May's shoulder, and she was
speaking to her in a coaxing tone, when there came a knock
at the door. Entering at the bidding of his mistress, the footman announced that Parkins, the constable, was below, and
requested an interview with Lady Snaffle, upon very pressing
and particular business. Perhaps it was the knowledge that
this man had been somehow mixed up with Tom Scarlet's
affair, and the possibility that the roving sailors might have
returned and fallen into his charge, that induced the lady,

after a moment's consideration, to grant his request, and direct the footman to show him into the library in which they were.

"The man," said she to May Bullfinch, "is a blockhead and a bore, a pragmatical fellow; but he is upheld in his office by the magistracy, some of whom, my dear, are none too wise themselves. I will learn what he wants, and speedily dismiss him, after which we will resume our little conference."

Parkins entered rather boldly, but, as if suddenly checked, he hesitated and made a low bow. He was surprised to see May Bullfinch there, and was rather disconcerted by finding Lady Snaffle's eye on him as soon as he was within the room. His face was redder than usual. It might be the effect of the wind and weather; but his nose was of a lively purple, and that might be the effect of his having taken what he called "a little summut" several times in the course of the day. As his eyes were bright but unsteady, and as there was a rapid winking of the lids nearly all the time, it was probably *not* the effect of the weather which caused the change in his appearance.

"Now, Mr. Parkins, come forward! Your business, sir? What do you want to state?" said Lady Snaffle.

"Well, my lady!" replied he, with another profound bow and a sort of jackdaw look of wisdom, "Sir Jerry being absent, I made bold, knowing your ladyship's influence with the higher authorities——"

"Never mind the preamble. To the point! What is it you want?"

"Your ladyship's influence and orders in a certain cause which is, I may say, before the authorities, and yet not before 'em—half and half, as a tapster might say."

"And what is it about, sir?"

"About two men that have been took up—took up *wrongful*, my lady. Very few is ever so took up—none that I pulls myself, although they all pretend to be. This here case, however, I have investigated, and the men is took up wrongful, and ought to be discharged."

"And what of that, sir! I cannot discharge them. I am not in the commission of the peace," said Lady Snaffle.

"True, my lady! I wish you was; for since the Admiral left, what with Sir Jerry being always so busy with his horses, and his hounds, and his matches, and Mr. Jericho being, as his man says, engaged night and day with his history of the antiquaries of the primitive church, there is a kind of a vacancy in the heads of the bench," replied Mr. Parkins.

"That will do, Parkins. You must take the men somewhere else."

"They a' been took up wrongful," said Parkins.

"I cannot help it, sir."

"These men be from America, my lady."

"Ah!" said Lady Snaffle, while May Bullfinch started.

"And they be sailors, my lady," said Parkins, with much emphasis.

"Sailors from America! May, I declare I do not perceive any harm in seeing them. Parkins, the case is altered," said Lady Snaffle. "As the Admiral is not here, tell me all about it. Come to the point and be brief."

"My lady, I will. It's a pleasure to speak to you in a cause, as if your worship was on the bench in earnest. From information I received this morning, I goes to Moleskin's lodge in the woods this forenoon, and finds him and the prisoners, the sailors from America, took up wrongful. Moleskin says the men be poachers, and tells me to take 'em and lock 'em up. The sailors say they isn't, and tells me to take 'em before Sir Jerry Snaffle. I tells the sailors that Sir Jerry Snaffle is absent. 'Then,' says the sailors, 'to prevent being clewed up fore and aft, we claim the right and privilege of being taken before Sir Jerry Snaffle's wife. She's an Admiral's daughter and knows the ropes.'"

"My dear," said Lady Snaffle, laughing, "it is just sailorlike. Parkins, what is the case against them, as alleged by Moleskin himself?"

"Moleskin, my lady, charges that the men were in the cover for the purpose of poaching, but the sailors tell another story. The sailors say, my lady, that coming to London in a ship from New Orleans, they were intrusted with certain presents, to wit, a gun and two bottles of rum, very old Jamaica, for Gypsy Jack, a friend of theirs."

Parkins paused, and the ladies being now greatly interested and all attention, waited for him to proceed.

"Finding himself in this neighborhood lateish in the evening, and hearing that the gypsy camp was about the middle of the heath, the sailor says—that is, the spokesman says—he took the way through the woods by a short cut, and his gun going off by accident, Moleskin came up and nailed 'em."

" A trifling, absurd story, Parkins, with nothing to corroborate it," said Lady Snaffle. " I doubt whether these men are sailors at all. Have they corkscrew curls all round their heads?"

" No, my lady. Their heads are as smooth as bullets and about as hard," said Parkins.

" May, my dear, all the fellows with curls, in sailor's clothes, are impostors, and ought to be sent to the treadmill. My father always told Sir Jerry so."

" And, my lady, there is something to corroborate what the sailors say," remarked Mr. Parkins.

" And what may it be, sir?"

" The rum, my lady, and the gun," said Parkins. " There's one bottle of the old Jamaica left. As one of the authorities, I tested the spokesman's credibility with the other, and found it sound and all right. Besides, he's intrusted with a token and a message to Tom Scarlet, or, in his absence, to his next friend. That token the sailor refuses to show; that message he declines to deliver to me and Moleskin."

" You did right to come here, Parkins. Do you think the sailor will intrust the token and the message to me?" said Lady Snaffle.

" To you and the young lady, Miss May Bullfinch, now present and occupying a seat on the bench, as I may say, he will, because she is the next friend, by name mentioned and set forth in the indictment as the party the token and message are to be delivered to in Tom Scarlet's absence. He'll stand and deliver, like a true man, will this sailor, if your ladyship will influence Moleskin to let him go away without further trouble."

" I will see Moleskin. I will see the men. Are they here?"

" They are, my lady. I left them in the hall, eating of roast beef and mince-pie, drinking your ladyship's health in ale, and gammoning the gals."

" Parkins, for shame!"

" Well, my lady telling of 'em long-winded stories about pearls and mermaids, and what not."

"Go and fetch Moleskin and the sailors here," said Lady Snaffle. Then she exclaimed to May, "now, my darling, I feel that we shall hear the truth. The men are real sailors. Their conduct in the hall among the servant maids proves it. Now we shall learn the facts."

When the prisoners made their appearance, preceded by Parkins and followed by the keeper, one of them pushed the former aside without ceremony and walked up unabashed to where Lady Snaffle was sitting. May Bullfinch immediately recognised the sailor Cox and Lady Snaffle did so in a few moments. His scarred face was flushed, and there was a merry twinkle in his eye as he made his bow, and stood turning his glazed hat over in his sinewy hands. The fact was, that he was about "half slewed," as he would have said himself, for besides drinking her ladyship's health often in strong ale, he had, at the instance of the cook, fortified himself with half a tumbler of cherry brandy. Moleskin had remonstrated with the cook against the last, but she replied that sailors must be treated well in that house. It was Lady Snaffle's express desire. And besides, as she had often heard Admiral Broadside say to his daughter, "they plough the raging seas, while the gentlemen of England do live at home at ease."

The demeanor of Cooper was different. He looked down upon the carpet, stood at a respectful distance, and seemed disinclined to face the Admiral's daughter. The man had been in action and had always done good service in storm and battle, but he was hardly equal to the present occasion. Lady Snaffle addressed herself to Cox:

" Young man, I understand you are a sailor—a real sailor?"

" I am, my lady. If your ladyship's father, Admiral Broadside, was here at this minute, he would say so. Man before the mast, and have been for years."

" You are recently from America, are you not?"

" Just arrived from New Orleans, madam. Anchored in the Downs last Sunday, and was paid off in the West India Docks on Tuesday. Discharge all ship-shape," replied Cox.

" My father was very fond of sailors," said Lady Snaffle, looking steadily at Cox.

" So I've often heard, my lady. He took such care of good

ones—men able to do topman's duty and be captains of the guns—that when they was once in the fleet, what with prize money and strong grog and the bounty afloat, and the press gang ashore, they could never get out of it again. However, he was a fine old fighting captain, such as the sailors like."

The other sailor mumbled something, and Lady Snaffle looked inquiringly at him.

" This is your shipmate?" she said to Cox.

" No, my lady, we only hauled alongside in London. This man, for all he looks spoony here in this presence, is a man-'o-war's man, and was captain of the foretop in the Racehorse, double-banked frigate, just paid off at Spithead. He knows your ladyship's father, the Admiral, well, he does."

" Bless me! come forward, my man. So you know my dear father well?"

" Yes, my lady. Admiral Broadside, Rear-Admiral of the Blue; hope to see him Vice-Admiral of the Red before he dies. So says every good man in the fleet," said Cooper. " He ought to fly the red flag at the fore!"

" My dear May, this is the genuine sailor, the real man-'o-war's man. You served under my father?" she added, to Cooper.

" I'll tell her all," said he to Cox, stepping forward. " Madam, I was taken to sea out of jail by Admiral Broadside eighteen years ago, being sentenced to transportation for fourteen years. I've served the king and the country ever since, and just came home to see my sister, Rose Tanner. My name is James Cooper."

" I remember, there were three brothers. Cooper, wait until I have heard this man. What is your name?" continued Lady Snaffle to the other.

" Harry Cox, my lady. Born at Oxford, and was one of the fancy before I went afloat," he replied.

" The fancy! what may that be?"

" The ring, my lady. The lads as follows prize-fighting as a profession. Have given it up now, and never fight except somebody wants a licking uncommon bad."

" You are charged with having been in the preserves for the purpose of poaching. Parkins thinks it is a mistake."

" Parkins is right, Lady Snaffle. It is a mistake on the part of the keeper, Mr. Moleskin here."

"Moleskin," said Lady Snaffle, "what do you say to this? The sailors allege that they entered the preserves merely to make a short cut. I believe it is often done."

"A good deal too often, my lady," replied Moleskin. "As to this man Cox, he had a gun."

"A present to Gypsy Jack from America," said Cox.

"He is a sailor, Moleskin, and I do not see how a sailor can be a poacher," said Lady Snaffle.

"Pheasants on him, my lady," replied Moleskin, without any change of feature. "As for the other, I believe Cox led him into it. Cox had the gun and shot the pheasants."

"Only two old cocks," said the sailor to Moleskin, in a surly, reproachful sort of tone. Then turning to Lady Snaffle again he said, "My lady, I know you are a sailor's friend, and I'll tell you all about it—from end to end, right off the reel, and never a kink. I was in the preserve just about sundown four bells in the dog-watch. Your ladyship knows what time that is, though the keeper and the constable are so ignorant that they don't. I had a gun, but it was a present sent to Gypsy Jack by a planter of the Arkansas bottoms named Langlois. I had two old cock pheasants, and they are the rocks ahead. Cock pheasants do more harm than good in the spring of the year, there being too many of them. But we'll slip that, and bear away. This is the real truth—born in these parts, and being fond of all sorts of sport, when I made out those pheasants, perched in a larch tree, I was bound to try the gun. My lady, I couldn't help it! I may be sent to jail, but I can do better service out of jail; and as you are an Admiral's daughter, I hope you'll tell Moleskin to let me clear for the salt water again. Cooper had nothing to do with it."

"Just so! being took up wrongful," said Parkins.

Lady Snaffle held a short conference with Moleskin, and the latter departed, taking Parkins with him, much against that dignitary's will. When they were gone, Lady Snaffle said, "I have procured your release. I am now about to request something in return of you, Cox—merely information. I am informed by this young lady—that is, by her father, through her—that you have some knowledge of Tom Scarlet."

"I have, my lady. I sailed in the same vessel that took

him out to America—clipper brig, belonging to Baltimore, where he and I parted, after I had introduced him to a good man."

"Who was that man?"

"A gentleman by the name of Sassafras—Western man."

"An Indian?" said Lady Snaffle.

"Thundering guns, my lady, no! As white as you—no, not as white as you, but as white as I be!"

"Have you seen Tom Scarlet since you introduced him to the man you mentioned—Sassy——"

"Sassafras, my lady. No, I have not. My chief business here was to see him. I hear he has not yet returned from the other side. In that case I was to deliver what I brought to Miss May Bullfinch, and I shall be glad to do it in your ladyship's presence."

With this the sailor placed his hat on the floor, and, drawing a knife from some part of his clothing, he ripped open the inside of his monkey-jacket and produced a small ornament, the head of a red horse, curiously carved out of a piece of stone. He held it up before the ladies on the palm of his hand, saying:

"As Tom Scarlet is not here yet, Miss Bullfinch is to take charge of this, and deliver it to him when he comes."

May whispered to Lady Snaffle, and the latter said:

"There was a rumor here that Mr. Scarlet was killed."

"So there was at Orleans, but I don't believe it. In fact, I know it wasn't true. He's all right, and will very soon be alongside of this young lady," said the sailor.

"Who sent the ornament you hold in your hand?"

"A friend of Tom Scarlet's, my lady. Cinnamon, by name, usually," replied Cox.

"Usually! Do you mean to say that he goes by more than one name? Who and what is he?"

"He's a Western man—large landowner, my lady. Hundreds of thousands of acres. Named after one of their productions."

"Does his land grow spice, then?"

"Why, no, my lady! I believe it chiefly produces bears and buffaloes; but I have never been on it."

"Cox," said Lady Snaffle, sharply, "I believe you are speaking of an Indian—a wild Indian!"

"I am, my lady. A chief—a very great chief! Friend of Sassafras and friend of Tom Scarlet. Called Cinnamon because when he was a papoose he had for his playfellow a cinnamon bear. He sent the totem."

"He sent the totem!"

"Yes, my lady. The totem of his tribe, the Cheyennes, for Tom Scarlet, signifying that Tom is adopted into his tribe, and that if any man injures him Cinnamon will have that man's scalp or know the reason why. It would have been given to Mr. Scarlet before he left the West, but certain ceremonies had to be performed, and it was sent afterwards to New Orleans, to me, through the agent of Langlois, who was in that country with Tom."

"We are very anxious about Mr. Scarlet. Do you know nothing more, Cox?" said Lady Snaffle.

"I know he's all right, my lady, for two reasons. One is that Sassafras had him in tow, and wouldn't let him come to harm. He'd take desperate chances sooner than see him injured. The other is, that if Tom had been clewed up, killed out there, instead of sending the Cheyenne totem to Tom as a live man, and one of his own tribe, Cinnamon would have sent the scalps of them as done it, as a satisfaction to this young lady and his other friends about here. He was no more killed in that country than I was, who was never there, though there was a scrimmage and one or two were killed. He has been detained by head winds. It hung in the east for a fortnight, as it often does about the chops of the Channel in the spring. It is now west-nor'west, and you may look for him every tide."

"We thank you, Cox," said Lady Snaffle.

"It's all right, my lady—all right, Miss Bullfinch! With this wind upon the larboard quarter they would make up the leeway very fast, and Mr. Scarlet will soon be a-riding all snug in harbor at your apron-string!"

"My dear," said Lady Snaffle to the blushing May, "the man is a sailor. What he says is just like a sailor. It was said, also, that Miriam Cotswold was carried off by Indians."

"My lady, Cooper can contradict that. Speak up, Jim," said Cox.

"If your ladyship pleases, I can contradict that. In coming from the Islands to Halifax we looked into New York bay for two or three days. While the frigate lay off the Battery she was boarded by a young woman and a man, and the word was passed for me. The young woman said she was my cousin, Miriam Cotswold."

" And the man—was he of florid complexion, with auburn whiskers?"

" No, madam. He was nearly as dark as I am, and his face was as smooth as mine. It was the man Cox named, Sassafras. They said they were bound to England. And they ought to have been in port before now."

CHAPTER XXXV.

> " He looked over fell, and he looked over flat,
> But nothing, I wist, he saw,
> Save a pyot on a turret that sat
> Beside a corby craw.
>
> " The page he looked at the skrich of day,
> But nothing, I wist, he saw,
> 'Till a horseman gray in the royal array,
> Rode down the bazel shaw."

YOUNG BULLFINCH had taken dinner and dressed himself in his best suit rather earlier than was necessary, in order that he might set out on his ride to the Hall as soon as he could reasonably convince himself that he would not arrive before Lady Snaffle and his sister would expect him. "It is rather too soon to start, but I can go a foot-pace," said he, as he surveyed himself with some satisfaction in the pier-glass over the mantlepiece in the parlor. There was a titter at the door, and Jack saw, with a blush, that the housemaid was looking at him. He wheeled quickly around and faced the girl.

" Well, you be, and everybody knows it," said she, with a laugh.

" Be what ?" said Jack sharply.

" Why, handsome, that you be! for a boy," she replied. " But, Master Jack, Tom told me to tell you that the gypsy, Rose, is coming along the lea at a great pace, and he thinks she wants to see you."

He met the gypsy in the orchard. She was evidently excited and out of breath, but declining to go into the house, she laid her hand on his arm and said:

"Now, Young Squire, now's the time! mount and ride fit to split the wind! He's come and the others can't be far off!"

"Your brother is come, Rose! Well, I'm sure I'm very glad; but you see I must go over to Sir Jerry Snaffle's first. I'm pledged to it."

"Ah, I knew that would be the way you would keep your word. But never mind; he's there himself before this time, so order out your horse, and don't spare him."

"Do you mean that your brother is at the Hall, Rose?"

"I do, and in custody. He fell in with that roving rascal Cox in London, and when they came down on the coach yesterday that fellow allured him into the covers at nightfall, and there they are, pulled for poaching by Moleskin and Parkins. I wish that Cox had been drowned before he led my Jim into this, but no such luck—'born to be hanged,' you know, as the old saying goes. Order out your horse. You can get Jim off. I know you can, you and your sister May. If you don't get him off——"

"Oh, I'll get him off if I can, Rose. And I think I can, but not by riding straight to the Hall. Tom, saddle Young Cowslip," he shouted, over his shoulder. "Rose, the hounds threw off at Stratton. I'll bet a guinea that I can hit the line of the hunt somewhere or another, and come up with Lord Doomsday."

"And what the d—l good will that do?" said Rose.

"Why, his influence is immense, and he'll do anything for me," said Jack, stoutly.

"That for his influence!" said the gypsy, snapping her finger and thumb. "You boys and men are so stupid. Don't you see that Lady Snaffle has got more influence with Sir Jerry, and good reason, when she chooses to use it, than all the lords in England. Sir Jerry will hold the examination when he reaches home from his hunting. Get there first—I say, get there first! And let Lady Snaffle know the rights of it before the baronet arrives. Mind and let her know that Jim's a great favorite with the Admiral—served under him, and all that. That'll go a great way."

"By George, Rose, I believe you are right!"

"I know I am," said the gypsy. "Besides, at the Hall you can see Moleskin. He thinks more of your father and of May and you than of all the other folks in Ridingcumstoke. If his evidence is light, they'll get off with a fine, provided the lady favors 'em and there's been a good run to-day

"Oh, there's always a good run when they meet at Stratton, Rose. But what has that to do with it?"

"Do with it! why, if there's been no run, Sir Jerry will be in one of his tempers, and Lady Snaffle will not interfere until Jim is committed. Then it will be too late."

"Yes, that's true; but there *has* been a good run. I'll lay anybody ten to one on it," said the lad. "Why, Rose, the men who stopped the earths in the copses and gorses about there last night passed here at daylight. I gave them a pint apiece, and asked them what the prospect was for foxes, and they said: 'Young master, the covers be full on 'em.' So you see that's all right. Now, here's my mare. I suppose you are for the Hall, too?"

"No, I can't go—not even to see Jim. I've promised to meet a man at a certain place—the Grange—and I must keep the tryst. I *must* keep it."

"Who is the man?" said Young Jack.

"One you never saw, but you will soon. Mount and ride! Let nothing stop you!"

His hand was twined in the mane of the mare, but he paused and said: "Rose, how about the twins, while you're going here and there?"

"They're all right. My eldest gal watches 'em, and Jenny gives 'em suck. You'll see me again to-morrow," said the gypsy, waving her hand and walking away with long strides.

"She's a rum 'un—a reg'lar rum 'un, she is!" said Tom, as his young master mounted; "and if I was you I'd keep a good lookout, coming home with Miss May after dusk."

"Oh, you don't understand Rose. I do," replied the lad, as he rode through the orchard gate into an adjoining field.

The weather was still gloomy. A thin rain, cold and pricking to the skin, was falling slantwise from the low-flying drift, when young Bullfinch rode through the lanes and over that portion of the heath which his sister had passed earlier in the

22

day. The lad had a horseman's coat on over his best clothes,
and cared nothing for rain or wind.   He galloped on, sometimes whistling cheerily, and sometimes humming a verse of
some ditty popular in the country side, and celebrating fox-
hunting.   Jack had nearly crossed the heath and was nearing
the woodland which lay beyond and bounded it, when he saw
a dark form moving stealthily among the bushes to his left.
It was that of a person flitting from one bunch of gorse to
another, and apparently trying to elude his observation.   The
lad was bold and fearless, but he knew that suspicious characters sometimes lurked about the neighborhood of the heath,
and at first he thought of riding on.   He had, however, a
desire to know who it could be that was endeavoring to steal
away like a fox from cover, and determined to give pursuit.
He felt certain that the person was no gypsy, for he was known
to all the band, and there was no reason why any of them
should avoid him.   Whoever it was, he now lost sight of the
figure for a moment, in a hollow where the gorse was thick
and high, but saw it make a dash up the slope beyond, and
quicken the pace.   Pulling out of the road, he put the mare
to a smart gallop over the wet sod and through the gorse.
The other party seemed resolved to foil the chase, and turning
round with a quick double, made for the woodland with swift,
sure foot.   The fence was at no great distance, and before the
youth could come up the pursued reached it, climbed a gate,
and disappeared on the other side.   The lad saw by the long
garments, as the person mounted the gate, that it was a woman.
" Well !" said Young Jack, " I *will* see who this quean is, now."
He touched Young Cowslip with the spur, and riding at the
hedge, went crashing through the top of it into the cover.
The woman, blown by her sharp run, and believing that he
would not follow, had stopped to draw breath near the edge
of the wood, and stood leaning against an ash-tree, as Jack
and the mare came driving through the fence.   Uttering an
exclamation, she darted away again at speed, and plunged like
a deer into the underbrush.   But she was at a disadvantage,
for the ground was boggy, and she was compelled to take to
the open ride again.   The lad soon came up with her, and
flourishing his whip, he cried, " Stop ! you can't get away from
me !   Who is it ?"

"Lord, Master Bullfinch! who should it be?" said the woman, stopping and turning about.

"Miriam! heart alive! Is this you? Why did you run away from *me?* You surely knew me!"

"Knew you? yes. Run away! good lack! What for, indeed!" said she, panting. "I knew you were going for your sister; and as the night will grow on apace, by and by, you have no time to lose. Ride on, Master Bullfinch. Good-day."

"Is this all?" said Young Jack, looking at her with some surprise. "Come, we must have a little speech together."

There was a change in the appearance of the gypsy since he saw her last. She looked older—less the girl, and more the young woman; less wild and frolicsome, though there was a smile upon her lip and a merry twinkle in her bright black eye. A warm flush, from her recent rapid running, shone in her nut-brown cheek. She was not dressed as the gypsy women and girls commonly are, but wore a gown and cloak of dark merino, while a hood of velvet, trimmed with fur, covered her glossy black hair. She stood before the lad as if undecided what to say or do; seemed anxious to be rid of him, and yet could scarcely control an inclination to laugh.

"And so you're back among us again, Miriam," said Young Jack. "I'm glad to see you—very glad!"

"Thank you! I thought you would be. But time wears, Master Bullfinch, and you had better ride on. You can talk to me another time, you know."

"Ay, but I want you to talk to me now. You have been away nearly a year. Tom Scarlet has been gone as long, and I want to hear all about it. He has been reported dead, and Lady Snaffle and May will want to know what you say to that."

"Master Bullfinch," said the gypsy, with her dark, bright eye full and intent upon him, "I think you had better not mention to them that you have seen me. My presence here is not known to any one except our people and one or two others, and there are good reasons why it should not be for a few days. So oblige me, and say nothing about it."

"Miriam," replied the boy, "it can't be done. There's too much mystery going on—too much in-and-out running. Tell me where Tom Scarlet is. Is he come back too? That's the question."

" Bless us, Master Bullfinch ! you talk as if his coming and going depended on me. You didn't expect me to bring him back, did you ?"

The gypsy moved towards the road, and Jack walked his horse by her side. They approached the beaten way, and he said, " Come, Miriam, no more of this winding about a hollow bush, and crying a holloa when there's neither fox nor har What do you know about Tom Scarlet ?"

" I know he's a fine young man—worthy of your sister—and that is a great deal to say," replied Miriam.

" Yes ; but where is he now, when he ought to be here ?"

" On his way home, no doubt. I hear he is expected every day. You may tell your sister I said so, if you mention having met with me at all, which you had better not do."

" I can't help mentioning that, lass. I wouldn't keep it secret for anything. May's my sister, and Lady Snaffle always behaves very handsomely to me."

" Ah !" replied the gypsy, " see what it is to have to do with a boy instead of with men. I'll warrant, now, that if Sir Jerry and your father had seen me here, and heard me say what I have said to you, they wouldn't mention it to her ladyship and your sister. But you want to be at the ladies' apron-strings, telling them some nice gossip. Good-day, Master Bullfinch ; ride on."

Young Jack was nettled at this, and not the less so as the gypsy laughed at the angry expression of his face. " Very well," said he ; " You want to put me off. I won't be put off. You *shall* give me some news of Tom Scarlet before you are out of my sight. I'll follow you till dark, and then again till daylight, but what I'll have it. You shall see whether I can't stay away from the ladies' apron-strings."

" Master Bullfinch," said she, " don't be so put out with an old acquaintance because of a jest. One of the greatest pleasures I looked for when I came back here was meeting you again, and seeing your sister, May, well and happy. At present I cannot say more. Shake hands, and ride on. I can stay here no longer. I expect a man to pass, and he must not find us here, holding conference in the shadow of the wood."

" Your uncle !" said Young Jack, extending his hand. " I can make it all right with him in two minutes."

"Not my uncle," she replied, shaking his hand. "Another man."

"What man? Who is he? Miriam let us have no more mystery."

"Well, I can't give his name. I promised not to give it for a few days. He's a man from America."

"It's Tom himself!" cried Young Jack. "Miriam, I know it is."

"Master Jack, it is not," said she, earnestly. "'Tis a man you never saw in your life, for he never was in this country before. If you meet him on the road, as I think you will do, you'll see a man different in looks and ways from folks about here. Something like our people on the moors and heaths in some points, but still no gypsy. A man rough and ready, but as true as steel. You need not be afraid of him if he stops you on the road."

"Me afraid! I'll wait with you till he comes."

"No, no! Ride on, and make speed. I'll see you again ere long, and tell you more. Perhaps news of Tom Scarlet. Touch spur, Young Jack, and away!"

"By George, Miriam, you speak like yourself again. And you think Tom is all right?"

"Yes, I hope and believe he is," she replied, walking off a few steps.

"One word more. How about Jagger? Is he come back?"

"Jagger! Oh, Master Bullfinch, he is dead! He died as the fool dieth. He was killed when Tom——"

"When Tom what? And who killed Jagger?"

"A man in America. Good-by."

With this the girl drew her cloak about her, turned back, and hurried away deeper into the wood. Young Jack looked after her for a moment. He then gained the highway, and rode on at a strong gallop.

He had not gone above half a mile when another horseman approached at speed equal to his own. The man wore a blue coat of pilot cloth, buttoned up to the chin. His face was dark, his eye bright and keen as that of a hawk, and locks of black hair appeared under the rim of his low-crowned glazed hat. He sat his horse with the ease and power of one who had been accustomed to riding from early youth. As they neared each other the man and the boy checked the speed of their horses, and after a good look, pulled up together in the middle of the road.

The man spoke first. His eye seemed to be all over the lad and his horse in an instant, and he said, in a clear voice and prompt manner:

" You seem to be in a hurry, young gentleman. You ride fast."

" No faster than you," replied the lad, with some undefinable feeling of uneasiness at finding himself face to face in the lonely road with this man.

" Well, considering that I hardly know my road, I was going pretty fast, I allow," said the stranger. " But where may you be going to at a gallop? Anybody sick ?"

" No, sir, nobody sick. I am going to Sir Jerry Snaffle's," replied the youth, with some assumption of dignity, and a movement as if he could brook no more delay.

" Hold on! I shan't detain you more than a minute. Sir Jerry Snaffle! It seems to me that I have heard of him."

" I should think you have," said the youth, with a shade of emphasis which the stranger marked, but did not notice in reply. Indeed, he changed the topic, saying:

" That's a nice young mare you're on. What's her name ?"

" Cowslip," said Young Jack, somewhat surprised at the free and easy way of the stranger, in thus putting to him the question; " Young Cowslip."

" O! then old Cowslip's at home? Dam of this mare, no doubt ?"

" No, sister of this mare, and not old, either. Neither is she at home, for father has her out hunting."

" Ay, ay! hold on a bit. I want you to tell me my road in a minute."

With this the stranger produced a flint and a dangerous-looking knife, and striking fire on some very combustible substance, lit a cigar.

" I reckon your name is Bullfinch, young sir ?"

" That is my name," replied the youth. " What is yours ?"

" Well, that is nothing to the purpose," said the stranger. " You live in these parts, and your name is naturally of interest to a stranger to these parts. I don't live here, and so my name is nothing to you, don't you see! Bullfinch is a good name—a very good name. I hope your father and sister are well. By the by, I suppose you left your sister at home?"

"No, I didn't. She is at Sir Jerry Snaffle's. I am going there to see her home, and must not delay any more."

"Hold on! hold on another minute! you have not told me the road. No doubt you can show me which is the way to a place called the Grange."

"The Grange! why, that is Tom Scarlet's place."

"So I've heard! What of it?" said the stranger, coolly.

"He's my friend! My father's friend! My sister's very dear friend! You bring news of him, I hope. You come from America."

"I never told you so, my lad."

"No matter! I know you do. Now tell me news—do tell me good news of him," said Young Jack, earnestly.

"Good news! Well, I have *heard* that he may be here soon. That is what they say. It may not be good news to some. I've heard that there are people who do not like him in these parts. What do you say to that?"

"I say everybody likes him that is of any consideration. You should hear my father relate what Sir Jerry said about him at the hunt dinner, when it was reported that he had been killed in America."

"Ah! they reported he was killed. Well, if he wasn't it was a miracle, for he was shot in the head and went down into the rapids of the Neosho. If he lived after that he's the only man that ever did."

Young Jack's countenance fell. He looked at the stranger, but there was no sign of emotion in the dark, strong-cut face of the man who sat in the saddle and smoked the segar which diffused a fragrance all around.

"It may be a mistake! It may have been another man," said Jack.

"Englishmen are not plenty out there in the Indian country," replied the stranger.

"It may have been another," said Jack. "There was one Jagger. Do you remember such a person about there?"

"I ought to. I killed him," said the stranger with much indifference, "but he was not the man who went down the rapids. That was Scarlet. After all, it is but a man gone, and no doubt there are plenty better left about here."

"There are none—not one better—not one as good. Poor, poor Tom! Oh, what shall I say or do?" cried the lad, with a quivering lip and a very sad expression of face.

"Why, if I was you I would say nothing at present. Mind, I don't aver that he is dead. He may be alive, and come forward when least expected."

"Ah! if he does everybody will be so rejoiced."

"Everybody! why don't you know that the backers of the Duke, in this great steeple-chase match I hear about, would as soon see the devil as Tom Scarlet in the saddle."

"No!" replied Young Jack. "The Duke himself likes Tom, and would sooner lose the match than be convinced of his death."

"Very well! I hope the Duke will lose it. I shall lay against him if I happen to be there. Sir Jerry will have the best horse and the best rider, and by all accounts he's the best man of the two. Which is my road?"

"Straight on till you come to the heath. You'll see the glow of the fires at the gypsy camp to the right. The people there will tell you the way from that point. You needn't be afraid of the gypsies. You will not be, I think."

"I think not," said the stranger, with a smile. "You are a likely lad! Give my regards to your father, and my respects, my very particular respects, to your sister. Good-by, Master Bullfinch. I shall see you again."

"But I cannot tell my father and sister who you are. I don't know your name," said Jack.

"True, I had forgotten that. You can say a man from America. And you may add that, in spite of all that has happened, Tom Scarlet may be all right, and turn up when least expected. It's true he was shot, but I have been shot three or four times myself, and here I am alive and merry. He also went down the rapids, and it had such an ugly look, that at one time I gave him up as gone, past all hope. But there is a man out there, well known he is to me, who went down through a canyon of the Colorado, and that's worse. So he may be alive. There's always hope about a man thought to be dead, until the body has been found. Good-by, Master

Bullfinch! Good-by, Young Jack! Take care of Young Cowslip, Jack, and do all you can to cheer up your sister. We shall soon meet again."

With this the stranger struck his horse with the whip, and dashed away. Young Jack looked after him until he disappeared, and then said, "For a man who has killed another or two, not in war time, and has been shot three or four times himself, this is the coolest person I ever heard of. After all, I have hopes of Tom. Miriam said this man was true as steel, and there was something in his manner that meant more than he said. I noticed how he looked up and smiled whenever he mentioned May. It made his face look pleasant. He does not seem to be a bad fellow. I'm glad I didn't mention Miriam to him, for a glint came into his eye at times like the light from that of a cat in the dark. There's no telling how he would have taken it, if I had told him I chased and pounded her. What will Lady Snaffle and May say to all this?"

CHAPTER XXXVI.

A SHARP gallop of twenty minutes brought young Bullfinch to the Hall, where he proposed to see Moleskin before he presented himself to Lady Snaffle. But before he could make any inquiry as to the keeper and his prisoners, a footman announced to him that Lady Snaffle wished to see him in the library. Thither he went, and the lady of the house, receiving him graciously, desired him to take a seat. Young Jack would have postponed the interview for a short time if he could have found a plausible excuse for doing so, but none occurred to him at the moment, and Lady Snaffle said:

"Master Bullfinch, we have had quite an adventure since your sister's arrival. Moleskin and the constable came here, bringing two prisoners—sailors from America."

"O, yes, my lady. I heard of it from Rose Tanner. She came to Hawk'ell in a great to-do about her brother, who was led into it by Cox. She says she wishes Cox had been drowned before he got her brother into that trouble, but there was no

such luck, because he was born to be hanged. If your lady·
ship pleases, I should like to see Moleskin for a few minutes
before Sir Jerry arrives to hold the examination of the men."

"Master Bullfinch, Moleskin is gone, and the men are gone,
too."

"Not to prison, I hope—I do hope not to jail," said Jack,
with alarm. "Much depends upon Rose and her brother, and
perhaps on Cox."

"Why, your sister and I had no power to commit them,"
said Lady Snaffle, "so we discharged them—set them at liberty. At least, we procured their discharge."

"Thank you, Lady Snaffle! Rose said you could do it,"
said the lad, with much animation. "Yet I should have been
glad if I could have seen Cooper before he left here. I think
he could have helped us at this pinch in regard to the safety
and present whereabouts of Tom Scarlet; for Rose said that
when he arrived she should know something without the
trouble of consulting the stars. Here he would have told all
that he knows; for Rose says his gratitude to the Admiral
and his respect for all the family are very great."

"Master Jack, he has told us all he knows," said Lady
Snaffle. She then related the incidents which had occurred,
and repeated what Cox and Cooper had said.

"Please, madam," said Young Jack, "I want to see the
totem. May, show me the totem. Ah! the head of a red
horse! My lady, that's significant. I have had an adventure
myself on the road here, and have seen two other persons from
America."

"Indeed! Who were they, Master Bullfinch?"

"The first, my lady, was Miriam Cotswold."

"Oh, dear!" said May. "Then *she* has got back?"

"Go on, sir. What did she say in regard to her adventures,
and to others?" said Lady Snaffle.

"Very little indeed, my lady. She tried to avoid me; but
I ran her down, as I may say, being well mounted. Then she
was mysterious, and wanted to get rid of me, telling me not to
mention to you and May that I had seen her, as she wanted to
be secret for a very short time. But that, of course, was out
of the question. Then she became very friendly—said she had
come back mainly to have the pleasure of meeting me and
seeing May happy as the day is long."

"My dear May," said Lady Snaffle, "is this gypsy an artful, treacherous person—one likely to have adopted these professions as a means of deceiving your brother and blinding us?"

"Dear lady, I think not," said May, after a moment's consideration. "She was always thought frank and bold, rather than crafty and treacherous. But the habits and nature of those people lead them to deal in mystery and roundabout ways. Miriam will do no harm. She was often brought to our house by her mother, before she lost her, and before I and my brother lost our dear mother."

"May, you are right. I know you are. I am sure Miriam is friendly to us," said Young Jack.

"Perhaps so—I hope so," said Lady Snaffle. "But what else did she say?"

"My lady, I do not judge so much by *what* she said as by her voice and the look of her eye when she said it. She said she hoped Tom would soon be here—that she was satisfied he would."

"And what else?"

"That Jagger was dead—killed in America."

"Jagger! Who is Jagger?"

"The man who ran away with the White Horse and her uncle's money, besides a great deal more," said Jack.

"What more said she, and where was she going?"

"She was going to the camp on the heath, and she told nothing more," replied Jack. "I pressed her hard, but she said she couldn't—she was under a promise. Now, Rose said she was under a promise, too, my lady; and I think I know the man to whom their promises are given. If Rose's brother was here now he would tell your ladyship what these promises are about, if your ladyship commanded him to do so; for, as Rose says, 'he honors the Admiral, and obeys orders.'"

"I, however, should hardly be able to compel his obedience," said Lady Snaffle.

"Oh, yes, your ladyship would, for he has been in men-of-war for the last eighteen years, and in Admiral Broadside's absence he would consider your ladyship as in command. Besides, my lady, he has been away from the gypsies long enough to have dropped their mystery and in-and-out running methods of dealing. As it is, I must look up Rose early in the morning, and with her and the twins I shall find Cooper."

" And to whom are the gypsy women under promise, Master Bullfinch ?" said Lady Snaffle.

" To the man that I met shortly after I parted from Miriam, my lady. She said I should probably meet a man on the road, and I did. He was a sinewy, strong man—well mounted and a capital horseman, as I could see at a glance."

" Who was he ? Let us know that first. Tell me directly, Master Jack. Was it not Tom Scarlet ?" said Lady Snaffle, impetuously.

" Bless me, my lady ! no. 'Twas a stranger to these parts— a man from America."

" What man from America—this makes three in twenty-four hours or less ?"

" Oh, Lady Snaffle, the man who killed Jagger. He told me that he was."

" What ! he killed a person, and avows it ? May, my dear, you must not think of going home to-night, with this fearful man on the road."

" If your ladyship pleases, there will be no danger at all ; I shall be with May," said Jack. " And I think this man may be a very good man, though he did kill Jagger. People say that your ladyship's father has killed some hundreds in his time."

" Master Bullfinch, I desire you not to compare this blood-thirsty man from America to my father. He was an officer in the fleet, a captain under Nelson. It was in the course of war and duty, and those they killed were Frenchmen and Spaniards !"

" Jagger was a rogue," said Young Jack, and then added hastily : " But please forgive me, my lady. I only meant that the man might not be so very bad after all. I'm sure I hope not."

" You are a good, brave boy, Master Jack. But, my dear May, I do not like it. The killing a man, not in battle, and then announcing it off-hand to a strange youth, is dreadful. You must not go home ; at least not until Sir Jerry comes."

" Please, my lady, I am sure we need fear nothing at the hands of this man from America. He had heard of Sir Jerry. He spoke highly of my father. He sent his respectful regards —his particular regards to May. He praised me and Young

Cowslip; and he said I should see him again. And Miriam Cotswold said before I met him that he was rough and ready, but as true as steel."

" Did he say anything of Tom Scarlet ?"

" Yes, madam, that he heard he would soon be home," replied Jack, with some hesitation and confusion.

" Master Bullfinch, tell me all he said about Mr. Scarlet."

" O, my lady! O, my dear sister May! Tom was shot in the head, and fell into the river above the rapids, and the peril was fearful. But the man says he knows one in America who went down a canyon of the Colorado, yet is alive at this day, and Tom may have escaped. And, my lady—May, my dear sister—I know he escaped. I feel certain that he did, and he will soon be here."

" How do you reach such positive belief?" said Lady Snaffle.

" My lady, I reach it because this man knows all about the steeple-chase match, and because he said that he would bet against the Duke, for that Sir Jerry would have the best horse and the best rider, and was the best man of the two."

" Then I do not believe him," said Lady Snaffle, hastily. " I mean, my dear May and Jack, about the bet and the horse and rider," she added, with a smile.

" Dear Lady Snaffle," said May, with a confiding look, " can you not guess who this man is? The sailor Cox spoke of one in America who was Mr. Scarlet's fast friend, and would take desperate chances for him."

" The Indian, my dear ?"

" Oh, no, dear lady; the white man, Sassafras."

" My dear May, I think you are right. The man your brother has met is Sassafras, and Scarlet cannot be far off. When you spoke, I thought of the Indian—what is his name, Nutmeg, Allspice, Cloves—what was it ?"

" Cinnamon."

" So it was. Now, I shall have much to tell Sir Jerry, and you and Jack will have much to tell your father—the sailor Cox, and his statement, and the story he told of the Indian, and the delivery of the totem. The boarding of the ship of war, according to Cooper, by Miriam Cotswold and Sassafras; the meeting of Master Jack with Miriam, and what she said; and what Rose Tanner, the gypsy with the twins, said; the meeting of your brother and Sassafras, and what the man from America said—oh! it will be a charming narrative," said Lady Snaffle. "There is one thing, however, my dear, that rather perplexes me. Men are so matter-of-fact and incredulous. Sir Jerry will call for the production of the sailors, the gypsies and Sassafras, in order that they may be required to produce Tom Scarlet. Master Bullfinch, do you think you can produce these parties at short notice?"

"My lady, I can do almost anything in reason," replied Jack, "and I think I can do this, when Sassafras is willing. My belief is that I know where the sailors, Miriam, Rose Tanner and Sassafras are now, this very minute."

"Where, Master Jack?"

"At the Grange, my lady. Or at the camp not far from the Grange."

"Then Tom Scarlet must be with them."

"I doubt it, Lady Snaffle," said Young Jack. "Please, my lady, these four have just come from America, like birds of passage, and settled down here like—like plovers we'll say, though it's too soon for them yet. Now, my lady, if you please, they may have good reasons for keeping Tom away for the present."

"Sir Jerry will insist that they produce him."

"Oh, my lady, I think not. Suppose what they do is part of a well-planned and beautiful 'plant' in regard to the great match. Madam, besides the stakes, two thousand guineas, the honor of our hunt, and of all this side of the county is involved. Oh, my lady, depend upon it that Tom and Sassafras have concocted a beautiful scheme and 'plant,' by means of which to win the great match. I'm sure Sir Jerry will never be the man to defeat such a thing."

"Right, young Bullfinch!" exclaimed Sir Jerry Snaffle, as he came forward. He had entered unannounced, and with him there was a much younger gentleman. They were in the uniform of the hunt. Lord Doomsday appeared to be rather confused as he bowed low to Lady Snaffle and to Miss Bullfinch. "You see, my lady, I have been able to prevail upon Lord Doomsday to come and take a family dinner with us. If Miss Bullfinch and her brother will stay we shall be a nice family party."

"I am delighted to see his lordship," said Lady Snaffle. "You know our young friends, my lord. I have heard the history of the great run with the Fringford Gorse fox, from Master Bullfinch, and my goddaughter, May, has told me of the enjoyment you have afforded her father."

"I think the greater part of the enjoyment was mine, Lady Snaffle. I have had the pleasure, the great pleasure, of meeting Miss Bullfinch and her brother at their father's house several times," said the young man, frankly.

"May, you will stay, will you not?"

"Oh, no, my lady, we cannot. My father will expect us, and he would be lonely," said May.

Lady Snaffle knew that when May said anything positively, it was of little use to try to change her determination. She, therefore, recounted briefly and rapidly to Sir Jerry all the events of the day. The baronet listened with much interest, and so did Lord Doomsday. When the lady had finished her narrative, the former said, "I wish the sailors had been detained until I came home—not that I would have them punished, but with them in custody we should have some sort of hold upon the women and the American. It is clear that some of them, certainly the American, and the girl, Miriam, and perhaps Rose Tanner, know all about Tom Scarlet, and it concerns me to know it, too, and that very soon."

"Surely, as a magistrate, chairman of the bench, you can make them give information, Sir Jerry," said Lady Snaffle.

"Why, I could have done so, but you have let the means go. The sailors cannot be arrested again. The women have done nothing, that I know of, except held interviews with our young friend, Master Jack. Neither has the American."

"Sir Jerry, I'm surprised! The American, by his own confession—nay, his cool avowal—has killed a man, and surely he can be taken up?"

"Not at all, my dear. I have no jurisdiction. Ask Doomsday."

"Then how are we to find where Mr. Scarlet is?"

"I wish I knew how. We cannot well send the bellman round to cry a reward for him."

"Sir Jerry, you are too absurd. I wish my father was here. He would soon make them produce him."

"Laura, I know what your father would do. He would very soon get out of the man-of-war's-man all that he knows, which is very little, for, according to his own account, he never saw Tom Scarlet, and did not know Miriam when she boarded his ship with the American at New York. The Admiral would then turn to the gypsy women, if he could catch them. But we can do with them all that he could do, and, I think, more. He could not well read the articles of war to them, and threaten the cat-o'-nine-tails if they did not split. As for the American, he would be certain to defy the Admiral to his teeth. Miss Bullfinch, tell me your opinion of this American. He seems to me to control the gypsy women and the sailor, Cox."

"I have never seen the man, Sir Jerry, but my brother has, and he has quick perception."

"Please, Sir Jerry, I have. May is right. I pronounced Lord Doomsday a good one from the first time I saw him," said Young Jack, briskly.

"Let your sister proceed, Master Jack. Her opinion in this matter will be of more value, I think, than that of all the rest of us."

"My brother's opinion of the American is very favorable, Sir Jerry, and I have still greater faith in him."

"Why, my dear young lady ?"

"Because of his character, Sir Jerry. I first heard it last spring when Cotswold told my father of him, and delivered two letters from Mr. Scarlet. In these letters he was spoken of in the highest terms. The gypsy spoke of him as such men never speak of any one who is not brave, honest, and true to his professions. He is a horseman—a great horseman! and Oh, Sir Jerry and dear Lady Snaffle ! I never in my life knew a really great horseman who was a treacherous, pitiful rogue. It would be against nature !" said May, with emphasis.

"Now, thank you, May Bullfinch, for speaking such a sovereign truth," said Sir Jerry,

"And in this I heartily join," exclaimed Lord Doomsday. "It is a truth."

"I really think it is," said Lady Snaffle, "for my husband, John Bullfinch, and Major Fitzgerald are instances."

"So is Tom Scarlet, my lady ! And, Lord Doomsday, you're another, as the saying is," cried Young Jack.

"Ay," said May, "there is no truer heart than that of the man who is absent, and none (dropping her voice) more generous and kind than that of the young nobleman who is present. Since we never doubted Mr. Scarlet, why should we doubt his friend? The sailor said to-day that he could not be dead because Sassafras was with him, a man who would take desperate chances rather than have him hurt. Sir Jerry, I have full faith in this man from America. If he had done wrong, or deserted his friend at need, or even if he had bad news to relate, he would not have sent the message to my father and —to me."

"That's as clear as the sun at noonday," said Sir Jerry.

"And he would not be going to bet against the Duke in the match," said Young Jack. "Oh, Sir Jerry, consider the bearings of the match!"

May Bullfinch drew nearer to Lady Snaffle. She blushed and was a little shame-faced, having done speaking. How came the insight and apt reasoning from one who was usually distinguished for maidenly reserve? Why, she would die for Tom Scarlet; and the man, Sassafras, from all that she could learn and divine, would die for him too, at need. "A fellow feeling makes us wondrous kind," and sometimes eloquent and wise as well.

"I must sleep upon this, and then determine how to act," said Sir Jerry. "Lady Snaffle, we had a great run to-day—a grand run. Lord Doomsday was in at the death."

The ladies and young Bullfinch congratulated his lordship.

"My lord, I'm so glad," said Young Jack. "Of course the country was stiff."

"I should think so. We found at Stratton and he went right through the Bicester Vale. *All* the fences are big there," said Sir Jerry.

"I wish I had been there," said Jack. "I was upon the point of trying to come up with Lord Doomsday to ask for his influence in favor of Jim Tanner, but Rose said—said something."

"And what was it she said, Master Jack?" said Sir Jerry.

"If you please, Lord Doomsday and Sir Jerry, I hope it won't give offence. She said, 'That for his influence! (snap-

23

ping his fingers) Lady Snaffle has more influence with Sir Jerry, and reason good, than twenty lords!'"

The baronet laughed heartily, while Lady Snaffle and the young lord had some difficulty in refraining from laughter themselves. The gentlemen then retired. In a few minutes, however, the footman announced that Sir Jerry wished to see Master Bullfinch for a moment.

"Now, Master Bullfinch," said Lady Snaffle, "you must not say that there is a beautiful scheme, a plan, in pursuance of which Tom Scarlet is to be kept concealed. I *insist* upon it that he shall be produced. Tell Sir Jerry that."

"Master Jack, do you happen to know where Jack Cotswold is at present?" said the baronet, as the boy entered his room.

"Why, no, Sir Jerry. Stop! Rose said at Christmas that he had gone to Lancashire. I have it, Sir Jerry! Where he is Tom is, and please, Sir Jerry, they are watering the 'plant.'"

"Watering the 'plant.' Then there is a 'plant?'"

"O, if you please, Sir Jerry, I forgot. I was not to mention that, and I must not disobey her ladyship for anything."

"You imagine Tom Scarlet is in England, and will be here to ride in the match?"

"Yes, Sir Jerry, and that he will bring the horse he is to ride. He was to bring the White Horse, and no doubt he has got him. He went for him," Jack replied.

"My own thought, Master Jack. What else could the American intend when he said he should bet against the Duke? Say nothing of this."

"O, not a word, Sir Jerry. But if The Bagman keeps on going well, and if Tom and his horse should not come to time, I think, please, Sir Jerry, you had better get Lord Doomsday to ride."

"Too young and too modest, Young Jack."

"Please, Sir Jerry, he's not as young as he looks, and that is the case with me. I could show him over every line in the vale, and whichever the gentlemen choose, he would know the rights of it. I think they will choose the one right down this side of Brill Hill, so as to have the big brook and Barker's bullfinch towards the finish."

"I think it very likely, Master Jack. Good-by. I may be

at Hawk'ell to-morrow, perhaps. If not, I shall be on the third day, unless I see your father at the meet on the day after to-morrow."

CHAPTER XXXVII.

"O, tell me how Love cometh—
Like dew from Heaven sent.
And tell me how Love goeth—
That was not Love which went."

AT the rising of the moon, as May Bullfinch and her brother rode home, there was a change of the wind and of the weather. The breeze veered six or eight points at the going down of the sun, and riding on the sharp breath of the north came a frost which seemed rapidly to convert the mud into a thick crust, and to cover the pools with a thin skin of ice. John Bullfinch had reached home, after the capital run with the hounds, long before his children arrived. As he welcomed his daughter, he saw that she was excited and somewhat agitated. After supper, Moleskin called in, and gave an account of the sailors, whose release he now seemed to regret. John, however, maintained that he had done quite right. The keeper denied it, but declared that he derived great consolation from the belief that one or both of them would be wounded by a spring-gun or caught in a man-trap before many days. Upon this a debate arose. The worthies contradicted each other, got heated, and each declared that the other was the most unreasonable man in the neighborhood. To this the keeper added that, concerning John Bullfinch, it was no wonder, for nobody ever heard of a Bullfinch who would not fly into a passion when confronted and confounded by cool argument. They then got sulky over their pipes, and looked at each other for some time more like bulldogs than two middle-aged men who had a strong regard for each other. Gradually May Bullfinch and Jack unfolded to them all they had to tell concerning Cox and Cooper, Miriam Cotswold and the man believed to be Sassafras. The farmer was sorely perplexed. "It beats me clean," said he. "I can't make it out. If Tom Scarlet is alive and well, as Southdown maintains to

be beyond argument, and as Sir Jerry himself holds to be
nearly certain, why don't he come home and show himself? It
appears that other people have lately come from America.
Here's this sailor chap and the man-of-war's-man—here's
Miriam Cotswold; here's this man that killed Jagger, and
makes no bones of telling of it. They have come—why hasn't
Tom Scarlet come?"

"The sailor told Lady Snaffle that contrary winds had no
doubt prevented," replied Young Jack.

"Contrary winds didn't prevent *him*, it seems," said John,
with his eyes fixed ruefully upon his daughter's face, and a
little surliness in his tone. "I say contrary winds is no answer. I want to know why Tom Scarlet doesn't come, if he
can come? He has nothing to be ashamed of, has he?"

"No," said Young Jack, boldly; "Nothing at all."

"Hem!" replied the keeper. "Nothing as I know of, except that if he could come, he has stayed away such a long
time that he feels himself to be in the wrong as regards—as
regards your daughter, May, and hangs fire like."

"I should think he's no such faint-hearted fool as that,"
said John Bullfinch. "But now, Dick, as you are cool again,
and are a long-headed sort of man, and well up to some things
when your prejudices are not involved, give me your opinion
of the sailors, the gypsy, and the man from America, and
what they say."

"I will," said Moleskin. "In the first place, the sailors are
poachers; and I have no faith in anything said or done by a
poacher. It's true I let them go, more fool I. But it was at
the request of Lady Snaffle, and her ladyship's wishes are a
sort of law to me, in anything reasonable. What the sailors
said is to be looked upon as gammon—nothing but gammon!"

"Cox produced the totem. May has it," said Young Jack.

"Well, as far as the totem goes, we'll admit what he says;
though, as he's a poacher, and a bad character in general, as
all poachers are—he kicked up a row at the races, when here
in the spring, and punched Parkins in the head—I might decline to admit so much. But that admitted, what does it
amount to? Nothing at all. He has not seen Tom Scarlet
for nearly a year, nor anybody who has seen him. Then
there's the gypsy! We know what gypsies are. Miriam,

Miss May is going to say, is different from the common run. There is a difference, for she's bolder and more artful than others of the band. Think of her setting off to America all alone—if she was alone—and staying there alone for a year!" May Bullfinch hid her face in her handkerchief. Moleskin saw it, but went on like a surgeon who, with a knife in hand, cuts away, caring nothing for the quivering of the nerves or the flinching of the muscles. "Therefore," said he, "we must look at her as just as any other gypsy, but more dangerous and deceitful than common. You can't hatch a pheasant out of a crow's egg, no matter where you set it. So what she says is of no more use than a flash in the pan. Not so much, for it is to be taken contrary ways. And I'm very glad she didn't say more. If she had said plump that Tom Scarlet was well and would be here to-night, and had offered to swear to it, I should have considered it good proof that he was as dead as a red herring."

"Go on to the other fellow—the man from America," said John, gruffly.

"The other fellow," said Moleskin, "is, by his own showing, a dangerous and suspicious character, a sort of wild beast in a neighborhood like this."

"No, no! a civil man! a well-spoken man!" said Young Jack.

"A man who has killed other men and brags about it," returned Moleskin. "Who has been shot four or five times, and isn't dead yet, which is of itself enough to set peaceable people on their guard against him. It is to be hoped that he's had nothing to do with Tom Scarlet, for if he has, it's ten to one that the young man is dead as a door nail, and this man and the gypsy have come over here to try and get hold of his property. Didn't you say the gypsy told you that you would meet him? and didn't you say that he asked the way to the Grange?"

"I did," replied Young Jack, "but what of that? Why, if he was, as I hope and believe, Tom Scarlet's true friend in America, and is his friend and our friend now, he would ask that."

The keeper was about to reply, when John Bullfinch interposed.

" Dick," said he, " Jack is right in that remark. May, my dear, the argument we have heard from Moleskin seemed strong, very strong, for a time. But it reminds me of one made to him and me by Parkins, when Tom Scarlet first went away, which proved that Tom was murdered then, and that Gypsy Jack had done it."

" What the man says himself doesn't seem to give ground for any reasonable expectation that Tom Scarlet will ever be seen here again," said the keeper. " I'm sorry, very sorry to give Miss May pain ; but the sooner she ceases to remember him the better. Not but what she may have a kind of hope, just as you and I hope that our cock will win his battle, when everybody else about the pit is ready to pound him. There may be hope, but I can't see that there is any grounds for reasonable expectation."

The keeper soon after left them, and the farmer and his children sat silent until the clock struck ten. May Bullfinch then kissed her father and went up-stairs with her brother, while John removed into the kitchen and established himself in the chimney-corner. The boy did and said all he could to reassure his sister, and insisted much upon the look and manner of Sassafras. They knelt together and said their prayers. Never since the time of her early infancy, when her mother used to put her little hands together, before she could talk, and repeat the Lord's prayer, had May prayed more fervently, or with a more serene confidence in the wisdom and mercy of God, than on that night. She bade her brother an affectionate good-night, and prepared to undress. Then she drew aside the curtain at one of her windows and looked out. It faced towards the south. Beneath it was the paved court-yard, then the garden : to the left the orchard, and in front of all the meadow called the Lea, which extended down to the blackthorn brake surrounding the Hawk's Well, from which the ancient house and farm derived its name. The moon, now high in the heavens and nearly at her full, shone brightly down upon the brake, and there for an instant the maiden saw the figure of a man in the tall bushes, whose face in the moonlight was pale. She started back, like one who had been struck. In a moment, however, she collected herself, and looked out again. No form was there. But at that instant a drift of clouds was passing over the moon. She waited until it was gone, but even then she could see nothing save the dark outline of the bushes which formed the brake. It was the place where she and Tom Scarlet had often walked in the gloaming, and a strange feeling, neither fear nor dread, but akin to both, shot through her. She reasoned that the appearance resulted from her over-tried and agitated imagination, and falling on her knees she prayed again with fervor.

Meantime, the mastiff, Fury, which had been sleeping before the fire when John Bullfinch seated himself in the chimney-corner, arose and paced the room like a tiger in a cage. Once or twice she came to the farmer, and laying her great dark muzzle on his knee, gave a sort of moan. She grew so uneasy and went so often to the door, that John Bullfinch rose and let her out. Instead of barking, as was her wont, she turned and looked him in the face, until he closed the door upon her. Then with noiseless steps and long strides, she took her way to the brake by the well, and there paced round and round a muffled man, who stood among the bushes with his eyes steadily fixed upon the light at the window of May Bullfinch. A quarter of an hour passed, during which the man still watched the light, seemingly hoping or fearing that the maiden would come to the window again, when the mastiff stopped in her walk, and with fire in her red eye, gave a low deep growl.

"Quiet, Fury! a friend!" said the man, as the rustle of the bushes gave note that another was approaching.

"Against orders!" said the new comer. "Quiet that big dog. She's twice as big as a Spanish bloodhound, and looks four or five times as fierce. You were to wait for me at the Grange."

"I know that, but I couldn't do so, Sassafras. So near her, after such a long absence. Such doubt and fear as there's been about me, and such faith and trust as she has shown—I could wait no longer. I couldn't stay away from her another minute. Look here! this is from my picture, taken when I was a boy. She put it there with her own hands on Christmas eve."

"Ay, ay! a good girl!" said Sassafras, taking a sprig of holly, and holding it in the moonlight. "If you remember, I always said she was a good girl, when you talked of her at our camps, and so did François. But as you are here, why not go to the house, and let the jolly old farmer bring his daughter down to welcome her wandering lover?"

"Ay, why not!" replied Tom Scarlet. "I see by the light below that John Bullfinch is in the kitchen, no doubt smoking his pipe in the chimney-corner. Fury found out somehow that I was here, for I heard the back door shut just before she came, which must be half an hour ago. I've been watching that light at her window. She came to it once."

"Watching the light! Why you're as silly as the fellow who sat on the bank all day waiting for the river to run by. Why don't you go to the house and watch her?"

"The truth is, Sassafras, that I feel timid—what you may call shy, and afraid to present myself before her, having been away so long. I ought to have come when we first landed."

"You ought not to have come now, I think," said Sassafras. "A man of your pluck—a young fellow like you! after the adventures you've gone through, been at death's door, and three parts of the way in, to be afraid of a young girl who loves you, is the greatest nonsense I ever heard of."

"I knew you would say so; but so it is! It's my love for her, you know."

"Love! Ain't I in love? Look at me! Am I afraid?"

"You're not in love with *her?*" said Tom, with emphasis.

"Why, no! If I was I shouldn't stand chattering here in the chill moonlight when I might be by her side at the fire," replied Sassafras. "If this is to be the effect she'll have on you, Sir Jerry must get another rider, for you'll break your neck in the steeple-chase to a certainty, after a few hours at her apron strings. If you've got a flask of brandy about you, take a good swig and settle your thoughts."

"I have none. I need none ; and after our meeting is once over, I shall be as bold as a lion and as cool as a cucumber for the steeple-chase. With her eye on me, I can't lose it."

"Well, that's more like the Tom Scarlet I have known. This little rascal love plays the traitor though, to some bold hearts, and courage goes out as he enters in. I suppose I must go to honest John myself. It's lucky I met his son—a likely lad—since I left you. Keep that dog back, and keep her quiet. When I whistle come to the door."

John Bullfinch was still seated in the chimney-corner, and not in a cheerful frame of mind, when there was a guarded knock at the door. The farmer wondered that there was no alarm from Fury; but he was insensible to fear, and thought it might be one of his men, come there for some reason. He opened the door, and there stood Sassafras, in his pilot coat and glazed hat. At first appearance the face of Sassafras was not one to strike an Englishman of the rural parts favorably. The strong, bony features, the deep-set, bright eye, and the matted, black hair were such as were seldom seen in the Midland Vale.

"What do you want?" said the farmer.

"Your pardon for what seems an unwarrantable intrusion at this hour," replied Sassafras. "After that a few words with you, and a word or two with your son, Master Bullfinch, who has a sort of a promise from me."

"And who may you be?" said John Bullfinch.

"I'm the man he met to-day. I suppose he mentioned the man from America?"

"The man from America!" said John Bullfinch, with an air of surprise and abstraction. "Yes, he mentioned that man."

"Well, Mr. Bullfinch, I am the man in question—Sassafras, the friend of Tom Scarlet."

"You are quite sure of that last, eh?"

"I am," said Sassafras, returning the farmer's steady look.

"Come in," said John; "I fully believe you. I'll call my son down without disturbing his sister."

"Wait a bit, Mr. Bullfinch," said Sassafras, as they entered together. "There's another man from America outside, and he's more bashful than I am, so I came first."

"You mean Tom? God bless my soul and heart alive! He isn't dead, and he's come at last," cried John Bullfinch. "I've said so all along. I told 'em so! I said to Moleskin this very night—says I, 'Tom is all right, and the man from America is his friend.' Sassafras, bring Tom in!"

"Gently, sir; speak lower. Miss May Bullfinch had better not be alarmed of a sudden."

"You're right! It's well be-thought of. My daater has been anxious and disturbed, in a sort of pale and pining way. We must have a care for her."

"It will be easily managed," said Sassafras. "You call Master Bullfinch down-stairs handsomely—that is, with no more stir than needful, and I'll have Tom here in no time. Then your son shall go up and call his sister to hear what his acquaintance, the man from America, has got to say. She will see, by the boy's face and manner, that the man from America has good news. At the foot of the stairs you take her in your arms with a fond embrace, and carry her into the sitting-room. She'll know then who's here, and Tom may go in and tell her the rest, while I explain matters to you by the chimney-corner."

"It's jest the thing!" said the farmer, in a husky voice.

He stole softly up-stairs, while Sassafras went to the door and gave a low whistle. Before Tom Scarlet was there the farmer had returned. When the young man came he shook him warmly by the hand, without a word, and then drew him into the room.

"Tom, my boy, I'm glad to see thee back. We thought at times you would never come. But it was contrary winds, no doubt. When did you land?"

"Nearly a month ago," replied Tom, rather sheepishly.

"A month ago? And not come here till now! Why not?"

"The truth is, sir, that Sassafras would'nt let me, and I'm ashamed of it. Still, I've got the horse in the way of good condition by staying down there in Cheshire."

"Ah, the horse. Is he a good horse, Tom? As good as The Bagman?"

"Better, sir. At least two stone better over a real stiff country. Barring accidents, Sir Jerry will win."

The entrance of the farmer's son cut short further observations on that head, especially as Sassafras stood forward and said:

"Hullo, young Bullfinch. Here we are again, Young Jack! And you see I've brought the man who was shot in the head and went down the rapids of the Neosho."

Young Jack flew to Tom Scarlet, saying:

"Oh, Tom, what a joyful thing this is. You're back! Now they'll believe what I say. I told 'em so all along! I told Lady Snaffle and May this evening, and I told May to-night, the very last thing I said, and after we had kissed each other at the chamber door, that it was all right."

" You are the boy for me !" said Sassafras. " Now you go to your sister's room, and wake her up handsomely—gently, you know. Don't rush in like a bull at a gate, but handsomely ; and say as quietly as you can, that the man from America is down here and wants to see her. You may mention that he's rough and ready, but as true as steel."

" I have already told her that a score of times, since Miriam said it," replied Young Jack.

" Go, my son, and be gentle. I'll meet you and May at the stair foot," said John Bullfinch.

The lad and his sister were heard on the stairs sooner than they expected, for May Bullfinch had not undressed. She had heard her father talking to Sassafras, though unable to distinguish what he said. Heard him call her brother up, and heard the latter go down-stairs. Fond kisses as he carried her into the sitting-room, and many affectionate little pats on the back when she was seated, together with the joy she saw in his bluff face and blue eyes, told her all. He said nothing but this, " May, my dear, he's outside, and all of a flutter. Afraid, the man from America says—afraid of you. I'll go and send him in here."

After Tom Scarlet had gone to May, her father sat on one side of the fire and his son on the other, and both had their eyes on Sassafras, who was in front of it.

" I said I should explain," he began. " He was a long time away, and thought to be dead. He was as near death as any man may be and pull through. Shot in the head, but by a glancing ball, he went down the rapids. If ten thousand men went into them wounded as he was, I don't believe there would be another saved. The river, however, was high, and an eddy carried him on to a shelving rock, where he lay insensible. It was even then falling. The streams out there rise and fall very rapidly. His senses came back to him, but he was unable to get up the steep, rocky bluff. Keeps and Kirby found him there the next day ; and Keeps, a handy fellow, but no better in other ways than he should be, rigged a purchase and got him up the bluff. They fed him and nursed him, and sheltered him as well as they could, all through the storm of the next night, which was one of the hardest that ever raged there."

" It was well done of them," said John Bullfinch.

"Ay, it was! But he was their salvation. Their lives hung upon his and they knew it. On the morning after the storm, I started Cinnamon and a band of his Indians on their trail, while I went to look up the man who had planned the raid upon us, and who as he believed, had killed Tom Scarlet. The chief was painted for war, and it was a hundred to one that the hair would not be on the heads of Keeps and Kirby forty-eight hours longer. Miriam Cotswold, however, insisted that I should send François with the Indians to look for Tom's remains, and went herself. It was well, for she recognised Tom just as the Indians had got the other party corralled, and had loosed their knives and tomahawks for a spring."

"Bless my soul!" said John Bullfinch, while his son sat staring upon the narrator.

"Cinnamon was naturally disappointed, for he meant business, and when the Cheyennes mean business they go for blood; but he had taken a great liking to Tom Scarlet, and at his earnest entreaty, he let Keeps and Kirby slide. We travelled to my plantation at St. Jo., and after the necessary preparations came here. We have brought the White Horse, and the White Horse and I prevented Tom from coming to see you right away."

"The White Horse!" said John Bullfinch.

"Ay, the White Horse. He had to be trained, you know, for this great match between the Duke of Jumpover and Sir Jerry. We have kept him at strong work near Chester, and in about a week you and Sir Jerry must come down quietly, and see a little trial."

"The White Horse!" said John. "So this horse he's brought that can beat the Bagman two stone, is the White Horse. Sassafras, I have my doubts about him. He's an unlucky horse, and I have my doubts."

"Sir, you'll have none when you see him take off at a rasping fence with Tom upon his back."

"Maybe so, Sassafras. But is he a water-jumper? You see, my experience is, that many a good fencer is not good at water. I mean big natural watercourses. There will be an ugly brook in this business, twenty-five feet at least, and the Duke's horse is a real good water-jumper, as good almost as Cowslip."

"Fire or water, this horse will face anything," said Sassafras, "and so will his rider when Tom is in the saddle."

"Say you so?" said John. "What's his breeding?"

"Well, sir, the full pedigree I cannot give, but he is quite thoroughbred. He was got by Stumps."

"Hold on!" said John, "you begin well. The Whalebone blood, to begin with as a foundation, cannot be excelled. From Whalebone's son (Stumps) comes the color."

"His dam was by Master Henry."

"Why, good again!" cried John. "It couldn't be better. There you bring in Old Orville, a horse of ten thousand."

"Grandam by Tramp," said Sassafras sententiously.

"Why, better yet! This'll suit John Gully, Isaac Sadler, and Ransome exactly. Why, Tramp got the Little Red Rover and Dangerous; and he was grandsire of Glencoe, with whom Lord Jersey challenged for The Whip at New Market, last year. Sassafras, you must see Ransome."

Sassafras laughed, and said, "Well, sir, to tell you the truth, I have seen him. We sent a special request to him to come down and look at the horse a week ago, and there he is now, taking care of him while we run up here."

"Oh, father, what a beautiful plant!" said Young Jack.

"Why, so it is. But, Sassafras, Ransome is no trainer. Now, if you had sent to me, I could have got Will Chifney and John Day to go down."

"Yes, and half England would have known it. Mr. Ransome don't attract the public eye. Why, the people in the coaches on his journey down took him for a banker. Besides, Tom says that he is the best judge in England of a horse for cross-country work, and of his proper condition."

"Sassafras, I believe he is, except Tom himself. Tom is an extraordinary young man. Still, he ought to have let us known that he was well and at hand."

"I'll explain that," said Sassafras. "A letter was sent to you from St. Jo. by him, the direction by another hand. That letter was lost at sea, there is every reason to believe; and when he learned through Miriam that you had heard nothing of him, and that Miss Bullfinch was unwell, I could hold him in no longer. He has been going to bolt the track above twice a week ever since we landed, and when he found that his letter

had never reached England, come here he would. We must
go again by the mail coach just before day, leaving you to
explain to Sir Jerry Snaffle."

"I'll ride over and do so," said John. "You mentioned
Miriam Cotswold. It is almost a pity that she has come back
to these parts. A gypsy camp is a queer place."

"Farmer Bullfinch," said Sassafras, "she is not going to
stay back. After Tom's affairs are settled she will return to
America with me. I'm going to marry her. She will suit
me and suit my plantation as its mistress. She can put up
with my way of life better than any other woman in the
world. A little while in the gypsy camp here won't hurt her.
Miriam can take care of herself anywhere. She was in an
Indian camp when I first saw her."

"You will be married here, of course."

"No, sir ; in King George county, Virginia, where I was
born, there is a little church, and in the graveyard round that
little church my forefathers are buried. Miriam and I have
settled it that we'll be married in that little church. In fact,
she insists that it shall be there."

"Give me your hand again, sir," said John Bullfinch. "I
shall see about a wedding gift for Miriam. My daater May
will help me to see about it. Her mother, who is dead and
gone, used to have Miriam here when she was a child. Sassafras, you're the right sort of man. And if you did kill
Jagger, it's a matter for your own conscience as to whether
there was justifiable cause."

"In regard to that there was," said Sassafras. "I could
kill three or four more like him, in the same circumstances,
without the least compunction. The man was a villain—a
thief and a coward, and a murderer at heart! We'll say no
more about him. As to the match, you come down with Sir
Jerry and see the horse. Meantime, we will keep our own
counsel, and come upon the Duke's party next month like a
thunder-clap in the night."

"So it shall be. Jack, you mustn't split," said John,
seriously.

"Me split! Never fear me! But I must ride over with
May when she goes to tell all this to Lady Snaffle, so that I
may caution her ladyship," replied Young Jack.

"It may be as well. We will all three go to-morrow after dinner. And I say, Jack, you needn't mention to her ladyship what Sassafras said about killing four or five more such as Jagger, nor about the disappointment of the Indian because he couldn't go for blood. Ladies, you see," he added to Sassafras, "are apt to be prejudiced in such matters; and the Indian has sent over a message and a token, claiming Tom as a sort of enlisted man, or what not."

"The totem of the tribe has come, then! I'm glad of that. Tom is now one of the Cheyennes!"

"Sassafras," said Young Jack, "don't you tell that to our May. She won't like it to be said about here that Tom is an Indian."

"I see! Young ladies may be prejudiced on that point," replied Sassafras. "But it's much the same as when your king has a man kneel down, and with a touch of a sword makes him rise up 'right honorable.' I'm a Cheyenne myself in the way that Tom is. I earned the distinction on the warpath against the Sioux, in the Rocky Mountains. Some day, Young Jack, I'll tell you about the battle we fought in Hell Gate Pass, when the Blackfeet had nearly come in third hand, and put us all to the axe and scalping-knife. I can tell you some beautiful things about Cinnamon, for, as a warrior and hunter, there's not his equal among the tribes."

While the roving hunter of the West was interesting John Bullfinch and his son, there was sweet communing and some tears between May and Tom Scarlet in the other room. They sat side by side and hand in hand, and Fury was at her mistress' feet. As he told his tale she looked fondly in his manly face. When he added that he must leave her before the dawn of day, she said:

"Oh, Tom! so soon, and after such an absence, when some thought you had forgotten all about us."

"'Tis but for two or three weeks," he replied. "And O, May, my life and love, I never in one waking hour ceased to think of you. I was scarcely at Liverpool when your image, always in my mind, had liked to have lured me back. But I said, 'If I go back bootless what a fool she'll think me.' Then at sea, when I was sick, no better than a dead man, in the gale, and the brig groaned and pitched as if she was going down head first to the bottom of the sea, the thought of you was all I had to set against much misery. In the West, upon the great plains, hundreds of miles from the habitations of men, with a feeling of boundless freedom, in boundless space, it was happy to sit with Sassafras by the camp-fire at night, and, while the wolves howled in the dark shadow beyond the light, to talk of you, May. And when I lay, torn and bruised, on the rock in the rapids, and with returning consciousness, that seemed to come just as I was about to gasp out my last, your form came with it, like a soft vision in my sleep, and gave me heart and strength. Dear May, it was a joy, and I said, 'I shall not perish here in the wilderness to be the prey of wolf and kite, for my love lives for me in the Vale at home, and I *will* live for her."

"O, Tom—poor Tom!" said she, with her face on his shoulder.

"So May, my life and heart! one little parting, and then I return for good and all."

"And then you will roam no more ?"

"No more. Here is my home. Here is my love—better than home itself! Home would be nothing—less than the western wilds without her," he replied. "I shall never wander more."

"Not even to go to see Sassafras, Tom ?"

"Ah, May, Sassafras, the best and most unselfish of friends, will come sometimes to see you and me, and bring Miriam with him. He is a born rover, and neither of them seems to suffer from the sea."

They sat and talked on. Young Jack came and hinted that a little of Tom Scarlet's company in the kitchen would be desirable; his father came and asked May whether she had not better go to bed. But there she sat, with Fury's great head in her lap, and her hand in Tom Scarlet's, until Sassafras came to the door and said, "Time's up!"

CHAPTER XXXVIII.

"Say, by what name men call ye,
    What city is your home,
That in such guise ye come to ride
    Before the ranks of Rome?
By many names men call us,
    In many lands we dwell;
Well Samo Thracia knows us,
    Cyrene knows us well.
Our house in gay Tarentum
    Is hung each morn with flowers;
Over the masts of Syracuse
    Our marble portal towers.
But by the proud Eurotas
    Is our dear native home,
And for the right we come to fight
    Before the ranks of Rome."

THE Ides of March had come, the date for the great steeple-chase between the horses to be named at the post by the Duke of Jumpover and Sir Jerry Snaffle. The day was not unfavorable, for the sky was tolerably clear overhead, and the brisk March breeze had dried the ground, except in the low places. The Vale was famous for its grass lands, its stiff fences, and its wide and deep brooks. Timber fences—that is to say, posts and rails—there were next to none; but the "bull-finches" and ox-fences—mostly double thorn hedges, with ditches on each side—were heavy and thick. The line chosen by the umpires was a noted one for the stiff fences which would be encountered; and there was one brook of more than ordinary width and difficulty when the stream was swollen, as was the case that day. The distance was from four miles and a half to five miles. It was a famous line of country in the times of the old, straightaway steeple-chase courses, which are now totally fallen into disuse and superseded by roundabout courses, mainly devised to enable the spectators to see the horses all the way from a stand. These partly artificial courses are not nearly as well calculated to try the powers of the horses and to test their capabilities as fencers, as the old straight lines were, and a different class of horses are now entered. Still, the danger is quite as great—perhaps greater

24

—for the pace is stronger, and a tired horse will sometimes fall at a comparatively small fence. This course was not quite straight. The horses started from a field by the roadside, and ran for over half a mile towards the southwest, which brought them two or three fields from the road; the line then went due west, the fences being very heavy for over two miles. Then it turned northwest for half a mile, and approached the road again at the deepest and widest part of the brook before mentioned, over which the road was carried by a stone bridge.

This was a critical part of the race. But there was another very critical point a mile further on, where, within a field of the winning flag, there was a great leap to be taken over, or rather through a very thick double fence, with its ditches, called Barker's Bullfinch. It was a noted place, and many a good horse and bold rider had been brought to grief by it, as they were commonly nearly done up before reaching it by their previous violent and long-continued exertions. The fences over this line of course were numerous as well as heavy, for the fields were not large. But there was this advantage —it was nearly all grass land, there being but three or four ploughed fields in all the line. What plough there was, however, was heavy, for the ground was the fat, loamy clay of the Vale, the strong land which will grow horse beans, and not the light loam in which barley delights. The attendance of spectators was very great. The match had long been a fruitful and favorite topic with the gentlemen of the hunts presided over by the Duke and the Baronet, and many were in attendance from the Pytchley, the Heythrop, and the Quorn hunts. These were all well-mounted men, but they could not hope to keep up with the matched horses except by keeping mainly to the grass on each side of the road, and thus avoiding the strongest leaps and some of the distance. The riders of the horses engaged were not allowed to go over a hundred yards along the road at any one time, and therefore they were never in it at all, as they would have lost ground by jumping into it. Besides the gentlemen of the hunts, there were many farmers and farmers' sons, well-mounted, and great crowds of foot people. The latter congregated most about the bridge and at Barker's Bullfinch, though there were also many men and boys up in trees all along the line. Those at the bridge saw with a sort of satisfaction the yellow, turbid current rushing along between steep banks, partly undermined by the stream and fringed with alder bushes, and chuckled to themselves as they said, " They must be good 'uns to clear this ; one or both will get a ducking." While those who surveyed the thick, leafless, double hedges of Barker's Bullfinch, composed of whitethorn, blackthorn, crab-tree, dwarf maple, and a great variety of briars, were equally well pleased with their own point of vantage, remarking, " A steeple-chase is nothing without falls, and my opinion is that both on 'em 'ull get ' croppers' at this here bullfinch." All the line was down the Vale. It was not by any means a flat surface, for the ground was undulating, and upon a range of hill to the southward there were many spectators. Upon this hill stood two windmills, and the houses of the millers. All the windows in the houses and the galleries of the mills were occupied by the wives and daughters of the neighboring farmers, and they had a good though rather distant view of the steeple-chase.

The hour for naming the horses had almost come. The stewards, Sir Harry Plowden and Captain Fane, were in the field, surrounded by many men on horseback and some on foot. There was a buzz of expectation as the Duke of Jumpover came up, accompanied by a number of his select friends, mostly country gentlemen of large estates and pedigrees much more ancient than those in the stud book. The Duke was a handsome man, with frank expression. With him came two very fine, weight-carrying hunters, prepared for the race. He had not declared which he would name, but the attention of the trainer and the glances of his chosen rider, a gentleman of name and fame from Melton Mowbray, indicated to the assemblage that the chestnut horse Belvoir, a thoroughbred of great size and power, would be the one. The rider, Mr. Coplow, was known to be one of the best gentlemen across a country in England. His fame was much more widely spread than that of Tom Scarlet had ever been, but his knowledge of the Vale and his experience at its very heavy fences was not so large or so thorough as that of the man whose absence the people of the neighborhood began to deplore. The general opinion was that Sir Jerry would name The Bagman and that his rider would be Mr. Stilton, a very good man, but without that inspiration in moments of difficulty, and that magnetic touch upon the reins, at supreme efforts, which informs and revives the horse. These Tom Scarlet was thought by his friends to possess. The Bagman had arrived and Mr. Stilton with a careless air walked up and down near him as he was led along. It was a sight at which Mr. Southdown and the farmers who looked upon Mr. Southdown as an oracle were somewhat disturbed.

The former saw The Bagman, and he saw Mr. Stilton playing with his whip, but he did not see Sir Jerry, nor John Bullfinch, nor Ransome, the great man among horsemen, who presided over the famous stud of Lord Jersey, at Middleton Park. Mr. Southdown looked glum, and told his friend from London, a sporting tavern-keeper, who had come down to see the match, that his mind was *not* made up as to the result.

"Southdown, things don't look well for your party," said the Londoner. "The Bagman is a good horse, but there isn't enough of him to beat Belvoir, and Mr. Stilton seems to think so. Sir Jerry hangs back. Perhaps he'll forfeit."

"Sir Jerry never hung back in his life, sir," replied Mr. Southdown. "It wants almost half an hour yet to the time set for naming the horses. They can start anything that was regularly ridden to hounds last year."

"Ay, I know; but Sir Jerry has but The Bagman here, and your watch is slow, I think."

"It's no such thing, sir. Your Lunnon time is fast. You're a good deal too fast in everything. But I shan't argey the p'int," said Mr. Southdown. "What's that?"

It was a bustle and a cheer from the road, as Lady Snaffle's phaeton with four horses and postilions and an outrider, in the baronet's colors, dark blue and silver, came in sight. These colors had been selected by the Admiral, as representing the ocean out of soundings, and the moonlit surface of the silver sea. There was another loud cheer as the carriage dashed up and Lady Snaffle was recognised. The Duke, Sir Harry, Captain Fane, and others raised their hats.

"Who's that lady?" said the Londoner.

"Who's that lady, sir!" said Mr. Southdown, with undisguised contempt. "Is it possible that you've come down here on this occasion, and don't know the Admiral's daughter, when she appears in state. I think you said, just now, that Sir Jerry would pay forfeit. You're a nice man! but it ain't worth while argeying the p'int with a Lunnoner."

In the carriage with Lady Snaffle was May Bullfinch, together with her brother. This arrangement, when first proposed, did not quite suit Young Jack. He had intended to be on Young Cowslip, to show Lord Doomsday the best line for Blue Peter, but had been overruled, in order that he might stand up and describe to her ladyship the moving incidents of the steeple-chase as they occurred. The postilions had not long pulled up, when Jack Cotswold came dashing along on the road towards the bridge in a gig, with a young woman by his side.

"Please, my lady," said Young Jack, "there's Miriam and her uncle. And, O, here's Rose and those twins," he added, looking back.

There indeed was Cooper in his best uniform, patiently leading a donkey, in whose panniers sat the twins, while Rose strode along by their side in a black velvet bonnet profusely decorated with the blue and silver colors of Sir Jerry Snaffle.

"How do you do, Cooper," said Lady Snaffle, while May Bullfinch smiled and nodded.

"I'm hearty, my lady, thanks to you. I've heard the Admiral has hove up anchor, and is standing for this roadstead, under a press of sail. Being in duty bound to report to him, I've come myself, and lent Rose a hand to steer this donkey and take care of the children."

"As if I couldn't take care of my own twins!" said Rose, with some contempt.

"But why have you brought them here, Rose?" said Young Jack.

"Why have I brought 'em? Why to let them see good horsemanship. Haven't my twins got as good right to see it as other people's children? You and Meg Southdown are here."

Young Jack blushed up to his eyes, and said in a low voice, "O, my lady, let this woman go along. Let Cooper take her away."

"I'm sure I am willing," said Lady Snaffle, with a low laugh.

Just then there was a louder cheer than that which had greeted Lady Snaffle's arrival, and it came from the road in the opposite direction. All eyes were turned that way, and from a lane to the right of the road there came six horsemen, followed by a trooping crowd of men, boys and gypsy women, all shouting and clamoring.

Sir Jerry Snaffle, John Bullfinch, Lord Doomsday and Major Fitzgerald were immediately recognised, but the dark man on John Bullfinch's left hand and the whiskered person on Sir Jerry's right were not, save by Lady Snaffle, May Bullfinch and Young Jack. As the clamoring crowd drew nearer the other parties made out the words, "Scarlet! Scarlet! Tom of the Grange!" and Mr. Southdown dashed his spurs into the sides of his horse, crying, "By George! he's come! My mind's made up!"

He was still more excited when he saw behind the gentlemen, a led horse in clothes, beside which Mr. Ransome rode, with the solemn, anxious face he always had when attending a racer of mighty promise on a great day. At a sign from Lady Snaffle, the whiskered man went to the carriage side, and would have remained there some time had it not been for the expostulations of Sir Jerry and John Bullfinch, The dark man and Ransome proceeded into the field with the horse in clothes between them.

"What the d—l is all this?" said Sir Harry Plowden.

"In the first place, it is Tom Scarlet, and I am glad he has reached home safe and well," replied the Duke. "In the next place he seems to have not only come himself, but to have brought the dark horse about which there have been many rumors in respect to this match."

"What a d——d rascal! I have got two hundred bet at evens with Major Fitzgerald," said one of the Melton Mowbray men.

"Rascal!" said the Duke, "nothing of the sort! The match always contemplated the naming of any horse that was qualified by having been hunted with last year. If Sir Jerry Snaffle has been able to get one better than The Bagman it may be the worse for me. I would name a better than Belvoir if I knew where to find him. I know of no gentleman who would feel called upon to do more than comply with the terms of the match, and this Sir Jerry has done.

"Exactly!" said Captain Fane. "Our friend here seems to think that Sir Jerry ought to have sent the bellman round to tell the people that he had a better chance to win than some supposed. He may not win. I have known dark horses deceive their owners. But here he comes."

"Sir Jerry," said the Duke, as the Baronet rode up, "I sincerely congratulate you upon the arrival of Tom Scarlet. His horsemanship is better known to you, but hardly better appreciated than by me. He has sometimes hunted with my hounds, and I hope he will again."

"I thank your grace for him," said Sir Jerry. "He seems to be too busy just now with his neighbors and friends to come here and do it for himself."

"We suppose you are now ready to name?" said Sir Harry.

"I believe so," replied the Duke. "Gentlemen, I name Belvoir, hunted with my own hounds last year. Mr. Coplow will ride him."

"And I," said Sir Jerry Snaffle, "name the White Horse, now called St. Jo., hunted with the Vale of White Horse hounds last year, as you, Sir Harry Plowden, and you, Captain Fane, will see if you go and look at him."

"It is needless; still, we will go and have a look at this champion and rover," said the Duke. "I'm told by Sir Jerry that the horse has been to America, and come back after many adventures among Indians and hunters," he added, after a few words with the Baronet.

The group moved towards the crowd surrounding the White Horse. The latter was now stripped and being saddled and fitted out by Sassafras and Ransome. His bloodlike appearance, and the immense power he displayed—a big horse on short legs—were quickly noted and commented on.

"You seem to have got him there, Ransome," said the Duke.

"I think we've got a pretty good one, your grace, but the test will tell. If he's as good as he looks, and as Tom Scarlet thinks, Belvoir and Mr. Coplow will have hard work to win," Ransome replied.

The Duke, Sir Jerry and the stewards drew off again, taking Tom Scarlet and John Bullfinch with them. The latter invited Mr. Southdown to go also, but that gentleman was the subject of another attraction. He had heard of Sassafras from May Bullfinch and Young Jack many times of late; and now that he was in presence, the ponderous grazier kept close by his side. There was no small contrast between the dark, lithe, black-eyed, and black-haired man of the Far West, and the towering, massive grazier of the midland English vale, with his full, ruddy face. Yet they were types of the same race; the former modified, or rather intensified, by the residence of many generations in the hot summers and bilious autumns of America.

"See the Duke's horse—that's Belvoir," said Ransome to Sassafras.

"A grand horse," replied the latter—"a noble specimen of the thoroughbred. But don't you think that for this business, over such a distance of ground and such a difficult country, he is a little too leggy?"

"It may be so. He has more daylight under him than the White Horse, though no bigger in frame."

"That's it. And then, to my mind, St. Jo. is stronger in the back and loins, his big quarters are more turned under and better calculated to send him over, when his fine shoulders lift him into the air. But here comes Tom!"

Mr. Southdown did not wait for Scarlet and John Bullfinch, but tearing himself, by an effort, from the side of Sassafras, he struggled into the midst of a thick cluster of farmers and hunting men, and, mounting his horse, proclaimed, with a stentorian voice and cast of countenance impregnable against all assault:

"My mind's made up—fully made up!"

"So is mine!" said an opulent yeoman from the borders of Whittlebury Forest. "Belvoir will win it! Don't tell me about your White Horse and rider and trainer from America, and other humbug! I say Belvoir and Coplow will win it!"

"Dick King," replied Mr. Southdown, "I shan't argey the question. I'll bet fifty guineas Belvoir and Coplow don't win."

His friend was about to take the bet, but before he had said "Done!" he heard the clear, cutting tones of Sassafras, as he led the White Horse up to the stewards, Tom Scarlet in the saddle, in the blue and silver, and let go of his bridle.

"Gentlemen," said the man of the West, "here's St. Jo., and here is his rider. Everybody can see them now, and I'll bet a hundred ounces they win this match!"

" Who is this man, and what does he mean?" said the Duke
to Sir Jerry and Tom Scarlet.

" He is a friend of mine, your grace ; a very gallant, devoted friend, too," replied Tom. " He is a planter and a great
hunter and a lover of good horses. His plantation on the
Missouri river is as beautiful a place as you would wish to
see—that is, all natural."

" A planter, eh ! What does he mean by one hundred
ounces ?"

" Ounces of gold, your grace. About four hundred pounds."

" Can he afford to lose it ?" said the Duke.

" Yes ; but he thinks he can win ; and I think so too," said
Tom.

" I'll take his bet though," said the Duke.

He then walked up to Sassafras and said :

" Sir, I'll take the bet of a hundred ounces you have proposed."

" All right, your grace ! I'll put my money up into the
hands of Mr. Bullfinch here, or anybody's."

" There is no need, sir. It is perfectly safe with you—as
safe as mine is with me."

With this the Duke mounted his horse; and St. Jo. and
Belvoir being all ready, and Sir Harry Plowden mounted and
flag in hand, Sassafras said a few words to Sir Jerry Snaffle,
threw himself into the saddle of The Bagman, and galloped
away towards the west, over the fields between the flags and
the road. And now the impatience and din of the crowd
increased, and swelled up like the rush of winds, or the roar
of swift-running waters. Some horsemen stole ahead, unwilling to leave the neighborhood of the start, especially with so
many eyes on them, but fearing that if they did not, they
might be away in the rear at the finish. The men and boys
in the trees rustled among the twigs, and craned their necks
forward. The ladies in the windows and galleries of the mills
pressed upon the rails. The postilions of Lady Snaffle's carriage sat in their saddles, looking over their left shoulders,
and with their whips ready to fall. Her ladyship stood up
for a moment, then sat down again to speak to May Bullfinch.
Then Young Jack cried, shrill and loud, " Off they go, my
lady !"

CHAPTER XXXIX.

HURRAH! hurrah!" shouted the men and boys in the
trees. "Clear the way! By your leave there! Clear
the way!" cried the horsemen in the road, spurring forward,
and narrowly missing the knocking down of some foot people.

Crack! crack! like the report of two rifles, went the whips
of the postilions, and Lady Snaffle's carriage, cheered to the
echo as it passed along, was whirled away with the four horses
at a gallop.

While the riders of Belvoir and St. Jo. kept the true line of
the course outside the flags, the stewards and many horsemen
well mounted, with some not as well mounted as they thought,
took the shorter way over the fields and fences, on the inside
of the flags. The horsemen and foot people streamed along the
road so fast that they could hardly look at the contestants
away to the left; but whenever Belvoir and St. Jo. made a
good leap, the men in the trees swung their hats and shouted,
and the ladies at the windmills waved their handkerchiefs with
delight and glee. The incidents were commented upon to
Lady Snaffle and May Bullfinch by that sharp observer and
competent critic, Young Jack.

"They have got into the straight going, my lady, and are
running due west. The pace is improved. They are nearing
the big ox-fences of the line. They are just going at the first
real rasper. Belvoir clears it. So does St. Jo.! My lady!
such a jumper. Now the pace is good. Coplow keeps the
very crown of a land, while Tom gallops on the south slope of
the next. Good judgment that, my lady; for the sunny side
of the lands is better going than the very top in our deep soil,
as Mr. Coplow, and his horse will find out. Now they are
coming to the brook above the bend. It's no great thing of a
jump, but it has spilt some already. There are four men in
it, this side of the flags, and their horses are loose. Cowslip
takes it beautiful! There's a girl at the windmill leaning
over the gallery rail so far, that she'll be clean over directly;

and it's forty feet to the ground. I hope it isn't Meg South-down. Belvoir is across the brook! So is St. Jo.! He over-jumped at least six feet, my lady, and is pulling hard. Now the pace is *strong*. They are coming to the bullfinch, where Tom pounded Lord Doomsday. O, my lady! O, May! Coplow only just missed a cropper! His horse stuck in the middle, and blundered through. Tom rode at it as a bull terrier goes at a badger. The White Horse smashed through, like a cannon-ball! It's the best steeple-chase that ever was seen. Now Tom draws up closer to Belvoir. He is at his hip, and forces the pace. My lady, they will soon be at the brook below the bend. Let us be there first, and see the game from the bridge."

"On, boys, on!" The whips of the postilions smacked, and the steaming horses galloped. The first great crisis of the race was near at hand. The horsemen in the fields sought the road, to avoid the brook at this its widest and most difficult part. The Duke, Sir Jerry Snaffle, Sir Harry, and John Bull-finch came sweeping by, while the foot people cheered lustily. Near the bridge the press was great. A hulking fellow brought the carriage to a standstill, by getting before the leaders in the middle of the road. He caught at the heads of the horses. The postilions swore. Young Jack stormed. The sailor Cox parted the crowd like a wedge; caught the fellow by the collar; with a straight left-handed hit, sent him stag-gering into the ditch, and touched his hat to the Admiral's daughter. Now they had attained the very keystone of the bridge, and over the heads of the foot people saw the yellow, turbid torrent, as it came rushing down towards them. Lady Snaffle looked a little anxious, and May Bullfinch grew paler. About two hundred yards to the south the steeple-chasers were coming to the brook above the bridge. They were nearly neck and neck. The crimson and strawberry leaves of the Duke were nearest, but the blue and silver of the baronet were dearest to the men of the Vale. The interest was intense. The people held their breath. Lady Snaffle and May Bull-finch stood up, while Young Jack was too excited to speak. Tramp! tramp! The very ground seemed to shake as the powerful horses strode on. Belvoir led a trifle. As he came to the bank, and heard the wild rush of the waters, he refused the leap, swerved round to the left, and, striking the haunch of St. Jo. with his shoulder just as he was leaving his ground for a grand leap, tumbled him and his rider heels over head into the flood. A shout! a yell! a shriek! May Bullfinch fell back into her seat, covering her eyes with her hands. Lady Snaffle grasped Young Jack by the shoulder. The White Horse was seen gallantly breasting the current, and making for the bank he had meant to reach by his leap; but his gallant rider, helpless, stunned by the hoof of his own horse, was floating down the stream. A man came running down the bank swift as an arrow, and while Lady Snaffle's gaze was still upon the patch of blue in the middle of the yellow waters, a dark form cleft the air and plunged into the stream.

"There! the man! the man!" she exclaimed. "I think it was the sailor!"

"O, no, my lady!" said Young Jack, tearfully, "that was Sassafras. And see, he'll have Tom out."

Close to the bridge, unseen by the spectators upon it, and by almost every one else, Parkins, half drunk as usual, performed a sort of dance, jumping up and down and shouting "He's in, he's in!" Whether his exclamations proceeded from joy did not exactly appear. He had never liked Tom Scarlet before he went to America, and it was doubtful whether he liked him much better now that he found the young man had returned, for the opinion of Parkins in regard to America was not high. Rose Tanner concluded, however, that Parkins was rejoicing over Tom Scarlet's mishap, and while the constable continued to shout "He's in, he's in!" she rushed at him crying "Drat that man!" and with a vigorous shove with both hands sent him headlong in himself. Her brother, Cooper, got hold of him as he rose to the surface, and "hauled him aboard," as he called it.

Coplow had managed to get Belvoir over, and the stout White Horse had attained the west bank farther up, when the powerful arm of Sassafras carried Tom Scarlet to the shore. The blood was running down his cheek. He staggered when set upon his legs, and looked around confused. Sassafras put his mouth to his ear and shouted aloud:

"Come, Tom, rouse yourself! I'm here! Sassafras! and May Bullfinch is looking on. Put your fingers in your mouth and call up St. Jo."

The young man did as he was told, and at the loud whistle the horse came up. With the assistance of Sassafras, Tom Scarlet was remounted. The seat upon the horse appeared to revive and steady him, while the flow of blood helped to do so.

"Tom," said Sassafras, "you can win this yet. The other horse is a good way ahead, but he is already sinking, and tires at every stride. I think he'll very likely fall before he gets home. St. Jo. is fresh, and will stand the pressure to the end. Close up gradually. What do you call that last big fence?"

"Barker's Bullfinch."

"Very well! creep up by degrees, keeping in powder enough to close with him when he nears that. Your horse is much the freshest. You are none the worse for the bath. You know the lay of the land, and I think you'll win it yet. Be cool and steady. When you believe that you have the race safe cry Cinnamon's war-cry."

The young man nodded, and away he went with the White Horse. For half a mile the people at the bridge could still see the horses as they galloped over field after field and took the fences, Belvoir with a large lead. Sassafras walked to the bridge and took a station on the western pier on the south side, looking steadily at the White Horse, who was going with long and powerful strides. The relative positions of the horses seemed to the crowd unchanged, and neither Lady Snaffle nor May Bullfinch had any hopes of final victory. The experienced eye of Young Jack detected, however, that the White Horse was gaining on the chestnut, and that Mr. Coplow was beginning to force his horse, and he said, "O, my lady! O, May! he gains at every stride. He jumps as strong and as well as he did at the first leap. If it were but a quarter of a mile further he couldn't lose it, and there's a chance as it is!"

"Chance, young squire! I say it's a certainty," cried Rose Tanner. "Coplow 'll come down a reg'lar cropper at Barker's Bullfinch."

"I say, Rose, how do you know?"

"Well, you see, I consults the stars."

The horses were now out of sight, having passed over a low hill towards the northwest and the last half mile of the course.

The carriage remained upon the bridge, for there was such a press of horsemen and foot people on the road beyond it that it was almost impassable. Still the figure of the American remained upon the pier, intent upon the northwest, and rigid as a statue carved in granite. At length, over the hubbub and clamor of the multitude, there rose from the distance a wild, shrill, echoing cry, at which Lady Snaffle started, and Sassafras jumped to the ground.

"Oh, that fearful cry," said she. "Some other accident, more dreadful, has happened."

"No, madam," said Sassafras. "'Twas the warwhoop of the wild Cheyennes, and Tom has victory in his grasp!"

"O, my lady! I know it's true," said Young Jack. "It's a great pity we couldn't see them take Barker's Bullfinch. Please, my lady, let me take Wingfield's horse and go and see. I'll be back with the news in two or three minutes."

Lady Snaffle would not consent to this, and they remained in uncertainty for some time. Then pouring over the hill, half a mile away, and stretching from one side of the field to the other came a great throng of people on horseback and on foot. Young Jack saw a group marching proudly, as it were, in the centre of the line.

"O, my lady, my lady! O, May, my dear sister May! It's all right—there they come. Sassafras leads the White Horse, my father rides on one side of him and Mr. Ransome on the other. Tom's afoot—he leans upon Sir Jerry and Major Fitzgerald, and Lord Doomsday is with them. O, if we had only seen them take Barker's Bullfinch I could die happy!"

"Better die game, Young Jack," said Rose Tanner, as she marshalled along her brother with the donkey and the twins. "If Tom had been drowned he would have died game. If Coplow has broken his neck at the bullfinch he has died game."

Soon there came spurring by men on horseback, fiery hot with haste, each intent on being first to carry the news to Aylesbury, and shouting "Scarlet, Scarlet for ever! Sir Jerry and St. Jo.! He won with his ears pricked."

"Thank God!" said May. "O, I hope Mr. Coplow is not hurt."

"Home, home!" said Lady Snaffle, with her handkerchief to her eyes.

The carriage was wheeled around, and away it went, while Young Jack said :

" Well, concerning Coplow—I'll lay two to one that it's nothing serious. Some such slight matter as the collar-bone, my lady, or a rib or two, and you know hunting men are used to it. When father was brought home on a hurdle ten years ago he said to the doctor, 'I'm all right. It's Cowslip that I'm anxious about. If young Tom Scarlet will ride over to Middleton for Ransome I shall be easy in my mind respecting the mare.' "

The narrative of Master Bullfinch was interrupted by the stoppage of the carriage. It soon appeared that Parkins was in the road in such a condition that he might have taken himself up on the charge of being "drunk and incapable." He had come to the steeple-chase provided with a bottle of gin, and the greater part of this he had swallowed as soon as he was hauled out of the stream by Rose Tanner's brother. He was now brought to the wheel by a couple of young ragamuf fin gypsies, who seemed to enjoy his plight very much.

" Parkins, what a condition," said Lady Snaffle, " for one in your position ! You have been drinking."

" Yes, mum, madam, my lady, I has—about two gallons in the bruk."

" Sir, you are intoxicated !"

" If water from the bruk will 'toxicate the authorities, my lady, I may as well admit that I be."

" Sir, you are very drunk," said the lady with difficulty repressing an inclination to laugh.

" I think not, my lady. I'll leave it to Master Bullfinch and these gypsy boys. I was never drunk in my life, except at harvest homes and such like gatherings, where no true man keeps sober. I may be on this occasion a little gammoned, but——"

" Boys," said Lady Snaffle, " take him to the nearest farm-house You shall be paid for doing so. Home ! home quickly !"

CHAPTER XL.

"Say, why are beauties praised and honored most,
The wise man's passion and the vain man's boast?
Why decked with all that land and sea afford,
Why angels called, and angel-like adored?"

LADY SNAFFLE was with May Bullfinch before a bright
fire in a spacious drawing-room, handsomely furnished,
and adorned with fine paintings. They chiefly related to nautical subjects, and to those landscapes of woodland, field and
stream which were, in a measure, connected with the turf and
chase. There was, however, none among them more beautiful
and pleasing than the picture presented by the elegant lady
and fair young girl who sat side by side and chatted pleasantly
over the cheerful blaze. Her ladyship was richly, though not
showily, attired, and in her soft armchair she evidently enjoyed
luxurious comfort and repose, and was well pleased with herself and every one else. She tapped the thick carpet with the
tip of the dainty slipper just visible beneath the lace flounce
of her satin dress, and played with the costly ruffles that, falling over her fair hand, vied with the fretwork of the frost, or
the delicate tracery of white foam on the falling wave. If
there was any exception to the general satisfaction the lady
felt, it was caused by the fact, that she had been waiting for
her husband some time; and this was a thing which the wife
of Sir Jerry Snaffle frequently had to do. On this occasion,
however, his delay had afforded an opportunity for a cosy conference and conversation with May Bullfinch—a thing in which
her godmother took much pleasure. For some time nothing
was heard but the kind tones of the Baronet's lady, or the
rustle of her satin skirts, save the sweet voice of May in reply; but Young Jack then entered, and informed the lady
that Mr. Ransome had reached the Hall, on his way home to
Middleton. Lady Snaffle desired that he might be requested
to wait on her for a few minutes, and the trainer soon entered.
He was close shaven, booted and spurred, a model of neat-
ness, although but lately he had been bespattered with mud.

His face was thoughtful and keen, and there was a sort of depth in his hazel eye, as if contemplating great things to come. It was a look well becoming to the man who had in charge the famous mares Trampoline and Cobweb. The former had borne Glencoe, and the last-named had at her foot her mighty son Bay Middleton. Young Jack looked up to the trainer with profound respect; his sister esteemed him as one of her father's nearest friends; Lady Snaffle held him in regard as a man of worth and ability, confided in by Lord Jersey, and by his countess. Ransome was a man who did honor to his profession, and though his name was seldom seen in the sporting journals and magazines, as Lord Jersey's horses were sent to New Market for their final preparation at the hands of Edwards, he could not well have been spared from that worthy and able fraternity. John Bullfinch had sometimes observed to Lord Jersey, that all the ploughing, harrowing, sowing and tending, was done by Ransome at Middleton, and Edwards merely had to put the sickle in, and reap the harvest. To this the earl usually replied, that what with the brood-mares, sucking foals, yearlings and two-year-olds, Ransome had too much to attend to at Middleton, to be spared for the purpose of looking after the fortunes of two or three-year-olds. "And, besides," the stout earl would say, "Lady Jersey would not bear of it, Farmer Bullfinch! Without Ransome at the park she would never be satisfied when we are away."

Now, Lady Snaffle was the most intimate *country* friend of the illustrious countess, who had been one of the most brilliant ornaments of two or three courts, and therefore the deference shown by the trainer was only exceeded by the respect manifested in every word and gesture of the baronet's wife."

"Oh, Mr. Ransome!" she said; "such a day! such events!"

"Wonderful, my lady! glorious! I would have given anything if Lord Jersey and the countess had been here to see it! We never had anything so good before. We have often had great steeple-chases, with large fields of horses and much fine riding, but never one that came up to this."

"What do the gentlemen say, Ransome? and where is Sir Jerry Snaffle?" said her ladyship.

"The gentlemen have all gone to the Barleymow, my lady, to talk over the events of the day! They are all much delighted—that is, all but a very few who lost on the race. That class of the people never ought to bet, my lady. If they win they crow and brag over it, as if *they* had brought the thing off. If they lose, they grumble and look black, and make insinuations. I am sure the Duke's horse was well trained, and Mr. Coplow rode well."

"Never mind the grumblers, Ransome," said Lady Snaffle. "We are very much pleased. I wish Lady Jersey had been present, just to see a young man of her own neighborhood ride. What is said of Mr. Scarlet?"

"I just stayed to hear his health proposed, and help to do honor to it, and then came away, my lady."

"Who proposed it, and how was it received?"

"The Duke proposed it, my lady, in a beautiful little speech. It was received with three hurrahs, such as the fox-hunters can give. The Duke said Tom Scarlet's riding, after the spill at the brook, was the finest thing he ever saw—a masterpiece of art."

"May, my dear, you hear this! The Duke of Jumpover and Sir Jerry Snaffle are as good judges of noble horsemanship as any in England. I am so pleased!"

"So am I, my lady!" said Young Jack; "and I know, too, that the Duke and Sir Jerry are as good judges as Ransome himself."

"Yes, indeed," said Lady Snaffle, with a smile. "And now, Mr. Ransome, tell us what was said about the American."

"Something handsome, my lady, I'll warrant; but I didn't stay to hear it. There is but one opinion. Everybody likes the man, when they come to know a little of him. I took to him in two hours, for I found out that he had that sound judgment and knowledge and love of horses that goes further with me than anything else. My lady, he's a clever man. He trained that White Horse to perfection. I told them that he couldn't be improved, as soon as I saw him go a four-mile gallop. And Sassafras, to-day, dressed Tom Scarlet's head with equal skill. He's a very clever man, my lady, and if he was to set up in the surgical line about here, where a good many broken heads and limbs are going, especially in the holiday and hunting seasons, he would beat Doctor Dose all hollow."

" Was Mr. Scarlet's head hurt?" said Lady Snaffle, gently restraining May with a light hand on her arm.

" Badly cut by St. Jo.'s hoof when they were in the water, which made Tom incapable, my lady; but Sassafras has dressed it with brandy and brown paper and a few drops of a balsam he got from the Indians. It is now tied up in a red silk handkerchief, and everybody is satisfied that it is a beautiful case."

" Mr. Ransome, I am not so satisfied myself," said Lady Snaffle, with promptitude. "The young man should have been brought here. I dare say he was drinking?"

"The doctor, my lady—meaning Sassafras!—said a little would do him good, and Sir Jerry concurred in the opinion."

"It is just like the—sailors, I was going to say; but my father, the Admiral, now that I remember, always prefers rum to brandy for an injury to the head, to be taken as well as applied. I shall send John with a message to Sir Jerry, requesting him to bring Mr. Scarlet here without delay."

"If your ladyship pleases," said Young Jack, "it will be better to send *me* instead of John. If John goes and delivers the message, Sir Jerry will just say to him, ' Very well give my compliments to her ladyship, and tell her we will be there very soon!' and then, my lady, he'll just turn to the Duke or the Major or Sir Harry or Lord Doomsday, and forget all about it. But if I go, my Lady, I shall just say to Mr. Scarlet, ' Tom you are desired by Lady Snaffle to come to the Hall directly; and, Sassafras, you are requested by my sister to see that he does so, *right away!*'"

" What's ' right away?'" said Lady Snaffle, with a laugh.

" My lady, it is what I have heard Sassafras and Tom say. It means forthwith, without delay, instanter."

"Your ladyship had better send Master Bullfinch than John," said Mr. Ransome, laying his hand fondly on Jack's head, "and I will see him mounted and started."

" Go, then, Master Bullfinch, and bring Mr. Tom Scarlet and Mr. Sassafras here *right away!*"

With this Lady Snaffle made a graceful and gracious inclination to Ransome, and the latter with Young Jack left the room.

" My dear," said Lady Snaffle, " your brother is a very nice,

clever boy—so prompt and alert. My father is much pleased
with him. The Admiral was always very fond of sharp boys,
and he wanted to place Master Bullfinch on board of a man-of-
war. He has professional notions about boys, much better, he
says, than those of tutors and schoolmasters. We went once
to see a cousin of mine at a great school, and when we came
away I said: ‘My dear father, I know you are pleased with
what we have seen. The young gentlemen are so well man-
nered, so well informed, so very nice and polite.’ But he
said: ‘Pshaw! Laura, there ought not to be any such thing
as a nice young gentleman; there is no use for such a person
as a nice young gentleman. Here, now, has been a great waste
of capital material for reefers and topmen, which last are the
hardest to come by.’ Reefers are midshipmen, May; topmen
the sailors who handle the great sails and man the heavy
guns. And the Admiral added: ‘Well-mannered, Laura!
Nothing to my boys, my young reefers on the quarter-deck of
a first-rate, especially when they had been mast-headed for
an hour or two. Every one of those boys could make a bow-
line knot, and look into the muzzles of the enemy’s guns, in
broad-side or battery, without winking. Young gentlemen,
indeed!’ But I said: ‘My dear father, these young gentlemen are getting a superior education.’ And then, my dear,
he burst out: ‘Superior education! Fiddlesticks and frying-
pans! The place for a superior education, Laura, is the quarter-deck of a fighting ship. Look at me! Your grandfather,
a very wise man, sent me aboard at ten years old. Racehorse
frigate—Sir Jerry’s father was a reefer in her too. I should
never have been the man I am if I had gone to school ashore
—I know I shouldn’t!’ And I believe, my dear,” Lady
Snaffle added, “that my father is quite right on that point.”

The lady’s reminiscences, touching the opinions and sentiments of the gallant Admiral Broadside, as good a man as
ever heard the rush of the round shot and the whistle of the
grape, were cut short by the announcement that the Admiral
had himself arrived, and he was ushered in attended by his
valet, a superannuated coxswain. The Admiral was tall
and portly, very red in the face, with white hair, bleached by
sixty years service at sea, and he walked with a limp from an
old wound which had shattered his left hip. He kissed his
daughter, shook hands with May Bullfinch and said:

"Here I am, Lady Laura, arrived in the nick of time for the steeple-chase."

"I wish you had seen it, papa," said Lady Snaffle.

"Seen it, child! I'll warrant I saw more of it than you did. Finding what was going on when we reached the hill, I stopped the chaise, and by means of a rope and ladder Mainbrace and I hoisted ourselves into the maintop of King's mill, where we could survey everything with the good glasses we always travel with."

"O, dear papa, how dangerous?"

"Dangerous! nonsense! No danger at all, unless the mill had blown over, and it was not a reefing breeze. We saw everything."

"Then you saw Tom Scarlet's plunge."

"Ay! ay! They were nearly yardarm and yardarm, when the chestnut horse broached-to, and falling aboard of the White Horse, sent him in."

"We thought we had lost then, papa, and that the accident might be fatal."

"Fatal! It did him good—did him good, Laura. Not so much as if it had been salt water, but some good. The man who jumped overboard after him is a gallant fellow, too. Who is he?"

"An American, my dear sir. A friend of Tom Scarlet's."

"Ay! ay! a sailor, no doubt. I knew he had been to sea, by the way he hauled Tom up the west bank. No landsman could have done it. But you did not see the finish, Laura. I did. It was a stern chase, but Scarlet gradually overhauled the other just this side of Barker's Bullfinch, and when he ranged alongside he rose in his stirrups, flourished his whip, and gave such a halloa as would do credit to the best boatswain in the service. 'Boarders away!' said Mainbrace; and boarders it was, for the White Horse shot ahead and went through the bullfinch like a thirty-two pounder. Those who came by the mill road said that the leap was measured and found to be thirty-three feet in the clear."

"And Mr. Coplow, papa! did you see him jump it?"

"Lady Laura, I saw Coplow—if that's his name—brought up all standing in the middle of it, and I am told that he is hurt. Still, it isn't a man expended, for he has only a shoulder dislocated and a few bruises. Now I'll go to my room."

Tom Scarlet, Sassafras and Young Jack soon arrived. They were shown into the room, and, after greetings and compliments, Tom Scarlet informed Lady Snaffle that Sir Jerry and the Duke, being very busy, could not leave the Barleymow just at present, but would be there in the course of an hour. He added that they were making a handicap for a steeplechase, to be run by the best twenty horses in their hunts, and when the weights were satisfactory to the owners of them, they would wait upon her ladyship.

"And when do *you* think that will be, Mr. Sassafras?" said Lady Snaffle, with a pleasant smile.

"Well, my lady, about this time next year, from what I heard some of the owners say," replied Sassafras.

"Sir Jerry and the Duke told me they would be here in an hour after we arrived, and desired me to wait for them," said Tom Scarlet.

"I desire it myself, sir. I wish to hear of your adventures."

"My lady, they both want him to ride for them. Your ladyship may depend that's it," said Young Jack.

"It may be the case; I should not blame them after what we saw to-day. But, Mr. Scarlet," continued Lady Snaffle, "I find that you have not yet given an account of your adventures abroad and on the seas, even to my dear daughter in the church, May Bullfinch; and now, if you please, as your head does not pain you, we will hear the narrative. Mr. Sassafras, I delight in narratives of adventure—my father is a sailor—reefer at ten years old in the Racehorse frigate—afterwards an admiral—Rear-Admiral of the Blue! I believe you are a sailor, sir."

"No, my lady, that's Cox, the man who brought the totem over," replied Sassafras. "I did once, however, go upon a trip in search of a small island, near the Grand Cayman, where the buccaneers buried a lot of gold."

"Did you find it, Sassafras?" said Young Jack.

"Well, we did and we didn't! We found the island as laid down by the bearings, but not the gold. My lady, it was a sort of Mother Carey's chicken expedition—what you may call, Miss Bullfinch and Master Bullfinch, a wild-goose chase!"

"Mother Carey's chicken! O, yes, May, the name the sailors have given to the stormy petrel, a bird never seen near the land, nor in fair weather. Now, Mr. Scarlet, let us hear of your voyages to and fro, your travels by land, moving accidents by flood and field, and so on."

"My lady, I've heard it myself, and Sassafras having been engaged, knows it all," said Young Jack; "so if your ladyship will permit us to go into the library, Sassafras can tell me about the expedition after the hoard of the buccaneers, and about Cinnamon and the Sioux, and the bears."

"Very well, Master Bullfinch, as you please. I suppose Mr. Sassafras is too bashful to hear his own exploits related by his friend to the ladies."

Young Jack ushered his American friend into the library, and they established themselves before the fire, in large, high-backed chairs, lined with soft green leather. In about an hour Lady Snaffle had heard Tom Scarlet's account of his adventures, and leaving him and May to discourse of love, she proceeded to the library. She found Young Jack and Sassafras engaged in animated conversation, the former speaking clear and shrill, and the latter replying with a deep, hearty voice. Neither heard her soft footfall on the yielding carpet, and she could not help hearing and being amused by what was said. It was as follows:

Young Jack.—"Then, as Cinnamon is the best hunter and the boldest warrior that you have ever heard of, tell me what he is just like as a man."

Sassafras.—"You mean in appearance. He is tall, and finely formed for strength, activity and endurance, dark in color even for an Indian, and not much given to fine clothes. He likes his war-paint best; and his is black and crimson. He is a capital horseman."

Young Jack.—"But I mean, what is he like in disposition?"

Sassafras.—"O! Well, he's just like one of us—Tom Scarlet and your father and me. There's no difference between a good Indian and a good white man in natural disposition. They are alike, but in different circumstances, and affected by different belongings."

Young Jack.—"Do you mean to say that the wild Indian chief of the plains and Rocky Mountains is like my father?"

Sassafras.—In disposition? yes—very much like him! And in courage, generosity and simple nobility of character he's just like Sir Jerry Snaffle and this Duke. Now, don't go and tell Lady Snaffle I said this, for I want her good opinion, and ladies are naturally prejudiced against Indians from hearing that the warriors maltreat their wives. It isn't the real truth; but then there's a color for the assertion, especially as regards the bands who loaf about the settlements and get drunk."

Lady Snaffle was about to come forward and speak, but Young Jack went on with great animation.

Young Jack.—" You will, of course, tell Cinnamon all about us, when you and he arrange for the presents to be sent over?"

Sassafras.—" Oh, he's heard about the most prominent. The chief understands a hundred times as much English as he can speak, and he heard Tom Scarlet and François talking by the hour about your sister and your father and Sir Jerry and Lady Snaffle."

Young Jack.—" And about me, too?"

Sassafras.—" No doubt you were mentioned; but, you see, the Indians think nothing of a boy until he has killed an elk, a bear or a buffalo, or drawn blood from a man. But he'll hear a good deal about you when I meet him again, and as Miriam's your staunch friend, she'll fix the chief for you when she sees him."

Young Jack.—" Ay! but the mention of me to the chief will come best, in the first place, from you, Sassafras, because you were on the war-path with him against the Sioux. But now tell me—as Cinnamon has heard about Sir Jerry and Lady Snaffle—let me know what he thinks about my lady. He may be a little prejudiced, too, you know."

Sassafras.—" The d—l a bit, Young Jack! I never heard him say what he thinks of her. I dare say nobody else ever did. It is not his custom to speak of such things. He's a man of few words, very few."

Young Jack.—" I know! like Mr. Southdown—but he talks as much as anybody else when he feels inclined, and is no way backward of giving his mind about other people."

Sassafras.—" I never heard Cinnamon *say* anything of Lady Snaffle, but I can tell well enough what he thinks of her. She is to him just about what the Queen Adelaide of England is to the chiefs and head men of the tribes north of the Canadian line. He pictures her as something great, beautiful and good; and he's right!"

The lady had heard too much to speak now, and yet she could not retreat. A blush of pleasure, but something of embarrassment mingled with it, mantled on her cheeks and tinged her neck. She knew not what to do, and the conversation between the others went on.

Young Jack.—" I may tell her ladyship what you say about that Sassafras."

Sassafras.—" No! no! not on any account; but it's all true, though."

Young Jack.—" I will tell May."

Sassafras.—" We will compromise this matter. You shall tell your sister after I am gone. If you must tell somebody before then, tell Tom Scarlet and Miriam."

Young Jack.—" What's the use of that, when they know it already? But now as to those presents—I am not to be forgotten."

Sassafras.—" O, no! You shall be remembered."

Young Jack.—" A pair of elks for Sir Jerry and Lady Snaffle; another pair for the Duke and Duchess; a buffalo bull and cow for my father; but the bear, the great grizzly bear, is to be sent to me? Remember that, Sassafras."

Sassafras.—" The elk and the buffalo will be all right. We could send a small drove of each, upon a pinch, if there was ship room. But a great grizzly bear is an ugly customer aboard, and the cotton ships roll so. I'm thinking that you had better have a cinnamon bear. It's more rare, more handsome, and, I reckon, more of a curiosity in natural history."

Young Jack (with discontent and vexation).—" Sassafras, a cinnamon bear won't do for me. I don't want a handsome bear. I don't care about natural history. I read the natural history of this country, and a good deal of it is all humbug. I want a great grizzly bear, like the one you and Cinnamon killed at the pass of the Rocky Mountains."

Sassafras.—" I see you know it all, Master Bullfinch. Well, Cinnamon and I must have a pow-wow over it, and by bringing in Pierre Langlois and his agents at Orleans, I dare say it can be done."

Young Jack.—" Thank you, Sassafras. And if you want to send over any animal for its beauty, send it to Meg Southdown. A very nice girl, Sassafras—she nearly fell out of the windmill to-day, while looking at Tom's riding. And, Sassa-fras, there is one thing more I want to say."

Sassafras.—" Very well, say it! I like to hear you talk."

Young Jack.—" When you are married to Miriam, and have reached your plantation at St. Jo., she will be four or five thousand miles from all her relatives and old acquaintances and friends. But we shall be glad for all that, Sassafras ; be-cause we shall know that, come what, come may, you will always love her and cherish her. Miriam has always been a good girl. I know the gypsies well, and I am sure of it."

Sassafras (red in face, and with lightning in the eyes).—"O, Young Jack ! there's more gold in your heart than the bucca-neers buried near the Grand Cayman. O, my boy ! you shall have the big bear, if I'm obliged to come over to bring him my-self !"

The Western man grappled the English lad to him with a sort of fond hug, and as he did so Lady Snaffle retreated towards the door. Sassafras rose, and began to apologize, although he did not know for what. But the lady then came forward with a smile, as though she had but lately entered, and extending her hand said : "I have heard of your gal-lantry. May I, too, call you friend ?"

It is very likely that Sassafras felt more overcome just then than he had ever done at the warwhoop of the Sioux and Blackfeet ; for even Young Jack was either unable to understand what he said in reply to the baronet's lady, or he had, when questioned by his sister May and by Miriam Cotswold, unac-countably forgotten it.

CHAPTER XLI.

" We were very, very merry,
  As we went to the ferry,
  For all our men were drinking;
  There were three men of mine,
  Two of thine, and three more
  Men were belonging
  To old Sir Thom of Lyne,
  And all our men were drinking."

WHEN the company at the Barleymow broke up on the evening of the day on which the steeple-chase was run, not a few of them were in case to sing the old catch quoted above. Still, they were steady on their legs and in their saddles, for the sportsmen and three-bottle men of that age were not easily shaken. Sir Jerry Snaffle was accompanied to the Hall by the Duke of Jumpover, Sir Harry Plowden and Major Fitzgerald. Lord Doomsday excused himself; but from John Bullfinch and Mr. Southdown, old and opulent tenants of his own, and freeholders in their own right, the Baronet would take no denial. Lady Snaffle received them, and the Duke, advancing, said: "I am requested, by many gentlemen, to thank your ladyship for honoring us with your presence at the steeple-chase to-day. We were all much gratified. The presence of the ladies on such occasions is always appreciated."

"The ladies, your Grace, are pleased with the sports in which our countrymen delight and excel. At steeple-chases there are few, for but a small part of them is usually to be seen. On the flat, however, we take the field in force; and while we rejoice in the success of our favorites, our regrets do not last very long when they lose. I was never before so excited as on this occasion. At one time Miss Bullfinch and I wished ourselves away. At the brook it was a fearful scene for a few moments, and we feared the worst, my Lord Duke; but in the instant of great peril we saw Mr. Scarlet rescued by the strength and skill of his friend here. It was grand, but terrible."

"It was, my lady; and no one rejoiced in the safety of Mr. Scarlet more than I," said the Duke; "but I hardly bargained for the defeat of my horse afterwards. The presence of mind, judgment and resolution of Mr. Scarlet, displayed after the accident, equalled the daring of his friend at the moment of his danger."

"And were a good deal more difficult to command, your grace," said Sassafras.

"I dare say they were, for I understand feats of daring and perilous adventure have been frequent with you. Mr. Scarlet's splendid riding at the finish routed me. All is lost but honor, Lady Snaffle. I have lost the stakes to Sir Jerry, a hogshead of Burgundy to Major Fitzgerald and a hundred ounces of gold to Sassafras."

"But not your good humor, duke," said the major. "Now there is a party from Melton gone off in the sulks on account of two hundred guineas I won of him. He had said something about the bad taste of gentlemen acting as stewards who had bets on the event, and but for Sir Jerry I should have requested him to explain what he meant, in which case an invitation to a morning walk in one of the sequestered glades of Wootton woods might have followed. But 'twas a glorious day, my lady; a Waterloo for our hunt. I would have lost my other arm sooner than have missed it."

"A loss we could not afford, major," said Lady Snaffle. "What would the ladies do if you had no longer an arm to offer?"

"Your ladyship is right, as you always are. I need it for the service of the ladies, and for the reaching of me glass of wine or punch."

There had been some general conversation, during which Mr. Southdown and Young Jack had got Sassafras a little on one side, and were putting questions touching buffalo bulls, bears and Indians, when Lady Snaffle crossed to Sir Jerry and said something in a low tone.

"By all means! It is kind and proper," said the baronet.

Lady Snaffle turned to Sassafras and said: "There is a young person I should like to see soon—this evening, if possible. I mean Miriam Cotswold. If she is at hand, with your permission, I will send for her."

"My lady, she was on the road, in a gig, with her uncle," said Young Jack. "The camp is in the hollow, close to Sir Jerry's ash spinney."

"I am grateful to your ladyship," said Sassafras. "A few words of counsel and encouragement from your ladyship will cheer her and do her good."

"Then I will send John."

"If your ladyship please," said Young Jack, loud and brisk, "it will be better to send me. The gypsies do not know John, and he does not know them. I know them all, men, women, lasses and children—from Dark Janet's mother to Rose Tanner's twins."

There was a laugh from the gentlemen and Lady Snaffle smiled. The man of few words rose with much gravity, and standing at his full height, with his great bulk displayed, he prepared to address her ladyship. At any other time he would not have ventured upon a speech to her, but he had virtually nominated Sir Jerry for the county, and what was more he had imbibed a great many glasses of gin and water at the Barley-mow.

"My lady," said Mr. Southdown, "the gentlemen laughed at what Young Jack said, but it is really no laughing matter. Among the gypsies there are some rum customers, as the keepers and constables find. Now, Young Jack knows them all, and he is a good boy. Sassafras, my lady, a man of large experience in boys and what not, agrees with me in this."

Her ladyship bowed, and looked archly at the Duke, then with a smile at May Bullfinch and Tom Scarlet. The latter was rather red in the face, and John Bullfinch had attempted to pull Mr. Southdown back. But the man of few words stood like a tower, and went on:

"I say, my lady, that Jack's suggestion is good, and it isn't the first time that one of the Bullfinches has aided this house in council or battle. On the monument to the four baronets of this family who were killed in the wars of the Roses, it is stated that when they marched to battle along with the stout Earl of Warwick, the Bullfinches always went with 'em hundreds strong."

"Southdown, you are right; the family is as old as my own in the county," said Sir Jerry.

"I know I'm right; my mind's made up on the p'int, your honor. If it was not, I should not venture to go on in this way to her ladyship. The Bullfinches being of a good old family, and John being a tenant of Sir Jerry's, as well as holding his own farm of Hawk'ell, when May was christened your ladyship stood godmother to her. When Young Jack was christened I stood godfeyther to him. A year after that my youngest daater, Meg——"

"Margery, Mr. Southdown, a beautiful old English name," said Lady Snaffle.

"Yes, her mother and sisters call her Margery, but I call her Meg, my lady, and so does Young Jack. When Meg was christened, John Bullfinch stood godfeyther to *her*. Well, my lady and gentlemen all, what naturally follows? Sassafras, as good a man as ever put boot in stirrup, means to marry Miriam Cotswold. Tom Scarlet, another out-and-out good man, means to——"

Lady Snaffle interposed and prevented the grazier from completing the sentence.

"Well, then, my lady," said he, "I'll come to the real p'int. Here's Young Jack! as good a boy as ever was—capital rider, and the best judge of the p'ints of a horse or a bullock, of his age, in these Midland counties. They may have boys in Lunnon who know more, or in Oxford college."

"Sir, they have got none who know any more anywhere, except aboard the men-of-war," said the Admiral, stalking in with Mainbrace in close attendance. "My sentiments on this subject are well known to my daughter, Lady Snaffle, also to Sir Jerry, whose father went to sea at fourteen in the Seahorse. I was ten."

"Very well, Admiral and my lady, and gentlemen all, Young Jack being an excellent boy—pattern to the youth of the country side, and a real good bred 'un, and my youngest daater Meg being a good girl, comely lass, and so on, my mind's made up. John Bullfinch's mind's made up. So is my wife's. If your ladyship has no objection, when the young people come to years of—of what you call it——"

"Discretion," said Young Jack.

"Ay, to years of discretion, their minds will be made up."

Lady Snaffle shook Mr. Southdown's hand and patted Young Jack on the head, whereupon the grazier said, "I was agoing to say something touching the wedding between——"

"Meg and me?" said Young Jack.

"No, between May and Tom Scarlet, who——"

Mr. Southdown was here interrupted by John Bullfinch, and he concluded somewhat abruptly by recommending that Young Jack should be sent for Miriam.

"And for company's sake, if Lady Snaffle pleases, I will go with him," said Sassafras.

"A moment," said the Duke. "When you return from the camp I shall be gone. Before you leave England I should like to show you my horses and hounds. Visit me. I will mount you well. Do you know that you are unlike the Americans of books and of the stage?"

"Duke, I never met a man in America, or anywhere else, who was not unlike them, and Tom Scarlet will say the same," replied Sassafras. "That which I have seen in books and on the stage, as the language and manners of Americans at home is just about as much like them as what goes on in the Punch and Judy show is like life as I see it here in England. Besides, there is fun in the Punch and Judy, but none in this kind of books and acting."

" I suspect you are right in that."

" If your Grace and Sir Jerry Snaffle could visit America and join me at St. Jo., we might have fine sport among the elk and buffalo, to say nothing of the bears, which are large and fierce. With Cinnamon and some of his young men for guides and escort, we could hunt the parks of the Rocky Mountains, and shoot where a white man has hardly ever fired a rifle shot."

" I thank you, Sassafras," said the Duke. " The offer is a tempting one, but we should find it almost impossible to spare the time. Visit me if you can, and be assured I shall always wish you well."

After a drive of four or five miles in one of Sir Jerry Snaffle's numerous vehicles, Sassafras and Young Jack drew up near the camp. The tents were pitched and the fires were blazing brightly in a sheltered glen, bounded on one side by a thick growth of young ash trees, on the other by clumps of gorse. Sassafras jumped out, and at the same moment two or three young gypsies, the scouts of the tribe, came out of the fern and underwood and saluted him with a sort of shy deference as he passed on towards the tent of their chief.

About half an hour later he reached the Hall with Miriam and Young Jack. Lady Snaffle's footman received them, and in a few minutes her maid advanced to conduct Sassafras and Miriam to her ladyship's cabinet. The lady's maid was a brunette, rather small, but with a well-rounded and graceful figure, handsome features, and deep, black eyes. She was a favorite of Lady Snaffle's. In fact, this young girl had been brought up at the Hall. Her grandfather, a sailor, who had married a Spanish girl in the Indies, had been killed at the battle of the Nile. The widow and her daughter found refuge on the Admiral's estate when Lady Snaffle was a girl. The daughter married one of the Admiral's coxswains, a younger man than Mainbrace, and Miss Kitty Ruffle was their child. What passed in Lady Snaffle's cabinet in the presence of May Bullfinch, Miriam Cotswold and Sassafras, the lady's maid did not know. She assured the housekeeper, the cook and the butler, however, that the interview must have been very touching as well as long, for when Sassafras and Miriam came out it was plain that she had been crying. She was then, however, calm again, and looking very well content and happy. "And the American," Miss Ruffle continued, "looked very much pleased. As indeed he ought to be, for he will have the countenance of my lady in marrying, he owns an estate of hundreds of acres in America—thousands, Master Bullfinch says—and he has won a hundred ounces of gold from the Duke."

"Then, miss, he ought to be ashamed of himself," said the butler.

Later in the evening Lady Snaffle inquired of Sir Jerry where he had left her father. "My lady," said Sir Jerry, "the Admiral has left me, and taken the Major with him. He sent for the topman Cooper, and the sailor Cox, and is now in his room expounding the rules of the service and fighting the Battle of Trafalgar over a huge bowl of rum-punch compounded by his man."

CHAPTER XLII.

"Through the house give glimmering light,
 By the dead and drowsy fire,
Every elf and fairy sprite
 Hop as light as bird from brier."

"Thus passeth yere by yere, and day by day,
 Till it fell once, in a morne of May."

"When the merry bells ring round,
 And the jockund rebecks sound
 To many a youth and many a maid
 Dancing in the chequer'd shade."

ONCE again stout John Bullfinch sat in his great arm-chair, alone, near the middle watch of the night. His daughter, May, the good, the fond, the bright, the beautiful, was to be married the next day, and John was full of thought and reflection. He recalled all the stages of her growth and

being, from infancy and prattling, toddling childhood to that
very hour—that budding hour of womanhood, when she was
so like her mother, as he had courted and married her more
than twenty years before. The same sweet face and wealth of
clustering hair; the same lithe, rounded figure; the same glad
and kind disposition. The fire had dwindled low upon the
hearth, and all was still. The great mastiff, Fury, sat upon
her haunches, and with her deep-set eyes looked up into her
master's face, as though she knew they were about to part with
the Rose of Hawk'ell—the one fair daughter of the brave old
house. She put her head upon the farmer's knee, and when
the clock struck twelve uttered a low growl, as if to protest
against the interruption of the solemn silence. Soon she rose
and walked gravely and silently to the door. The farmer, following, opened it. The light of the May moon and the song of the
nightingale from the bosky blackthorn grove came rushing
into the house. A step was heard, and then John Bullfinch
saw the erect form of the keeper, as he came along by the
hawthorn hedge.

"Dick, this is kind, very kind and thoughtful!" said John,
as they passed into the house.

"I thought," said Moleskin, putting his gun gently down,
"that you might not object to see an old friend of the family
to-night. To-morrow there will be many people here."

"Nobody who'll be more welcome than you, Dick."

The keeper shook John's hand, and there was a curious
movement of the muscles about the mouth and at the corners
of his eyes, as if the cast-iron visage was being acted on by
the heat and glow within.

"Having made my rounds and found all reasonably safe,"
said he, "I determined to walk over here. I never sleep 'o
nights. When you go to bed I shall keep ward here, and can
call you betimes for the preparations of the morning."

"I have no inclination for bed," said John. "I have been
sitting here listening to the ticking of the clock, and thinking
of all May's life and pretty ways, and what she has been to
me, and everybody else in this house, since the sad day I lost
her mother. You know she is just like her mother; and it
almost seems as if I was going to lose *her* over again. Yet

26

there's no reason to doubt May's happiness with Tom Scarlet, is there?"

"None at all. My opinion is, that they'll be very happy. She has that winning way with her that'll always prevail with him; and mark my words, John, she'll rule her husband! Therefore, they'll be very happy."

"Sir," said John, "you speak like an ignorant old bachelor."

"Very likely. I tell you I conclude that happy will be their lot, from the fact that she'll rule him. The lightest touch on the bridle and he'll obey the bit. No more sauntering and dawdling along by the cover sides o' moonlight nights when the leverets play and the pheasants crow upon the larches. No going out with Gypsy Jack and Rose Tanner's man to dig out badgers. No more goings off to America without so much as by your leave. Still, I can understand your feelings. She will be looked up to hereafter more as Tom's wife than your daater. The preserve is poached into, you see. On the other hand we may say, 'A mantrap has gone off, and he's caught for life.' That's how things stand, eh?"

"Another time I should have been angry," said John. "Mantrap!"

"If you could get into a passion and blow somebody up sky-high, it would do you good," said the keeper. "Where's Young Jack?"

"He went up-stairs with May. They went hand in hand," replied John. "I heard them talking since, and was twice at the stair-foot, softly. I wouldn't have stopped them in their conversation for the world. It was all about me, Dick. The boy mentioned Tom, once or twice, as near as I could make out, but May's talk was of her father?"

"It was natural," said the keeper. "She is about to leave you, in a measure; and her heart clings to her father, though she is about to have a husband to cleave to. Then a woman can have but one father; whereas, though I dare say it never occurred to May, she may have two or three husbands before she has done."

"If you talk like that I would prefer to be alone again," said John.

"Sitting here all alone, in the middle of the night, has not been good for you," said Moleskin. "It has made you melancholy."

"Serious, but not melancholy," replied John. "It did not appear to me that I was alone. My children were above-stairs, and I felt as though the spirit of their mother, my wife, was near—come back to comfort me, and be as a guardian angel to her daughter at this time. You will think this a strange fancy of mine, but I had it strong."

"Not so strange," replied Moleskin. "I am myself a lonely man, and pass many nights in the still woods or over the embers in the solitary lodge; yet it often seems at such times that I am not *all* alone. Considering what a good woman—one of ten thousand—your wife was, and how she loved you and her children with all her heart, I think that at this time she may be near."

There was a silence of some minutes after this, broken by John Bullfinch:

"You mustn't leave the house in the morning. There will be people enough about, but I want you and Ransome; he is to be here to breakfast. Southdown will not come so early, but his wife and daughters will drive over betimes, to take charge of May. Mrs. Hickman and Mary will also be here."

"I have come to stay," said the keeper. "My best things are in the pockets of this shooting-coat, and ten minutes in your room will be all I shall want. But now about Tom—how does he seem to stand it?"

"Wonderful! wonderful!" said John. "He was here till ten, and would have stayed till now, mayhap, if he had had his own way. He's very cool and pleasant, and not at all bashful."

"He never was, that I know of," said the keeper.

"Yes, he was; not in a general way, but I remember when he would sit and look at May, and have never a word to say to her, though he could talk glib enough to me. I think he's a little disappointed, because Sassafras couldn't stay. I would give a twenty-pound note myself to have him here."

"To my mind, he's just as well away," said Moleskin. "The man himself is a good man, straightforward in manner and action—word as good as bond; but——"

"But what, sir? I like the man, and you had better not let Southdown hear you say anything against him. If you do, you'll find that his mind is made up."

"The man himself is a man I would trust anywhere," said Moleskin, "even in the best preserves in October, though he's a dead shot, and could cut a pheasant down with a rifle ball off the tallest roost, every time; but I can't answer for some of his cronies. As long as he was here I had little rest. Gypsies, roving sailors, and other fellows, whose presence bodes no good to the health of the game, were always straying about. Out of respect for Sir Jerry and you, and considering that he was well liked by the ladies, I said nothing; but that gypsy camp was here too long at one time. Then that Cox and Jim Cooper, instead of going off to blue-water and staying there, as they promised to do, they comes to an anchor, as they called it, in this neighborhood, and got three or four more like themselves, drinking and skylarking, and setting a bad example generally. When the American went the whole covey took wing. The American was well enough. I liked him. He had a very true eye, and the proper insight into the ways of birds and animals; but he was not up to the nature of our English scamps."

"It could hardly be expected," said John. "He associated with no one, to speak of, except Tom and Southdown, and you and me."

"Didn't he! I say that when occasion offered, or chance threw them in his way, he was well met by every poacher, fighter and loose-liver in these parts. I never told you of the supper they gave him at the Running Horse, over by Heyford Leys. I have it from Lord Jersey's keeper that every known scamp in Buckinghamshire, Oxfordshire, Northamptonshire and Warwickshire was present. That fellow Tom Barton had come up from Warwickshire with one Ford, who has been in America—known poachers both, as the keepers of the Duke of Grafton and Lord Southampton are well aware. After being introduced to Sassafras, this fellow Barton proposed that they should do honor to the Crown and to Major Fitzgerald and the Admiral, by being presided over by the Army and Navy. So they put the recruiting sergeant of the Fusileers into the cheer. If he had only enlisted the company there and then, it would have been a good thing. Jim Tanner was vice-president, and the fun was fast and furious. The fact is they drank everything the landlord had in the house, and at break of day brought off a little battle, for a sovereign a side, between two of the serjeant's new recruits. The keeper at Middleton says that, next to the American, the most respectable man in the room was Jack Cotswold."

" Wasn't Tom Scarlet present ?" said John.

" He was not. You'll observe that since his engagement to your daughter was made public, and the wedding generally spoken of, he has been at your house every night."

" It is true," said John, rising. " Now, Dick, I'll go to bed. Call me, softly, at break of day."

" Break of day will be here in no time."

" The sooner the better. Call me at the earliest flushing of the dawn."

Morning bright and beautiful! A flitting up and down of beauties just as bright, about the young bride's chamber. Mrs. Southdown and her two eldest daughters had arrived in fine array. Mrs. Hickman and pretty Mary had come in brave attire. And there were other ladies and young maidens, pretty and fluttering, talking in hasty half whisperings. The toilet of the bride began. One of Sir Jerry Snaffle's carriages drove up and the housekeeper and lady's maid stepped out of it. The old lady, stiff and stately in brocade, curtesied with antique ceremony to the other ladies as she entered the bride's room. Miss Ruffle minced daintily in, and with sparkling eyes surveyed and comprehended everything. The bridesmaids, already dressed, and much too elegant and helpless to be of assistance to their principal, were favored with a nod of approval. The other ladies, endeavoring by advice and counsel to direct Patty, the housemaid, in her feeble efforts to bind and compel May's luxuriant tresses, were not so rewarded, for Miss Ruffle stared and said, " O !"

Had Mrs. Southdown been gifted with the powers of her husband, she would, no doubt, have replied to this exclamation; but she was not. Besides, the stout and rosy lady was "worrited" about her youngest daughter, who had been left at home by her father's express command, to come with him. Mrs. Southdown had remonstrated, and pointed out the fact, that Margery was the fourth and youngest bridesmaid, but her husband had replied : " My mind's made up ! John Bullfinch will never let his daater leave for the church before I get there."

So, unable to reply to Miss Ruffle's exclamation, Mrs. Southdown stood with a ribbon in one hand and a frill in the other, and looked at the black-eyed invader. She had not long to look, for by virtue of certain pearls, certain laces, certain wreaths, certain satin shoes, etc., derived from Lady Snaffle, "lessor of the plaintiff," as Mr. Doublefee would have called her, Miss Ruffle brought her action of ejectment, *Kitty Doe* v. *Rachel Roe et al.*, and, taking possession of the bride, proceeded to adorn her according to her own art and mystery.

Mr. Southdown pulled up his gig at Hawkwell, near a group of about half a dozen of the cousins of John Bullfinch, who were standing in the morning sunshine, talking, not of bridals, but of the condition of the crops and the state of the markets. They were florid, festive-looking men, with the large noses and strong jaws of the family; all were booted and spurred, and all had nosegays of Mayflowers in their buttonholes. John Bullfinch, Ransome and Moleskin had rushed out at the sight of the gig, and they exclaimed, cousins and all, "Late, Southdown!" as he pulled up.

"Late be hanged! I shan't argey the p'int! I ain't late, but still I see no use in wasting time in argeyment," said Mr. Southdown, taking John's arm and striding to the door. "I saw Sir Jerry's carriage; he and Lady Snaffle will be at the church."

He forgot all about his daughter Margery, youngest and fairest of the Southdown flock, who was left sitting in the gig. But Young Jack, very smartly dressed, as he had been from an early hour, came forward. The maiden took his hands and jumped out, bounding up about a foot when her toes came to the ground, and laughing gleefully.

"I was so disappointed when your mother and sisters came without you," said Jack.

"Were you? O, dear! how smart you are!"

"To be sure! We will walk together, you know."

"Yes, we will. I've been so put about. The dresses didn't come home until late last evening. My sisters—mind, this is a secret—couldn't sleep, and got up in the night to try theirs on. This morning there was such a time. It was Margery here, Margery there, and they were so long, that they had to go before I could be dressed. I had no one to help me dress but our maids Dolly and Jane, but we managed it, with father storming at the stair-foot. How do I look, Jack ?"

"Beautiful! charming! You'll beat all but May, I can tell you," said he, as the laughing maiden spun round, and shook her muslin flounces.

"Shall we go in now ?" said she.

"No," replied Young Jack. "We'll just step to the stables : I want to show you something I have got there. Mind, it is a secret !"

"What! is the bear come, Jack ?"

"Why, no. There hasn't been time yet. Sassafras isn't much more than landed in America. Come along."

Miss Margery was picking her way upon the tips of her slippers, by Young Jack's side, when a housemaid came down upon them full sail, ribbons and frills below and aloft, crying, "Miss Margery! Miss Margery Southdown !"

"I say, Meg!" roared the grazier from the parlor window, and the maiden stopped in dismay. The housemaid, red as her own ribbons, said, "Lord bless us, miss! Your ma and sisters be in such a taking. The bride's dressed! The bride-groom and his young men are here! The ladies are a'most ready to come down stairs, and you a rambling round with young master !"

The gentlemen stood near the parlor door. There was the whisper of voices, the rustle of muslin and silk above, and down came the bevy about the young bride. May, leaning on her father's arm, passed out, and as she crossed the threshold her hand was laid upon the great head of the wise, faithful mastiff, Fury. Mrs. Southdown followed with Tom Scarlet, who looked like a lord, as the servant maids declared. Then the brides-maids, and at a little distance a lot of friends. It was a walk of more than a mile to the church. On the bush at the gar-den gate merrily piped the linnet. On the plum-tree bough, all among the blossoms, the goldfinch made sweet music. All along the spangled hedgerows of the pasture-land bullfinches flew and whistled loud and clear, in salutation to their name-sake, the bride. The young colts and heifers stopped in their frisky gambols to stare at her. Over her head the skylark sang "a dropping from the sky." And she was beautiful? In her fair face mingled the blooming badges of two lines of kings, for—

> " The red and the white rose
>   As all the country knows,
> Were the emblems of the foes
>   In a long and bloody strife !"

They rose the hill, and over the elms of the old churchyard came the merry peal of the marriage bells from the stout stone tower. Sir Jerry and Lady Snaffle met them at the church door and walked up the main aisle to the chancel with them. The Rev. Mr. Jericho was ready. The church was full. The housekeeper, the cook, and the ladies' maid from the Hall were in a front pew in the gallery, from which all the proceedings could be seen. The cook was eloquent over the beauty of the bride, the handsome face and fine figure of the bridegroom, with a few remarks upon the bridesmaids. The ceremony was over. " Fast bind, fast find." Tom Scarlet and May Bullfinch were man and wife. " He has kissed her !" said the cook. " So has her father! so has Sir Jerry!"

" The idea of mentioning it, ma'am," said the ladies' maid.

" Why not? It is proper and customary, my dear—the kissing of the bride—to a certain extent; and so you'll find when your turn comes. What next!" she added, hastily. "Of all the boys of that age, for coolness he bears the bell."

" What boy, ma'am? and what has he done?"

" What boy! why, Young Jack. He'll come to the altar himself—that I plainly see—and before long. As he paced down the aisle, as large as life, with Meg Southdown on his arm, he cocked his head to one side, and winked up here."

"Shocking! the audacity?" said Miss Ruffle. " If he had a mamma she should be told of it. I have a great mind to tell Lady Snaffle."

" You had better not," said the housekeeper. "I have found Master Bullfinch a very well-behaved youth, and my lady has often said as much. There must have been a mistake as to his winking up here. If he did wink up here, it must be attributed to the agitation of the moment, and his respect for the family."

" Ay, perhaps that was it," said the cook. " He could hardly wink at Sir Jerry, especially as his honor's back was to him then, and so diverted his respect to us."

The wedding party had walked to the church, for that was in conformity with custom, with prognostications of luck, and with the settled notions of John Bullfinch, Mr. Southdown and all the cousins, male and female, of the Bullfinch blood; but they went back to Hawkwell in vehicles and on horseback, amidst the plaudits of the people, and attended by the joyful pealing of the bells. Mrs. Hickman took upon herself the marshalling of the guests to the great tables spread indoors and out. It was not then the custom, which has been heard of in some places since, for the bridegroom and bride to stand up for a while before the company, and then take an opportunity to escape by stealth, as if they had stolen the old people's spoons, or done something else to be mortally ashamed of. No, Mr. and Mrs. Scarlet would have the places of honor at the feast. When they left for a little excursion to Stowe, the seat of the Duke of Buckingham, the slippers would fly out after them, while tabor and pipe struck up, and the lads and lasses began their dances in the orchard. And when at night, on their return, with their bridesmaids and grooms, they reached the Grange, the door-posts would be hung with myrtle, and Tom, taking his bride round the waist with his strong arm, would " over the threshold lift her in."

This order of events was a little delayed by the sudden arrival of Mr. Doublefee, who, fiery hot with haste, rushed up to Tom Scarlet and May, and shook their hands.

" Hem! you were about to sit down," said he. " I crave a delay of a few minutes on a matter of great importance. Mr. Bullfinch, Mr. Southdown, I bring intelligence of weight and import to the future standing and happiness of the amiable couple whose nuptials are the occasion of general joy. I endeavored to get here before the wedding——"

" The villain!" said old Mrs. Oatford to her niece. " He would have stopped it if he could."

" But," continued the lawyer, " though I flew upon the wings of——"

" Love!" said Young Jack, with Meg Southdown's arm snugly tucked under his own.

" Not exactly love, my young friend. We can hardly call it love in the pleadings. Let us rather say the wings of law and equity and testamentary proceedings."

" What have they to do with this wedding?" said Mr. Southdown. " There's nobody dead!"

"Yes there is, though!" replied Mr. Doublefee; "and what is more the deceased made a will, as my client Mr. Scarlet and Miss May Bullfinch that was, now *feme covert*, will find, duly proved."

"*Feme covert!*" cried Mrs. Oatford, "what does the man mean? I declare it's an insult."

"Nothing of the kind, madam. It means female joined in wedlock—a married lady."

"Go on, and come to the p'int, sir," said Mr. Southdown.

"Hem! I may say that I came to that a day or two ago; but I shall now do so as briefly as possible. Some fifty years ago a certain *feme sole*, a spinster of the Scarlet family, offended her relations by running off with the mate of a West India-man and getting married to him. Nothing was heard of him or her for many years.

"Now stop!" said Admiral Broadside, from the great arm-chair. "You say this man was mate of a West Indiaman fifty years ago."

"I do, sir; and I can prove the fact to the satisfaction of any intelligent jury."

"Then, sir," said the Admiral, "that mate must have known the landlady's daughter at Port Royal, who was very beau-tiful, and just like the bride of to-day. This will corroborate the case, sir."

"Thank you, sir!" said Mr. Doublefee, and continued: "Young Crosstree and his wife soon removed from Bristol, and the mate, promoted to be captain of a brigantine, sailed out of Liverpool, trading to the west coast of Africa. Mrs. Margaret Crosstree, the captain's wife, was energetic and industrious. She took possession of her husband's money every time he was in port, and invested it. The captain, a man of jovial disposition, with a constitution capable of en-during any—a—a——"

"Climate," said Young Jack.

"Yes, climate, too; but I was about to say any amount of hard drinking—became a great favorite with the African chiefs—kings of Bonny, Old Calabar, &c., and especially with the renowned potentate Ja Ja Jumbo. He made much money for his owners, having a sort of monopoly of some sorts of trade whenever he was there, and he also made a good deal of money for himself. In fact, it was more than sufficient to buy a snug estate of three hundred acres, arable and pasture, with a substantial dwelling-house and appurtenances. Mrs. Margaret made the purchase. The captain contented himself with naming the place, which he called the Cameroons. Mrs. Margaret lived in the house. The land was let at a fair rental. Some years passed, and at length the worthy captain died, in the Bight of Biafra, of the coast-fever, the sailors said, but the surgeon of the man-of-war then upon the station said, 'of too much rum.' But dead he was, and his will was proved, leaving the Cameroons in fee to Mrs. Margaret, together with all his personal property. She continued to live at The Cameroons, with two female servants and a gardener, and as she grew old became eccentric. The fact that she abused her relations was nothing, because it is very common. But she talked of leaving all her property to some benevolent society. It is not certain that she would ever have been able to determine which; but something occurred quite recently to divert her intentions. From her windows she saw, one day in January, two men and a boy come into the dairy ground of The Cameroons with a White Horse, which was mounted and galloped. The trespass was complete, and Mrs. Margaret had a mind to compel her tenant to sue; but she first sent her gardener to question the parties. Before he got to them, one of the men, the boy, and the horse had regained the public road; but he returned to Mrs. Margaret with the other man, one Sassafras."

" I thought it would come to him when I heard of the White Horse. Eh, Southdown?" said John Bullfinch.

" I remember the place well enough. It is within nine miles of Chester. We went there because we observed that the dairy ground was good going when our usual working place was hard from frost," said Tom Scarlet.

" Hem! I do not mind your admitting that, but as to anything further, I beg of you to consult your legal adviser, myself," said Mr. Doublefee. He then continued: " What I am now about to disclose is not only of vast importance to you and Mrs. Scarlet, but will be of great interest to all the ladies and gentlemen present, who may be said to be counsel in the cause. Mrs. Margaret fancied that Sassafras was a good deal like her late husband when she first saw him, and asked him if he was not a sailor."

"He looked like one," said Tom.

"I protest against any further admissions on your part, Mr. Scarlet, until we have had a consultation. Sassafras said he was not a sailor, but admitted that he had once gone upon an expedition to an isle in the Carribbean Sea, near what is called—the name escapes me at the moment——"

"The Grand Cayman!" said Young Jack.

"Yes, the Grand Cayman. Mrs. Margaret mentioned the trespass and directed her handmaid to set out a bottle of rum. They discussed the subject matter. Sassafras took his neat and cold. The venerable lady had hers in the shape of hot toddy, compounded by the maid, whose practice had been large. Sassafras recited the history of Tom Scarlet, his love for Miss Bullfinch, and the engagement of the White Horse. The venerable relict of the worthy captain asked many questions, and made a few comments. When Sassafras left she arose, and with what he called a lightning flash in her eyes, said, 'If he's a true Scarlet, and the man he ought to be, he'll win this race!'"

Loud applause interrupted Mr. Doublefee, and Tom Scarlet was about to speak, but the former interposed, hastily saying, "No admissions! Not a word! Now mark me," said Mr. Doublefee, with a triumphant air, "five days after the steeple-chase, to wit, Mrs. Margaret sent for her man of business—meaning her attorney—and upon his arrival she then and there executed a will. It devised handsome legacies to her servants, and then bequeathed all the rest of her estate, real and personal—The Cameroons of three hundred acres in a ring fence, with much valuable timber, constituting the former, and the latter consisting of money in the funds, and in a bank in Liverpool—to her well-beloved cousin, Tom Scarlet of the Grange, but upon the condition that he married May Bullfinch, whose grandfather the testator had known in her youth. The conditions really amounted to nothing, for he is next of kin, and would have taken in that capacity if the will had failed. Mrs. Margaret's health failed rapidly from the time she made her will, and ten days ago she died. If she had survived a month longer, it was her intention to invite Mr. and Mrs. Scarlet to the Cameroons, and put them in possession. As it is, her man of business and myself have put everything in proper train, and I now announce, without hesitation, that my client, Mr. Thomas Scarlet of The Grange, residuary legatee and survivor of Mrs. Margaret Crosstree of the Cameroons, recently deceased, has an indefeasible title."

"Sir, you are a credit to your profession," said Mr. Southdown, "and it now appears to me, that what with the Grange and the Cameroons, Tom Scarlet is a rich man."

"And that makes no difference to him except so far as it may please his wife," said Tom. "We really owe this estate to Sassafras, for I never saw cousin——"

"No admissions! Not another word!" cried Mr. Doublefee.

"Now, I think," said Young Jack, "if everybody pleases, that it's all owing to the White Horse, and as I have him in the stable, next box to Cowslip, I propose to bring him out when we have eaten the wedding breakfast, and distributed the bride-cake."

CHAPTER XLIII.

THE finishing of "THE WHITE HORSE OF WOOTTON" will be but the winding up of a tale that is told, as he made no more races, but remained at Hawkwell, the admired of John Bullfinch, Tom Scarlet, Southdown, Ransome and Young Jack. His sons out of Cowslip and Young Cowslip were famous hunters and steeple-chasers. Sassafras reached America after a stormy passage, and was married quietly to Miriam Cotswold in the presence of a few friends of his father and mother. A week after the wedding he presented himself at the office of Mr. Leith, greatly to the delight of Duncan, who had the account made up. The truth is that Duncan had been in sore trouble in respect to Sassafras for some months. In the preceding winter old Mr. Leith had come in one morning in a heat, and told Duncan that they must "haud the gear together" for Sassafras; for, said he, "he's awa' aff to England wi' anither daft loon of the same stamp and a race-horse, and ye ken, Duncan, they English would just tak' the eyes oot of a man's head in any dealings about race-horses, and the like of things that goes on at Newmarket. Why could na' the chiel stay here ?"

" Aweel, sir," said Duncan, "Sassafras is no' that easy to beat in regard to horses and racing, as I have heard from mair than ane. He may beat tha Southron bodies at their own game at Newmarket."

" I have na muckle hopes of ony such thing, Duncan. Ye'll find he'll come back a broken man."

Therefore, when Duncan found Sassafras in presence, his joyful greeting was mixed with lamentations over the losses he supposed the Western man had incurred.

" Losses !" said Sassafras, " man alive, what losses ? I'm richer by thousands of dollars than I was when I went away."

" Save us, Sassafras ! Ye dinna mean to avouch that ye ha' beat the English at Newmarket ?"

" Why, no ! not at Newmarket, but in the Midland Counties, Duncan, the famous Vale of Aylesbury. We won a steeple-chase for a thousand pounds a side, and I had a bet with the Duke of Jumpover for a hundred ounces of gold."

" Lord save us ! a thousand pund sterling ! I'd gie a bawbee if oor Mr. Leith was in the day. He's awa to New York, but in course ye'll wait his return. A hundred ounces of gold ! And of a Duke, too ! I hope he didna pay ye wi' a bill ! Tha Dukes is no' that sure of a cash balance at their bankers."

" He paid in Bank of England notes, and here they are," said Sassafras. " The man is a trump—real gentleman ! so were all that I met with in the little Island over yonder. I want to deposit these notes with you for the present."

" My certie, Sassafras, the sight of them is gude for sair een. Ye ken we've nae sich banks here as yon Bank of England."

Sassafras then explained that he had won a wife, as well as the wealth, and meant to take her out to visit a cousin in the country. When he returned they would have a settlement as to the tobacco, robes and furs.

" And thereby, man, I hae a tale to tell," said Duncan, eagerly. " Ye'll mind the silver fox-skins ye made a present of to oor Miss Janet ? We sent them to Lunnon to be dressed and made up. At the beginning of the winter they were returned. Miss Janet first wore them to church. Sassafras, ye shuld hae seen all the leddies eyeing the silver fox furs, and ready to faint wi' envy. Ye see, the puir bodies had naething on but mink and otter—the very best of them—and some naething but red fox and muskrat, while oor Miss Janet was just resplendent in the silver fox fit for a princess. Man, the vera minister could na' tak' his eyes aff her. Mr. Leith was fu' o' pride—mair sae than was proper for the place. As for Angus McTartar—he's coorting her, ye ken—when we got hame he just threw aff his hat and coat and daucit the Hieland fling while the young leddy was up-stairs. 'Twas wrang on the Sabbath, Sassafras, but ye see tha Hieland lovers hae na that reverence that beseems the day."

Sassafras and his bride spent a week or two at Pierce's, and Elizabeth was much pleased with her cousin. On the evening of the day they left for the West, Pierce stood behind his bar, intently regarding his man Jake. Finally he produced the peach and honey, and, with a pantomimic gesture, signified that the negro should help himself.

"Mrs. Sassafras, Jake, may not have *all* the accomplishments of Mrs. Pierce—Elizabeth—but she's a very beautiful woman."

"Dar' no handsomer young 'oman, sa, in de Ole Dominion," returned Jake.

"And her manners, Jake, and her style, are superior."

"Why, of course, Pierce," said the voice of Elizabeth, from the stairs. "My cousin, Miriam, is not only an English lady, but in some sort a daughter of the Old Dominion, Pierce, being a descendant of Captain John Smith and the Princess Pocahontas, Pierce!"

It was some years before Elizabeth was undeceived as to this matter.

Five months after Sassafras and Miriam reached the plantation there was a meeting at the trading-post between them and the Indian chief, who had come eastward with a band of his young men for the purpose of greeting his old friends. He brought many presents for Miriam, and there arrangements were made for the shipment of the elk, the buffalo and Young Jack's bear upon the Arkansas. The precise locality of this post is in dispute. Some think it was in Arkansas, some in Missouri, some in the territory of the Cherokees, and some carry it much further west into Kansas. The precise place of the events related is not of much moment. The post is like Prospero's Isle.

"Since that time the Isle hath been
By wandering sailors never seen."

When Sassafras became a father he gave up his roving habits to a considerable extent, though he still went West nearly every fall to hunt with the chief of the Cheyennes about the forks of the Canadian river.

Once only Cinnamon visited him at the plantation near St. Jo., but he did not remain long. He was soon head chief of his great tribe, but nothing could ever induce him to pay a visit to his "Great Father at Washington." The only white man, besides Sassafras, for whom the chief had a high respect was the late General Harney. Much communication was kept up between Sassafras and his wife and their English friends. When the Duke of Jumpover's nephews visited America, and the plantation at St. Jo., to hunt with Sassafras and go out upon the plains to Cinnamon's country, the young lads who went with them were called respectively Tom Scarlet Sassafras and John Bullfinch Sassafras, and the beautiful dark-eyed young girl whom they left with her mother at the plantation answered to the name of May. The Frenchmen, Jules and Antoine, were also of the party, and many trophies of the chase were secured.

It was on their return from this expedition that Sassafras brought the party to a halt in a wild and broken spot, and said: "This is the very place where the Choctaw killed Captain Staples. You see, the captain had hired the Indian to track Tom Scarlet and me; and when the old man sought his camp, after the doings at the ford, he found the Indian there. The fact is that the Choctaw found he had been duped in the pay. A difficulty arose. The captain pulled a pistol, but he was too slow, for the Indian jumped in with his knife, and that settled it."

The elk, the buffalo and the bear had arrived in England long before that time, and the former bred in Sir Jerry Snaffle's park and in that of the Duke of Jumpover. But the bear was not a success. At first, from his huge size and his fierceness, he was the wonder of the country side, and the delight of Young Jack. But trouble soon began. Moleskin complained to John Bullfinch, as they sat over their pipes and ale, that the bear attracted all sorts of rough characters to the neighborhood from Oxford, Banbury, Birmingham, Coventry and the Black Country. The truth is that for some time the "fancy" of those parts could not be persuaded that their bulldogs and mastiffs were not equal to the baiting of young Bullfinch's bear, and on a Sunday some twenty or thirty men, with as many dogs, used to assemble at the saw-pit, in which the bear was chained. Finally matters came to a climax. Barton and Ford arrived with four powerful bull mastiffs, descended from the famous bitch who had taken the lion Wallace by the hock, and made him roar with anguish, when he fought the six dogs at Warwick for a thousand pounds. Ford protested that Bullfinch's American bear was not a fair bear, and claimed that the four dogs should be slipped at once. If it had been a "Rooshian" bear, he protested that he would have been content to let go one at a time. After some altercation Young Jack stipulated for two at a time, and down the slope into the pit they went, set on by Barton. The others were furious, and Ford, pretending that he was unable to hold them, let them go too. A desperate fight ensued. Finally, the bear broke the collar to which his chain was attached, and climbed out of the pit. Before he could be got in again he hurt three or four men and a short-horn bull, and was eventually shot by Moleskin in the brisket.

But if Master Bullfinch experienced some disappointment and a failure in regard to the bear, he soon had a notable triumph in another respect. His was a busy life for a youth. In spring and summer and in the ripe time of harvest he was a-field early and late, and during the winter, in the hunting season, he was chief confidant and adviser of young Lord Doomsday. On the great day when Lord Doomsday with Blue Peter beat his brothers-in-law in a steeple-chase down the Vale, Jack was in his glory. Tom Scarlet had trained the horse, and Master Bullfinch had ridden him in his work. The line was the same as that over which the White Horse ran. The brothers-in-law not only got into the big brook, but fell at Barker's Bullfinch as well; but, as Rose Tanner remarked, they were ready "to come to time," and said, after it was over,

27

" Let Doomsday lend us the money, and we will run again in a month."

Rose's brothers in Australia continued to prosper. They became possessed of great tracts of land and vast flocks of sheep. They sent money every year to Rose, but it was always remitted to John Bullfinch, as the gypsies continued to harbor doubts touching the honesty of the parson of the parish. Jack Cotswold was soon very well off. His horse-dealing was carried on with much shrewdness and success, and a great venture on Bay Middleton, through hints from John Bullfinch and Tom Scarlet, who continued to be very intimate with Ransome, netted him a large sum when that famous colt won the Derby. But what most excited the admiration and delight of the good people of the Vale at the time of that glorious event was the fact that Lady Snaffle's maid, Miss Kitty Ruffle, won five hundred pounds. Being in waiting on Lady Snaffle at Middleton during her usual winter visit to Lady Jersey, Miss Kitty learned the opinion of the countess in respect to the prospects of Bay Middleton. She requested Sir Jerry Snaffle to bet twenty-five pounds for her, probably moved thereto by the Spanish blood in her veins, stood it out when the odds got short and the baronet advised her to hedge, and won five hundred pounds. On the same race Lady Jersey's coachman, the Duke of Grafton's coachman, and Lady Snaffle's coachman won heaps of money ; but nothing was so much talked of from Aylesbury to Whittlebury Forest, and from Belvoir Castle to the classic courts of Oxford, as the gameness of the little lady's maid in standing the bet out and winning a handsome marriage portion. Intelligence of this was written to Sassafras and Miriam by Young Jack, and he concluded his letter by stating that he should have got as much put on for Margery Southdown, only his father and his sister May forbade him. It is to be regretted that Parkins did not very long retain the confidence and countenance of the higher authorities. As he got older he grew more and more addicted to captious meddlesomeness, and retaining at the same time his devotion to " No. 1, brass tap, right-hand side of the cellar," he was ousted of his office. John Bull-finch continued to entertain Moleskin very frequently. When his daughter was at the Grange John rode over every day, but she and her husband were often at Hawkwell. One, two, three times John took pen in hand to announce to Sassafras and Miriam that there was an increase in his daughter's family. The first child was a boy, and by the sage advice of the keeper the child was christened John, for said he: "You thereby knock down four out of the covey. There's you, John Bullfinch, and if the baby takes after you he'll do. There's John Sassafras in America, also a good man and true. There's John Scarlet in the old churchyard, and there's Young Jack, so-called, his real name being John."

"I shan't interfere in regard to the name, sir," replied John. "My daater is not likely to choose any outlandish name. Your arguments are good, so far as they go. But May will be apt to please herself."

"Jest so!" said the keeper, "I always said she'd have her own way, in spite of you or Tom either."

"None of that, sir," said John, with some severity. "My daater is now a mother, and is more like her own mother than ever."

"And a little like her father, too, as her husband will find if he ever takes occasion to contradict her, which, like a wise man, he has not yet done," said the keeper. "Now John is a good name—a good eldest-born, son-and-heir sort o' name. There's two estates in the family—let May call her baby John, after you, after Sassafras, after Young Jack, after Captain John Crosstree of The Cameroons, and after the late John Scarlet. I have said my say. You may put it out of the way by obstinacy, but not by argeyment, not by argeyment."

With this the keeper replenished his pipe, drank a great draught from the tankard, and looked John in the face.

"John, sir, is a good name—a very good name. Nobody has said anything against the name," replied John Bullfinch, with some heat, "but it is not the only name. There has been many a Charles in our family time out of mind——"

"So there has," said the keeper, striking in, "and what's more, there is now. There's Charlie Bullfinch of the Mill. He's a known man—none better in the county at a feast or a fight. Then there's Charlie of Cherwell side, better known as Charlie-over-the-Water, most likely because he never drinks any. O! the Bullfinches have got their Charlies in the country still."

"Sir," said John, with a little dignity, "nobody ventures to say anything against the miller and the grazier in their presence. Besides, sir, my uncle Charles, of Bath, was one of the most eminent physicians in this kingdom. He was often called in to attend royalty."

"As often as it had the gout!" said Moleskin, "and I've heerd that his treatment was esteemed in that family because his favorite prescription was took in brandy and water. But who said anything agen Doctor Charles?"

"Nobody can say anything against him, sir, and my daater May may wish to call her boy after her learned and distinguished grand-uncle, or she may wish to call him after his father, Tom. Or, as Sir Jerry and Lady Snaffle have been always very kind to her, treating her, as she says, almost like a daughter, she may call the boy Jerry."

"I object to Jerry," said the keeper. "But if you j'ine the two names and make it 'Tom and Jerry,' the boy will be popular in these parts. You advise Mrs. Scarlet to call the young 'un Tom and Jerry."

"I will first advise you not be a fool, sir," said John Bullfinch, sternly. "She may wish to call the boy Richard," he continued, raising his voice and rising from his chair. "Do you object to Richard, sir? Have you anything to say against Richard, sir? There have always been four or five Richards in our family, and there are now."

"Then that's plenty," said the keeper, "especially as Rough-riding Dick of Heythrop is one on 'em."

"I think it is likely this child may be called Dick—I mean Richard," said John. "Four of my cousins will take it as a compliment. Besides, there's Richard Southdown, family connection as will be; and your own name is Richard, to boot. What do you mean by abusing the name of Richard, sir?"

A reply was prevented by the entrance of Young Jack, who had been at Southdown's, where indeed he was very often, much to the scandal of the older Misses Southdown, who never ceased to insist upon the fact to their mother that Margery was but "a *child*."

"I know, my dears," the good lady replied. "Still, she and young Bullfinch may be said to be engaged. Your father's mind is made up, and when Young Jack is twenty-one they will soon be married. There now, it's out!"

May's first-born was called John. The next child born at Hawkwell—for May went *home* on these occasions—was a girl, and by general acclamation of all the family and friends this baby was called May. And then, behold! in fulfilment of a prediction by Rose Tanner, after long consultation of the stars, came female twins, and these were called Margaret and Miriam. That was a christening! Lady Snaffle was again godmother; Lord Doomsday stood godfather. Presents rich and rare were showered upon the infants. The young mother —beautiful as ever, paler than usual, still blooming like the red and the white rose—was the object of a hundred toasts. From all the country round there was a great flight of the Bullfinches to the christening of the twins. Best of all, Sassafras "happened over," as he called it, at that time and was present. Then it was that he struck hands with Charlie of the Mill, Charlie over Cherwell Water, Rough-riding Dick and a score of other Bullfinches; and there and then observing that while Master Bullfinch was still "Young Jack" with the cousins, Mr. Southdown and the keeper, his name had ripened and mellowed into "John" upon the lips of May and his brother-in-law, and those of Lord Doomsday, Mrs. Southdown and her daughter Margery, the Western man remarked to John Bullfinch, Sr., "I see that I shall soon have to come across again, and bring Miriam!"

THE END.